CAUGHT IN THE MIDDLE

REDEEMABLE SERIES

Curry & Rice

ANNETTA LINCOLN

Cover design by: Ivana Knezevic exclusively for Annetta Lincoln

DEDICATION

To all those girls who really want to hate the cruel villain
but still want a morally grey man to love and gasp at when he fights for the girl
and wet themselves over when he takes control of her,
plus a golden retriever to snuggle up with on cold rainy nights...
This book has all three just waiting for you...
Come and meet them.

WARNING

Mentioned throughout this book are several triggers including;

A lot of swearing
Racial slurs
Intimidation
Submission and humiliation
Non-con
Sexual assault
Bondage
Whipping
Gagging
Forced Proximity
Forced body tattooing
Kidnapping and imprisonment
Gun Violence
Knife Violence, stabbing
Gratuitous Violence, fighting
Explicit sex scenes MM, MMF, MF
Double Penetration
Anal Play
Grooming

Prologue

I own you!

"Quinn, I need you to come and have a talk with me please, tonight."

I looked at the message on my phone from my step-father and didn't know whether to laugh, cry or run for the hills.

It had only been four weeks since my mom's funeral and I had already packed up my stuff ready to move out of my step-father's mansion. I knew I wasn't actually part of the family. He had been nothing but kind to me for the six years I had lived with him and my mom, but I knew what he was. As I had grown older I had become more aware of the things going on around me.

My step-brother, Antonio, had moved out of the house permanently six months ago. He was taking over their 'family' business and so had moved to New York City while his father, Augusto, planned to retire. Then my mom had taken ill, diagnosed with cancer she had sickened and withered quickly taking us all by surprise and now I was alone surrounded by dangerous violent people who I thought didn't want me around any longer.

Augusto had never fully accepted me, not being of his blood but the daughter of some other man. He had been quite possessive of my mom when they first met and kept her almost like a prisoner in his large house, allowing me to live there had felt like a compromise on his part and I kept a low profile. He never called me his daughter, not once. I had never taken his name, keeping my own father's last name of Malley.

Antonio had never seen me as a sister either. He was seven years older than me and I had only been twelve at the time of moving in, him already practically an adult and attending college coming home for the holidays. I had developed a crush on him. He was tall, lean, dark-haired, hot Italian blooded, sexy and handsome and he knew it and had a toxic personality to go right along with it.

He was an outrageous flirt, a player, but at twelve I didn't really understand what that meant, I only saw the fact that he always had a different girl on his arm every week he was around and guys seemed to idolize and admire him, acting like it was a privilege to be able to hang out with him.

As I got older I realized more about the dangerous family that surrounded me, I became to notice the unobtrusive guards that paced the grounds and followed both Antonio and Augusto around wherever they went. I noticed the gun holsters under their jackets and the menacing expressions. As I reached into my teenage years and was sent to an all girl's high school I got told by Antonio to guard myself and was strictly controlled when it came to extra-curricular activities and my schedules were tight and organized, but I wasn't followed around like they were.

I also blossomed in my teens, I confess, I know I'm pretty and the fact that I did ballet and a little bit of inter-school competitive swimming I had a great body developing. This seemed to cause my step-brother's control over me to become tighter as boys became interested in me, mainly because Antonio suddenly started looking in my direction back at me too. I know now it was naïve of me, but to finally have my crush pay affectionate attention to me when I was fifteen years old...at the time it was a dream come true.

Antonio at twenty two years old took my virginity at fifteen.

Don't get me wrong, it was consensual, but had I known the spider's web of depravity I was getting myself into at the time I would never have let myself get swept up by him, because now...well, let's just say I'm in for a big surprise. He opened me up and trained me into a darkness of submission and bondage that I was taught was normal, although our relationship was kept secret right up until now...he owned me, controlled me and possessed me in the bedroom whenever he was home most weekends and controlled me in my daily life with strict rules I had to abide by...although nothing prepared me for what was about to happen as I prepared to leave them all behind and head off on my own now I was nearly nineteen and my mother was gone. I had made these plans with her, but had not told the Ferrantes.

And why should I? Antonio had been gone now for six months with no contact leaving me confused, hurt and deeply ashamed at what he had groomed me into. Augusto, I had heard, was planning to retire and move back to Sicily. What was a meant to do but plan my own future without the Ferrantes in it?

As I entered the home office of Augusto Ferrante, head of the New York faction of the Italian Mafia, I felt my stomach drop to the floor to see Antonio also waiting for me in the room. I had no idea he was even here.

His dark gaze hit me with a perverse smirk and my mouth went dry. He was standing by the window, his hands held casually in the pockets of his pants, sweeping his suit jacket back and showing off his trim waist in the tight fitting waistcoat he wore. I rarely got to see him in his work attire but it always struck me how damn sexy, yet darkly dangerous, he looked. He had filled out since I first started crushing on him, his shoulders had broadened and his chest had expanded and he had gotten taller stopping at six foot two. He worked out in the gym plus did boxing and a bit of Jiu Jitsu so his physique was top notch. I should know, I've seen that body change and develop over the years of sleeping with him just like he had with mine.

I downcast my eyes, knowing my cheeks were blushing at his direct look. I was his play thing, had been from the moment I had slept with him as a virgin and giving him my everything. He allowed no other guy to come near me, but played with me like a toy. He always said that I was to remain pure only to him.

I resented him for it now I was reaching a level of understanding as I matured, but I was already caught by him and his dark world, caught in the web of training, submission and fear. I had hoped with him moving out permanently and getting his own place in Manhattan and that I was heading off to college in a couple of weeks that this would be the moment I would get to finally leave and put this dangerous and possessive family behind me.

"Quinn, please come in and sit down." Augusto said as he sat behind his large oak desk that was a replica of the one in the white house, apparently.

I quietly sat down, wiping my sweaty palms over my denim clad thighs and looked up at Augusto with apprehension. He gave me a small smile.

"Did you like the funeral I did for Maria?" He asked gently, leaning forward and putting his forearms on the desk, his hands clasped together.

I nodded and looked up, smiling back gratefully. "I did, thank you so much for dealing with all that, I know Mom would have loved it too, it was beautiful."

He nodded in response. "Good, I'm glad to hear that, I loved your mother."

"I know..." I breathed.

"I understand you've made plans to leave here and have been accepted into Tuck School of Business up in Hanover?" His voice seemed a little annoyed and his eyes narrowed as he looked at me.

My stomach dropped in a panic to realize they knew! I licked my lips nervously, glancing sideways at where Antonio was, his gaze was piercing and I had to quickly avert my gaze.

"Ah, yeah, that's right...I spoke about it with Mom a month ago before..." I trailed off, looking down at my hands as I fidgeted with a ring on my little finger.

"Were you planning on telling us?" Augusto enquired.

As I looked up at him I frowned, confused. "I thought my leaving here would be a given now Mom's gone and you're selling the place?"

I flinched as I heard Antonio cluck his tongue. "The nerve of you..." He muttered but got shushed by his father. Those few words sent chills down my spine that I had made a very grave error in judgement.

"I don't understand..." I start but Augusto shut me up as well with a finger raised in front of me.

"You don't get to just walk away and leave, Quinn. You're in this for the long haul now, you know too much."

"I don't know anything!" I breathe back startled, feeling a nervous swirling in my belly.

"Oh, you know...you've been fully aware since you started going to high school, don't try to act all cutesy and naïve now, Quinn." Antonio sneered. "Besides, how dare you think you can just up and leave me behind...you're just getting useful now I've trained that sweet little body of yours."

"Antonio." Augusto reprimanded.

I gasped at his words, looking up at him with real concern, turning back to Augusto realizing he knew everything when I thought our strange sexual relationship was a secret.

He smirked at me. "Yes, I know Antonio has been sleeping with you...I told him he could have you."

"What?" I gripped the arms of the chair, my head feeling a little light.

"You are the daughter of a great man, Quinn. The blood in your veins secures an alliance that was started and forged by my marriage to sweet Maria. You must stay in the fold, stay by Antonio's side and do what will be required of you as Antonio moves into top position."

I was shaking in fear. "What do you mean?"

Antonio walked over and placed his hands on my shoulders, leaning over me from behind and bringing his mouth to my ear. "It's time to earn your keep, little Quinn, now you're finally coming of age."

I felt a heavy dark cloud pass over me at those foreboding words.

"I have enrolled you into a very special college for those that can afford it, one that houses the children of important people that would be under threat of kidnapping and assassination, it has serious security and several peace treaties in place amongst organized crime syndicates as a non-aggression zone...it's here in New York, just outside New York City and is a division of Columbia University, so is an Ivy League college...I will put you in a nice little apartment and you will continue to learn business management and corporation law, for the benefit of the family. In exchange you will be under Antonio's care from now on. When he calls you, you go to him and do what is required of you. Understand?"

I looked at Augusto mortified by what was being implied. "No." I blurted out.

I was always one to speak my mind, I wasn't normally scared or a wall flower, I was confident, strong willed and showed an aptitude to become a leader except where Antonio was concerned. He scared me.

I stood up facing my step-father, my fists clenched with the shock of what he was saying. "I refuse."

My skin crawled as I heard Antonio chuckle ominously behind me. Augusto slouched back in his large leather chair, appraising me with his dark eyes as I felt a hand press to the back of my head and dig into my hair.

My head was pulled back viciously as I felt my legs get kicked out from under me and I fell heavily to my knees. I looked back to see Antonio standing over me with a gun pointed to the side of my head.

"There is no refusing a direct order made by Don Ferrante, it's time you learnt your place, little cannoli."

"P-please...I'm sorry...please don't..." I begged for my life.

He crouched down behind me, yanking my head back further until it was on his shoulder. "You're mine, Quinn, you always have been from the moment you stepped foot inside this house my father gifted you to me as an apology for marrying a second woman after my mother was killed."

I couldn't believe the words coming out of his mouth, but the next words chilled me to the bone.

"Your mother agreed to it, she sold your freedom away for the promise of a better life than the one she had with your father."

"Please, I really don't understand what's going on...you...you're hurting me..."

"Let her go, Antonio." Augusto commanded. Antonio clucked his tongue then planted a kiss on my cheek before letting me go and standing up, putting his gun away.

I looked up at Augusto, tears flowing down my cheeks. "Is that true?"

He looked at me sternly. "Yes, it is. Do you know who your father was?"

I shook my head. "Mom never told me and I knew she was scared about me finding out about him, I assumed he was abusive...I know that he's dead."

"He ran a gang up in Boston." He said vaguely.

I looked at him completely speechless, in shock that my mother had been involved with not one dangerous gangster but two!

"So you can understand your importance to our continued peace." Augusto said firmly. "You will remain in our family under my son's care and you will do your part within our organization as required to earn your keep, later you will marry and give Antonio an heir."

I dropped my gaze to the floor as my heart shattered, all my dreams shattered and I felt a coldness seep into my heart and blanket my emotions.

"You will enter our company once you graduate from college with a Bachelor of Business and Law which should take you four years until then Antonio will need you to help him in building alliances and securing contracts and agreements as he builds his own standing within our organization as the new Don."

"By doing what exactly?" I asked with trepidation making me feel sick.

I felt Antonio's hand come round my throat as he pulled me up to my feet. I gripped his wrist in fear but he didn't squeeze tight enough to choke me out, only tight enough as he usually did when he was rough with me during sex.

"Doing whatever I order you to do...you belong to me. Come when I message you and you'll have the rest of the time to live independently while attending college but be careful you don't have too much fun, this body is mine."

He pulled me up on my tiptoes and brought me up to his mouth, kissing me controllingly like he always did as I obediently opened my mouth to him.

"Antonio..." Augusto growled.

Antonio pulled back and grinned as he licked his tongue out over his lips, giving me that heated gaze that made my body pool heat deep in my core.

"What? She loves it...don't you, petalo?" His thumb stroked over my windpipe and pressed.

I couldn't lie, when he looked at me like that I was lost, groomed to obey his touch. "Yes, sir." I breathed, making Antonio chuckle and let my throat go.

"Brara rageizza...go get your things you're heading back to New York City with me to my new apartment for the weekend before I take you to your new place near the college on Sunday."

He pulled a set of keys out of his pocket and held them up in front of my eyes. "You'll also be needing a car to get around...you like Mustangs, right? If you're a good girl for me this is your reward." He grinned as my eyes widened to see the black car key on the keychain with the apartment key. I looked up at him stunned, he had never bought me anything but something he could use on my body.

"Say thank you, bambina."

"T-thank you, Antonio."

"I look after you now, Quinn, in every way...get going." He reached out and grabbed my waist pulling me forward, passed him and towards the door then smacked my butt. "Hurry up, I leave in five minutes."

I made my way to the door, too overwhelmed by everything to speak. I glanced back as I opened the door to see Augusto and Antonio, Don and heir, staring at each other silently. The aura in the room one of smug satisfaction.

I swallow my fear and apprehension for my own future down and practically ran from the room, knowing my life was never going to be what I wanted.

1
The way it is, marked

"Make yourself comfortable for a moment, I have to make a phone call." Antonio said as he ushered Quinn into his apartment, took out his phone and wandered off up the long hallway.

She looked around at the vast living area stunned. It was a split level area with steps down to the living area. Couches sat in front of a gas fire place with TV above on the stone wall, with a dining area and large black kitchen on the same level as the entrance foyer. She wandered over to the large glass windows, they stretched up for two stories and looked out over Manhattan harbor. A large chandelier sat pride of place high above the living area. The space was huge!

"Shit, this place must have cost about ten million!" She muttered.

"More like twenty." Antonio's deep voice came to her and she turned to see him walk back in. He had shed his suit jacket, tie and vest and was rolling the sleeves up on his shirt.

"Want a drink?" He asked as he went over to the kitchen and opened a cabinet that contained a bottle of Macallan scotch. He pulled it down and grabbed himself a chunky square glass from the glass frosted cabinet housing lots of different glassware. He looked up at Quinn from under his brows as she didn't answer.

"I have that white wine in the fridge that you like." He lifted his head and gave her a sultry smile. "Relax, Petalo, you've been quiet all the way here."

"What do you expect?" She accused as he lifted his glass and sipped his drink. He lowered it slowly, his top lip twitching irritably.

"Have you forgotten your manners?" His tone changed to a menacing one and Quinn realized her mistake.

"Sorry, sir." She dropped her eyes to the floor.

"Answer my question." He said firmly, staring at her with those dark eyes.

"Yes, please, sir. I would like a glass of wine...sorry I was rude." She talked quickly, coming towards him and standing before him, her eyes downcast.

He reached out a hand and placed it on her head. "I'll forgive that little outburst in light of today's revelations to you..." He stepped away and got the wine from the fridge and a glass from the cabinet, pouring her a glass before stepping back in front of her and holding it out.

She took it from his hand carefully, with both of hers. "Thank you."

"Hmm, I've got you all weekend..." He thrummed as he whipped an arm around her waist and pulled her into his body. She startled, making sure the wine didn't spill as she held it out to the side and looked up at his cruel smile and glittering eyes. "...I have plans for you before I let you go and live by yourself...so drink up and get relaxed."

She swallowed hard as he lifted her wine glass in her hand to her lips and made her drink. He kept pressing the bottom of the glass, tilting it up so she drank almost half of it before he let it go and chuckled darkly.

"I've spent quite a bit of money to renovate a special room for you here...are you looking forward to seeing it?"

Quinn felt heat pool in the depths of her core and she bit her lip, her eyes searching his face. "Yes, sir..." She said hesitant and nervous.

He smirked, pleased at her answer, and ran his fingers down her cheek and to her throat circling them around to the dip at the back of her skull and pulled her up to his waiting mouth. He kissed her languidly, his tongue exploring her mouth until she whimpered out a breathy moan. He pulled back and that smirk seemed satisfied.

"Good girl...now loose the clothes." His order was deep and smooth as he stepped back, lifting his whisky glass and waited for her to comply.

"You are forbidden to wear clothes in this apartment from now on, you will lose them at the door when you enter."

Quinn put her wine glass down, butterflies in her stomach making her feel nauseous and moved out of the kitchen to stand in a clear space on the other side of the island bench. She toed her shoes off and removed her socks then pulled her sweatshirt off and her t-shirt then undid her jeans and removed them placing all her clothes over the breakfast stool.

"That's enough, come here." Antonio instructed, leaving her in her underwear.

Quinn walked back around the kitchen bench and he grabbed her waist, lifting her to sit on the bench top and lifted her feet around his waist as he stepped between her legs. She placed her hands on his shoulders as his hands came to her breasts and he kissed her again, more passionately this time, more controlling.

She closed her eyes and kissed him back as he pulled the cups of her bra down and played his fingers over her nipples. He pulled his mouth from hers and kissed down her neck before devouring a nipple with his mouth.

Her head tipped back and she moaned out a breath of pleasure. He looked up and smirked. "You're needy tonight, Quinn, have you missed me while I've been here for the past six months?"

"Yes, sir." She replied, honestly. Her body absolutely craved him, no matter how much her mind screamed at her and wanted to focus on the conversation in Augusto's study, his touch, his scent, his voice, his heat made her forget everything but him.

He chuckled as his fingers slipped between her legs and under her panties, stroking through her pussy and round her clit. She gasped and moaned.

"You're so wet...I doubt I even need to prepare you for me, I bet I could just thrust straight in." He kissed her neck, sucking on it, then nibbled on her earlobe as his fingers slid inside her and he slowly twisted them. She bucked against it, gripping onto his shirt. "Who do you belong to, Quinn, I want to hear it?" He whispered in her ear.

"You, Antonio." She breathed, starting to pant, her body getting hot.

"That's right and I'm going to imprint that on your body tonight so you never forget it while you're off at college during the weekdays."

She opened her eyes, a little startled. "You want me to come back every weekend?"

He leaned back from her, making her arms drop and he pulled his fingers from her wet pussy and pressed them to her lips. "Lick." He ordered and she obediently complied. "Of course I want you here every weekend, what else would you be doing?" He grabbed her by a fistful of hair and yanked her head back, leaning over her intimidatingly now he snarled in her face. "Don't think for one minute I'm going to let you free enough to go to parties and see other people, Quinn."

"I'm sorry, sir...I didn't mean..."

"Shut it...follow me." He stepped away and stalked up the hall he had walked up before when on his phone. Quinn dropped off the kitchen counter and followed with a flutter of apprehension. He could be a really good lover but he could also be cruel and she could never tell his moods he was also closed off emotionally like a brick wall.

He led her down the hall and paused at a door with an electronic keypad, he punched some numbers in and opened the door, pushing her in front of him and making her step into the room first. She tensed up immediately and stumbled forward as he pushed her all the way in.

A sex room!

Equipped with several pieces of BDSM furniture that Quinn had never seen before. There was a huge X thing in one corner, a chair that looked like it should be in a doctor's office as it had foot stirrups and a thing that looked like a pommel horse or small massage table yet had places for restraining knees and arms and made her feel very nervous. The most normal thing in the room was the bed, but even that had a cage over the top with restraints attached to it as well as restraints attached over the mattress. She hadn't even let her eyes roam to the things that were displayed on the walls and in shelves.

She took an involuntary step backwards but hit the brick wall of Antonio's chest. His hands gripped her shoulders as he rested his chin down on top of her head.

"What do you think, Quinn? Are you nervous? Trying to escape already?"

Quinn licked her dry lips trying to form some sort of reply. "I...ah..."

He guided her further into the room and to the bed, turning her around and lifting her chin to look at him. "Answer me...I want to know what you're thinking?"

"Ah...this is...umm...quite a big step up from..."

"From what we've been doing? Yes, it is, but now I own you." Antonio stated, letting her go and stepping back to stare at her body with a twisted smirk. "How about you lose the underwear and get on your knees like a good girl."

Quinn was trembling, she wasn't actually sure if it was from fear, nerves or excitement. She decided it was from all three and that combination was making her wet. She stripped, placing her underwear on the end of the bed and sat on the floor on her shins as Antonio shut the door.

He turned back and his eyes sparkled to see she had been obedient. "This room is soundproof and I intend to teach you how pain can become pleasure...up until now I've been pretty tame with you, a little spanking and light flogging, nipple play and my favorite anal play, but from now on you are going to have to learn to accept my full depraved personality."

Quinn swallowed hard, staring at the floor. She wanted to run but how do you run from such a dangerous man without him finding you and doing even worse things to you, she was still getting over the shock of having a gun to her head.

He crouched down in front of her and lifted her chin again, his eyes darkened to see tears brimming hers. One lone tear dropped off her eyelashes and ran down her cheek. "Ah, petalo...you are beautiful. Do you understand what I've told you?"

"Y-yes, sir."

He saw she was trembling as he wiped the tear from her cheek with his thumb. "Don't worry, petalo, I'll start off easy and even let you use a safeword. Now get on the bed and spread your legs."

He stood in the middle of the room with his hands in the pockets of his pants and watched her as she crawled up the bed and lay down on her back, bent her knees up and then spread her feet wide letting her knees fall open and display herself fully open, wet and ready for him. Antonio merely chuckled before turning away and walking over to a set of shelves where various toys were laid out.

"I had thought you were trembling from fear, but I can see by how your naked pussy is glistening that you're excited...that's good..." He turned back with something in his hands and walked over. "You're a good girl, petalo, we're going to have a lot of fun in this room together."

Antonio's phone bleeped as a message came through and Quinn thought it weird, he usually turned his phone off when they were busy. He lifted his head from between her legs and wiped his mouth with a satisfied smirk, getting up and undoing the Velcro straps on her ankles. "Relax for a moment..." He said as he went and checked his phone then took a fine nib ink pen and came back to her, flicking the Velcro straps on the restraints to keep her legs straight and closed. He leaned over her and wrote his full name on Quinn's skin, low on her belly angled between her pubis and hip bones. He scrawled it out long in cursive and looked at it with a satisfied smirk then lifted his gaze to meet Quinn's inquisitive one.

"I said I was going to imprint my name on you tonight..." He said cryptically then walked to the door and left, leaving her stretched out and feeling like something she wasn't going to like was about to happen and now she was tied up and unable to do anything to stop it.

Her heart was hammering in fear as she heard voices in light conversation as the door opened and Antonio returned with a man with a long ponytail and tattoos covering every part of his skin including up his neck and parts of his face, accompanied by Matteo, Antonio's right hand man, who was watching the guy carefully with a grim expression.

The guy grinned widely at the sight of Quinn stretched out on the bed, tied up and now trembling. "Smells like sex in here..." The guy chuckled as his eyes swept the room.

Matteo slow blinked at the sight of her and looked away, standing like a statue by the door as he closed it.

"A-antonio?" She breathed in fright.

"Relax...this is Jimmy, he's here to tattoo my name permanently into your skin, so stay still!"

"What! Wait, Antonio...no, please, don't do that!" Quinn started to panic but Antonio ignored her and instructed the tattooist to set up and get on with it.

Jimmy opened his bag and started setting out his gear on the little trolley table Antonio had pulled over next to the bed, before putting on some black latex gloves. Antonio came to Quinn's head and stroked his hand over her hair, brushing it back from her sweaty face. "Stop freaking out, petalo...you'll be fine, this doesn't hurt anywhere near as much as I've even hurt you before."

"But..." Quinn breathed, trying to see what Jimmy was doing.

"Eyes on me, baby..." Antonio intoned making Quinn look up at him and calm. "Good girl...I need this reassurance in order to let you go to college, understand?"

She bit her lip and nodded.

"Quinn?" He growled.

"Yes, sir." She replied meekly.

She heard Jimmy chuckle. "Wow, I've read about this sort of thing...you're crazy man!"

"Just shut up and do your job, I'm paying you plenty to keep your mouth shut and work fast!" Antonio barked at him. Quinn squeezed her eyes shut to stave off tears when the tattoo gun buzzed to life as Jimmy checked it then set out the black ink ready.

"Okay, I'm ready to start...just this name, right?" He traced his fingertips over Quinn's skin causing her to jump and flinch with a small yelp. "Wow, okay...that can't be happening..."

Antonio lay a hand over Quinn's sternum. "Eyes, Quinn...breathe." He looked down on her as her eyes opened and locked with his.

Jimmy watched for a second feeling a stirring in his pants and grit his teeth. Fuck this was erotic...he had done some real private tattoos on chicks before but nothing ever seemed this provocative before. He tentatively touched the girl's skin again and felt her stiffen but she didn't jump like last time.

"I'm going to keep my hands on you so you get used to it, okay?"

"She's fine...hurry up and don't talk to her!" Antonio growled intimidatingly, looking back at Jimmy with a dangerous glare.

Jimmy swallowed hard, knowing the guy standing at the door who had escorted him up in the lift was armed with a gun. "Okay, don't make me nervous, man!" He breathed out, his fingers stroking across Quinn's skin and then he stretched it out between finger and thumb and turned the tattoo gun on. It buzzed to life and he heard the girl whimper.

The asshole in charge murmured to her and she stilled again as Jimmy collected some ink and started the tattoo.

It only took a few minutes and Jimmy was cleaned up and ready to go.

"Just keep it covered and dry." He instructed as Matteo opened the door and waved him out before following.

Antonio walked around to her hip and stared at his name etched into Quinn's skin. "È cosi bello il mio piccolo cannolo" Antonio breathed.

Quinn strained her head up trying to see. "Please, sir...can I see it?"

He looked up under his brows. "Not just yet...I have you in this position for a different reason remember and I believe we were only half way through..." He adjusted the straps on her ankles and opened her legs again. "You let that stranger smell your excitement..." He stroked his fingers over her wet pussy. "Lucky he couldn't see your juices, you're soaked..."

Quinn panicked at the deathly calm tone. "I'm sorry, sir...forgive me...I'm..."

"Quiet..." He ordered and she shut up instantly, her heart hammering in her chest.

2
Cory and Reese

First day of the new semester and Cory was sitting on the hood of his F250 pick up watching all the newbie chaos when a black motorbike cruised up next to him and the rider got off, removing his helmet and then leaned on the side of his truck. It was Reese, the one guy in this whole damn college he felt awkward talking to, they had been best mates up until high school and had drifted apart because their dads were on opposing sides of the law, as well as other reasons. Reese was a gangsters son, while Cory, his dad had just become New York Police Commissioner two years ago, hence the breakup of their friendship.

"Hey." Reese said, sweeping his dark hair back from those pale golden hazel eyes that the girl's all went nuts about.

"Hey." Cory answered nonchalantly, not taking his eyes off the people walking back and forth.

"Babe watching?" Reese asked amused.

"New talent observing..." Cory corrected with a smirk.

They both heard a rumble of a nice V8 engine pull up on the other side of Cory's truck, he turned with interest as a platinum grey Mustang pulled into the car park two down from him.

"Nice car..." He muttered to himself.

He sat up as he saw a girl with long chestnut colored hair tied up in a high ponytail, dressed in khaki cargo pants with the bottoms rolled up, chuck tailors and a singlet top with a large white hoodie unzipped halfway down making it slip off one shoulder to expose golden skin.

Cory whacked Reese on the shoulder and indicated over to the hot chick as she closed her car door and lifted her head to look around the campus getting her bearings, revealing amazing pale green eyes set into long dark lashes.

"Dibs." Reese called it.

"What the fuck? I saw her first." Cory exclaimed.

"I called dibs first." Reese chuckled. They watched as she pulled a lollipop out of her pocket, unwrapped it and stuck it in her mouth then took her phone out. Her calm attitude screamed confident with a tinge of 'don't talk to me' moody angst.

"Oh? You think you have a better shot at her than me, is that it?" Cory huffed. He was quarter back in the football team for the Lions over at the main campus of Columbia University and was basically the most popular guy in this college campus and a player who thrived on it. His dirty blond hair and blue eyes, athletic build and roguish smile helped out a lot of course.

Reese shrugged. "You're just a fuck boy...she looks like she would see you coming and eat you alive."

"Ha! You think you're 'oh so Alpha dominant male' huh? To what...get her to submit to you and your weird kinks?" Cory said sourly, Reese was the other popular guy on campus, known as the Prince on campus due to his tall, lean, MMA fighter's body, black hair that fell into those pale eyes and his ability to stare into ones soul with them. He was also President of the Student Executive as much as the school hated the fact a gangster was in control of representing students for any disciplinary offenses, it was voted by the students and Reese loved the power it gave him.

Reese chuckled a deep sexy rumble. "It's Sigma...I dominated you, didn't I?"

"Once, asshole! You took advantage of my drunken ass. I should report you!"

"Yeah, except you've simped for me ever since."

"In your dreams, asshole...you know I'm the best fuck you ever had!" Cory teased back, sliding off the hood of his truck and facing Reese.

Reese laughed. "In your dreams, Curry...but if you let me I'll show you how to improve." His eyes seemed to brighten into a golden glow.

"Fuck off, Rice! Stay the fuck away from me!" Cory shuddered and Reese's smirk widened.

They noticed the girl start to walk towards the main entrance of the administration building joining the small crowd of freshmen from around the world that made it in to this special campus for the rich and infamous.

Reese laughed, dropping his arm around Cory's neck and walked off dragging Cory along with him. Cory grinned and elbowed Reese in the side.

"So does this mean we're going to compete?"

"Fuck yes." Reese thrummed deeply.

"She's hot, huh?" Cory said watching her ass.

"She looks fucking gangster..." Reese confirmed in his own way, licking his tongue over his teeth. She oozed sex appeal but looked sweet and demure under a hard shell that Reese really wanted to crack and expose the real her. It was obvious to him she had a mask up, not wanting to draw too much attention to herself.

"Oooo, exciting...I haven't had no gangster chick before. Hey, do you think she could really be into that weird shit you are?"

Reese smirked and licked his lips as they followed her up the stairs, looking at her perfectly round yet toned ass in those cargos. Reese's eyes dipped to her muscular calves as she flexed them going up the stairs on her toes.

"Oh, I hope so...but I can teach her."

Cory chuckled and broke away from Reese's arm. "Game on, bro." He held his fist out.

"Game on." Reese fist bumped him as the girl disappeared inside.

"Reese!" A voice called out making him stop and look back as Cory grinned at the opportunity to get the jump on him and went inside.

Reese saw it was his mate Jacob and turned back, moving swiftly down the steps and approaching him, cursing for being seen with Cory. They greeted each other with a quick manly hug and pat on the back.

"Hey, how was it over the break?" Reese asked.

"Not too bad..." Jacob sighed.

"Yeah, I fucking hate it when I have to go back for the holidays." Reese chuckled.

"But, good news, it means we have our first party up this Saturday, welcome back party!"

Reese shook his head. "Let me guess...the jocks?"

"Yeah, did Cory not mention it to you, I guessed that's why he was talking to you."

"Nah..." Reese said cautiously.

Jacob shrugged. "Anyway, guess what the theme is?"

Reese gave him a look to just say it.

"Bring a freshman."

"Oh, fuck...hazing party? Seriously, they still do that shit?"

"Looks like it, so will you be going?"

"Not sure, depends if I can wrangle a freshman..." Reese commented, his gaze going back to the admin building.

"What? You going to join in?" Jacob seemed surprised.

"Well, it doesn't say the freshman has to be the same sex, right?"

"The hell!? You already eyeing up new meat?"

"Maybe..." Reese answered with a coy smirk.

"Do tell...what did I miss?" Jacob laughed, looking up at the admin building knowing the new students to this college would all be special in some way. Genius, connected, rich, only the children of special families around the world got to be here, usually their parents signed them up here if they were famous in some way or at risk of kidnapping and extortion.

"Nah, I'll keep it to myself for now...catch up later." Reese side-stepped and walked off across the lawn and around the side of the admin building heading to his locker on the other side, easier to avoid the crowd and go in the side doors.

Quinn made it up to the desk and got her class info and campus map including her locker code then was filed into a large auditorium to listen to the welcoming address. She noticed the security was high at this campus, but the students seemed relaxed and quite nonchalant about it. No individual security was allowed on campus, certainly no weapons so she guessed everyone felt safe within the closed gates.

When Augusto had told her that this special college was off the map but formally a branch of Columbia University, an Ivy League college it had made her happy to attend this forced enrolment. It also meant students had an opportunity to compete as normal in any sports or activities as long as their own parents were aware and allowed them to attend team practice over at the actual university grounds. It was featured that the football team, the Lions and their cheerleader squad would both be speaking today for any freshmen interested in joining up.

She looked around the auditorium with curiosity. There were only a small number of them entering this secret campus and maybe two looked like football players.

A girl nudged her elbow and sat down next to her.

"Hey there, my name's Vanessa, I'm co-leader of the cheerleaders of the Lions, you look like what we're looking for?"

Quinn pursed her lips together looking over the bleached blond in her short flared skirt and tight blouse with a judging glare. "Ah...no offense but..."

"You look like the type..." Vanessa rudely interrupted Quinn's rejection. "Are you a dancer or something?"

"Used to do a bit, yeah."

"Perfect, you'll enjoy hanging with us." Vanessa gave Quinn a worldly look. "So, who's your family?"

Quinn's mouth pressed into a hard line. "I really don't think..."

"Oh, are they that serious? Say no more..." She interrupted again. "...well, anyway, I saw you enter and knew that body type was what we're looking for, you're a good height and you have a great face too, so come along to our first casual meet up and audition...if we like what we see then we'll organize going over to Columbia for a proper audition with the coach."

"No thanks." Quinn said in a rude tone, standing up and pushing passed Vanessa's knees to get out. "I have to go find my locker."

"Rude..." Vanessa stated, tossing her hair back.

Quinn grit her teeth to stop the words that wanted to come out. She didn't want to make enemies of the clearly popular cliques in any college, but if that girl had interrupted her one more time!

She breathed in a calming breath and looked at her map orientating herself before heading off in hopefully the right direction. She had a couple of the recommended text books in her bag and it was getting heavy. She was glad when she finally found her locker and it unlocked with little effort just as the tone sounded for first hour, although classes on day one were more about just orientation and meeting the professors, TA's and other teachers, they were still expected to find their way to class on time.

She fiddled with the key pad lock, changing the code to one of her own as instructed to do and put her books into the locker, pulled out a lollipop, stuck it in her mouth and closed the locker door.

She startled as she found a face staring at her from behind it, smiling roguishly at her, his beautiful blue eyes twinkling brightly. He was handsome, clearly a footballer and she wondered if he had followed her from the auditorium.

"Hi, I'm Cory." He declared as he leaned on the lockers and folded his arms without a single care to anyone else trying to get into those lockers. He was clearly beyond reproach.

Quinn appraised him silently, one eyebrow slowly arching as her eyes went to his feet and slowly rose to his face. She twirled her lollipop around her mouth with her tongue, clicking it off her teeth. By the time her eyes met his once more he was actually blushing. She slowly took the lollipop out of her mouth and smiled at him. She pressed the lollipop against his lips making him open his mouth startled, his eyes widening in surprise. She let go of the lollipop and turned away.

Cory frowned confused as he took the lollipop out of his mouth. "Huh? What the fuck!"

She glanced back at him with a lazy smirk. "That's as close as your lips will ever get to mine, blue eyes." She purred and sauntered off to find her first class.

"Damn!" Reese laughed, clapping Cory on the back as he quickly came over from where he had witnessed the rather amusing scene.

"That cheeky bitch!" Cory stared at the lollipop, grinned then put it back in his mouth.

"I told you she would eat you alive!"

"Well, if that wasn't a challenge to prove her wrong, I don't know what is...?" Cory grinned like a loon around the lollipop sticking out of his mouth. "She's so fucking hot and her lollipop is delicious."

"What's it taste like?" Reese laughed, shaking his head.

"Strawberries and the promise of great sex." Cory mused.

"Still dreaming then..." Reese scoffed, walking off.

Quinn was left wondering what that guy was all about getting up in her face only an hour into her first day. He was clearly a senior. She had got the feeling from the other people in the hall that he was one of those untouchable types, obviously a powerful father and as part of the football team probably ruled campus, so she didn't want to piss him off.

He was cute, really cute, not that she could have anything to do with cute thanks to Antonio. She stepped into her first class, a small lecture hall and was handed a leaflet from a cheerful looking girl with strawberry blond hair.

"Hey, this is an invite to a special meeting put together by a few of us freshman girls to get together to get to know each other. Girls looking out for girls and all..."

"An invite to what?" Quinn asked, looking at the paper.

"It's just a fun night ten pin bowling...we just want us girls to all get along and know who each other is."

"So who are you?"

"Oh, sorry, I'm Lizzy." She beamed a cute smile. "Daughter of Logistix Conglomerate, based in Ontario, responsible for data protection of some pretty major companies and government departments worldwide."

"Right..." Quinn wasn't used to people introducing themselves in such a fashion.

"And you?"

"Ah...Quinn."

Lizzy gave her a patient look waiting for the rest.

"Um...of Zortex Industries and Construction, I guess..." That was the legitimate business of the Ferrante family.

Lizzy's eyes went a little wide. "Oh, wow...they're big, government contracts big."

"Are they?" Quinn didn't know. "How do you know this stuff?"

Lizzy frowned at her. "It's important to know this stuff."

"Huh, okay...well I might actually go, thanks..." Quinn waved the paper invite at her and wandered off to find a seat.

Lizzy gave her a wave and stepped out of the room, making her way up the hall. A tall dark haired Adonis stepped out in front of her making her halt her steps with a flinch to avoid bumping into him.

Her eyes widened at the sight of him. "Reese O'Shea?"

"You know me, freshman?" He smirked at her.

"Of course, my sister goes here...Lila Waterman, Logistix Conglomerate. I'm Lizzy."

Lila and Lizzy...of course, you look alike too, both cute."

She blushed and dropped her gaze making Reese chuckle. "Do me a favor, Lizzy?"

She looked back up at him. "What is it?"

"Tell me what you found out talking to that girl just now?"

"Girl...just now? Which one?"

"The last one at lecture room four, with the long red ponytail and the combat pants."

"Oh! Her...Quinn. She said she was from Zortex, can you believe that?"

"Zortex?" Reese frowned darkly. "Thanks..." He wandered off leaving Lizzy blinking in confusion.

"Quinn, eh...cute name. Rich too, uber rich, although you don't look or act like it?" Reese mused to himself.

3
A bet is made

Reese wandered over to Cory's truck after his classes had finished for the day to find him already there and waiting for the new girl to appear.

Reese collected his bike helmet from the back of Cory's pickup and came up to lean on the driver's door to talk through the window.

"So how did you go today, Curry?" He called his rival by his old nickname.

Cory rolled his eyes. "Apart from a glimpse across the cafeteria for like twenty seconds I didn't manage to see her again, what about you?"

Reese smirked lopsided and cocky. "I found out her name is Quinn and get this, she's supposedly something to do with Zortex..."

"Zortex? Fuck, that's a serious family, my dad is all up in contracts with the Ferrante's...all sorts of dodgy waste management, garbage collection, construction, real estate...they're a serious no go zone."

"But only a son, right?" Reese asked.

"I'll do some research." Cory grinned and did a little head flick in the buildings direction.

Reese turned to see Quinn walking back to her car. A lollipop once again in her mouth. "I wonder what's with the lollipops?" Reese murmured under his breath.

Quinn seemed to feel their eyes on her and looked up as she approached her car. She recognized the blond inside the truck, but the mean-as looking biker dude holding the skull motorbike helmet made her take pause and blink.

He gave her the most understated grin, yet it was so sexy, tempting and strangely hypnotizing with those pale hazel eyes peering at her from under that dark fringe of black hair she felt like the devil had noticed her, something about him reminded her of Antonio, it made her shiver.

"Quinn, isn't it?" Reese called out. He relished the fact she had taken pause to look at him properly, it was obvious she liked what she saw.

"Ah, yeah..." Quinn answered as she opened her car door and threw her bag in across to the passenger seat. "I'm not even going to ask how you know that, I'm just going to leave."

She got in her car and slammed the door shut.

Reese's hand gripped around the jaw part of his helmet as he sucked on his teeth feeling a little annoyed. "Well, fuck you, princess."

Cory laughed. "Ha! You were so confident when she looked at you like that..."

Reese scoffed. "She's not normal, that's for sure."

"She's got amazing green eyes..."

"She's got amazing tits." Reese said as he watched Quinn back her car out and drive off to join the rest of the vehicles trying to get out onto the road through the security barrier gates.

He slipped his helmet on and walked to his custom Ducati, starting it up and deliberately cruising up next to Quinn's Mustang.

She had the window down, enjoying the breeze while she sat in the queue and looked sideways at him as he rolled up. He lifted his visor and their eyes met. He was struck by her beautiful green eyes, they were quite pale like jade and as they caught the sun he could almost see flecks of gold in them.

"Hey!" He said. "There's a party Saturday...I want to take you."

She scowled at him. "No." She said and raised her window on him.

Reese wasn't going to make it look like her rejection bothered him so he flipped his visor down and accelerated forward, clicking down a gear and passing all the cars in the line to exit the car park quickly and was gone with a roar of his engine.

He was annoyed.

She was rude.

Maybe she was a Ferrante after all...

Later that same evening Cory turned up with beers and a guy from the football team to Reese's condo. He had a pretty sweet place not too far from campus and it was in a small complex of eight units that all faced into a pool area. The fact that he was practically a mobster meant he ruled the complex and even the manager groveled at his feet, so his friends came and went at all hours and they partied loud and obnoxiously most weekends.

"Hey, it's Rice!" The footballer said as he came through the security gate to see Reese lounging by the pool, smoking and drinking. A couple of his own mates were there and a huge one stood up to confront the guy.

"Hey! Not just anyone gets to call this guy, Rice, dickhead! Watch your manners or you might just accidentally drown in the pool."

"Easy, Tank..." Reese drawled. "He's a friend of Curry."

"Yeah...this is Will." Cory added. "He's here for some green."

Tank nodded in acknowledgement. "Ah, okay, you've come over from Columbia?"

"Ah-huh...we've just finished training." Cory sat down on a pool lounger next to Reese as Reese sat up and grabbed a small zipped bag that was beside him. He tossed it over to Tank, who caught it by reflex.

"Take this inside and sort him out will you, I need to talk to Curry."

"Sure thing, boss." Tank inclined his head to Will and they stepped inside. There were two other ominous looking guys by the pool, wearing singlets and showing tattoos. Reese inclined his head at them with a piercing look and they both stood up and walked inside.

Cory watched them go and gave Reese a curious glance. "This seems serious?"

"Nah, not really...I just don't want them to know about your father, it makes their types nervous."

Cory laughed. "Yeah, I get it, sorry I should have messaged you first." He looked Reese over, his eyes narrowing at the tattoos on Reese's shoulders and upper arms. "Did you get more work done?"

Reese looked at one arm and grinned. "Yeah...looks good, eh? I said I was going to get it all to join into one...just need to finish the back now and then do some breast plates..." He sat up and pulled his singlet up to reveal the large tiger tattoo taking up his whole back.

"You look like a real gangster..." Cory huffed.

Reese shrugged. "Nothing that can be seen when wearing a shirt..."

"Hmm...I guess...still it makes you look like an old Japanese gangster or something..."

"I've always liked the yakuza style of tatts so..." He shrugged again, taking a sip of his beer straight from the can. "Want one?" He held the can up and indicated to a cooler next to him.

Cory reached out and grabbed a beer from the cooler, opening it with a satisfying sound and drank deeply.

"So did you get to ask your dad about Zortex?" Reese asked.

"I haven't really seen him, he wasn't home when I got there and I had to go to training so..."

"Hmm." Reese frowned and looked away.

"Was it urgent?" Cory studied his body language.

"Guess not...I just think it's weird how that girl said she was from Zortex...maybe she's not a Ferrante, she might be the daughter of someone else in the group."

"So what if she is?"

Reese looked at Cory with a strange expression. "You do know the Ferrante's are mafia?"

Cory gave him a startled look. "Oh, is that your concern?"

Reese snorted. "Not concern exactly, just have to tread lightly, is all."

Cory laughed. "Maybe we should forget about her..."

"You backing out of our competition?"

"I thought that's what you were trying to do?" Cory chuckled.

"Not at all, in fact let's sweeten the deal. The guy who gets to fuck her first gets ten grand from the loser."

Cory sat back. "You think I have that sort of money, asshole? You gangster fuck...just because you're rolling in it..." Cory looked down purposely at the Audemars Piguet watch on Reese's wrist.

Reese laughed, cockily shaking the watch on his wrist before running a hand through his hair lifting it from his eyes. "Oh, come on...I know you get a good allowance from Papa Police Commissioner and you don't spend it."

Cory grimaced. "I'm saving for my own place, ya jerk."

Reese looked at him seriously. "Okay, let's make it five then?"

Cory sighed, flicking his finger over the tab on his beer can. "Yeah, okay..."

"Unless you know you're going to lose?" Reese teased with a smirk.

"Fuck off...I saw her wind her window up on you!" Cory laughed and Reese chuckled darkly.

"Yeah, she's rude...a real stand-offish bitch, I don't know though if its caution or arrogance..."

"Hmm, yeah, she's arrogant...look what she did to me."

"Perhaps she needs a little lesson in just who we are." Reese thrummed, his eyes taking on a bright sparkle.

Cory grinned. "Yeah, you're going to be aggressive? Alright, bring it on."

"Let's see if either of us can get her to Luke's party..." Reese added.

Cory nodded. "Okay, you're on."

4
Be more polite

As Quinn pulled into campus on day two she noticed Cory's truck had a black Camaro parked next to it rather than the motorbike of that guy that pestered her. The one with the sexy bangs and intense gaze, she hadn't ever seen anyone with eyes like those before, they certainly stuck in one's memory. Hopefully that meant he wasn't there today as she looked around and couldn't see the bike in the carpark.

She walked around the side of the main building heading straight to the easiest entrance to the lockers. She looked up the stairs to the stoop and paused in her tracks as there he was. He was wearing a different black leather jacket, one with a white strip down the sleeves, dark blue denim jeans and a crisp white t-shirt. He really was amazing to look at, he had a great body, that was obvious and his confident swagger was sexy and alluring. However, he was surrounded by girls at this precise moment all vying for his attention. He was leaning on the wall, his phone out like he was collecting numbers as the girls giggled and chatted with each other, batting their eyelashes at him. All the while he stared at his phone oozing a calm indifference.

Quinn's face deadpanned as she walked up and stepped up the steps, passing the group. As she went to step in the open door she felt a hand curl around her wrist, clamp tight and yank her back a step.

She looked to her right and met Reese's sparkling golden gaze, hers narrowing as she glanced down to where he gripped her wrist with a filthy look. The gaggle of girls had gone silent, some surprised, some scowling at her, they were all juniors and seniors and wondered who this new girl was gaining Reese's attention. As she looked back up at Reese he smirked sexily like he had been waiting for her eyes to come to him.

"Are you just going to walk passed and not say hello? I'm your senior and president of the executive, you should really be more polite, Quinn."

Quinn was stunned as the girls started whispering in agreement to him. "Ah...sorry, I didn't realize, I don't even know who you are..." He hadn't been at the welcome yesterday with the other executive members.

"How can you not know him?" One girl asked. "This is Reese O'Shea, our prince of campus!"

Quinn's gaze slid to the girl and back to Reese. "Wow, seriously..." She managed to free her wrist from his grasp and rubbed it. Lucky she was wearing arm warmers and covering her bruises, but that hurt, he had some serious power in that grip and she wondered if he knew just how much force he had applied.

"Sorry, I didn't realize you were so important..." Her tone was facetious but Reese chuckled. "Hello." She stated looking straight into his eyes.

"Hello and good morning to you, Quinn."

She managed to look startled. "How *do* you know my name?"

His smirk widened. "I wouldn't ask a girl to go to a party with me without first knowing her name...I asked around after seeing you in the carpark yesterday morning."

This startled Quinn and shocked the girls around him. They all looked at Quinn with a level of open hostility that made Quinn wish he would just shut up, she didn't need to be singled out on day two. She dropped her gaze to the ground and a faint blush tinged her cheeks in her embarrassment.

"You're putting me on the spot, I don't like it." She stepped away quickly and entered the corridor making her way to her locker.

She heard the girls behind make varying comments and some exclaimed startled, by what Quinn wasn't going to turn around to find out.

As she went to open her locker a large hand with long dexterous fingers reached around her and slammed it shut. She turned, shrinking back in fright to see Reese glaring at her darkly.

"What now?" She demanded, but her voice cracked with fear. Her heart skipping a beat as Reese towered over her. He was really tall and managed to use his height to crowd in on her and make her feel a little intimidated. He reminded her a little of Antonio with his intenseness and that scared her more than anything.

As she flinched back on instinct Reese saw the fear in her eyes as reactionary from being triggered by something. Her hard cold exterior suddenly made sense as he saw the flash of vulnerability and he dropped his hand from her locker and pulled back.

"I didn't mean to scare you...I just wanted to ask you again about Saturday, I want to take you." His voice was calm, gentle and husky.

Quinn breathed in deeply, letting her heart even out. "I have plans already, sorry."

"You do...what?"

"Ah, it's a family thing." She answered uncomfortably.

"So not a party?"

"No, it's a dinner with some politician..." Quinn said not making eye contact.

"So, if you weren't busy?" Reese smirked, his eyes smoldering darkly.

She looked up at him and blinked. He was really intense and his smile was damn hot. She took in his beautiful manly face close up regretfully. "I'm..."

"What about Friday?" He interrupted.

"No, sorry, I'm going out that night too..." She opened her bag and pulled out the invite to ten pin bowling. He took it and read it, as she watched his jaw muscles tick. He had a slight growth of stubble that she couldn't help but wonder what it would feel like between her thighs. She gasped in a breath and squeezed her thighs together feeling suddenly hot.

Reese's eyes snapped up to hers at the little gasp of breath. He studied her sudden flushed face and his smirk returned, his eyes darkened a little into that smolder that made her breath hitch.

So she did find him attractive...

He heard Cory's voice in the hall call out and the smile dropped from his face.

He handed the invite back to her looking cold and she took it with a little frown. "Shame...maybe some other time."

"Hey. What's going on?" Cory asked as he approached, looking around Reese's broad shoulders and seeing Quinn. "Oh, it's you, lollipop girl...how's it going? Is Rice bullying you?"

"Don't be ridiculous." Reese growled as Cory grinned boyishly at Quinn, coming beside her and leaning on the lockers like yesterday.

Quinn's little frown was adorable as she smiled slightly up at Reese. He grit his teeth at the change that came over her face as it softened and her eyes glittered like pale gems. "Rice? Did he just call you Rice?" She looked at Cory, she had heard people talking about him and the football team. "And people call you Curry? Curry and Rice?" She giggled, making them both stare at her silently. "Are you like a couple or something?" She saw both their faces go deathly cold. She coughed and stifled her amusement taking their stares as annoyance. "Sorry..." She beamed a smile at them.

"Wow..." Cory tersed.

Reese wiped a hand over his face. "Fucking hell..." He grumbled behind his hand.

"I'm sorry." She blurted out, grasping her bag and pulling it in front of her protectively.

Reese flicked a dark gaze at her from under his hair making her hold her breath. His gaze slid to Cory who was still staring at Quinn. "Don't fucking giggle like that!" He growled out and stalked off down the hall.

"W-what?" Quinn breathed, confused as she watched his back. She stiffened as she felt Cory's presence lean in to her.

"It's a cute sound...he hates anything cute. Ignore him."

Quinn moved away a step to her right. "Oh, really? So you guys are known as Curry and Rice?"

"Yeah, we called ourselves that when we were kids playing together, it just kinda stuck."

"So, you're friends?"

"Hmm...not really...kind of...it's hard to explain." Cory sounded uncomfortable.

"Okay, well I have to get going..." Quinn pointed over her right shoulder and stepped away.

"Wait, I..." Cory went to try and keep her talking but a group of girls that were a part of the popular group of cheerleaders and influential daughters leaped over and curled their arms around Quinn's and walked off with her.

"Quinn...just the person we were looking for..."

Cory huffed and folded his arms as he straightened up, his football mates, Lucas and Harry coming over. "You like that girl, huh? Seems Rice does too..." Harry was laughing.

"Yeah, we're competing to see who can get her first."

"Fuck, really?" Lucas asked with a look of concern.

"Yeah..." Cory grinned.

"Won't Reese just have her kidnapped and whisked away to Paris or something?" Harry joked.

Cory gave him a baleful look. "What the fuck...he's not that desperate to win."

"Are you?"

Cory scowled. "Don't you think she's worth a little effort to compete against him, she fucking gorgeous."

"You guys have never crossed paths on campus, why start now?" Harry asked.

"Yeah, you may break the peace." Lucas agreed.

Cory scoffed. "It's just a freshman slut...what's to get all worked up over, it's just a friendly competition."

"If you say so..." Harry said unsure.

"That cheerleader, Mila, didn't look happy as she dragged the girl away." Lucas mentioned.

Cory rubbed his jaw, feeling a little uneasy. "Fuck, you think she's going to bully the girl?"

"Over you? Absolutely." Lucas scoffed.

Cory rolled his eyes. "Shit..."

"Let me go, what the hell!" Quinn struggled against the arms of the two girls as they led Quinn around the corner and into the girl's bathroom.

They let her go with a slight shove, pushing her in front of them as they barred the exit. There were four of them all together, Vanessa included. Quinn met her gaze and she smiled vapidly.

"Seems you have gotten the attention of both Curry and Rice...that's going to be a problem."

"I don't see a problem." Quinn straightened her shirt. "I'm not interested in either of them, I'm just here to study and get my degree."

Mila's eyes narrowed. "If that's so, good...but we'll be watching."

"What's the deal with them?" Quinn asked.

"Cory is mine." Mila stated.

Quinn huffed. "Good for you, then go get him...look I don't want trouble, okay?"

"Fine, neither do we, right Mila?" Vanessa affirmed.

"Whatever." Mila rolled her eyes and flicked her hair back.

"The Prince and Cory are off limits, simple." Vanessa announced, turned with a flick of her blond hair and walked out of the bathroom.

"We'll be watching!" Mila said with a twisted smirk and they all left as Vanessa's shadows.

Quinn let out a breath of relief that hadn't escalated, leaning back on the vanity.

A girl came out of a toilet stall, peeking out before stepping out. "Are you okay?"

Quinn looked up at the girl dressed head to toe in designer brands. "Fine...I just wish I knew what was what, you know...I've been here two days and already pissed off the princesses obviously...through no fault of my own."

"Yeah, the top girls are pretty obsessive over who hangs out and talks with the footballers and with Reese's lot."

"So they don't hang together?" Quinn asked.

"Hardly...that's the joke...curry and rice should go naturally together, but they're more like chalk and cheese, they are the polar opposites of the school...like jocks versus outcasts, you know? Although apparently they used to be best mates in middle school. That's where the nicknames come from."

"Huh...I thought that Reese guy was on the executive?"

"Only because, as much as he's an actual bona fide gangster, around here he's actually top academic of campus."

"What the hell?" Quinn exclaimed.

The girl giggled. "Yeah, I know...he's a freaking genius and the school board and faculty hate it!"

Quinn laughed. "Oh, I bet they do..."

"Yeah, and Cory McMillan, is the King of the sports faculty, it's rare to have the star quarter back over here doing a law degree rather than a sports one seeking sponsorship..."

"Hmm..." Quinn nodded, her expression falling into a frown of concern. Somehow she had got herself caught in the middle between the two main factions of the students here. "...great." She sighed.

"Good luck." The girl waved out as she left the bathroom.

"Yeah..." Quinn huffed, rolling her eyes. "Guess I'm not joining the cheer squad now..."

5
Don't ignore me

As Quinn walked to the café on campus to get a coffee during a break in her class schedule she received a message and pulled her phone out.

She saw it was from Antonio and felt her stomach drop and roil in uneasiness as she opened and read the message.

A - **I've bought a dress for you for Saturday night. You will come here to get ready. Danny will pick you up at 4, make sure to book into Patricia's Beauty Salon**

She sighed out a heavy breath, feeling sick as she wandered into the café. She didn't feel right about going to some high society event with Antonio, he had never taken her out anywhere, ever, now suddenly he wanted to show her off in a fancy dress that cost thousands...she was uncomfortable about it given everything that had happened over the weekend together in that room of his. He had turned things up a notch and quite frankly she was scared by it all.

"Quinn! Over here..."

She looked to see a couple of girls in her classes. She smiled at them and stepped over.

"Hey..." She replied awkwardly.

"Hi, we were just grabbing coffee before Prof Leinster's class too, join us." The girl that had introduced herself the other day as Lizzy and handed Quinn the invitation that had saved her from Reese called her over in a jovial tone.

"Thanks." Quinn said gratefully, looking at the other girl with Lizzy.

"I'm Emma." She said with a smile. "I'm in Leinster's class too."

"Quinn, nice to meet you."

"So are you going to come to bowl's night?" Lizzy pressed.

"Well, I..."

"Oh, come on, it will be fun, just us girls."

Quinn could probably do with some friends now the popular girls on campus had chosen to outcast her thanks to Curry and Rice.

"Yeah, sure...I'll come." She was sure it would be fine with Antonio if it was a strictly girls only invite they could be her future study partners. She decided she would take a pic of the invite later and send it to him to ask permission.

"Awesome!" Lizzy exclaimed enthusiastically.

"Heads up, the prince is here." Emma said under her breath, looking down at the table then glancing up with just her eyes.

Quinn shrank into her seat and peeked around behind her seeing Reese with a couple of his mates walk in like they owned the place as everyone in the café hushed and moved back.

"Wow, he's really scary, but so hot!" Lizzy whispered, looking at Quinn.

Quinn looked back at the table keeping her head down looking uncomfortable.

"You know, Quinn...he asked me about you yesterday."

Quinn looked at Lizzy with a frown. "Is that how he knows my name?"

Lizzy looked apologetic. "Yeah, sorry..."

"I'm going to go before he turns around." Quinn announced.

"Why?" Emma asked. "If he likes you, stay. My god, he's so hot!"

Quinn's expression looked like she was going to be sick as she stood up, slinging her bag over her shoulder and as discreetly as possible made her way to the exit as Reese was at the counter ordering a coffee to go.

He turned just as she made it to the door and saw her.

"Quinn!" He yelled out in a deep authoritative tone that silenced the entire café.

She flinched but kept going through the door and ran.

"Fuck!" Reese spat and ran off after her.

"Oh my..." Lizzy breathed. "What's going on there?"

Quinn was spun around by a forceful hand on her shoulder, lucky it was gripping her hoodie otherwise she would have probably reeled backwards and fallen on her ass.

"Quinn, wait." Reese growled as he steadied her on her feet. He looked pissed, those pale hazel eyes looking dark. "Haven't I already told you about ignoring me?"

Quinn calmed her rapid breath and shook his grip off her clothes causing her oversized sweatshirt to fall off her shoulder and show skin as she was wearing a string strapped singlet underneath. Reese's eyes were drawn to the skin that was exposed and Quinn yanked her sweatshirt up again indignantly. Her skin wasn't the usual pale white you would expect from a girl with red hair, her skin was golden and sun-kissed, but then her hair wasn't the normal red either it was dark and lush and her ponytail looked like the tail of a chestnut horse...she was an exotic creature and just as flighty it seemed. It infuriated him but he really didn't know why and that pissed him off even more.

"What do you want?" She demanded, yanking her sweatshirt back up.

"I just told you..." He smirked, clearly amused to be teasing her.

Quinn huffed, blowing her hair from her forehead, it wafted up and then settled back down. Reese's fingers twitched to touch it and brush it away. "Don't you have enough girls hanging around you to annoy? Leave me alone."

"None of them are as beautiful as you though." His smirk turned into a sexy smolder as his gaze intensified and seemed to darken and become more golden at the same time.

Quinn stared at him for a moment lost in those eyes then looked away with a small sardonic chuckle. "I'm already taken, okay, so stop."

"You have a boyfriend?" Reese asked with a dark tone.

Quinn paused. "Not in so many words...look it's not any of your business, I've already been hassled by the queens of campus, I don't need trouble in my life and you..." She looked him up and down with a haughty glare down her nose as she pointed up and down at him. "...are all sorts of trouble."

His chuckle in response was the sexiest damn thing Quinn had ever heard and the fact that his tongue licked out over his teeth and he raked his hand through his raven locks all at the same time made her body react and melt inside. Fuck, he really was hot.

"Any other complaints while you're at it?"

"I hate to damage your over inflated ego but just because you have a fan club of fifty girls following you around that call you the prince does not mean I should automatically want to join them and fall faint at your feet." Quinn stepped up to him grabbing the open edges of his leather jacket collar and pulled him down to her height to be face to face with her, aggressively.

His eyes widened, the pupils contracting in surprise and Quinn got an all up close and personal look at the gorgeous golden color of them. She lost her momentum and stared, hypnotized as the amazing scent of his cologne drifted into her nostrils and made her skin goose bump.

Reese recovered his shock and found himself staring into the most beautiful light green eyes he had ever seen, they looked unreal...they were so pale and flecked with gold but had a deep sea green depth to the middle of them that surrounded her pupils that he felt like he was falling into them, pity she was doing this to obviously yell in his face.

Wait, why wasn't she yelling?

Quinn blinked as she noticed the slow sexy smirk curling up Reese's lips and snapped out of her reverie, shoving him away. "I'm not interested!" She yelled and stormed off feeling flustered and hot.

Reese straightened up, putting his hands in his jacket pockets and leaning his weight back on one leg. "Bullshit you aren't!" He yelled back at her. "Fucking hell...what was that?" He muttered, raking a hand through his hair feeling a little flustered himself, his heart was thumping, this had never happened before. "What was that connection just now?"

Later that day Quinn was out on the large grass quad in the middle of the three main buildings finally enjoying some quiet time to have a look at the chapter of the law book she was supposed to read before tomorrow's class when two girls came over and plonked themselves down either side of her.

"Quinn, I've been looking for you."

She looked at the one who spoke and cringed inside to see it was Vanessa. "Why?"

"Look, we got off on the wrong foot...I would like to rewind back to our first meeting and the offer I gave you."

Quinn closed her book and gave Vanessa a strange, confused look. "I said I wasn't interested in being a cheerleader for some mid football team."

Vanessa's face contorted into a sneer before changing back to a smile as she laughed. "Yes, I remember, silly...no I wanted to ask you where you're staying, because if you're having to rent some overly expensive tiny apartment in some godforsaken surrounding town miles away might I suggest to you that we have a room available in our house right here in Scarsdale."

"Ah...why?" This was out of left field.

"Because you're obviously what we look for, like I said...you fit with us, so I'm giving you another shot at joining us."

Quinn looked dubiously at her. So I'm rich enough, was that it? I'm not though...I don't have a penny to my name.

Vanessa rolled her eyes at Quinn's suspicion. "Look, you're really cute, the boys obviously already think so, you're fit, smart and obviously fairly well off...you did say to Lila's sister that you're from Zortex Industries, didn't you?"

Quinn couldn't help but laugh. "So I fit your criteria to be a part of you clique, is that it?"

Vanessa grinned, completely unashamed. "Exactly, we're not above putting our differences aside for the greater good, girls like us should be together on the same side. So, will you move in to our house, it's really big and has a pool?"

"So, you're like a sorority?"

"Yeah, we're with the AOII, founded at Columbia..."

Quinn stifled a laugh. "Look no offense, but my brother bought me a nice place in an attached townhouse type complex on the north side of this 'godforsaken town' and he provides everything I need, so I'm good, I prefer to be able to study quietly by myself anyway and I won't have a lot of free time to spend doing whatever with you guys. Thanks anyway."

Quinn got to her feet, grabbed her book and bag and walked off.

Vanessa clucked her tongue and looked at the other girl. "What a bitch, well can't say I didn't try."

"Shit, she has a townhouse on the north side...how rich is this brother of hers? That would have to be a couple of million, right?"

Vanessa folded her arms in a huff. "Shut up...this is war! Did you hear, Reese fucking ran out of a café chasing her this morning!"

6
Just come quietly

The very next day as Quinn approached the side entrance of the main building to go to her locker she saw Vanessa and her gaggle of rich girls standing on the stoop like they were waiting for her.

Quinn never really cared about brands or fashion and just wore what she wanted, mainly based around comfort and now hiding the rope burns and bruises from spending her weekend with Antonio. So today she was wearing jean tights and an oversized t-shirt from an energy drink company, as well as her favorite grey and black striped arm warmers with the thumb holes that kept them covering her wrists. Her hair was up in her usual ponytail with the front few strands free to frame her face but usually ended up being tucked behind her ears. She knew her look was edgy, but she really didn't care.

As she passed the girls on the step Vanessa gave her a little twisted smirk and Quinn just knew something was going on even before one other girl spoke out in a shrill voice.

"Oh my god! You look so trashy today!"

Quinn stopped and looked at the girl with her tight miniskirt and see-through blouse. "I believe you had better look in the mirror and get a dictionary to look up the word trashy because you..." She waved her hand in a circular motion at the cheerleader. "...are the one that's all over that word." Quinn walked off inside leaving the girls all stunned and gaping at her.

Vanessa hissed and stormed off down the stairs.

In the cafeteria at lunch Vanessa saw Quinn enter and looked across the way to see that Cory was with the football team. She elbowed Mila and whispered in her ear. Mila looked up and saw Cory had noticed Quinn and was watching her.

"Quinn! Quinn!" Mila called out, waving her arms and bouncing in her seat getting the attention of both Cory and Quinn. Quinn frowned at her and Vanessa as they beamed huge friendly smiles at her. "Come sit over here with us!"

Quinn turned back to the counter, paying for her chicken salad to go and walked off. Mila glanced at Cory and he frowned at her in question as Quinn ignored her and walked out to find somewhere else to eat. Mila gave Cory a little innocent shrug and smile and he walked over.

"What was that about?" He asked.

Mila draped her hands over his arm, squishing her boobs up against him. "We've been trying to be friendly with that freshman, but she's quite nasty."

"Yeah, I even invited her to live in the house with us..." Vanessa added.

"You did?" Cory asked, surprised.

"Of course, she's fit...right? Should be one of us, don't you think?" Vanessa's smile was like a snake.

Cory scratched his nose. "Yeah, she should be part of our group...I think she's just shy, quite reserved, you know? Keep trying, I'm sure she'll come around, she is only a freshman after all."

"That's what we thought." Mila said, putting on a fake pout.

Cory disentangled himself from Mila and gave her a smile. "Cool, you guys are coming to Lucas's party, yeah?"

"Of course."

"Wouldn't miss it." They both beamed huge smiles.

"Okay..." Cory walked off back to his mates and they made their way out to the grass quad. He saw Quinn sitting at a table with a group of freshman girls and smiled to himself to see she wasn't alone. She looked up and caught him looking.

He waved out at her but she looked away quickly. Maybe she was just shy?

He wandered over to say hello and gave all the girls a sexy smile, sweeping his golden locks back from his face.

"Hello ladies...I'm Cory, quarter back of the Lions, you probably saw me at your welcome ceremony but I just wanted to take this opportunity to introduce myself to you all on a more personal level." He leaned over and reached out to grab Quinn by the hand and pulled her off her seat and started walking away dragging her with him. The other girls descended into whispers and giggles wondering what was going on.

"What the hell are you doing?" Quinn hissed under her breath, looking around and seeing that the popular girls were all watching through the large glass windows of the cafeteria. She pulled against his grip of her hand but he had interlaced their fingers and when he squeezed more firmly Quinn whimpered in pain.

"Just come quietly." He said in a tone that made Quinn's body tremble. She went quiet and let him take her away and around the building to a quiet corner.

He finally let her hand go as she noticed he had her boxed in against the wall. He finally saw the fear in her eyes and his clouded with remorse. "Shit, relax, okay...I just wanted to talk and...fuck, why are you so scared?"

"Ah...because you physically dragged me here and hurt my hand!" Quinn quailed, she was trembling and looked like a scared rabbit cornered by a vicious wolf.

"Sorry." Cory reached out and took her hand gently, rubbing it and checking it over. "Are you alright?"

"I'm fine." She snatched her hand back before he lifted her sleeve.

"I just want to talk...and I know it's insane but it's best to do that away from the crowds and I want you to be nicer to the girls is all."

Quinn looked at his guilty expression as he rubbed the back of his neck, he seemed genuinely sorry for hurting her, that was something at least. "You know those girls weren't sincere about being nice to me?"

"What makes you say that? I can see them really trying to be friendly with you and being a freshman it should be a big deal."

"Are you fucking serious?" Quinn snapped.

"Yeah, look if you get in well with them then it means I get to see a lot more of you as well." He looked up under his brows and grinned.

"Oh, I get it..." Quinn folded her arms over her chest and leaned her back against the wall. "Is this place really that cliquey?"

"Yes it is, trust me, being in the wrong group here could impact future success...think of this place as an opportunity to network for future prospects."

"Network what? Where to get my hair bleached and my nails done?" Quinn sneered.

Cory chuckled. "Wow, you're vicious, aren't you...like a real alley cat."

Quinn looked startled for a moment then her gaze dropped to the ground dismayed. "I have my reasons." She muttered quietly.

Cory noticed the sudden gloom mellow her attitude and frowned in curiosity. "I would really like to find out about those reasons and other things about you?"

Quinn blinked and looked up at him. He was gorgeous, fit and muscular, a real boy-next-door type but with a very powerful protective aura.

"Can I get your social media info?"

"What?" She startled like a cornered rabbit again. "Um...I don't really..."

"Hey..." His calm soft tone brought her attention back. "It's no big deal, you know...everyone has everyone's here, especially these days, right? Just give me your Insta..."

Quinn was chewing her bottom lip nervously not sure what to do. Cory's eyes were intently fixed on it as he licked his lips wishing he was licking hers, they were full and pouty, naturally and looked soft and pink.

"I won't let you leave till you at least give me that." His voice was strange and husky and Quinn's eyes widened. He saw her pupils dilate out. He coughed and cleared his throat awkwardly feeling like a predator.

"Here..." She said suddenly, taking her phone out and scrolling to it and holding it up, her hand shaking.

Cory quickly added her and grinned in triumph. "Thanks, so your name is Quinn Malley?"

"That's what it says..." She said, back to her abrupt self. "Can I go now?" There was a desperate pleading in her voice and Cory started to feel bad.

"Sure, thanks."

"Whatever." Quinn pushed passed him and made quick her escape.

He wandered back around the corner and bumped into Reese.

"What the fuck's that goofy grin on your face for?" Reese asked in a surly tone.

Cory pointed back down the other side of the building and Reese saw the back of the red ponytailed girl retreating in the other direction. "Just got her Insta..."

"Fucking prick." Reese breathed in shock. "You're a real jammie bastard, give it to me."

"Fuck off, get it yourself...if you can. I had to practically kidnap her back there and not let her leave until she gave it to me."

"You fucking what?" Reese chuckled unbelieving. He clucked his tongue and rubbed his forehead. "If this shit keeps up she's going to report both of us for SA."

"What SA? All I've done is hold her hand, what the fuck have you done?" Cory's tone was accusatory.

"Not much more...but I think it's time to escalate things." He grinned, licking his tongue over his teeth.

Cory knew that look. "What are you planning?"

Reese gave him a piercing look. "Give me her Insta..."

Cory huffed. "We're supposed to be competing..."

"Okay, I'll see you around then..." Reese wandered off looking cocky and Cory worried about what plan Reese had cooking.

Quinn it seemed was easily scared and that invoked strange feelings to well up inside him.

Mila watched as Quinn came out from the little through-way between buildings and walked off. She grit her teeth at what she had heard. Cory was interested in this girl!

There was no way she was going to listen to Vanessa any longer and be nice to this bitch! It was all on...

7

Be nicer!

Quinn pulled into the parking lot to find her usual space taken up with a white BMW. She cursed as she saw the blond haired Mila get out of it and look back with a shit-eating grin and wave at her before she flounced over to Cory's truck as he was sitting in it still. He met Quinn's eyes as she drove past and his expression seemed flat before he looked away to Mila and gave her his usual roguish smile.

"Is everyone here fake as shit?" Quinn muttered to herself as she went further down and parked her car. She couldn't believe the crap she had to put up with for the last few days, did they not know she had bigger problems in life than if they liked her or not?

She knew Antonio tracked her phone and her movements and could at any random moment send someone to check up on her. There was no way in hell she was going to take any risk of being caught in a compromising situation with any guy. No matter how damn cute or hot they were. Not that she wasn't flattered to have the interest of two amazingly handsome guys as soon as she started college, but she was already caught in one spider's web.

She saw Mila move across the grass to meet up with a couple of other girls and stop, look back at her and then stay put.

Oh, great, are they waiting for me?

Quinn stuck a lollipop in her mouth and got out of her car with a heavy sigh, making her way over to the side entrance. She was wearing army green tights, doc martins and a black fine mesh t-shirt with a black and white plaid shirt tied around her waist, her wrists were clear of marks now so her arms were bare. Her hair was down and one side was braided back. She had chosen this outfit especially to try and piss off the fashionistas and it worked.

"What the fuck are you wearing, are you an emo now?" Mila's whiney voice called out as her friends twittered and giggled. Quinn noticed Cory walking up with a little frown etching his fine features.

Quinn smiled, friendly at Mila. "Oh, I wore this outfit today because you tried to be friendly yesterday, so I thought this fit would let you know how I feel about that and tell you to fuck off without me actually having to say it. Was I wrong?"

"You bitch!" Mila stomped her foot but hesitated as they all heard Cory's laughter. He sauntered up and hooked his arm around Mila's neck making her blush and look up at him with Bambi eyes.

"I don't know, I think your fit looks badass...especially the black mesh tee with the black bra underneath, nice touch." He unashamedly eyed her breast's nice curves.

Quinn scowled at him, turned with a flick of her head, causing her braid to fly around in a circle and stormed off.

"Cory...why did you have to say that?"

Cory tightened his arm around Mila's neck and brought his mouth to her ear. "Listen, Mila...leave Quinn alone."

He walked away leaving Mila with tears in her eyes at the threat in his voice.

"What does she have that I don't? That fucking bitch is going to pay for stealing my man! Just wait for next week!"

Cory caught up with Quinn, trotting up beside her and matching her walking pace. She flicked a sideways glance at him and her lips pursed into a disapproving pout.

"Hey, are you busy this weekend? There's a welcome party for all freshmen being held by us, the footy team..."

"Yes, I'm very busy this weekend, sorry." Quinn said as she walked.

"Shame, it was for just the guys, a hazing really, but then we decided to open it up to the girls as well..."

"Cool..." Quinn said quite noncommittal. "I'll let the others know..."

Cory's mouth twisted. "Can't you cancel whatever you're doing?"

Quinn stopped walking and turned to face him with a sour look. "Did you not hear Mila just now? I'm being picked on, because of you."

"I just told her to leave you alone." Cory shrugged. "She's a little obsessive..." He grinned like it was to be expected given his good looks.

Quinn's mouth twisted. "Wow! Ego much..."

She turned away and walked off the path onto the grass in a different direction hoping he wouldn't follow.

"Hey!" He called out.

Quinn stopped and looked back at the harsh angry tone more from reflex than anything else.

Cory was glaring at her. "Perhaps if you could be a bit nicer to people you wouldn't be having all these problems...take my advice...be nicer!"

He walked off, raking a hand through his hair feeling annoyed at her brisk attitude.

Quinn stared at his retreating back for a moment, chewing on her lip. A million come backs swirling around in her mind before it was too late and he had gone. She sighed to herself.

'I can't be nicer...I can't encourage you.' She thought regretfully.

Quinn had offered to pick up a couple of the other freshman girls from the business faculty and take them to the ten pin bowling arcade so she didn't have to turn up alone. She knew she probably wouldn't have gone if that was the case, she hated having to turn up to social events alone and awkward.

Emma had insisted on going with Quinn as she really wanted a chance to ride in her Mustang and the other girl, Tania, somehow managed to get dragged in by Emma as well.

It was good and had Quinn relaxed and smiling as she pulled into the parking lot. She looked up at the building and couldn't help but laugh.

"What's so funny?" Emma asked, taking off her seatbelt and checking her makeup in her compact mirror.

"Strike Palace? It's a bit 60's isn't it?"

"That's the fun of it...this place is decked out retro style, like you're actually back there..." Tania said, looking out from the back seat. "Oh, look! Lizzy is here."

She jumped out of Quinn's car and walked over to where Lizzy was parking her Tesla.

Quinn watched with a small frown.

Emma saw and snapped her compact closed. "What's the problem? Is it V8 against electric or something?"

"What?" Quinn looked around with a scoff. "No, nothing like that, just her sister lives in the AOII house with the cheerleaders, doesn't she?"

"Yeah...but Lizzy isn't bitchy, she's nice why else would she organize this freshman bonding thing?"

"Hmm, I guess so."

"You've been getting a hard time from those bitches, huh? Is it because of Reese O'Shea or Cory McMillan?"

Quinn snorted at Emma wondering why she was asking. "Neither, it's a misunderstanding."

"Misunderstanding?" Emma laughed. "Okay..."

"What's with that sarcastic tone?" Quinn asked a little defensive. She took a lollipop out of her glove box and stuck it in her mouth.

"Nothing...but I saw Reese run after you out of that café the other day, remember. He clearly likes you."

Quinn gave her a hard look then got out of the car deciding not even to comment, what was there to say? It didn't matter if Reese liked her or not, she wasn't free to do anything about it. Just like how she felt about Cory.

She thought back to the night before and how she had gone onto Cory's Insta page and scrolled his photos. There were lots of him, practicing with the team but also lots without a shirt. Holy heck, did he have a good body! He also had lots of photos with girls, out at clubs, out at the park, around campus...everywhere. It made her think why was he chasing her? Was it just for the notch on his bedpost? She had heard the rumors that he was a player that got around with a different girl every other week, but then how was Mila so convinced he was her boyfriend?

8

We all have trauma

Inside the Strike Palace was a little more modern retro than Quinn had expected, it was all digitized with electronic score boards and the atmosphere was fun. The girls were all nice and since they had a fairly good turnout of eight girls they took up two channels and competed as pairs. There wasn't really anyone else in the place except for a couple of teenagers over at the old pinball machines and playing foosball in the corner.

Quinn had never played before so had to be shown how to bowl and she wondered why they had to wear special shoes...nevertheless she was having fun and making new friends and that's what counted. She exchanged contact info with everyone and was a bit stunned to hear them all say she was weird to only have Insta as a chat app. Most seemed to use several but Quinn didn't have a reason to have so many social media apps, she seldom really used any form of media. Posting photos, influencers and famous people didn't really interest her, neither did flirting or anything for obvious reasons so she never bothered with them.

The only person that actually texted her phone number was Antonio.

Quinn's mood rapidly declined the moment the doors to the place opened and a group of young guys walked in. The one leading them in like the leader of some notorious street gang, his hands in his pockets and swaggering like he owned the joint with a pleased smirk on his face as his eyes searched the place and landed on Quinn was none other than Reese O'Shea.

Quinn's mouth twisted in discontent as his eyes met hers and she purposely looked away. "What the hell is he doing here?" She muttered.

"No idea..." Lizzy said sounding legitimately shocked. "Didn't think this would be his sort of place to hang out?"

"Argh..." Quinn rolled her eyes and hid her face in her hand as she groaned. "Stupid me told him!"

"You did, when?"

"When he asked me out and I told him I was busy..."

Lizzy grinned. "He asked you out, the Prince asked you out and you didn't tell any of us?"

"What's to tell, I said no." Quinn glanced at him over at the shoe counter taking his boots off. She couldn't believe someone so cool like him would come here to ten pin bowl and wear these crappy horrible shoes.

She groaned and rolled her eyes again feeling a nervous twitter start up in her belly as he wandered over to the booth she was sharing with Lizzy, Emma and Tania. The girls in the other booth were all staring like they had just seen a celebrity walk in.

"Evening girls, how great it is that I have a free evening so I could come down and spend it with the lovely freshman girls of the business faculty...how about we all mingle and play together...I have a great game to get to know each other."

"We're already playing a game, it's called ten pin bowling." Quinn grumbled, folding her arms as Reese squeezed past her knees and sat down beside her.

"Don't be like that, this will make things more interesting."

"What is it?" Lizzy asked enthusiastically, her eyes sparkling with delight as the other girls all gushed and giggled.

"It's called Strike Truth or Dare...whoever gets a strike gets to pick one of their opponents for truth or dare."

"Sounds exciting, shall we?" Lizzy asked the other girls. "He is on the executive, we should get to know him a little..."

Quinn scowled darkly, seeing the trap. "I'm out...time to go." She went to stand up but Reese grabbed the back of her jeans and yanked her back down.

"You stay here." He growled in a deep sexy demand that had the other girls all gaping openly at him.

Quinn's mouth went dry as her brain left her and she felt her cheeks heat up in a flush. His hand was still on the small of her back and the heat permeating through from it was sparking heat in her womb. She glanced sideways up at him to see he was smirking at her as all the other girls agreed to the game and split into groups with the guys of Reese's gang leaving Lizzy with a guy called Mac and Emma with a huge muscly guy called Tank to play with them, Reese and Quinn.

Reese leaned in, lifting his hand up and placing it on the back of her neck making her gasp in a little breath. "Why are you so quiet and demure all of a sudden? No smart ass comments, no struggle?"

Quinn could barely breathe let alone speak. She moved her head and swiped his hand away. "Don't touch me like that!" There was another person who liked to hold her around the neck and it sent shivers through her enough to give her goose bumps.

Reese noticed and his eyes narrowed suspiciously as he chuckled. "Wow...fuck." He breathed out to realize she was actually submissive. "So all that mouthiness is just for show, huh, brat?"

"Shut the hell up!" Quinn hissed. She looked away to where Lizzy was organizing everyone and everything, that's what she was good at it seemed, a real mother hen type. "Why did you come here?" She looked back at Reese as he relaxed back into the seat once he knew Quinn wasn't going to try and leave again. Mac started the round and instantly got a strike.

Quinn felt a bad shift in the air that they had all been duped.

"I thought you were inviting me when you handed me that invite." Reese said smoothly.

"Bullshit." Quinn hissed under her breath.

"Ah, there she is..."

Mac grinned as he came back to the table. "Truth or Dare, Quinn."

She looked at the guy who was a complete stranger, stunned. "Me?"

"Ah-huh." Mac grinned like a cheeky little boy, dimples and all.

"Truth, I guess..." No way she was ever picking dare with this psycho sitting next to her.

"Alright, one for all the girls..." He looked at Lizzy and Emma. "When did you lose your virginity?"

"I was fifteen...he was hot, no regrets." Lizzy stated proudly.

Quinn was a little surprised and relieved, she hadn't wanted to say fifteen honestly thinking it would label her a slut or something.

"Same." She muttered. Reese's eyebrow's lifted in interest and he smiled at Mac who nodded.

Emma answered. "Eighteen, like literally two months ago, with my current boyfriend."

Reese leaned back to Quinn's ear, bumping shoulders with her. "So you like the back of your neck touched?"

Quinn shoved him away and went to get up but Reese laughed and held her in place with a strong grip on her thigh. "Stop, I was only teasing, man you're so reactive to every little thing...do you not get guys flirting with you?"

"I try to avoid it."

"Why?"

"I told you already..." Quinn huffed as Lizzy and Tank started their turns.

"The boyfriend that's not in so many words, what the fuck does that even mean?" Reese asked annoyed.

"It means leave me alone, I'm not interested."

Reese gave her an intense glare that almost made her forget how to breathe. "Oh? But I think you kinda are..."

Tank got a strike. "Yes!" He fist pumped the air and waltzed over. "Truth or Dare, Quinn?" He asked amused.

Lizzy giggled. "You're popular."

Quinn grimaced and glanced at Reese to see his amused smirk. Was this all a set up? "Truth." She muttered."

"I'll go easy on you." Tank said sounding quite gentle for a big guy. "Where were you born?"

Quinn gave a little cluck of the tongue. "Boston." She flinched as Reese suddenly stood up.

"Easy, babe...it's my go." He chuckled and walked off to pick up a ball. He wondered how come she was always so flighty, like she had been hit before. He knew all about how women flinched being used to being hit, he had seen it growing up plenty of times. That made his blood boil and he had to take a moment to close his eyes and calm down before taking his turn.

Quinn blinked in startled chagrin as the ball flew straight into the pins for an almost professional strike. Reese turned on his heels and gave her the most shit-eating self-congratulatory grin making her stomach sink as he wandered back over.

"Look at that! A strike!" Lizzy cried out enthusiastically. "Wow, so you get to pick someone for truth or dare...you guys are like pool sharks, huh?"

Quinn gave her a lethal look as Reese chuckled. "Quite right, little Lizzy...who do you think I'll pick?"

Lizzy's eyes slid to Quinn and she smiled coyly. "Perhaps Quinn?"

Emma giggled behind her hand.

"Bingo! You're good at this game." Reese praised her as Mac chuckled to himself.

Reese sat down and put his arm around Quinn's shoulder's pulling her into his side. "Truth or dare, Quinn, what will it be?"

She was engulfed by the scent of his expensive cologne and felt the hotness of her cheeks. She pouted her lips and sighed. "Truth I guess, I certainly don't trust what sort of dare you would give me."

Reese laughed a husky deep chuckle. "Spoil sport." He murmured, licking his tongue over his teeth.

He looked really carefree and handsome when he laughed and Quinn wondered why he always looked so dark and moody most of the time like something was weighing him down. She really didn't know anything about him because she had purposely not found out. She wanted to, he was being quite close but his rizz was quite infectious.

Quinn was looking at him with a weird pout waiting for his invasive question, but her eyes were sparkling brightly. His eyes seemed to darken in intensity at that look.

"Tell us your body count." He said with a smug grin.

Quinn frowned. "My what?"

"How many people you've slept with." Lizzy cooed, amused. Quinn thought she looked like she was enjoying this far too much, had she been in on this?

She frowned deeper and more serious. "I've only slept with one guy."

"Really?" They all sounded surprised and Quinn gave them all a strange curious look.

"Why is that so shocking? What's all yours?"

Reese chuckled. "Get a strike and then you can ask...it's your turn."

She huffed and stood up, grabbing the pink ball she had chosen to play with and walked to the alley.

"You think that was actually the truth?" Mac asked Reese as Quinn played her shot.

"She didn't look like she was lying." Reese shrugged, watching Quinn.

"She seems strangely innocent of a lot of things...was she home schooled or something?" Lizzy butt in.

Reese's gaze slid to Lizzy with interest. "Home schooled? Interesting theory, yeah, she seems quite out of touch with a lot but still sassy as shit."

Quinn managed to get three pins down and then missed the rest on her second shot returning to the table with a disappointed little pout.

"Maybe next time..." Reese teased. Quinn stuck her tongue out at him and dropped into her seat folding her arms with a huff. He chuckled deeply, wiping a thumb over his bottom lip. "Fuck, don't do that...I will not be responsible for what happens next."

Quinn flinched away and glared at him in shock. His intense gaze just gazed back and his eyebrow lifted as if daring her to do it again.

Mac had jumped up and started the next round, getting a strike. Quinn grimaced and her face fell to the ground. Reese frowned, perhaps this game had done its dash. He looked up at Mac with a look to not say Quinn but Mac frowned at him.

"I'm guessing Quinn will just choose truth at this stage." He said as he sat down. "So I have a question that I really have been genuinely interested in finding out about."

Quinn looked up with a sick expression on her face wondering what the fuck he was going to ask. Reese sat up with a grumpy look. "That's enough."

Mac grinned. "Nah, hear me out...I'm sure everyone has been wondering what's up with the lollipops?"

Reese's face looked surprised for a second and he turned to see that Quinn looked equally as shocked. She pressed a hand to her chest and laughed, relieved. "Shit, I was literally scared and ready to walk out of here..."

Mac just chuckled.

"So?" Lizzy asked. "We are all dying to know? Are you trying to give up smoking?"

"I thought maybe she was diabetic and needed the sugar boost, until I saw they were sugar free lollipops." Emma said.

Quinn smiled to herself, she hadn't realized it was such a big deal. "I'm not eating to try and fit into a dress for tomorrow night, I have a function to go to."

"You eat at lunchtime every day." Reese stated with a dark frown. "And you hardly need to lose weight..."

Quinn looked at him a little shocked to hear the vehemence in his voice. She wouldn't have to try and lose weight if Antonio didn't purposely always buy a dress a size smaller than she was, but she couldn't say that to him.

She just shrugged. "You asked...I eat one meal a day, but don't worry, I'll be back to eating normal on Monday."

"Hmm, I get it...I guess guys don't." Emma said in her defense.

"You want a drink?" Reese asked, like he wanted a reason to suddenly leave.

Quinn's eyes squinted suspiciously.

"I'm getting one for myself, probably for Tank and Mac too, Lizzy? Emma?"

"Sure, Coke."

"Thanks, Dr Pepper."

"Quinn?" Reese asked again, managing an innocent look.

"Fine, can I have an orange juice, please?" She gave him a pretty little smile.

Reese's head tilted sideways as he scrutinized her. "You're so polite, have you had etiquette lessons?"

Lizzy giggled. "I had to do those...god, they were such a pain!"

Quinn just seemed to blush and looked away awkwardly.

"A question for a strike, maybe?" Reese commented, smirking at her expression with interest.

Quinn startled and looked back at him noticeably distressed. "Please don't."

That made him scowl darkly. Something certainly wasn't right about this girl and he really wanted to get to the bottom of it.

Quinn looked away and searched out the sign for the bathrooms. "I'm going to the bathroom..." She fled leaving Reese bewildered.

Quinn really hoped he didn't push things otherwise she was going to have to lie and she was hopeless at lying. She certainly couldn't tell them she had never received etiquette lessons more submissive lessons, made to be polite when asking for anything of Antonio.

"Wow! She's so scaredy cat of social gatherings...does she suffer from anxiety?" Emma asked as she stood up. "I'm going to go see if she's alright."

Reese raked a hand through his hair and stood up. "I'm going to get the drinks, maybe some loaded fries too..."

"Cool..." Lizzy smiled. "Can I ask you something though?"

Reese gave her a challenging stare that made her stop breathing. "Get a strike first." He said walking off. "But just realize, I'm not here to talk to you."

Lizzy gasped at his back, stunned by his sudden coldness.

"Savage." Mac chuckled.

"Typical, Rice." Tank commented. "I bet he's going to the bathroom."

Quinn was staring into the sink, running her hands under the water and trying to convince Emma she was fine when the door banged open and Reese strode in. Quinn backed up to the side wall looking terrified as his heated golden gaze settled on her.

"Hey!" Emma shouted. "You can't come waltzing in here!"

"Get out." Reese ordered, his voice low and calm, but deadly. He didn't even look in Emma's direction but she knew he meant her. She swallowed hard, glancing at Quinn to see if she would be okay.

"Out!" Reese looked at her then and Emma jumped out of her skin, his order was so menacing and he looked like a werewolf glaring at her with those golden eyes through his fringe of dark hair, deranged.

"S-sorry..." She whispered to Quinn before she fled.

Reese slid his gaze back to Quinn, he didn't approach her, just leaned back on one leg, his hands dropping into the pockets of his leather jacket and tilted his head at her studying her like she was a new undiscovered animal on the discovery channel.

She looked completely terrified, vulnerable, yet there was a fire in her eyes as she returned his gaze, similar to a cornered wild beast ready to lay its life down.

"Are you alright? I apologize if I stepped over a line, we were just having fun, weren't we?" Reese's voice changed tone, it seemed casual, soft and Quinn blinked in surprise.

"Hey, I'm not going to hurt you? Why do you think I would?" His frown was offended.

Quinn shook her head, relaxing a little. "No, I don't...I just..." She stopped and her eyes dropped to the ground.

He raked a hand through his hair and he saw her eyes lift to watch his movements, like that cornered animal watching the predator. His smirk was smoldering and hot as he realized a small part of him was being turned on by this.

"Did you have strict parents? You've never done this sort of thing have you?"

Quinn breathed in a deep breath and folded her arms defensively. "I suppose you could say that they were, and no I've never been out with boys before."

Reese scratched his jaw. "How did you lose your virginity at fifteen then?"

Quinn paled at his affronting question and shook her head, biting her lip nervously.

He saw that reaction and his jaw clenched. Was her first time not a good experience? Had she been raped or something?

"Fuck, sorry...was it not a good thing?"

Quinn looked up at him with a wavering glance as tears threatened and welled up in her eyes. "I'm sorry...I just don't want to do this. You're being too much..."

"I..." Reese sighed and collected his thoughts. "I was hoping for a fun relaxed night playing bowls and a few sneaky little games to find out more about you...it obviously back fired...we'll go."

He turned away and walked to the door, opening it. He paused when he heard a little 'I'm sorry' come from Quinn.

"Look, if you actually want to get to know me come out of here, if you don't stay in here till I leave." He walked out leaving Quinn staring at the bathroom door.

"What...the...hell?" She breathed. He wasn't at all what she thought he was. She thought he was going to force the issue with her, try to kiss her or grope her maybe...instead he had backed off the instant he realized her trauma, apologized even and then put it all in her hands to decide what she wanted.

But what did she want?

What she wanted never mattered, she had never been asked what she wanted. When she tried to do anything for her own self it had been shut down and arrangements had been made for her for the benefit of the Ferrante family.

She liked him...

He seemed cocky and red-flag at first but he held himself to a moral code when it came to girls. He gave the same protective vibe as Cory did but in a much more violent and dangerous way.

Did she dare to go against Antonio and start talking to these guys?

If she kept her interactions with them within campus maybe she should risk it? She was practically an adult now...and she wanted freedom.

She dashed out the door of the bathroom and ran to the bowling alleys. She saw Reese and Tank were gone.

"Where's Reese?" She asked Mac.

"He's leaving..." Mac pointed to the exit.

Quinn ran off and threw herself through the door, looking out over the parking lot to see two motorbikes starting up side by side.

She was too late.

She sat down on the step, hugging her arms around herself and watched as the bikes drifted off to the exit.

She saw one stop as he seemed to be looking in his mirror then he turned his bike and headed her way as the other bike waited.

She stood up and watched as Reese came back, lifting his visor and idling his bike beside the steps. "You almost missed me...I'm glad I looked back in hope." His eyes were sparkling like golden light and she could see he was really happy.

She smiled. "I'm really glad you did to...but I need to do this at my speed, not yours...okay?"

"Sure, babe, just don't make it too slow..." He chuckled. "I'll see you Monday, don't ignore me."

"I won't and thank you for understanding."

"We all have trauma, Quinn, I get it." He said and banged his visor down, revved his bike and turned it around then took off.

Quinn stared after him.

He had trauma?

9
For the family

Quinn was standing beside Antonio wearing the deep red evening dress he had bought for her. It was hard to breath in it, it was tight and the corset she had on underneath because the dress was strapless was worse.

He grinned at her into the mirror after zipping it up for her and stroked a hand down her spine and across her buttocks to the back split and dipped his fingers inside.

"Open your legs...I have a surprise for you."

"What? But I'm dressed ready to go..."

Quinn watched in the mirror as Antonio dropped down to his knees and took a bright pink double bullet wireless vibrator out of his pocket.

"Oh god..." Quinn breathed in startled. "Please don't, this is my first time out with you...why?"

"Because I know everyone is going to want you...I need to make you remember who you actually belong to."

"I don't need reminding, Antonio..."

"Shut up and open your legs." He growled, stroking his fingers through between her legs across her panties.

Quinn bit her lip and stepped her legs apart, feeling his fingers pull her thong aside and push up into her.

"You're going to have to relax, Petalo..." He muttered. "Bend over...put your hands on the wall."

Quinn complied putting her hands either side of the mirror and closing her eyes, feeling the heat of her cheeks as Antonio played with her pussy and ass and inserted the bullets inside her.

He stood up, stroking her butt cheeks and pulled the remote from his pocket, turning it on. Quinn gasped as they buzzed inside her holes.

"People will hear them..." She whined in desperation.

"No, they won't. The din of so many in the room will diminish the sound...trust me." He stepped away, shutting it off and grabbed his suit jacket pulling it on over his waistcoat and straightening his tie in the mirror, bumping his hips into Quinn's ass as she dare not move until told to.

"Stand up, let's get going...I want to see if those can make you come in the car on the way..."

Quinn stood up and glared at him in the mirror as he turned away towards the door.

The event was a small soirée held in a very swank hotel banquet room. Quinn walked in on the arm of Antonio to a whole new world, her eyes wide as she looked around the room awestruck by the rich people chatting and drinking as champagne and hors d'oeuvres were walked around by stiff waiters.

The amount of people who turned to stare as Antonio entered with his bodyguard and right hand man, Matteo and Quinn on his arm made her want to curl up and hide, the leering smiles on the men's faces and the frowning dark looks on the women's as they all spoke in hushed whispers made her feel sick, let alone the fact she was standing in front of them with vibrators inside her holes, her panties soaked and her face flushed from Antonio playing with her in the car.

He chuckled a dark sinister little laugh. "See what I mean..." He muttered to her.

A man and lady walked up, she was about fifty and elegant, tall and slim with diamonds around her neck worth a small fortune, the man was clearly younger than her and Quinn wondered if he was a boytoy, but he wasn't quite that young.

"Mr Ferrante, I'm so pleased you could join us, I wasn't sure you would..."

"Mrs Whittaker...you're looking lovely as ever, how could I miss one of your grand soirées?"

Her eyes narrowed in amusement. "I don't doubt you're here for some other reason, but who is this lovely young lady, have you finally found yourself a potential wife?"

Antonio coughed and Quinn tensed up. "Maybe..." Antonio said coyly.

"Oh..." Mrs Whittaker exclaimed. "Well, this could be the gossip of the night, I wouldn't let her stray too far from your side."

"She goes nowhere." Antonio stated coolly making Mrs Whittaker flinch back. She gave him a benign smile and stepped away.

"What the..." Quinn went to object.

"Silent!" Antonio growled under his breath. "Observe and don't speak. These people are the scum of the rich...that woman makes her money selling young girls."

Quinn gulped at that and nearly choked.

He moved her deeper in talking to people as he went, introducing her by name only and never giving her leave to speak, answering for her if she was asked a question. Soon people got the message and started not trying to speak to her at all, just looking at her with predatory gazes.

She felt a small buzzing start up inside her and jolted, her back straightening up and her eyes flying up to Antonio. His dark gaze was watching her and he smirked.

"You looked bored..." He said as explanation for startling her in that way.

She bit her lip and shuffled on her feet.

"Don't do that!" He barked at her, lifting a hand and dragging her lip out from her teeth. "Do you have any idea how fucking sexy that is?"

Matteo came to his shoulder and whispered. "Senator Smith is ready to meet."

"Excellent...Quinn, come this way..."

"Where are we going?" She asked when he led her out of the banquet hall and down the hallway.

"To a private room, I have a meeting with Senator Smith regarding procuring a license for the new casino downtown."

Quinn grimaced. She really didn't want to be included in something so clandestine. She knew that whatever this discussion was it was negotiating on a corrupt level. She had already had the Senator leer at her when he had taken Antonio's hand in introductions earlier and with the little things inside her she felt vulnerable and exposed being here.

Antonio swept into the back room with his arm around her waist and directed her straight to a chair, sitting down beside her and lifting his piercing gaze to the Senator who sat across a low table from them watching them enter with a grand smile on his fat face.

Quinn thought he looked like a bull dog.

Matteo followed them in and stood behind Antonio's chair as the Senator's assistant stood nervously holding a tablet and a folder.

"Get this man a drink!" Senator Smith ordered. The assistant moved to where a small bar was set up and placed his things down before looking up with a questioning expression.

"What's your poison, Mr Ferrante?" The Senator asked.

"Just call me Antonio, no need to stand on formality..." Antonio's voice was even and calm. "And, let's leave the drinking until the agreement is done and the license is signed."

Senator Smith's face fell slightly. "Very well...I'm sure you know my first name...and the name I go by when signing into your Black Diamonds Club." He smirked wickedly.

Antonio merely slow blinked. "Indeed I do, Senator."

"Okay, well if the money is here that we agreed on, and the photo..."

"Both are here..." Antonio grinned viciously.

"There's one more thing before I agree..."

"What's that?" Antonio's voice cooled.

"How about a little dance performance by your off-sider here..." The Senator's gaze slid to Quinn.

Antonio's gaze hardened as Quinn tensed up and looked at Antonio with worry. "Pardon?"

"Come on...I know from spending time in your club you like to watch a pretty girl dance as well, I'm sure you've trained this one to dance very well, hmm?" Senator Smith chuckled at the reaction he was getting. "So my request isn't shocking, is it? I'm sure she will dance her sweet little ass off if you tell her to, hmm?"

Antonio's jaw clenched tight and Quinn's stomach dropped. There was no way he would make her dance for this horrible man, especially knowing what was inside her...surely. "Sir, no?" She asked tentatively.

"What's this? Do you let your subordinates talk to you like that, Antonio?" Senator Smith grinned sickeningly, taunting Antonio, testing him over Quinn and what she meant to him.

Antonio's top lip twitched in his growing ire at being snookered, if he refused it would tell the Senator he had a weakness, but did he have a weakness where Quinn was concerned? Only that no other man shall ever touch her. "Do it, Quinn."

"But..." Quinn startled.

He turned to glare at her with those dark eyes glittered coldly like obsidian. "Do it!"

Quinn nervously stood up, smoothing down her dress and feeling the toys inside her very acutely as they buzzed drolly.

"Of course..." Senator Smith drawled, enjoying this moment. "I expect her to lose the dress for this performance."

"No way!" Quinn blurted out, horrified.

Antonio's lip lifted in a vicious sneer and his little chuckle was menacing. "Yes, of course...I didn't expect anything less of you, Senator." Antonio's gaze burned into Quinn as she gasped at him. "Lose the dress." He ordered.

"Please, Antonio..."

His gaze lifted to Matteo, standing like an unemotional rock, his face showing nothing of what he was feeling. "Unzip the dress for her and if she refuses and pulls away rip the bloody thing off her!"

"Yes, sir." Matteo intoned emotionless and stepped behind Quinn, his eyes momentarily softening in remorse for her as she looked back at him. Senator Smith chuckled amused around his cigar as he licked and sucked on it repulsively.

"Oh, and..." He went to add.

Antonio stopped him with an audible cluck of his tongue. "Be very careful what more you ask for, Senator, I'm not in the best of moods all of a sudden..." His warning was very clear.

Senator Smith grinned like a Cheshire Cat. "No, no...no more demands...I wouldn't dare. This artistic performance is as far as I go...anything more could constitute inappropriate actions involving a very young woman..." His eyes sparkled creepily as he leered at Quinn.

"Quite right." Antonio hissed.

"I was just going to ask about the music?"

Quinn watched Matteo grab out his phone and hand it to Quinn. "Choose some music."

Quinn bit her lip, staving off tears and searched a tune as she felt Matteo flick her hair over her shoulder and unzip her dress. She could hear his breath catch as he realized she was wearing a corset and suspenders, the whole works, perfect for Senator Smith's perverted gaze to fully enjoy.

He took the phone back as Quinn wiggled out of her dress under the dark watchful gazes of the men in the room and stepped to the side, leaving it on the floor.

"Here, right here..." Senator Smith ordered, pointing to the coffee table. "Move this out of the way, I want her dancing right here in front of me."

Quinn felt sick and glanced at Antonio as Senator Smith's bodyguard moved the table. Antonio's dark gaze burned into her as if daring her to cry and make a fuss, he smirked a little and put his hand into his pocket.

Quinn gasped in a startled breath as the bullets vibing increased inside her. She blinked at Antonio as he leaned back in his chair. This bastard was enjoying this humiliation of her!

She felt her cheeks flame up with the embarrassment as Matteo started the tune and she stepped between the two powerful men, her legs trembling and started to sway her hips awkwardly trying to find her rhythm.

"Just like you do for me, petalo..." Antonio instructed in a deep serious tone.

Quinn's stomach flipped and she swallowed her tears back hard, hearing the Senator's gross groans of pleasure at the sight of her moving in front of him.

She bent over, keeping her eyes on Antonio's and showed her ass to the Senator, moving to the music and shaking her hips.

Senator Smith reached out to grab her ass.

"No touching my property!" Antonio growled like a feral beast. "Unless you want to lose your fingers, Senator."

The Senator gave a nervous laugh and retracted his hand as Quinn straightened up, feeling a little better in the fact that there would be no touching at least and turned around to face the Senator, cringing at the sight of him getting excited and sweaty, chewing on his cigar like his life depended on it. She saw his eyes drop to the tattoo of Antonio's name on her skin and he smirked slyly.

She couldn't wait for this song and dance to end.

The toys inside her were making her crazy and she knew she was getting wet, glad her thong was black and hopefully didn't show too much, but she didn't bend over for him again, instead she bent over for Antonio, showing the Senator her cleavage and opened her mouth, sticking her tongue out instead.

She heard a small growl come from Antonio and was a little turned on by it, but still glad when the music finally stopped.

She went to grab her dress off the floor but Antonio whipped out a hand and grabbed her wrist, yanking her over and forcing her down on his lap, facing the Senator.

Antonio brushed her hair from the side of her neck and nuzzled his lips to behind her ear making her pant out a little distressed moan hoping he wasn't going to play with her in front of all these people.

Antonio's eyes were fixed on the Senator. "Are you happy now, Senator?"

"Very...I'm quite ecstatic to see how much you value your sister." He chuckled darkly at his intended meaning.

Antonio's hand came to Quinn's throat and pressed her back into his chest as his other hand came to her breast. She clamped her thighs closed tight in panic.

"What sister?" Antonio drawled. "I have no sister...this is my assistant and my property, no more than that, Senator...don't get presumptuous. Now sign the license!" His tone was not to be argued with and Matteo bristled behind him making the threat very real.

Senator Smith waved a hand. "Relax, Mr Ferrante...I meant nothing by it." He waved his assistant over who had stood quivering over by the door the whole time. "Get the license."

Antonio looked back at Matteo. "The money..."

Matteo lifted a heavy envelope out of the inside pocket of his jacket, opened it to reveal a stack of cash and a photo of a woman with a man in an embrace then handed it over to the Senator. He put it quickly in his pocket. The assistant opened the file and took out a pen and held both out to the Senator who signed the papers. The assistant closed the file and handed it to Matteo.

"Pleasure doing business with you, Antonio...can't wait for us to talk again." Senator Smith stood up and gave Quinn a lengthy look over as she sat prone upon Antonio's lap with his hand still around her throat. "Miss Quinn, have a lovely evening..." His tone was vile as he looked straight at her pussy like he knew what was in there before walking away, followed by his bodyguard and assistant.

Antonio growled in Quinn's ear. "Fuck, I want to fuck you hard, right now!" He lifted his head and looked back at Matteo. "Get out!"

Quinn felt fear slice through her as she heard the door click closed.

Antonio stood up, spun her round to face the seat and pushed her face down into it. She managed to get her forearms under her in time and braced herself against his biting grip on the back of her neck. He grabbed her thong with his other hand and ripped the gusset in two then yanked the bullets out of her and thrust his hard cock straight into her pussy.

She grunted and gasped at the hard entry, closing her eyes against the sharp sting of pain before he started thrusting like a mad man. He pulled out and thrust his cock into her ass and she cried out at the intrusion as he thrust a couple of times then pulled out and went back to her pussy.

"I'm gonna make you not be able to sit down for a fucking week!" He growled in his anger, smacking her ass hard.

Quinn couldn't even get a breath to speak, her lungs were just working by his thrusts leaving her panting and moaning under him as her eyes rolled back in her head hoping this would be over soon.

She hoped she didn't come for him, but her body was already starting to betray her as tears formed behind her tightly closed eyes as he continued to thrust back and forth between her holes.

"Stay pure for me, petalo...I'm the only man that ever gets to fuck you!"

Quinn was dropped off Sunday afternoon by Antonio's driver, Danny and as soon as she closed her front door she collapsed in a heap on the mat. Tears fell like unstoppable rain as she hugged herself and screamed a hoarse voice-cracking emotive scream of vulnerable frustration.

She understood now, she got it. She knew what she was to Antonio. He had said it to Senator Smith on Saturday night.

Property.

That's all she was to the man she thought she loved, a play thing he could manipulate and make do whatever he wanted. Lucky for her he was a possessive narcissistic control freak otherwise she may just have ended up being tricked out to get that license for his new casino.

She felt worse than dirt and needed a hot shower to burn Antonio's sadistic touch from her skin. She lurched up to her feet and staggered upstairs to her bedroom and through to the bathroom. She stared in horror at the bruises on her neck.

How the hell was she going to hide those?

It was bad enough trying to hide the bruises on her wrists all the time under arm warmers and long hoodies.

She leaned into the mirror and touched her neck tentatively.

He had been extra cruel after the Senator debacle, like he blamed her for everything. Pissed at the whole premise that Senator Smith had made out like she was a weakness to him, he had taken it out on her right through the night and into early Sunday morning without a break.

She felt sore and tender all over and decided a Radox bath would probably be a better idea...

10
Something's off

The backward comments and jibes continued from the popular girls led mainly by Mila Monday morning. Quinn hadn't realized before but had found out through talking with the girls on Friday night that Mila was actually Vice Captain of the Cheer Squad, the only good thing about that was she spent a lot of time over at Columbia for practice as did Vanessa. Apparently she didn't even need to come to this special branch but did only because she had made her daddy enroll her here after her friends told her about it and its special rich status.

Quinn did her best to just ignore the comments, it didn't seem like anything was going to escalate passed that stage as long as she didn't react so she played it cool, she had taken to putting in earbuds to make out like she couldn't even hear them.

After Friday night's spectacle with Reese now the talk of the freshman girls she really didn't need any trouble from the popular girls so had decided to sit in her car during her lunchbreak. She knew there had been a party on Saturday night while she was forced to be a plaything for Senator Smith's pervert gaze and she felt a little jealous that they all got to have fun and drink and dance and be with others their age and flirt and kiss and carry on while she was put to use to get a contract signed.

She shuddered as memories of Saturday night came back and she cringed behind the steering wheel of her car resting her forehead on it as tears welled up, triggered by the haunting creepy feeling the memory left on her skin. She tried to break through it, but her breathing just couldn't get big enough, she knew she was starting to panic and gripped the steering wheel tight.

She startled as someone banged on the car window.

She instinctively looked up startled and met beautiful sky blue eyes with her red ravaged ones, tears streaking her face.

Cory's face darkened from that roguish grin to a serious grim expression at seeing her crying and he demanded she open her door as he tried the handle to find it locked.

She didn't want to face him but didn't want to fight either, so she unlocked the car and let him open it. He crouched down outside beside her seat and placed a hand on her thigh, the other sweeping her hair back from her face as she had dropped her forehead back to the steering wheel.

"Shit, are you okay?" He asked, full of worry. "What's wrong?"

Quinn sniffled and wiped her face with her hands, looking up with a deep breath and a fake smile. "Nothing, I'm fine...go away."

"Are you fucking kidding me?" Cory growled at her. "Stop this macho bullshit it doesn't suit you and I'm fucking sick of it!" He grabbed her chin and made her look at him. "Tell me what's happened." His tone changed to a caring soft murmur.

Quinn sniffed, startled by his outburst and brushed his hand away from her face, leaning over to the glove compartment and getting a tissue out. "It's nothing really...that time of the month."

Cory bit his tongue knowing she was lying to him. "Really...is that it?"

"Yeah, I'm fine...embarrassed you caught me in this state, but fine." She looked at him and ventured a smile, it looked more like a grimace.

He laughed. "You adorable idiot. Come on, get out, I'll walk you to your locker."

"You really don't have to..."

"I know that, but I want to." His roguish smile beamed at her and she couldn't help but give a small genuine smile back. His good nature was infectious and she was grateful for him appearing. He took her hand and gently coaxed her from the car then wrapped his arms around her in a huge comforting hug. He was quite broad shouldered and his arms fit around her completely encompassing her within his body making her feel safe.

"Oh god..." She groaned out a sob. His hug felt so good, he was so warm and he smelt awesome. She burrowed her face into his chest and sobbed. He cradled her, his head resting on hers, loving the feeling of her, she fit against him so perfectly.

"I don't know what's happened but at least take this comfort from me, just for a moment." He breathed out, closing his eyes, his heart tearing to hear her crying again.

"I'm sorry..." Quinn's meek voice came to him. He squeezed her tighter to his chest.

"Don't ever be sorry...just tell me if I can help you."

She shook her head.

He grit his teeth. "Okay...but I'm not happy about seeing you cry."

She looked up, having gained her composure and pushed away from him. "Nah, don't worry...truly it's nothing just got a little overwhelmed by...ah...family stuff, you know?"

"Family stuff? Sure, I get it." He lifted her chin and met her eyes. "If you ever want to talk, you know I'm over here waiting to get to know you better, I'm a good listener." He gave her his charming smile and let her go.

"Thanks...really...I needed that." Quinn looked away into her car. "I should go before I'm late, Ellery locks the doors on late comers to her class." She bent into her car and reached across the seat for her phone and bag and took her keys out of the ignition.

Cory shuffled backwards to let her close the car door. She glanced up at him. "Thank you, really." She said again, not sure what else to say.

He beamed a truly handsome smile at her. "No problem, anytime, don't just sit by yourself and be miserable, okay?" He reached out and stroked her cheek of a stray tear.

"Oh god..." She pulled her hoodie sleeves down over her hands and wiped her face dry, taking in a huge cleansing breath and releasing it. "Okay...thanks."

Cory laughed. "It's a good thing you don't wear makeup to school...if you wipe your face like that! Shit, eighty percent of the girls here would never be able to do that."

Quinn startled a little at that and pulled her hair forward around her neck, she would have to check the makeup that was hiding the bruising. "Ah...yeah, lucky me." She gave a little amused chuckle.

"Hey now, that's better, I even got a smile...are you really okay?" The concern in his voice almost made her cry again.

She scowled at him. "Stop with the concern already...going...bye." She turned and walked off slinging her bag over her shoulder.

Cory huffed at her scowl. "Adorable...you're like a bad-tempered bunny rabbit."

He watched her walk away, scratching his chin in contemplation. What family stuff would make a girl react like that? He had seen his real mother have panic attacks before when he was younger and knew what it was...although Quinn had snapped out of it easily with his quick distraction.

Something about it made him feel uneasy.

Mila threw her coffee into the bin and kicked the bin.

"What the fuck was that? Are they secretly dating? Did that bitch manage to steal my man from me? Is that why he's been so distant this semester?" She was screaming and pacing as the other girls around her looked on nervously. "And after all the effort I went to, to get him to finally sleep with me."

Mila had seen Cory hugging Quinn, comforting her over something, stroking her cheek and making her cheer up and smile at him.

"Argh!" She growled out. "She's going to pay, that bitch!"

Cory made his way up to the third floor of the admin building and walked up to the door labeled with a stick-on gold and black plaque that read 'Executive.'

He knocked on the door and opened it without waiting for anyone to tell him he could enter. He knew what to expect and when he saw Flipper and Mac both sitting on the couches in the room with girls making out he didn't even pay them any mind. They casually looked up at him as the girls panicked a little bit but relaxed when they saw it was just Curry.

Of course he had messaged Reese to talk, he wouldn't dare come up here unannounced and he looked up past the couches to the desks and saw Reese sitting at one, wearing his blue-light glasses and looking at the screen.

Reese swiveled his chair around and took his glasses off, indicating for Cory to sit in the gaming chair next to his own.

'Fuck, he looks sexy with glasses.' Cory's intrusive thoughts spoke to him.

"I thought this room was for the executive to meet, not a gaming pad for gangsters?" Cory said sarcastically.

Reese smirked. "It is whatever I want it to be."

"Ha! Figures." Cory rolled his eyes and sat down with a heavy sigh.

"Wow, what's eating you?" Reese commented, his left eyebrow lifting.

Cory glanced at the others in the room and back to Reese meaningfully. Reese's eyes narrowed and his expression deadpanned.

"Everyone, get out." He ordered in a firm deep tone.

With no argument the two guys instantly got up, grabbing their girls and their stuff and left quickly. Cory snorted, impressed. "Wish the boys on the team would be like that..."

"You have to whack it into them." Reese chuckled. Cory knew Reese was a mixed martial arts fighter for his father's underground fighting ring and was so far undefeated. "So what's got you so riled up on a Monday morning that you had to seek *me* out to fix it?"

"Nothing like that, settle down."

"Hmm..." Reese thrummed, amused. Cory never came here, never hung out with him on campus, so this was a real rare event happening.

"I just caught Quinn in her car crying and panting like she was terrified."

"What the fuck?" Reese's fists clenched tight and his eyes blazed with fire.

"Calm down...she said it was because of family matters, what do you know of the 'family' at Zortex?"

"Before that..." Reese commented. "Did you find out anything from your father? On Friday she said her surname was Malley...so not Ferrante."

"Yeah, I had a quick chat with Dad on Sunday. Unfortunately he didn't want to say too much, only that he was pretty sure the head, Augusto Ferrante only has a son, Antonio, who is said to be stepping into the head seat soon..."

"Yeah, that's what the word on the street is...he's maybe four or five years older than us..." Reese was tapping the desk with his fingers and thinking when he was that age he would be stepping into his father's shoes too. "A real sadistic prick from what I hear."

"Says the asshole who beats his men into line." Cory muttered.

Reese grinned viciously. "Maybe, but the problem with the Ferrante family is they're still stuck in the glory days of shooting anyone that opposes then, chopping off fingers and kidnapping family members."

"Fuck..." Cory looked bleak. "Well, good thing Quinn isn't a Ferrante than...still, we know she's something to do with them."

"Yeah..." Reese rubbed his cheek. "It doesn't sit well with me...they're rivals, although we have peace they do have a lot of legit businesses as well to cover and clean the money...hopefully it's just a simple executive or director she's related to."

"Should I be hearing this?" Cory looked at Reese a little uncomfortably but Reese just chuckled. "Anyway, I hope you're right cause whatever upset her made me want to punch someone."

Reese gave Cory a little sideways glance. "Is that so?"

Cory heard the surly tone. "Don't get all bossy on me."

"I want to throttle your neck and tell you to back the hell off!" Reese growled under his breath as he grabbed for his vape and stood up. "...but we have a competition..."

"That's right...and fuck when she smiled at me and thanked me for comforting her...man, I just about came!"

"Dirty fuck boy!" Reese spat as he opened a window then he inhaled on his vape and blew it out the open window as he leaned on the ledge.

Cory laughed. "Have you jacked off to her yet?"

Reese gave him a dark threatening look. "Don't talk your locker room shit with me! Get out!"

"Wait, sorry..." Cory laughed, holding his hands up in surrender before Reese tried to punch him. "Look, I came here to ask if maybe you should put a tail on her and make sure she is actually okay."

Reese's expression deadpanned again and he looked away out the window as he huffed on his vape again. Cory took the moment to appreciate the fine side profile of a truly beautiful man.

"Take a picture." Reese muttered before turning to look at Cory, his expression dark and heated. Cory swallowed his cheeky comeback at that expression. "You think this thing with Quinn is serious enough to warrant a tail?"

"What's serious enough? Her situation or my feelings?"

Reese grit his teeth causing his jaw muscles to spasm as that left eyebrow lifted and he tilted his head at Cory pensively.

"Yeah...I don't know..." Cory confessed. "Something just feels off."

"Hmm, alright then...it will be good to find out where she lives, if nothing else."

Cory grinned. "I'll take that as a freebie then, since it's something you want to know too."

"Nothing says I'll pass the info on to you, fuck boy."

"Says the dude that had a threesome with some random chicks at that party on Saturday." Cory spat back, offended.

"Well, instead of jerking off to thoughts of Quinn like a teenager, I would rather take action and fuck my thoughts away properly." Reese smirked as he wandered back over and grabbed his jacket and phone. "I'm off, so you need to leave."

"Fine..." Cory huffed and stood up. "...and thanks, I knew you would understand."

Reese stepped up behind him and inhaled into the back of his neck making him freeze and his skin to goose bump. "You smell good...new cologne?"

Cory placed his hand on the back of his neck as Reese stepped past him with a chuckle. "Fuck, don't do that! And yes...I bought that gold Jean Paul Gaultier."

Reese flicked an intense gaze at him. "Don't think this makes you winning this competition, just because she showed you her vulnerable side...she's still wrapped up in a gangster family and you're the Police Commissioner's son."

Cory shrugged as he walked to the door. "I obviously make her feel safe...you on the other hand are just the same as the dicks she's forced to co-exist with that give her panic attacks..."

Reese's expression changed instantly to violent seething. "Fuck you, prick!"

Cory flipped him off and left quickly.

11
A missed coffee

As Reese walked the halls of the business faculty building he was well aware of the fact that his eyes were constantly searching for Quinn Malley. After Friday's outcome he hadn't seen or heard from her and now it was after lunch he really wanted to be able to touch base with her and make sure she was still on board and double check she was okay after what Cory said.

It was quite obvious to him now that Quinn had suffered or was suffering from some sort of trauma, possibly from her childhood, she had said she was born in Boston but that didn't mean much. It was the way she flinched, the way she was suddenly quiet or polite to dispel any confrontation with men.

He sighed and berated his own invasive thoughts as they pointed out the fact she would make a great sub...

He loved delving into that world but had never fully immersed, most girls got nervous when you wanted to tie them up and smack their ass and he never spent enough time with just one girl to build the trust for anything more serious than a bit of hair pulling, throat holding and making them beg for his cock while on their knees.

He bumped into someone in the hall and snapped back to reality, looking around. He looked down to see a guy standing in the hall blocking his way as he stood with his mates all chatting right in the middle of the corridor. Being six foot four he was taller than most people and intimidating to boot.

"Sorry man." The guy blurted out and quickly moved to the side. His mates all staring at him and Reese with apprehension, expecting the worst.

"Nah, my fault...I was miles away." Reese flipped back then gave the guys an intense look. "But maybe next time don't have your chat in the middle of the goddamned hallway!"

"Sorry..." They all lamented as Reese ran a hand through his hair sweeping it back from his eyes and looked ahead taking a step to continue on his way. He paused, his hand falling as he forgot how to breathe for a second.

There she was...

Standing in the hall and smiling at him brightly showing her teeth, her eyes sparkling with great amusement.

Wait? Is she laughing at me?

"Something amusing to you, Quinn?" He asked with a little light-hearted scowl as he walked up to her.

"Yeah...even though that was your fault and you admitted it you still had those guys terrified."

Reese breathed out a little short laugh and licked his tongue out over his teeth.

Quinn's eyes tracked his tongue, god he was so damn sexy. She had never known anyone ooze male sexuality like this guy did. It made her wonder just how much experience he had. She knew Cory and the footballers were known as the fuck boys on campus, no surprises there, but Reese was known as the Prince and girls scrambled to get in his bed, and even guys if the rumors of him being bisexual were true.

Quinn realized they were just staring at each other and dropped her gaze, coughing awkwardly. Reese grinned, enjoying the candid moment. "I'm glad I caught up with you, I wanted to grab a coffee or something?"

"Oh, I'm on my way to the library." Quinn said, indicating a girl Reese hadn't even noticed standing beside her. Reese looked at the girl a little surprised and saw her watching their exchange with a little faint blush on her cheeks. "Me and Tania have been paired for an assignment."

"Oh, maybe later then..." Reese gave her a dashing smile.

Quinn chewed on her lip making Reese take pause.

"You want to say something, Quinn? Don't be nervous, speak your mind."

Quinn's eyes seemed to brighten and dazzled him as she slow blinked. "You could come with us if you weren't doing anything right now? We just need to do a quick outline, get a couple of books and then we're done."

Reese had to block his view of her adorable expression and covered his face with one hand. "You're asking me to join you?" He peeked out from between his fingers. "With that cute look on your face...damn, how can I say no?"

Quinn pouted a little at him making fun of her, but her friend interrupted their outrageous flirting. "I've only got a quick twenty minutes, so..."

Reese took his phone out of his pocket and held it out to Quinn. "Tell you what...give me your Insta and you can let me know once you're finished and meet me at the café 'Artifice'."

That was the café in the art faculty building that used the space to feature student's winning artwork.

"Okay." Quinn took his phone and added herself to his Insta then added him to hers.

"See ya later, babe." Reese quipped and walked off. He wanted to bounce and had to concentrate so hard to not fist pump the air. She seemed like a completely different chick today and he wondered if Cory had been the reason for her light mood, because she didn't look troubled to him.

Cory, that damn golden retriever!

Quinn followed Tania to the library and as they sat down Tania sat shoulder to shoulder, pressing in.

"Now spill, first Friday night and now you're openly flirting with each other in the halls?" She gushed. "And can I just say you two were so freaking adorable...I had no idea he could be so damn cute."

Quinn smiled. "Don't make a fuss...its early days, I still know nothing about him, I'm just curious that's all."

Her phone chirped with a notification and she saw it was a message from Cory on Insta. This was the first time since she gave him it that he had messaged her.

C - **Hey, just wanted to check you were doing okay?**

Tania looked over her shoulder and gasped. "You really do have Curry and Rice on the hook!"

"Shush, it's not like that...Cory saw me upset about something earlier, he's just checking up on me, it's sweet."

"Sweet...yeah, real sweet." Tania teased in a whisper. "Means he's sweet on you. I'm so jelly!"

Quinn gave a little awkward smile. If only she knew...

Quinn saw Mila and her waspish group come into the library. She deliberately sat at a table next to Quinn and Tania and gave Quinn a long facetious smile.

"I think your dress sense is awful." Mila stated with a condescending smirk. "You really wouldn't fit with us at all."

Quinn gave a benign smile back, was this really the only thing her small brain could come up with to comment on? "Lucky I don't give two flying fucks what you think, at least I don't go around showing my bare ass cheeks to all and sundry every time a gentle breeze blows."

Mila went red in the face. "That's it, I've had enough of your fucking smart ass comments back to me, freshman!"

"What's the matter, not used to someone telling you like it is? I told you on day one to fuck off and leave me alone, but no...you all had to try and be the big miss popular cheerleaders and try and bully me, but because it didn't work and every time you were left red-faced and embarrassed, now what? You going to step up your game?" Quinn stepped up and got into Mila's face. "Bring it, bitch!"

"Argh!" Mila pulled a face and stepped back acting horrified. "She doesn't even have the decency to cover up her ugly and wear makeup." Her friends all cackled.

"I don't need to...I have perfect skin." Quinn boasted with a savagery that made on-lookers snicker. "I'm not hiding a whole bunch of nasty acne behind a wall of clay."

Mila looked horrified as she palmed her cheeks. "I...I do not have acne, you bitch!" Mila grabbed Quinn by the arm.

Quinn tried to struggle free. "Get your filthy hands off me!"

Mila dug her nails in. "What if I don't!?"

Quinn winced in pain then saw red. She slammed Mila into a wall of books with a hand around her throat. Mila looked stunned and struggled to get free as Quinn squeezed. The other girls started screaming for Quinn to let go, a couple ran off to find help as the whole library erupted into chaos.

"This is your last chance to leave me the hell alone!" Quinn yelled in Mila's face.

"Hey, hey...no need to fight over me girls..." Cory came up and pulled Quinn's hand away, looking at her with a little surprise to see her ferocity. "Easy, babe."

Quinn flashed a terrifying look at him. "Keep your bitch on a fucking leash if you can't control her!"

"Hey!" Cory called out as Quinn stormed off.

He went to chase after her but Mila grabbed him tightly in an embrace and cried into his chest. "Oh my god, I'm so glad you came, I was so scared. She's crazy!"

He looked down at her, annoyed. She was hindering him but as she looked up at him with her glassy blue eyes he saw the red marks around her neck, clearly Quinn had been really trying to hurt her.

He touched Mila's neck with his fingertips. "Shit, are you okay?" He hated seeing any girl hurt.

"No! She tried to kill me!"

"Why would she do that, did you say something?"

"Why do you think I started it? She's a horrible person, why can't you see that?" She clung to him desperately.

Cory bit his tongue not wanting to escalate the situation any further but something was going to have to get sorted out soon.

Quinn made her way to her car, messaging Reese on the way to cancel their meet up. She wasn't in the mood now and decided it was best to just go home for the day.

Her phone chirped with a message and she saw it was from Tania.

T - ***I have several people's videos showing Mila grabbed you first in case she takes it to the Dean. Hope you're okay?***

Q - *I'm fine, but going home*

T - ***What about your coffee date with Rice?***

Q - *I've messaged him to cancel it. Talk later*

Just as Quinn closed her phone it chirped again. This time the message was Reese replying.

R - **What happened in the library, people are already talking about it?**

Quinn grimaced at how fast the grapevine worked and didn't want to talk about it. She was already not coping with her fucked up life, she didn't need any of this on top of it all. Maybe this was a sign to not pursue anything with either Curry or Rice.

She reached her car and got in, breathing in a deep breath and relaxing inside the protective shell of steel, taking a moment before starting the engine and driving out.

Reese reached the parking lot in time to see Quinn's car just leaving the toll gate and driving off up the road. He cursed and went to quickly grab his bike, intending to follow her like he had promised Cory he would.

As Quinn pulled her car up the shared driveway and into the garage of her townhouse Reese pulled up across the street and looked down the drive. Quinn's place was the last of four two-story townhouses that were all joined together down the private drive connected by their garages with house two and three sharing a wall. It meant Quinn's house had the most yard and her house altered from the floor plan of the other three slightly to make the most of having a back and side yard. Reese was surprised she was living in such a new build and so close to his own place, they lived practically around the corner from each other. He could even easily walk the distance...he was going to have to change his jogging route from now on to include this street.

He smirked to himself and drove off, heading home.

As he walked into his condo his phone rang.

"What's up?" He asked seeing it was Cory.

"Did you see what happened today with Quinn and Mila?"

"No, should I have?"

"It's all over the chat...hang on."

Reese's phone vibrated and he saw Cory had sent him a video, he watched it and then reconnected to Cory's call, livid. "Sort that little bitch out." He growled down the phone.

"Quinn had her by the throat, man...that was uncalled for. I know Mila grabbed her first but Quinn took it too far."

"I'll take it further, how about that? Why are you sticking up for a girl you fucked last semester?"

Cory sighed. "I'm not, I'm actually concerned Quinn could get in real trouble over this."

"You think Mila will dare take this to the college?"

"Maybe, she was really upset and her neck's gonna bruise."

"Fuck, okay..." Reese rubbed the back of his neck. "I'll contact the Dean and sort it if she goes to him."

"Cool, I didn't get a chance to talk to Quinn...I think she's gone home."

"Yeah, she has."

"Where are you?" Cory asked suddenly suspicious.

Reese chuckled. "At home...but I followed her to make sure she lived somewhere safe."

"And?"

"She's got a real nice place, better than mine and just around the corner."

"You're shitting me?"

"Nope." Reese grinned to himself. "Oh and I have her Insta now too, she was going to meet me for coffee after the library so I should be really pissed Mila interfered with that."

Cory huffed. "I should thank her then."

Reese hung up and rubbed his forehead. "Fucker..."

12

The car incident

Quinn bumped into Mila in the halls again the next day shortly after third lecture and Mila giggled obnoxiously making Quinn think she had been searching for her.

"Quinn, I'm surprised you're still going to class..."

"Why?" Quinn sighed, rolling her eyes expecting some drab insult. She was wearing black jeans and her striped arm warmers so looked quite edgy.

"Oh? You don't know yet! That's hilarious that no one has told you, don't you have any friends looking out for you?"

"What are you on about?"

"Your car's been vandalized." She gave a real shit-eating grin. "Seems I'm not the only person who hates you around here." She sauntered off with a toss of her hair as her friends all cackled like witches and followed her.

"What the fuck!?" Quinn ran to her car.

She stared at it in mortified shock as she slowed to a walk across the grass and onto the asphalt, walking around her car and seeing that all the tyres had been slashed and the paintwork keyed.

"What the actual fuck!" She screamed, kicking at one tyre as tears threatened and welled up in her eyes. She became aware of voices and looked up to see several groups of people filming her with their phones. She snatched in a breath, determined not to let them film her get upset or cry and stormed off to the admin building to report the damage directly to Chancellor Bayton.

She knew it was Mila who had organized it. Why else would she go to so much trouble to bump into her and say what she said? She had wanted to be the one to tell her! She had probably organized the people to film her reaction too...that bitch had gone too far!

She was going to have to inform Antonio.

Quinn felt sick at that prospect she could almost hear his words. He would use this against her but she had to get his help to get a tow-truck and get her car repaired. She didn't have any money to do it herself. Antonio kept her on a short leash and supplied everything she needed and didn't give her any money except for a small allowance for gas, snacks and coffees on campus. He even sent groceries to her house to make sure she ate correctly, the control freak!

As she sat waiting for the Chancellor to be free she messaged Antonio knowing he would be busy at work and certainly not wanting to disturb him, so she wouldn't ring directly.

Q - **Sorry to disturb you at work but when you get this can you please ring me, I need your help**

She chewed her lip in distress and jumped in fright when her phone started ringing almost immediately.

"Hello?" She answered tentatively, although knowing exactly who it was.

"I've got a meeting starting in five minutes, what's the problem, petalo?" His smooth voice came through calm and faintly amused.

Tears sprung up in her eyes and she wanted to cry her heart out to him. He doesn't love me, I don't love him.

"My car's had its tyres slashed, I need to organize a tow-truck and repair, please, sir."

"What the fuck? Who did this?" His rage flew over the phone immediately and full scale. Quinn just about dropped the phone, she had really thought he would find it amusing and laugh at her humiliation.

"I'm not sure, I'm just waiting for Chancellor Bayton now so I can report it and check the cameras."

"You must have some idea, Quinn. That sort of shit is usually personal vendetta stuff. What the hell have you been up to?" His voice settled into a venomous menace.

"I...um...I'm not sure, sir, please believe me." She begged, looking up as the Chancellor's door opened and seeing the secretary and the Chancellor staring at her with concern.

"Miss Malley, please come in now." Chancellor Bayton said curtly.

"I need to go now..." Quinn said to Antonio. "Chancellor Bayton is free."

"I'm coming to talk to him, tell him he better sort this out!"

Quinn hung up and stood up seeing the Chancellor's face looked bleak as he had clearly heard her conversation.

She walked into his office and he closed the door.

"Please sit down, I've been alerted to your unfortunate situation and we'll look at the security footage together now, I'm just getting security and maintenance up to recall the footage on the computer for us."

"Thank you..."

"Any idea who might have done this to your car, Miss Malley?"

Coming out of the Chancellor's office on the same floor as the student executive meeting room Quinn saw Reese heading along the hall. He stopped, surprised to see her and she looked upset.

"Quinn? What's happening, why are you coming out of Mr Bayton's office. Is this about yesterday?"

"Don't fucking talk to me!" Quinn hissed as she barreled down the stairs.

Reese chased after her, catching up on the landing between levels. He slammed her up against the wall and caged her in with his arms as he put his hands on the wall either side of her.

She leaned on the wall and rolled her eyes, avoiding his gaze.

"What is your fucking problem with me now?" Reese growled, his eyes blazing out from under his dark fringe.

"My problem is the Prince and the Star Quarterback are both playing with a freshman and causing me too much unwanted attention, leave me alone!"

"You could just pick one of us?" Reese joked, but saw her distressed expression. "Has something else happened?" His tone dropped. "Tell me, I'll sort it out for you."

"You think you're such a gangster! Please...you can't do anything to help me."

"What's that supposed to mean?" Reese's eyes blazed at the derogatory way she spoke.

"You want to see a true gangster? Watch who picks me up today..." She felt sick at that prospect and covered her mouth.

Reese frowned, going through the words she had spoken. "Pick you up?" He asked confused. "Didn't you drive?"

"Yeah, but thanks to that fucking maniac cheerleader who thinks I'm trying to steal her boyfriend and the prince at the same time my car has four flat tyres and the paint is scratched all to fuck! So my brother has to come pick me up and organize a tow-truck!"

She pushed out of his cage by yanking his arm out of the way as he was dumbstruck by what she just said. This was out of control...

"Hang on!" He called, grabbing her arm and halting her. "What fucking cheerleader?"

"Little miss Vice Captain, Mila."

"Wait...she thinks Cory is her boyfriend?" He said it like that was the most ridiculous thing he had ever heard.

She sighed and looked up at Reese. He was blown away by the amazing pale green of her eyes as they wavered with unshed tears. "She seems to have this warped sense of tradition that cheerleaders and footballers are to go out with each other, be prom king and queen, whatever...like she's in bloody high school. And don't get me started on how those other popular girls in that clique act over you!"

Reese changed weight on his feet, agitated but wouldn't let her arm go. "Let me get this straight...she said this to you?"

"Yes...a few times they've warned me off Cory and you and no matter how many times I tried to get through their dense bitch heads that its him and you annoying me not the other way around, she doesn't want to know...she's nuts and in denial that now he obviously slept with her he's moved on."

"And she slashed your tyres?" Reese's tone dropped dangerously.

"Probably not directly...I doubt she's got the gall to do it herself, but she certainly took the credit when she laughed at me in the halls just before."

"Fuck..." Reese looked away with a frown. "Curry is going to be pissed."

"I'm fucking pissed!" She shoved him off and stormed off. "Do you know how much those tyres cost? And I do not need any excuse for my *brother* to make me owe him back for anything! You have no idea what paying him back means!" Her voice sounded so distressed like her life was on the line as she yelled back while walking down the stairs.

Reese's golden gaze followed her with concern. "What the fuck? What does that mean, pay him back?"

13
A real gangster

Reese was sitting on a bench seat just off to the right of the steps leading up from the parking lot to the main administration building so had the perfect view when a blacked out Bentley was admitted through the security guard post and into the carpark followed by a large tow-truck.

The Bentley pulled into the space next to Quinn's Mustang as she got out of it, glancing nervously over at where Reese was plainly in sight before the driver of the Bentley got out and opened the back door for her and she clambered in and the driver closed the door. The tow-truck went about his business hooking Quinn's car up.

Quinn slid in beside Antonio and looked up at him with concern. "I'm sorry, I didn't mean to..."

"Quiet." He ordered in that low smooth tone. "I don't want to hear any excuses or apologies just tell me what happened." He was firm but calm and she knew that could mean trouble.

How did she explain this without admitting to Cory and Reese both being interested in her? Antonio would shoot them both dead.

"I have had problems with the junior and senior girls from a certain sorority...the specific group seemed to think I should be a part of their exclusive little clique and wanted me to join the cheerleading team and move into their frat house..." She knew it wasn't a lie but still felt a little like she was lying. She knew there was no way Antonio would ever let her join a cheer squad and wear those short skirts and flash her underwear to everyone.

"You refused I take it." Antonio said darkly as he clucked his tongue. He hated mindless stupid shit and this was all over that so Quinn knew he would be pissed on two fronts. "You should have told me you were having problems."

"I'm not having problems I can't handle...it would be worse if I had to call you in! Please...but it's gone too far this time."

Antonio sucked his teeth, appraising her answer. "Alright, I get that...I know what college is like I'm not many years out of it myself and I went here, believe it or not."

"You did? Huh, I guess that makes sense..." Quinn looked away, chewing her lip and watching the towie with her car.

Antonio's fingers curled under her chin and lifted it making her look back at him, he glanced at her neck and smirked to see she covered the bruises with makeup. "I'm going to need a proper thank you this weekend, something really special, petalo...but for now kiss me before I go speak to Chancellor Bayton in regards to what he plans to do about this and remind him just who I am and that perhaps he should be taking better care of you."

"He says the security footage doesn't show enough to do anything...it's clearly two guys, but they were wearing sheets over their heads like ghosts so it looked like just a stupid prank. I know Mila did this..."

"Well without evidence you can't accuse her..." His eyes narrowed. "Kiss. Now."

His dark eyes watched with amusement as she moved closer in her seat and lifted her mouth to his, pressing her lips on his and closing her eyes. His hand drifted from her chin to the back of her neck, threading his fingers into her hair at the back of her scalp and gripping tightly as he opened his mouth and licked along her lips.

She opened her mouth immediately to him and as he dipped his tongue inside her mouth, he pulled on her hair, tilting her head back and sideways so he could cover her mouth completely and dominate her. He kissed her for a full minute before moving away with a satisfied smirk, wiping her chin with his thumb, seeing her breathless, flushed and dazed. He chuckled. "Stay here with Danny, I'll speak to the Chancellor regarding this myself. Come, Matteo." He opened his own door.

Quinn looked at the driver, Danny and Matteo in the front seats and blushed embarrassed, but nodded. "Yes, sir."

As Antonio got out of the car with Matteo stepping out of the front passenger seat, he looked around the campus and buttoned up his suit jacket. There were a few students still hanging around and his eyes scanned them all with a slow disinterested gaze before he walked towards the main building. Heads turned and whispering started up, girls gaped and giggled behind their hands. He was an impressive sight and with Matteo behind him they looked dangerous and compelling.

Reese sat up slightly in shock to see none other than Antonio Ferrante get out of the Bentley after what felt like an eternity after Quinn got in. He must have been getting her full story. Reese wondered if that included him.

Why was Antonio here? She had said her brother...called him a real gangster...

"No fucking way! This is impossible!"

Reese felt like he might be in for an encounter he couldn't handle and watched as Antonio approached but kept walking.

Antonio's gaze slid sideways for merely a second as he past Reese by, not even giving him a change of expression before he was past and heading inside, but that momentary gaze had sent a chill through Reese.

That was a gaze of a true blooded killer.

"Fucking hell." Reese breathed as he grit his teeth and looked back at the Bentley where Quinn was. "What the fuck is going on here?"

He was glad he hadn't been recognized by Antonio, at least he hoped he hadn't...and he really hoped what Quinn had said about paying her brother back wasn't what was creeping up the back of his mind.

Quinn was sitting on Antonio's lap, her hands cuffed together and hooked over the back of his neck so she had to lie back on his chest, her legs spread over his as he played his fingers through her pussy.

"Are you going to tell me what really happened at college, Quinn?" Antonio breathed into her neck.

Quinn tensed up. "I did tell you, it was Mila, she's had it out for me since day one."

"Why? Because you're prettier than her?"

"I don't know...I think she thinks I'm acting stuck up because I refused their offer to join their sorority."

"Good thing you did, sororities mean fraternities, which means horny fuck boys, parties and drinking if I remember rightly."

"Exactly why I said no." Quinn replied hastily.

"Good girl...you really are a good girl, petalo." Antonio crooned in her ear. "But I'm still pissed at the car...so how about you get this sweet little ass into the playroom...I just bought a new paddle that I want to soften up on your hide."

He ducked his head out from her tied hands and pushed her off his lap and onto her feet. She stood up and looked back at him with wide scared eyes.

"It wasn't my fault..."

Antonio gazed up at her, sucking on his teeth. "And Christmas is in July...I don't care two fucks if you're lying to me about why someone took it upon themselves to vandalize your car, Quinn, because in the end I get to punish you for it regardless just for lying to me."

Quinn's legs started to tremble under her as he stood up and grabbed her throat, bringing his face down to hers. "But if I ever find out the real reason is actually because of some fuck boy, you and him are going to die slowly."

He shoved her back and she staggered. "Now move!"

14
Get over yourself!

When Quinn didn't turn up to classes the next day Reese sought out Cory to have a chat.

"Have you been messaging Quinn?"

"Yeah, of course. I wanted to make sure she was okay."

"So you know you need to sort out Mila Buick, right?"

"Yeah, yeah...I'll have a word with her if you really think she did it."

"Did she tell you that she goes around telling everyone you're her boyfriend after you slept with her at that party last semester? She tells every girl you act nice towards to back off behind your back."

"You're kidding me?" Cory rubbed the back of his neck anxiously.

"I'm fucking not...this is all your fault for not keeping your bitches in line." Reese thundered.

"Hey, easy man, I wasn't to know...I'll fix it."

"You better."

"Is that the reason Quinn's not here today?"

Reese's mouth twisted. "She says she wants to just stay away till the fervor dies down, but I don't know, it's hard to reach her when it's only by message...maybe I'll drop in on her after my last class, I've only three today."

"Take me with you."

"Fuck off...competition remember." Reese pivoted to walk off. "Sort that Mila slut out or I will."

Cory pulled up outside the girls' house and saw a couple of the cheerleaders on the front drive taking shopping bags out of their car. He jumped out of his truck and walked up.

"Need an extra pair of hands?"

They both startled then their eyes lit up to see who it was offering his help. "Sure." "Absolutely, thank you."

As they loaded his arms up one of the girls gave him a sideways look. "Are you here to see Mila?"

Cory's eyebrow lifted and he gave the girl a once over. "Why would you assume that? Maybe I'm here to see you." He gave her his roguish smile as she blushed prettily.

"Why would you be here to see me?"

"Aren't you going out with Mila?" The other girl interrupted, making the first one look away.

"Who says that?" Cory scoffed, so it was true. The two girls looked at each other confused.

"Ah...Mila says so..."

"Hmm...really? Is she in?"

"I think so..." One of the girls said with a huge grin.

God, they were all so catty, they couldn't wait for a chance to tear each other down. He rolled his eyes. "Don't sound too excited..."

The girl baulked. "Sorry, but if it's not true..."

"It's not." Cory turned and walked to the front door. "You better show me where you want this stuff..."

"Oh, right..." The two girls rushed in front of him and through the door.

They made a big show of the fact that Cory was with them and bringing in their shopping bags as they made him walk all the way into the lounge before dumping their bags on a seat.

"Thank you." They both battered their eyelashes at him and hugged his arms.

Mila stood up looking at them with a savage glare. "Cory! What brings you here?"

"I need to talk to you."

"Okay, well...should we go up to my room?" She gave him a coy smile, twirling her hair with her fingers.

"No, what I have to say can be said right here." His tried to make his voice calm but the anger he felt building up was spilling over.

She frowned at him and folded her arms. "If this is about yesterday..."

"No, this is about today..." Cory looked around, there were four other girls in the room and they were all looking on in rapture. "Did you have anything to do with Quinn's car being vandalized today?"

Mila placed a hand on her chest like she was mortally wounded. "How could you ask that of me?"

Cory's eyes narrowed. "Are you saying you didn't?"

"Of course I didn't!" Mila huffed. "Babe..." She went to step over to him.

"Don't call me babe." He growled stopping her in her tracks. Her face looking shocked as she glanced around the room. "In fact stop telling people we are going out together, I fucked you last semester, get over yourself."

Mila's mouth gaped open as the other girls in the room hid their grins behind their hands.

"If I wanted you as my girlfriend you would know about it, I haven't even messaged you for a month." Cory added just as Vanessa walked in.

"What's going on here?" She asked, seeing Mila start to get distraught from her embarrassment, tears pricking her eyes.

"Are you involved in giving Quinn a hard time too?"

"What? No...I wanted her to move in here and pledge but she wasn't interested."

"Well, I'm here to say to those of you that are continuing to give Quinn a hard time to knock it off before you piss me off...and if I do find out any of you had a hand in what happened to Quinn's car..." He glared at Mila. "Just know you'll have to answer to a higher power than me!"

"Why are you sticking up for that bitch?" Mila screamed.

Vanessa gave her a haughty suspicious glare.

"Don't call her a bitch..." Cory grumbled, wiping a hand over his face. "I like her, not you, get over it."

He turned and walked out of the house and made his way to his car.

Vanessa followed him out and he turned to look back at her with a questioning look. "What?"

She sauntered up to him with a conspiring smile. "I heard you and Reese had a competition going over who gets to fuck that freshman first, is that true?"

"Who the fuck told you that?" Cory asked a little stunned.

Vanessa's eyes sparkled. "So it's true...good to know, I won't say anything...I just think it's interesting..."

Cory remembered Vanessa was hanging around Reese at the last party. "Did Reese tell you that?"

"No, Reese told me to be nice to the girl, I guess I forgot to pass that message on to Mila..."

Cory huffed. "Well, she's really gone and done it now, if Reese finds out it was her, and I'm pretty sure it was, he'll come down on her."

"Why?" Vanessa asked, confused. "Why do you both care so much if it's just a bet?"

Cory stared at her darkly, then raked a hand through his hair and looked away over his truck. "Maybe it's not just a bet to me..."

Vanessa grit her teeth. "And for Reese?"

Cory looked back with a smirk, it was so obvious Vanessa was interested in Reese. "Reese doesn't fuck cheerleaders, haven't you worked that one out yet?"

Cory got in his truck and closed the door as Vanessa stood there with her arms folded and an angry scowl on her face.

He drove off wondering if his message had actually got through to them though.

Reese had spent the rest of the day gathering information rather than attend his classes...he knew several people had filmed Quinn reacting to her car being vandalized and also knew that the guys who did it were probably part of that, so he had a couple of the computer kids up in the executive room searching through everyone's social media and finding all the names that posted on it.

He had four names of guys that he suspected...

A knock sounded on the door and Tank got up from his couch and opened it. Jacob walked in tossing up and catching a USB stick over and over with a pretty little Asian girl walking in behind him with a bob of black hair and glasses. "Got it, Boss...all thanks to Yuki here."

Reese gave the girl a sultry smirk as Jacob walked over and handed the USB stick to the guy at the computer.

"Thanks, I hope the security guy wasn't too sleazy?"

She shook her head shyly.

"Nah..." Jacob said amused. "He was all for it to be as quick as possible, was maybe a bit rough though, eh Yuki?"

"I'm fine." She said meekly.

Reese frowned. "Rough?"

"Yeah, you know, like grabbed her head and shoved it down the back of her throat..."

"What the fuck?" Reese snorted. "You're embarrassing the girl."

"I'm not embarrassed..." She spoke up. "It happens all the time." She shrugged and looked at Reese expectantly. "I'll just take my money now..."

Reese's jaw clenched and he clicked his fingers at Tank. "Okay, then...and thanks for your help."

"Anytime if you're going to pay that much for a simple bj." She smiled coyly at him.

Tank handed her a fifty dollar bill and she took it with a smile before leaving.

Reese scratched the back of his neck. "Jesus...where did you find her?"

"Why, think she's cute?" Jacob laughed. "She is pretty cute right?"

"I guess..." Reese looked away to the computer guy who was plugging in the USB.

Jacob sat down and stretched his legs out. "She's one of the new girls down at Hummingbird."

Reese looked back over his shoulder with a curious gaze. "And what are you doing in Hummingbird?"

Jacob shrugged. "I wasn't...I waited for some of them to come out and asked them if they wanted to make a quick fifty bucks and blow off a guy."

Reese rolled his eyes. "Figures..."

"Hey, we got the footage, right?"

"Right...here it is." The guy at the computer said making Reese turn back.

They watched the screen as the two ghosts in sheets vandalized Quinn's car. Jacob and Tank came over to and peered at the screen.

"Good disguises, they could be anyone."

"Nah..." The computer guy said. "If you look close you can see their shoes...and one of them is tall and skinny."

Reese squinted at the screen. "Basketballers..."

Tank grumbled. "What now?"

Reese looked up at him with a smile that wasn't pleasant. "Just so happens that one of the social media accounts that posted Quinn's reaction to her car was one of the basketball team...I think it's safe to assume he was in on it."

"Who?" Jacob asked with a frown.

"Micky Dobbs." Reese spat.

Tank flexed his muscles and rolled his neck. "Right, let's go pay him a visit then."

The door to the locker room under the Bob Burchard Court at Columbia University banged open and Reese followed by Tank and Mac walked in looking serious and lethal. The guys from the basketball team all stood up with concern.

"What the fuck? You can't just waltz in here..."

Reese turned to the one that spoke and sneered in his face. "Gonna stop me?" He shoved the guy aside and he hit the row of steel lockers hard causing others to step forward.

Tank moved into a defensive position in front of Reese and cracked his knuckles. That made them all take pause.

Reese looked up from the guy now sitting on the ground holding his shoulder and smirked. "Relax...I'm part of the student executive...I'm looking for Micky Dobbs."

Just at that moment Micky walked out from the showers. He froze, taking in the scene of Reese and his off-siders standing in the locker room with his captain on the floor at his feet clutching his shoulder.

"Fuck." He turned and ran back the way he had come.

Reese chuckled. "Where the fuck does he think he's going?"

He strode through the locker room passed all the players like they were no threat to him at all and followed where Micky had run.

He found him standing against the back wall of the showers holding his hands out in terror. "Easy man, I don't know what you want but...fuck..."

"You know exactly why I'm here." Reese growled. "So get dressed 'cause you and me are going to take a little drive..."

"What? Wait...you're not serious?"

Reese lashed out a fist straight into Micky's face. The back of his head collided with the wall at the impact of Reese breaking his nose and he slid in a daze down the wall to sit on the floor, clutching at his face.

"What the fuck, man!"

"I only tell people to do something once...if you don't move you get hit." Reese stated in a deep calm menace.

Micky looked up at him like he was a monster. "Okay, okay...fuck..." He gained his feet, holding his towel to his bleeding nose and walked back to the locker room with Reese following him like a stalking beast.

In the locker room the players all gasped and started moving forward, yelling to back off away from their mate. Tank shoved a couple of them back while Mac took out a large bowie knife from behind his back and held it low and menacing. That made them all back up again.

Reese saw Micky pulling on some shorts, while gasping to breathe through his mouth and turned to Mac. "Put that bloody thing away..." He looked at the team in front of him. "Don't be heroes...a couple of you know why we're here and be thankful we don't have your name yet...don't be running off anywhere, it'll just make things worse for you." He stepped towards the door, looking back at Tank. "Bring him..."

"Wait you can't just take one of our team..." The Captain pushed forward again.

"He's wanted for vandalizing a car...get the fuck out of my way." Reese growled. "Unless you want me to fuck up more than just your shoulder...you want to continue to play basketball?"

"It's okay, Eddy..." Micky said grimly. "I'll go."

Reese looked back at him with a gleeful smile. "Good for you."

"Hey, I can't let you do that." Another guy pushed forward with a somber expression. "He didn't do it, he just recorded the girl's reaction...I did."

Reese's mouth twisted as his lip curled up on one side. "Nice of you to come forward, Ryan, but there was two of you."

"Fuck...just take me, asshole."

"Fine, you'll tell me the name of the other fucker soon enough." Reese smirked. "Let's get out of here."

Tank grabbed Ryan by the arm and pushed him forward to follow Reese out of the locker room. In the hall they were confronted by the coach and assistant.

"What the? Who are you, where are you taking Ryan?"

Reese reached into his pocket and took out a slip and handed it to the Coach. "I'm President of the Student Executive over at the Scarsdale campus, I have permission from the Chancellor to remove Ryan back there to face disciplinary procedures in relation to a car that was vandalized on campus grounds...expect him to be suspended, if not expelled."

The Coach looked at the slip and paled slightly looking up at Ryan's remorseful face. "You stupid idiot!"

"Sorry, Coach..."

Tank moved forward, shoving passed the Coach and Assistant and walked off holding Ryan's arm. Reese smirked at the Coach's bewildered expression.

"Have a nice day..."

"You know you still have no right to come here and just take a player from my court like this, I don't care who you are, I'll be filing a report about your attitude and conduct." The Coach yelled.

Reese just chuckled, licking his tongue over his teeth. "Go right ahead...and make sure to tell them my name...it's Reese O'Shea...don't get it wrong."

The coach stared at him in disbelief, who the hell did this guy think he was?

15

You picked the wrong car

Reese entered the warehouse with Tank and Mac in tow pulling Ryan in as he struggled violently in protest.

"What the fuck is this man, I thought you said I was going back to Scarsdale Campus?"

"Did I?" Reese chuckled as he took his jacket off and threw it over a long table that was set up against the wall, he grabbed an old wooden chair and dragged it into the center of the dingy warehouse and pointed to it. "Sit down. Let's have a chat."

Tank and Mac pulled Ryan over to the chair and threw him at it, standing in front of him menacingly as Reese wandered back to the table and sought out his vape from his jacket pocket then some boxing tape and started wrapping his hands. A thumping bang sounded on the steel door into the warehouse and Reese being closest unlocked it and Jacob came in with two others.

"For fuck's sake, come on man...it was just a car, you're acting like I killed someone!" Ryan stood up but was shoved back into the seat.

Reese clucked his tongue and looked back, his golden gaze burning with an intense rage. "Just a car?" He muttered darkly.

He stalked forward to stand in front of Ryan, still wrapping his hand. "You may think it was just a car, but you picked the wrong fucking car."

"Fucking hell..." Ryan licked his lips nervously. "It was fixable, no harm done..."

Reese's face dropped into an emotionless state. He turned away with a small growl deep in his throat. "The gall of this fucker..." He muttered causing a couple of the men standing around Ryan to laugh to themselves.

Ryan looked at Jacob distraught and fearing for his life. "What the fuck is his problem, it's not even his car!"

Jacob gave Ryan a strange look. "It's not the car, but the owner...you have no idea of the consequences of your actions. What made you do it?"

Reese had walked off to the other side of the warehouse where there was a small home gym set up and started punching the bag that hung from the rafters.

Ryan saw him and licked his lips again, nervously. "Mila paid me a thousand dollars to do it."

"Wow, just a thousand..." Mac commented snidely.

"So who helped you?" Jacob asked as the dull thudding of Reese warming up was clear in the background. Ryan couldn't stop watching him as he struck out at the bag with a deadly force every punch.

"Shit man...would you give up your friends?"

Jacob laughed, rubbing his cheek. "No. Just thought I would give you the chance, but that's fine..."

"What is he going to do to me?" Ryan asked feeling a little sick.

Reese walked over, rolling his shoulders and Jacob hauled Ryan to his feet. Ryan looked around at them all as they created a ring around him and Reese stepped into it.

"Guys?" Ryan apprehensively asked.

"You're going to fight me..." Reese said with a hoarse little laugh.

"W-what? I can't fight you!"

"Well, I'm not just going to beat someone up, who do you think I am, a thug?" Reese's cocky grin was facetious.

Reese stepped in quick and slugged Ryan right in the guts. He doubled over, over Reese's fist and collapsed to his knees when Reese stepped away. He coughed and gasped for air.

"Get on your feet." Reese growled.

Ryan looked up into the face of a monster, those golden eyes seemed to glow with a feral light from behind the curtain of black hair, and the way Reese licked his tongue over his teeth was pure animal.

"I'm sorry, okay! Fuck!"

"Get up!" Reese growled again. Tank stepped in and grabbed Ryan by the shoulders and yanked him to his feet.

He stood in front of Reese and feebly put his hands up. He was taller than Reese, being a Basketballer, and Reese flicked his head to move his hair out of his eyes as he looked up and focused on Ryan's face.

Ryan held his hands up and crouched down slightly. Reese dropped his hands, giving Ryan an opportunity to strike him. Ryan went for it, swinging out with his right fist in a quick motion forward. Reese blocked it, stepped close and uppercut Ryan in the chin with a solid punch.

Ryan went down like a ton of bricks, his eyes rolled back in his head.

"Fuck Rice, are you trying to kill him?" Mac jumped over and checked Ryan's vital signs then turned him on his side.

Reese clucked his tongue and stalked away. "You guys finish him off when he comes round, make him bleed, and make sure he knows this is Mila's fault...I don't want him to follow anything she wants ever again."

"Got it, boss." Tank replied coolly as Reese grabbed his jacket and left without even unwrapping his hands.

The guys looked at each other, no one saying anything until Ryan came round, coughing and spluttering. He grabbed his jaw and winced in pain. "I think he broke my jaw!" He cried out in a strange mumble.

Tank chewed his lip. "Fuck...let's just crack a couple of ribs and get him to a hospital."

Later Reese pulled up to the curb outside Quinn's place and walked up the driveway to the rear house that was hers, knocking on the door. He noticed a camera doorbell and pushed it, peering into the little camera lens with a cheeky smirk.

"What the hell are you doing here? Go away, you can't be here!" Quinn's panicked voice came through the speaker.

"I wanted to check on you. Open the door." Why was she so panicky?

"I'm fine, how did you even know where I live?"

"I can find out most things when I want to...open the door, Quinn, I'm not leaving."

"You don't understand...my brother will know."

Ah, so that's why she sounded panicky. "Who gives a shit?"

"I do, very much...please, Reese."

He grit his teeth against her plea. She was definitely scared of her brother. "Just open the door and show me you're okay and I'll leave happy."

"You promise you'll leave and not try to barge your way in?"

"Barge in? What do you think I'm here to do?" Reese was a little taken aback.

He glanced at the door when he heard a clatter and it opened to reveal Quinn standing there wearing gym clothes, her face sweaty. She had a sloppy cardigan on over the top, the sleeves pulled down over her hands and she held a towel up to her neck.

"You were working out?" He asked a little amused as his eyes tracked down the skin tight Lycra crop top and bike shorts. His mouth twitched into a sultry smirk. "I think I like you sweaty..."

Quinn groaned, appalled and went to slam the door shut on him. "Just leave!"

He put his hand on the door and stepped into the threshold. "Wait, sorry...I couldn't resist teasing you a little...come on...when are you going to relax around me?" He noticed she was keeping a tight hold on the towel and wondered if she was trying to hide something.

Quinn opened the door back up and pouted. "You promised you wouldn't try to barge in..."

"Actually I never did, but I won't...I just want to see you, make sure you're okay after yesterday and..." He ran a hand through his hair. "...get an explanation about how the fuck Antonio Ferrante is your brother?"

Quinn stared at him fearfully. "That's none of your business."

"You're clearly scared of him, Quinn."

"Wouldn't you be, you should be if you know who he is, especially with being here? He has cameras to keep an eye on my safety...you should go."

Reese grit his teeth at the tension he was feeling from her. "So the Ferrantes keep you hidden, is that it?"

"If you like." Quinn snapped, clearly getting annoyed.

Reese chuckled. "Calm down, what would he do? I'm just talking to you on your doorstep...does he govern who you can speak with?"

"Yes, he does...now leave." She went to close the door again but Reese put his hand up again to stop it, his face clouded with suspicion.

"Is that fucking sadistic prick hurting you?" He demanded, causing Quinn's expression to startle, her eyes widening and her grip on the towel became deathly. "I know his reputation...he better not be doing shit to you because of what Mila had done to your car!" He looked her over more carefully but he couldn't see any signs of her being hit except that damn towel and she was covering her arms and hands. He felt better about what he did to Ryan now and almost felt like going back and doing it again.

"He would if he found out she did it because of your mate...he's extremely over protective when it comes to me associating with guys...so if you don't want me to get hurt because of you please leave."

"Fuck...you're not shitting me are you?" Reese's eyes seemed to glow with an intense rage. "That fucking asshole..."

"Look, just leave it alone, you obviously know who and what he is."

"Yeah, I know...but you don't know who I am..." Reese backed up, looking dangerous and pissed. "But I get it...our family can be like this with the daughters too. I'll go, but come back to college if that's the only place I can talk to you freely."

"I'll be back tomorrow."

"Cool...take care of yourself, Quinn." Reese's voice held his sincerity and she smiled to hear it. He seemed like a nice guy under all that dangerous.

"That's what I'm trying to do." She said quietly, hugging the door.

He gave a little nod of his head and passive smile before walking off. He looked back to see her watching him leave. He waved back curtly and she smiled before closing the door.

Reese sighed bitterly.

Ferrante's fucking sister...hidden from enemy eyes by a different name but held in check and controlled heavily by Antonio, the new Don.

"Damn it to hell." Reese muttered as he got in his car and drove off. "Just as I was really beginning to like the chick..." He paused in his thinking.

Wait a minute...

Didn't she say she was from Boston?

Reese returned home to find Cory's pickup truck parked out front. As he drove his car into his reserved slot he saw Cory get out and walk up to him.

"Why are you here again, this is becoming a habit I don't like." Reese asked him with a surly tone.

"How is she?" Cory asked, instead of answering.

Reese clucked his tongue while locking his car. "You better come inside I guess."

Cory grinned and followed Reese through the entrance security gate and into the communal pool area, around the pool to his own apartment and he unlocked the large slider that was his informal front door. There was a formal front door down a path on the other side of the complex from the street but he never used it and neither did his friends.

Cory noticed there were two guys already lounging by the pool and one of the other residents was looking out their windows at them with a sour look on their face. Reese did a head flick to acknowledge the guys as they both greeted him, standing up.

"How do you get away with your friends letting themselves into the complex?" Cory asked.

Reese looked up and saw the resident looking, they ducked quickly behind the curtain. "What are they going to do? I've offered to help them move."

Cory chuckled, shaking his head. "You're an ass."

"Don't pretend to be anything else..." Reese shrugged as he went inside and dropped his jacket and bag. "Besides those two out there are my security."

"Oh..." Cory replied, looking back to see them both watching him.

Reese saw Cory's discomfort. "Don't worry about them, you arrived with me, but don't make a habit of these visits...want a beer?" Reese went to the fridge and grabbed a can holding it up. He hated Cory coming over, anyone could see him and start associating him to the gang, and that was one thing Reese did not want happening.

"Yeah, alright..." Cory said and Reese threw the can at him. He caught it and his mouth twisted. "Thanks, now it's going to froth up."

"Good catch though." Reese chuckled.

"Did you think I wouldn't catch it?" Cory asked a little offended.

"Nah..." Reese grinned and collapsed down into a comfy armchair, opening his beer and taking a swig from it as Cory followed suit, tapping the bottom of the can to dispel the gas before opening it and sucking off the froth that bubbled up.

"Quinn is Antonio Ferrante's sister." Reese muttered quietly.

"What the fuck!"

"I'm not sure why she has a different last name but it seems they are keeping her tightly controlled and off the radar."

"Smart..."

Reese's expression was tight. "He keeps tabs on her, cameras at her place, probably tracks her phone too...so if you want to keep this competition going we're going to have to get smarter."

"Do you really think it wise to keep playing with the sister of Antonio Ferrante? Not to mention that means she must be daughter of Augusto..."

"That doesn't bother me." Reese smirked before taking another swig from his can.

"It should..." Cory stated a little disturbed by Reese's lax attitude towards someone so notoriously dangerous and psychotic.

"Maybe I'll just go to Augusto and get his permission to date his daughter...it could be a great peace alliance."

"You would go that far?" Cory was stunned. "You'd be forced to marry her!"

"I don't know about that...the Ferrantes are traditionalists, but Quinn is not some virgin Mary and she's already said she has a boyfriend..." Reese sat up in realization. "Wait! It may be she's already been promised to someone..."

"An arranged marriage, seriously?"

"She said she was taken and when I asked if that meant she had a boyfriend she said 'not in so many words'. I asked her what that meant but she wouldn't elaborate...it makes sense, Antonio's over protectiveness, making sure she's not hanging around any strange guys." He frowned darkly. "Maybe her virginity is being protected..." Did she lie to avoid more questions?

"Fuck...that's not cool."

"Yeah, she's petrified of Antonio."

"With good reason I would say..." Cory huffed. "I don't know much about him but Dad's reaction in telling me to keep well away from Zortex and the Ferrantes is enough to know how dangerous they are...maybe we should drop this competition and leave her be."

Reese sucked on his teeth. "Something still doesn't sit right with me."

"Like what?"

"I don't know, it's just a weird vibe I got seeing Antonio yesterday when he turned up to get Quinn's car towed and talk to the Chancellor and the way she was acting just now." The way she hides her hands in her sleeves all the time...

Cory could see on Reese's face he was deeply troubled. "You're not going to let this go, are you?"

Reese's eyes lifted to Cory, looking at him from under that black fringe, pale gold and intense. "Nah, I don't think I can."

Cory smirked. "She's really got under your skin, huh? Reese the impregnable is falling in love!"

Reese's expression darkened. "Don't be a cock."

"Be honest...look at you, I've never seen you so caught up in feelings over a girl before."

Reese's darkened gaze heated slightly. "No, only by a boy..."

Cory coughed and spluttered, his cheeks reddening. "Cut it out..."

Reese tilted his head and gave a cocky grin. "So are you going to back off and let me have her then?"

"Not on your fucking life...I'm all up in those feels too, you know...I'm completely besotted by her. I find myself wondering constantly what she's up to, how she's doing..." Cory sighed and rubbed his face. "Damn...I hate this."

Reese looked away with a grimace. "Fuck's sake."

Cory grinned. "Who would have thought we would both catch feels for the same girl, huh?"

"I'm not going to fight you for her...I know she likes me."

"I'm sure she likes me too..."

Reese glared at Cory as Cory rubbed his cheek with concern.

"We need to get her to a party or something. Somewhere we can both approach her properly in a situation surrounded by people making out." Reese muttered darkly.

"Get her in the mood and see which one of us she kisses?" Cory chuckled. "Yeah, maybe...but how if you say her brother controls her movements?"

Reese tapped his fingers on his beer can, deep in thought. "I'll think of something."

16
Family Dinner for Reese

Reese huffed as he sat back in his seat and let his gaze wander the restaurant. He was bored and felt these little family dinners were a complete waste of time especially when it was cutting into his Saturday night. Why his father always insisted on him meeting every bloody new wife potential was beyond him. This one seemed to be a little bit crafty and was actually of a decent age for his fifty five year old father, she looked to be thirty rather than the twenty somethings he kept showing up with, and was decent enough to look at. He wished them all the best and good luck once the woman found out what his father, Cillian O'Shea, did for a living.

In the good old days it was extortion, booze running and illegal gambling, these days it was guns and drugs importing that the Irish Mob invested in and a healthy dose of money laundering through their various legitimate looking businesses, including restaurants, hotels and clubs.

Reese's eyes fell on a familiar face and he smiled in realization that he was witnessing something interesting and maybe something that he could utilize the information of later.

Emma Johnson was sitting across the room in a quiet romantic corner with a man having a very romantic little dinner for two by the looks. Reese couldn't see the man's face as his back was to him. The fact she was in this very swank and expensive restaurant and the man was definitely a lot older in years than little miss Emma, freshman in college, was what made Reese chuckle darkly to himself. He took his phone out and snapped a pic.

"What's so amusing?" Cillian asked, sounding offended.

"What? Oh, nothing about you or what you're saying, I'm sure what you're saying is very poignant and interesting, dad."

"No need to be facetious, Reese. What are you snapping?" Cillian went to turn around but Reese stopped him.

"Don't...it's just a little bit of surprise news that I wasn't expecting to have fall into my lap that I can utilize later...nothing to do with you."

"Hmm...well, it's good to practice your blackmailing skills." Cillian muttered behind his napkin with a chuckle of his own.

Reese grinned widely, showing his teeth. "Exactly!"

He saw the man stand up and button his suit jacket closed before turning around. Reese lifted his phone and got the perfect shot of the man's face as he put his arm around Emma's waist and motioned for her to go first. This definitely wasn't Emma's dad and in fact he was pretty sure there was absolutely no reason for Emma Johnson to be having an expensive romantic dinner with the Dean of Science unless they were fucking. Was Emma, the heir to a large pharmaceutical company having trouble passing her grades?

Reese stood up, downing the last of his drink. "Right, I'm off."

"Very well, son...keep up the good work." Cillian smirked at him, amused. Reese smirked back and left. Passing the table of the four henchmen that followed his father around at all times, they all gave him a polite goodbye. He had free rein to enjoy every aspect of his life for a whole other year until he graduated. Then he would be tied down to the way of life his father had in store for him. He intended to enjoy every fucking second of it!

He discreetly followed the car Emma and Dean Franks got into, a very nice Mercedes and got the pictures he needed the most. Them parking up in a secluded spot in the park and kissing while going for a little romantic stroll.

Nothing could be more perfect than the plan he had forming.

Quinn was kneeling on the floor between Antonio's feet, tears in her eyes and his huge hard cock in her mouth as he yanked on the leash that tightened the collar around her neck.

"Take it all in, petalo, swallow. Don't you dare even dribble out a single drop."

Quinn swallowed, her lungs starting to scream and let out a gasping cough, breathing in deep as he finally loosened the collar and dropped the leash so she could pull back.

He smirked and grabbed her chin in his hand, lifting her face back to look at it, admiring the tears and red cheeks. He swiped his thumb over her lips where spittle was still sitting.

"Beautiful..." He murmured. "Stand up."

Quinn gathered her feet under her and stood up. He grabbed her hips and dragged her naked body over his lap, grabbing his still hard cock and thrusting it inside her. She groaned at the rough invasion and settled her legs either side of him on the chair. He leaned back, admiring the view.

"Play with your breasts while you ride me, slowly...I want this to burn the insides of both of us as we're both held back from coming."

Quinn started a slow undulating dance on his cock, squeezing her breasts and rolling her nipples between her fingers, she dropped her head back, closing her eyes at the exquisite torture of him filling her. She would never deny that sex with Antonio wasn't great...even if he was the only person she had ever been with and had no comparison, she knew he was an expert at this and the things he had taught her she would be forever grateful for knowing.

She gasped as he reached up and grabbed the collar around her neck and yanked her forward. She had to slap her hands down on his chest to control her fall forward as his mouth devoured hers. She groaned into his mouth salaciously as he pushed the button on the remote in his hand and the butt plug inside her started to vibrate.

He pulled her away from his face with a fist full of hair held at the back of her head and grinned smugly at her as she ground down hard on him with the extra stimulation.

She looked up with hooded eyes as she was bowed forward rocking and grinding on him to see that sexy damn smirk directed at her.

"Fuck, you love it don't you? You dirty slut."

"Yes, sir." She breathed between pants.

"Look at you grinding on me...you're like a bitch in heat." He turned the vibrations up and Quinn let out a husky groan, gripping his shirt into her fists.

"No..." She breathed as her body started to tighten and her hips moved on their own seeking the pleasure that was starting to build. She knew she couldn't, he had not told her she could.

"Don't you dare come, Quinn." He threatened in a little growl of amusement. "I'm supposed to be punishing you...you were late getting home to your townhouse and so late being picked up."

"I'm sorry, sir...please..."

"I told you, you could walk home only if you weren't late with doing so."

"I'm sorry..." She mewled. He grabbed her hips and stopped her movements and pushed her down hard on him as he ground up into her.

She was desperate now and clung to him, her back curled and her head bowed. She dug her fingers into his chest through his shirt panting in need.

"What's the matter, petalo?" He tilted his head so he could see her face as her head was bowed low in front of him.

"I'm going to..."

He ground up in her again and her body spasmed as she cried out. God, another one of those and she was going to come undone.

He chuckled darkly, he knew it too and was determined to make her come without his permission just so he could haul her off into his playroom and bang her ass as punishment for the rest of the night.

She was so fucking delicious.

He was so fucking cruel to set her up like this.

He thrust up hard into her, one, two, three times.

Quinn arched her back and threw her head back as she came hard riding his cock in wild abandon for a few seconds, collapsing back into his chest again as her body twitched in ecstasy, crying.

"I'm sorry, please, I'm so sorry..."

Antonio chuckled as he gathered up the leash, curling it around his hand, pushed her off his lap and stood up. He yanked on the leash hard making Quinn yelp.

"Crawl..."

He didn't even have to tell her where as she stifled her whimpering and started to crawl on her hands and knees towards the hall.

"Good girl."

17
Convince her or go viral

Emma entered the Student Executive Office with a strange trepidation having no idea why she was being summoned first thing on a Monday morning. She knew she hadn't done anything to warrant this and she was nervous about having to face Reese O'Shea noticing he was alone in the room.

Reese smiled as she entered and stood up from the computer desk, indicating for her to sit on the couches.

"Emma Johnson, glad you could come and see me. Please sit down, make yourself comfortable, I'm just wanting to have a little bit of a personal chat with you. You don't mind, do you?"

He gave her a sexy smile as he sat down in the arm chair that faced side on to the couch and crossed his legs exuding a calm friendly manner that seemed to work on putting Emma at ease.

"Oh, okay...whew! I thought for a minute I was in trouble." She giggled nervously as she sat down, pulling her skirt down as much as she could to cover her thighs and gave Reese a responding smile. "What can I help you with?"

"I was just thinking last night about the other night at bowls, you remember, don't you?"

"Of course, you were teasing Quinn." She pouted like she wasn't approving.

"Yes, well...do you remember the question that was asked that all you girls at our booth had to answer?"

Emma frowned in recollection, tapping her lips with one finger. She was quite cute and had a rather large pair of tits.

"Oh, about losing our virginity?"

"That's right, and you answered just a couple of months ago with your new boyfriend..." Reese drawled, leading her to his point of reveal.

She frowned, instantly suspicious. "Yeah, so what? I wasn't lying."

"I'm not accusing you of lying but I am curious to know who this boyfriend of yours is exactly?"

Her eyes widened and she clutched her bag close, Reese knew her phone was inside. "What business is that of yours?"

"Not much..." Reese shrugged. "As you know I'm interested in Quinn."

Emma's frown deepened into confusion. "So why?"

"I'm not sure if you know too much about her back story, but her brother runs the family and is particularly controlling of Quinn's ability to...shall we say...socialize."

"She's mentioned she can't go out in the weekends because her phone is tracked but what's that got to do with me and my virginity?"

"Or lack of it..." Reese chuckled. "Nothing except that I need you to do something for me."

"Huh? What?"

"I need you to persuade Quinn that she absolutely must break her brother's rules and sneak out this weekend to a secret rave that's happening up in North Mount Levetto Forest."

"What? A rave...seriously?" Emma's eyes brightened.

"Of course you get an invite too...if you can get her to come."

"How the hell am I supposed to do that? She seems pretty adamant that every weekend she is busy."

"Busy?" Reese scowled at that. Busy doing what? "Well you'll need to be really convincing then."

Emma stared at him. "I don't know how you expect me to..."

He flipped his phone around and held it up, cutting her off as her words got stuck in her throat to see a photo of herself with Dean Franks on Reese's phone. "If you don't, this goes viral."

"How?" She gaped, horrified.

"That's not relevant, what is, is the fact that after doing a little research I found out Dean Franks used to work with your father and now it seems he's working you."

Emma glared at Reese. "It's not like that!"

"I'm sure and I don't really care but we all know contractually Dean Franks is screwed if this gets out, so how much do you like him?"

"You're a cold-hearted asshole!" Emma yelled at him, tears pricking her eyes.

"No argument here..." He chuckled. "So you get Quinn to that party and I delete the pics...easy."

"You don't deserve her, acting like this!" Emma cried, clutching her bag to her chest.

Reese chuckled in a chilling way that made Emma swallow hard. "Oh, I think that's not for you to decide so no saying anything to Quinn about me at all, got it?"

Emma huffed, wiping tears away. "Yeah, got it...can I go now?"

"Of course...as long as you understand your assignment."

"Yeah, got it asshole!" Emma stormed to the door. "You know I heard you were some mobster's son, I guess the rumors were right."

Reese smirked and licked his tongue over his teeth as the door slammed shut.

"Come on, you have to come with me!" Emma tried to coax Quinn about the rave.

"To a secret rave in some forest? No thanks." Quinn scoffed as she kept walking. Emma had been trotting along beside her all day trying to persuade her.

"I can't go alone!" She pleaded.

"So go with someone else, you seem friendly with Lizzy, ask her."

"But she'll tell everyone! I'm not even supposed to know..."

Quinn stopped walking and gave Emma a seriously intrigued look. "And how did you find out about it?"

Emma paled. "Ah...well, let's just say that information is top secret." She beamed a smile.

"So how do you even know it's a real happening thing?"

"My source is one hundred percent accurate."

Quinn looked at Emma dubiously. "I don't know, I don't think you should go...it sounds like the start of some sadistic horror film, like Saw or something..."

"Eww...don't even go there...nah, it's a legit party, it's gonna be dope...it's a birthday but I can't say whose."

Quinn squinted in distrust. "Regardless, I can't go."

"Why not?" Emma whined. "Just cancel whatever plans you have and come have fun...you've been at college for nearly three weeks now and have the two hottest guys on campus vying for your attention and not once have you ever let your hair down and come out to just enjoy yourself!"

Quinn's mouth twisted into a regretful pout and her eyes dropped. Antonio wasn't in New York this Saturday coming but he had specifically told her to stay at home, so she knew he would check up on her. As much as she would love to go and do something as exciting as a secret rave and possibly get the chance to actually spend some time with either Cory or Reese to actually flirt and maybe secretly kiss one of them...there was no way in hell she was ever going to risk it.

The punishment she could have received just from having Reese turn up to her door last week was enough to know she couldn't handle what Antonio could do to her is she snuck away to an actual party in the fucking woods! Matteo had paid her a visit on that one and told her in no uncertain terms that was her one and only warning, next time he would have no option but to tell Antonio everything. She was grateful but on edge now to know the cameras were definitely being monitored.

She sighed. "Sorry, I just can't."

Emma clucked her tongue. "Are you really going to let your brother control your life forever? You're legally an adult, what the fuck, Quinn!"

Quinn looked at her stunned, of course she didn't get it, how could she ever understand what was really going on but how did she know it was Antonio... "How do you..."

"It's a rumor all over campus that you're not allowed out because your brother says so...is that actually true?"

Quinn looked around herself at all the people passing them in the corridor and hushed Emma to stop talking. "Please shut up."

"Promise to discuss this later then?"

"Alright..." Quinn walked off and Emma looked pleased.

Reese moved through the crowd before he was noticed, a small smirk on his lips. He had to hand it to Emma Johnson, she was determined and persistent, this might actually work.

"Okay, now we're alone can you tell me the issue with your brother?" Emma asked after meeting up with Quinn after class and sitting in Emma's car.

Quinn fiddled with her bag strap wondering how much to tell Emma about Antonio. He had warned her to never mention their true relationship or that he was actually mafia and let people think he was her brother.

"Look, I can't say too much but my family are..." She paused. "...dangerous. There's no more simpler way to say it, and Antonio runs that family and the business now and it's just the way it is, the family head sets the rules the others all obey."

Emma's face was pale. "Shit, like mafia...?"

Quinn looked down and just put her finger to her lips.

"Holy crap! Are you serious? Shit, I had no idea."

"Well, of course no one has any idea, that's the point." Quinn said. "But I'm not allowed to get friendly with any guys."

"Just because you're going to a party doesn't mean you're going to hook up with guys...oh my god, this is like a conversation I had with my parents when I was fifteen!"

Quinn rolled her eyes. "I know, it's pathetic but I don't dare go against it."

Emma was starting to fret, what the hell was she going to do to get Quinn to that party? "If you could go, would you?"

Quinn's lips pursed as she thought about it. "Probably...I hate not being able to enjoy college life to the fullest."

"Exactly, and you should! Fuck your brother and his rules."

Quinn pressed her mouth tight. It wasn't that easy, it was so much more complicated than that. She felt that little pit in her stomach start to grow. She feared him and he was becoming crueler since her mother died and he declared she belonged to him, she didn't dare put a single step out of line.

Emma saw the fearful reluctance cross Quinn's face. "Shit, would he actually like hurt you if you disobeyed him?" She asked in worry.

Quinn looked up with a startle and Emma saw the truth in the glimmer of fear in Quinn's eyes. "No, of course not, but I would be punished in other ways probably..." Even her voice sounded off.

Emma wasn't buying it.

"Look, I'm sorry but I hope you understand now, I gotta go..." Quinn left Emma's car and walked off.

Emma looked over and saw Reese watching from the shade of a tree. She waved him over.

He seemed reluctant but wandered over and got into her car.

"What's happening?" He asked coldly.

"I can't do it!" Emma whined.

"You're not trying hard enough..." Reese growled, annoyed.

"Look, she didn't say it in actual words but, I think she might be being actually abused by her brother if she doesn't obey his rules."

"Hmm..." Reese grumbled. "I wondered the same thing...he's a violent person, I doubt he would hold back just because she's a girl or his sister." Reese spat, his fists clenching.

"So she's too scared...there's no way I can talk her into breaking the rules knowing she could get hurt just so you can have your fun, that's not fair to her!"

"You're right..." Reese conceded with a twist of his mouth. "Forget it, back off for now."

"For now?" Emma questioned.

Reese grinned at her. "You're being put on the back burner, but you're still useful to me."

"Are you fucking serious!?" Emma was outraged.

"Do I look like I'm joking?" Reese's scowl was deadly and made Emma stop breathing.

"You're probably just like how her fucking brother is!" She accused harshly.

"Maybe...except I don't hit girls."

"You blackmail them instead!" Emma hissed.

Reese chuckled. "Yeah, don't panic...I just want you to keep subtly working away at Quinn's resolve to not go against her brother's control."

"I just told you..."

"Yeah, yeah...there's another party coming up soon...I want her there, no excuses this time. Talk her into it, come up with a plan for her to sneak out without her brother finding out...leave her phone at home, leave her car at home, sneak out a window so there's no footage of her leaving her home...it can be done, it just needs more time." Reese was fully committed.

Emma gave him a repulsed look. "You sound almost like a stalker..."

"Bullshit, this is the opposite. This is getting Quinn out from under the scrutiny of a stalker brother..."

Emma was dubious. "You like her that much or do you just like the challenge? Because I don't want this to end with Quinn hurt by either her brother or by you. She's actually really sweet."

Reese's lip lifted on one side in a sneer. "Then refuse to do it and let me expose your dirty little secret." Reese grinned to see Emma pale and swallow hard at that.

"I hate you." She muttered under her breath.

Reese opened her car door and climbed out. "Lucky I don't give a shit."

18

A kiss and bruises

"Do I have to do this?" Quinn asked nervously. "You told me my weeks were my own, so why am I having to go to some charity auction on a Thursday? Who even does these things during the week?" She was standing in front of Antonio wearing a long dark blue dress that the shop assistant had recommended for the event and that the shop fitters were now hemming while they waited. This meant two nights were taken up by this, today being Wednesday and tomorrow the night of the event, both of which she could be studying.

He was sitting in a comfy chair, one leg hooked up over the other while he scrutinized Quinn in the stunning velvet dress that showed a lot of cleavage in a dipping sweetheart neckline.

"The rich with nothing better to do...and of course you do, you're my partner in this now...why do you dare to question me?"

The fitters glanced nervously at each other while they worked on the dress as Quinn stood still on the raised plinth like a display doll under Antonio's dark gaze.

She bit her lip, looking at Antonio with a nervous flutter in her stomach. "What happened last time...?"

She saw his expression tighten as his jaw clenched tight and she dropped her gaze to the floor.

"You did what was required to ensure the business got the needed licensing, what is wrong with that? It didn't cross any line you shouldn't be willing to cross for the good of the family."

Quinn chewed her lip and glanced at the shop staff awkwardly. He wasn't going to give her any reassurances that it wouldn't happen again.

She felt a justified anger boil up and she lifted her gaze at him challengingly. "I want to say that I will not allow you to use me like that ever again. I am not a stripper or a whore or your property that you can let other people humiliate me like that!"

She saw Matteo stiffen and grimace behind Antonio, closing his eyes for a moment.

Antonio sat up, putting his foot on the ground and leaning forward so his forearms were on his knees. His head tilted up and sideways as he regarded her with an amused menace.

"Is that right? It seems my little bird is trying to grow up and leave the nest..." He stood up and started advancing on her like a predator. "...little does she realize she's not a free little bird in a tree in the wilderness..." He grabbed her around the throat, pulled her down off the plinth turned her around and bent her over it as he loomed over the top of her and pressed his groin to her ass. "...she's trapped in a gilded cage of my making where she does as she's fucking told!"

"Antonio...stop!" Quinn struggled but the hand to her throat had moved to the back of her neck and squeezed tight, forcing her forehead hard against the plinth top.

Matteo shooed the staff out of the private fitting room and closed the door, putting his back to it to prevent anyone from entering. He grimaced as he heard Quinn cry out.

"Not one word of this to anyone or you'll find yourself homeless, jobless and alone." Matteo threatened the staff who cowered back looking at the door behind him with great concern.

"It's just a little lover's spat, nothing to get all worked up over...calm yourselves, ladies. I'm sure they're just patching things up as we speak, is all..."

He explained over the noises as a continued rhythmic thumping started up.

Quinn wore her hair down to college the next day, she knew she probably had bruises on the back of her neck that she couldn't see to be able to cover up, she definitely had one on her forehead. She cursed as she walked up the rise from the security gates to see Reese sitting on his motorbike, looking at his phone, he looked annoyed about something.

He looked up as if sensing someone watching him and looked directly at her. She gave him a little smile and he stood up off his bike immediately and walked over.

"Hey..." She called to him.

"Hey." He answered with a lick of his lips and a cheeky smile. "You're early today?"

"I have to get some things done so I can leave early today..."

"Oh?" His eyebrow lifted as his eyes narrowed slightly.

She tilted her head, squinting up at him in the sun. "Yeah...I have a thing..."

"A thing? Shit...that's amazing, you must be so proud."

"Ha, ha, very funny...you know what I mean." Quinn pouted at his sarcastic humor.

He chuckled. "Yeah, none of my business, right?"

"Got it in one." She beamed a bright smile at him.

He stared at her for a moment, dazed by her beauty. "Got time for a coffee first?"

"Sure...why not."

He actually grinned at the easiness in the way she accepted his offer. "Nice, that was easy...see how that works."

She pouted again, scowling at him making him chuckle. "Do you want me to refuse?"

"Nope..." He grabbed her hand and started walking. "No way your backing out...this just made my morning."

"Seriously?" Quinn scoffed.

Reese looked down at her next to him. She was a nice height compared to him...he guessed around five foot six or seven...with heels on she would still be shorter than him which was a good thing, but only by a few inches which would make kissing her easy.

"Ever wear high heels?" He asked as they reached the café.

She frowned up at him. "What made you ask that weird question?"

He shrugged and raked a hand through his hair. "No reason...just noticing your height...with heels on you would be at a perfect height for some serious making out."

She looked at him like he had just performed an impossible magic trick as a slow blush reddened her cheeks. He sat her down and bopped her on the nose.

"You're freaking adorable when you're speechless." He walked off to get coffee.

She swallowed trying to moisten her dry mouth as she tried to get control of her beating heart. What a thing to say! That guy seriously had some rizz, she felt out of her depth and swept up by him, but it felt fun and she couldn't help a small smile creep over her face as she pressed her hands to her cheeks feeling the heat.

He came back and placed an electronic disc on the table as he sat down. "How you getting on there, still blushing?" He teased with a cocky smirk.

She looked up into those pale hazel eyes dancing with amusement. "I thought about it, and no..." She replied, not wanting to lose and really wanting to see him shocked for once. "...I would rather be sitting to make out, preferably on your lap."

She got the desired result, and regretted it instantly as his expression deadpanned but his eyes seemed to become iridescent and lock on to her like an eagle locking onto its prey before swooping in for the kill. "You did not just say that to me, Quinn Malley?" He thrummed, his voice dropping in tone and becoming husky.

She felt her stomach flutter and she pressed her thighs together as she felt herself get wet at that sexy tone. "What if I did?" Her voice squeaked, belying her true nerves at the way he was looking at her.

"Fuck this!" He growled and leaned over the table, grabbing her around the neck and his lips smashed over the top of hers, his mouth open and his tongue licked her lips. She gasped and her mouth opened, her eyes staring at his, blurry in her vision but clearly still locked on to her. She felt his tongue dip into her mouth and caress her tongue, swirl around it like it was coaxing hers out and her eyes fluttered closed as she kissed him back.

It didn't last long, a few seconds and he pulled away, but he left her breathless and stunned, he was a great kisser...gentler than Antonio but with a similar controlling dominating way, it excited her. She opened her eyes as his hand drifted forward to under her chin and he stroked her cheek with his thumb. His eyes were sparkling now, a satisfied smirk on his lips as his eyes wandered her face with a wonder to them that left her gaping at him.

"Finally..." He growled out in a husky breath.

The electronic disc on the table suddenly went off between them causing Quinn to jump out of her skin and reel backwards.

"Easy babe!" Reese's fingers went to the back of her neck again, catching her and keeping her close. She winced as his fingers dug in a little too strongly. He instantly let go, standing up and stepping to her side and sweeping her hair back. "Fuck, sorry, did I hurt you?"

"No, stop!" Quinn cried out.

Too late...

Reese stood staring at the black bruises on the back of her neck, his face dropping into a grim and deadly expression.

"Who the fuck did this?"

"Stop!" Quinn pushed him away, sweeping her hair back over her shoulders to cover it and looking around the café embarrassed to see it half full of people and some of them staring and gossiping about them. "Not here."

"Then let's go somewhere to talk..." He pivoted around grabbing the disc off the table and stalked off to the counter to get their coffees.

"Shit..." Quinn breathed out as she stood up on shaking legs. What do I do now?

He stalked back holding the coffees giving her an intense glower with those amazing golden eyes. "Follow me." His tone was a definite order.

She sighed as she followed him out of the café. He headed around the back of the building and to a small secluded spot where a couple of people were vaping at a picnic table.

"Leave." He growled at them, putting the coffees down.

They took off and Reese pointed to the seat. "Sit."

Quinn huffed irritably and sat down, pulling her sleeves down over her hands. Reese suddenly grabbed her arm, yanking it up into the air and pulled her sleeve back. He glared at the bruises still faintly on her wrists then let her go, wiping a hand down over his face as he sank down onto the seat beside her.

"Fucking hell, Quinn...why didn't you say anything...to anyone?"

She tucked her hand back into her sleeve, staring at the table top. "What for?"

He turned, putting his feet on either side of the seat so he was facing Quinn and wrapped his arms around her. "Now I get why you are so damn scared of your brother..." He said quietly and calmly so not to scare her, but inside he was writhing with anger. "He did this, didn't he?"

Quinn didn't answer, but her eyes teared up and a single drop trailed down her cheek. Reese cupped her cheek, lifting her face as he wiped the tear away. "I don't think I can just sit on this and do nothing, Quinn."

"You don't understand anything." Quinn mumbled. "Can we please just pretend this didn't happen?"

"How the fuck can I do that, someone hurt you and I know who!"

"You don't know the why of it though, please, just drop it." Quinn looked up pleadingly into his eyes.

His jaw was ticking as he held himself in check at her miserable and fearful expression. He dropped his hand to her thigh, his other hand coming around her back and he pulled her closer as he widened his legs to accommodate her body, dropping his forehead to her shoulder. He took in a deep breath, smelling the sweet fresh scent of her hair, expelling it deeply.

"Tell me it's a one off and I'll believe you, babe."

Quinn chewed her lip, playing with her sleeves. They both knew it wasn't a one off but he was willing to let this go one time. "It's a one off..."

Reese closed his eyes as he grit his teeth. Why would she defend that asshole and cover up her abuse. He lifted his head and looked off at nothing for a moment then dropped his gaze to her. He saw her glancing up at him side on, her face full of worry. "Alright...I'll drop it this time, but only once, you hear me. If I ever see another bruise on you, you better be able to prove you tripped or bumped into something to back it up." He sounded pissed off and Quinn hated the funny feeling she was getting in her stomach.

"I just want us to go back to how we were ten minutes ago..." She murmured quietly.

He reached out and grabbed a large handful of her hair, trailing it over his hand and through his fingers. She had amazing colored hair, he hadn't ever seen anyone with this sort of dark red before...and it was so soft and bouncy. "I love your hair..." He said then, choosing to try and change the mood. He sat up, moving back slightly from her. "Drink your coffee, babe."

Quinn looked up at him and pouted in misery. "I'm sorry..."

He sucked his teeth as he gave her a look full of concern. "What for?"

"I think it's best if I just go..."

Reese didn't have the temperament to argue for her to stay right now. "You do you." He said rather coldly.

Quinn stared at him for a moment then stood up, and went to leave.

"Take the coffee with you." Reese grabbed it and held it out to her. She stepped back to grab it and he grabbed her wrist, making her startle and lock eyes with him.

"I'm sorry too, Quinn...I need time to process my anger, I can't be what you want right now. I suggest you go find Cory." His tone was begrudging.

He dropped his grip and she frowned at him. "Why would you tell me to do that?"

"He's better at the emotional stuff than me."

"So you actually know about him being interested in me too?" Her frown was suspicious.

He chuckled darkly and looked away, licking his teeth. "Yeah...I know. Of course I know, you've mentioned it before..."

"Please don't tell him about this..."

Reese shrugged. "I can't promise that, babe...I can only do this one thing and not act on it this once...I won't hide it like you, don't ask me to. I'm that person, I'm really fucking angry right now, just go."

Quinn could hear the anger in his tone as he spoke through gritted teeth. Tears welled up in her eyes again and she turned and fled in as quicker walk as she could not to attract any more attention than was absolutely necessary. She past the big guy that had accompanied Reese to the bowling alley and he gave her a shocked look before looking up to see Reese looking bleak sitting at the table.

Reese stood up and walked up to him. "Let's hit the gym...I need to thump something."

Tank turned, shoving his hands in his sweat pant pockets and followed without a word, he knew that expression on Reese's face.

On the way Reese took his phone out and messaged Cory.

R - **Find Quinn, now!**

19
Golden Retriever

Cory was just drying himself off in the locker room after his shower when he heard his phone go. He leaned into his locker and grabbed it, reading the message from Reese with a grim sigh.

"What the fuck have you done...?" He muttered and hurriedly dressed, grabbed his stuff and went to walk out.

"Hey! Wait for us, Curry..."

"Nah, got somewhere to be..." He said and dipped out quickly.

He had no idea where to even look for Quinn at this time of the morning...he made his way to the business faculty and scanned the corridors.

After a few minutes he saw the top of her red head cross the hall in the distance and he hurriedly made his way up to the intersection to see her walk into a class room.

He ducked in and saw her take a seat and take a folder out of her bag. No one was in the room and he guessed she was in here to drop some assignment notes off but she looked mentally spent as she sighed and closed her eyes.

"Quinn..." He called out, startling her and making her look up with surprise.

"Ah...hey?" She greeted back.

Cory saw the fleeting look of despair cross her face as she looked down at her hands and pulled her sleeves down. He walked up to her and took her by the shoulders pulling her up and into his chest before wrapping his arms around her.

"I'm really sorry to disturb you right now if you're busy, but I needed a hug from a pretty girl and I saw you from across the hall come in here, so..." Cory made up some excuse with a small smile to himself.

He felt Quinn wrap her arms around him tight and bury her face into his chest. Saying nothing she just clung to him. He stood there for a long time just rubbing her back, his chin tucked over her head with his eyes closed just enjoying the warmth of her body. Her breathing was steady so he wasn't in any great hurry to do anything else but wait and enjoy the moment.

Quinn didn't want to let go, there was something about this guy, something that just made her feel safe in his arms. She had never felt that in Antonio's arms and she never realized before how much she craved the feeling of safe before being hugged by this guy. After everything that just happened with Reese she needed this so much, it made her feel like she could face the world again, she felt re-energized by Cory's amazing supportive hugs.

Did he know what had happened with Reese? He hadn't made any attempt to talk to her about anything, he just held her silently and let her take the time she needed.

She finally lifted her head and stepped back to look up at him. He brushed the hair from her face and gave her a gentle handsome smile.

"You obviously needed that too, huh?" He said softly.

Her eyes narrowed. "Did Reese tell you to find me?"

He shook his head feigning innocence. "No, why? Did something happen with him?"

"You know he is trying to date me too, right?"

"Oh!" Cory managed to look surprised. "Is he? No, I wouldn't know, I don't have much to do with him these days..."

"So you aren't friends?"

"Not really, we used to be really close...but we drifted apart in high school. Why, are you interested in dating him?" Cory's voice dropped a little and hardened.

Quinn chewed her lip. Were they really as distant as they made out? She had seen them in the carpark talking to each other, but she hadn't actually seen them together anywhere else. She had no reason to not believe him. She shook her head slightly as she looked away from Cory to her bag and the folder on the desk.

"No, I'm just curiously interested I guess...I don't know, a part of him scares me."

"That's just him...he's a hard nut to crack, and he's never going to be soft and gooey...not like me." Cory grinned that boyish playful smile and Quinn couldn't help but laugh.

"Hey, there she is...look I wanted to ask if you've had any trouble with the girls lately?"

"No, actually, it's been pretty quiet on that front."

Cory nodded. "That's good."

"Did you say something to them?"

Cory rubbed the back of his neck. "Let's just say I had a little chat with Mila and sorted out what me and her are to each other, she was a bit confused."

Quinn gave a wry smirk. "I bet she enjoyed that conversation?"

Cory's mouth twisted. "Hmm, not so much...but at least it got through..."

"Yeah, thanks." Quinn picked up her bag and folder and moved to the front of the room, placing the folder on the professor's desk. She turned to look back at Cory and he smiled at her expectantly.

"I'm heading to the library..." She said.

"Sweet..." Cory answered, stepping towards the door.

Quinn gave him a strange look. "So you're coming with me?"

He shrugged. "I've got nothing better to do for a bit...can I?"

"Sure..." Quinn frowned a little and went to the door. Cory opened it for her and stepped out into the hall behind her.

The halls were relatively empty now and they walked down side by side.

"Are you going to the rave on Saturday?" Quinn asked out of curiosity.

Cory blinked as he put his hands in his letterman jacket pockets and looked ahead. "I was thinking about it...you?"

She shook her head. "I can't...I'm not free on weekends."

"Shame, not any weekend?"

"No."

"Can I ask why?"

She sighed and her head dropped. She really didn't want to have this conversation again. Cory seemed to understand and spoke up before she could answer.

"It doesn't matter...I get to see you here, and it's not going to be forever, is it?"

They had reached the doors leading out of the building and as they stepped outside Quinn stopped lost in the revelations of Cory's question.

Was it forever?

Was she truly stuck in Antonio's web forever, never to get the chance to be free and enjoy herself? Forced to obey his rules and do whatever he ordered her to do for the rest of her life...to marry him...to have his heir?

"Quinn?" Cory's startled voice jolted her out of her nightmare. She looked up bewildered as he stepped in close, his hands coming to her face and wiping her cheeks. She blinked, feeling wetness and realized it was tears, tears were streaming down her face.

"Quinn, are you okay? You're shaking, are you cold?"

Cory took his jacket off and put it round her shoulders, dragging her over to a bench seat on the lawn and sitting her down. He crouched in front of her, his hands on her thighs and looked up at her concerned.

"Shit, Quinn...you're scaring me."

She wiped her face and took in a deep ragged breath, letting it out slowly to calm her frantically beating heart. "I'm fine...I just..."

"You had another panic attack..." Cory stated, his voice firm. "This isn't a joke, Quinn, you need to talk to someone about this..."

"No, I'm fine...really, I was just struck by a memory..."

"A memory? Of what?"

"Oh...um...my mother..." She lied, hoping it would appease him to not keep asking questions. "She just died a few weeks ago."

"Oh shit..." Cory straightened up on his knees and pulled her into his chest. "I'm so sorry, bunny."

Quinn chuckled and lifted her head, her eyebrows furrowed but her eyes sparkling with amusement. "What did you call me?"

Cory let her go and stood up, raking a hand through his hair. "Ah, nothing..."

He looked down at her little smile and smiled back. "Are you okay now?" He held his hand out to her.

"Yes, thanks...I'm so sorry you had to see that."

"Don't be, it's perfectly understandable...I get it now, it must be hard?"

Quinn chewed her lip as she stood up, she didn't want to lie to him but how could she ever tell him the truth...now that Reese was figuring things out she was going to have to give him a wide berth.

"Come on..." Cory encouraged. "Let's get to the library and I'll sit with you until my next class."

"Thank you...you're really nice."

Cory beamed that roguish smirk and winked. "Only to the pretty girls."

Quinn laughed rolling her eyes. He really was a rogue, she had to remind herself of that...she wasn't sure if this nice act was real or just his way of getting a girl in bed, but for right now she needed it and liked it as it made her feel special, even if she wasn't.

Cory loved spending time with Quinn in the library, she was actually a lot of fun, with a witty dry humor and she was quite intelligent. He enjoyed watching her read, looking at her side profile...the concentration in her eyes, her pert little nose, the way she hooked her hair behind her ear and it flowed over her shoulder, exposing just a little of her neck. The way she kept shushing him as he tried to talk was adorable.

He felt a deep regret when he looked at his watch and realized he had to go. As he stood up he leaned forward and kissed the side of her head making Quinn look up at him with shock.

"I've got to go, this has been fun, we should do this again."

"Yeah, okay..." Quinn smiled up at him as he put his jacket on.

"Anytime you need, Quinn...find me, okay?"

She looked away shyly back to her books. "Yeah, okay...and thank you...I mean that." She glanced back up and found him grinning at her. He reached out and very lightly touched her face, trailing a finger down her cheek.

"Can I message with you tonight?"

Quinn startled. "No, I'm going out..."

"When will you be home, I'll message then."

Quinn chewed her lip for a second. "Late...I don't know."

"Hmm, okay..." He frowned. "Message me a good night, eh, no matter the time."

Her mouth twisted at the subtle command. "Okay..."

He smiled and turned away with a wave. "Look forward to it...see ya!"

"Bye..." Quinn frowned. He was smooth in manipulation, experienced in getting what he wanted in the end by being nice, that was a change.

Cory wandered out of the library and saw Reese sitting on a benchseat looking broody. He lifted his hand and flicked his fingers for Cory to go over. Cory grit his teeth at the silent command but did it anyway.

"Have you been sitting here waiting?"

"Yeah, how is she?"

"You know that's quite stalkerish of you, I'm shocked."

"Get over it and answer my damn question."

Cory looked around and sucked his teeth. "Did you know her mother just died?"

"What? No...she hasn't mentioned it to me."

"Answers why she has panic attacks, must be a grief response..."

"Panic attacks?" Reese growled. "Fucking hell, it's got nothing to do with her mother..."

"What do you mean?"

"Just do what your good at and be that lovable retriever when she needs it, okay..."

"Okay..." Cory frowned, he was missing something in this conversation.

Reese stood up coming face to face with Cory. "Sometime soon, we need to have a serious chat you and me...but not now." Reese walked off and Cory was about to yell out at him to explain what he said but saw Reese's mates Tank and Jacob walking up to him.

Cory frowned darkly, he didn't get how Reese managed to get those idiots in the gates, but somehow he had given them passes. It annoyed him that these thugs were here...

20

A charity auction full of surprise

Quinn was shocked at the swanky room Antonio led her into for the charity auction. The five star hotel that was hosting it was definitely for the uber-rich and she could feel the difference between this group of people and the people at the last soirée. These people were elegant and refined and exuded class. Quinn gripped Antonio's arm nervously.

He glanced down at her with an amused smile. "Don't worry, petalo, these people are pussycats...we are here to rub shoulders and shake hands and be seen in esteemed legal company."

She relaxed a bit and when the waitress came round with flutes of champagne she took one, taking a heavy sip.

"Take it easy..." Antonio warned. He knew she was no good with alcohol and bubbles tended to go straight to her head. Besides, she was technically underage, no matter how grown up and sexy she looked in that dress.

A man dressed in a fine three piece suit came up to Antonio and shook his hand. "Mr Ferrante, I'm glad you could make it..."

"It was short notice, but I wouldn't miss such a valuable cause..." Antonio said back in a smooth tone. "I thank you for thinking of me when the extra tickets came up."

Quinn pouted at the congenial way Antonio spoke, he was definitely acting. She looked up as she heard him introduce her to the man.

"Quinn, this is Senator Peloski, a good friend of my father."

Quinn heard the 'my father' and guessed she had been introduced as his partner not his sister, that suited her fine, she was neither really but certainly closer to partner than sister.

"Hello, nice to meet you." Quinn said politely.

"What do you think of your partner becoming a mayor?" Peloski asked her with a hearty chuckle.

"A mayor? A mayor of what?" Quinn asked surprised by the question as she looked up at Antonio to see him smiling amused.

"She didn't know anything about it yet...I don't want to get too excited about anything quite yet, it's a long journey." Antonio said, brushing it off as Peloski laughed and side winked.

"Quite right...there's a few steps of process to go, but you're on your way being here...being seen."

"Antonio!" Someone else called out and he turned around. Quinn peered around him as he had dropped her arm and turned so his back was to her.

"Mrs Wright, lovely to see you again." Antonio greeted, kissing the woman on both cheeks as Italians liked to do.

Quinn looked up and around the room. Matteo was beside her so she knew she couldn't just wander off. She glanced up at him and he instinctively dropped his gaze straight to her with that grim expression. She looked away instantly, she felt uncomfortable with him ever since Reese had knocked on her door...she felt like she owed him a favor for not telling Antonio, and this sort of man was not one you wanted to owe anything to.

She sipped her champagne and let her eyes wander as Antonio did his networking, occasionally pulling her into a quick conversation and introduction, but most of what they spoke about was politics and the charity, some cancer research institution that wasn't government assisted and helped people in some poor African countries get treatment while taking their experimental drugs. It was a great first step into the world of influence where politics was concerned for Antonio.

She felt Antonio's hand slide over her waist and his mouth come to her ear. "You can get one more drink...I'm just going to have a quick private conversation with someone, stay here. Matteo will stay with you."

"Okay..." She looked up as Antonio walked away. She saw a woman waiting for him by a side entrance and they disappeared together. She grit her teeth against the dip she felt in her gut at the sight of the woman's sultry smile and the familiar touch she gave him. She looked away bitterly, not wanting to admit it hurt but it did.

Her eyes landed on the one person in all the world she never thought to see here. He looked exceptional wearing the black three piece suit, his hair slicked back away from those fierce golden eyes as he talked to an older couple of some wealth judging by their clothing. He flicked his wrist, straightening his shirt cuff and lifted his eyes to the room.

Quinn blanched and stepped back. What the hell was Reese doing here?

Just as she tried to step behind Matteo to hide his eyes fell upon her. She held her breath as she saw his face go through a range of emotions like he didn't recognize her at first but then it slowly dawned on him. She knew she looked different when she was made up and wearing an evening dress, she looked older and the dress clung to her curves normally hidden under large sweatshirts. She remembered their conversation about wearing heels and a small blush crept over her cheeks.

He went from a casual glance to a sultry gaze to a frown then his eyes widened up to shock. He licked his lips and looked away before looking back again as if to make sure she was real.

Quinn pursed her lips and shook her head at him.

He dropped into a broody sulk, staring at her from under his brows with his head down like a wolf. He was distracted by a man approaching him and shaking hands, forced to look away from her.

She swallowed hard and turned her back, hoping the message to not come near her was relayed. Her stomach dropped when she turned and saw Antonio coming back, a sexy smirk upon his lips and the woman nowhere in sight.

Quinn frowned, that wasn't long enough for anything to happen, did she have it wrong?

Antonio walked up to her and slid his hand across her bottom and onto her hip, pulling her into his side. She lifted her chin and he gave her a dashing smile. He was in a good mood.

"You are the most beautiful woman here, petalo..." He breathed as he ran his finger under her chin and leaned down to press his lips chastely to hers.

She tensed up hoping Reese wasn't watching.

Antonio straightened up and with his hand on the small of her back guided her to another part of the room. There were plinths and display cases showing the auction items, some were jewelry, some were vouchers for holidays, clothing from esteemed designers that had featured in films, gold plated golf clubs, fifty year old scotch, plus other expensive luxury items. It all screamed at the wealth of these people to be able to donate such extravagance to the auction.

Antonio stopped in front of a large diamond encrusted watch having a good look at it. Quinn looked over her shoulder and saw a beautiful single diamond ring on display. It was huge and teardrop shaped and sparkled incredibly under the little spotlight it had.

Antonio leaned over her as he turned her way, his hands coming round her and clasping together over her stomach. "You like that, petalo?"

"Yes, it's beautiful..." She gaped in awe at it.

He nuzzled his face into her hair. "You're more beautiful than any diamond...do you want it?"

"W-what?" She spun around to look at him to see if he was serious or just teasing her. His dark eyes glittered with a smoky smolder.

"It could be your engagement ring..."

Quinn baulked at that but Antonio straightened up, wiping his thumb across his bottom lip and laughed at her. She felt the tease now and pouted, looking away as he took her hand and pulled her on to look at something else.

Quinn stopped breathing as she saw those golden eyes glaring at her with a dark menace as Reese stood off behind them, his hands in the pockets of his suit pants, the jacket swept back behind his forearms showing his trim waist. He sucked on his teeth, turned and walked off.

Quinn felt sick, how was she ever going to explain this away?

She stumbled as Antonio pulled her and he turned his head to look at her with a frown. "Please, Antonio...I need the bathroom."

He glared at her for a moment then nodded, letting her hand go. "Go, quickly...the secret auction is about to close and I want to bid on that watch." He stalked off leaving her to go fill in the required form. She looked back and Matteo was right there on her shoulder making her flinch. He pointed to the left.

"Over there."

"Oh, thanks..." She ducked her head and had to concentrate on not running for the door.

The hallway she stepped into had an exit door out onto a small balcony with a fire escape and she rushed off out there to get some fresh air, her stomach swirling in fear and nerves.

She stepped to the balustrade and gulped in air, closing her eyes and enjoying the cool air on her face as it was hot and no doubt red.

"Quinn, what the fuck!"

She spun around as Reese growled behind her. Her heart skipped a beat at the fierce look in those golden eyes, they seemed to almost glow in his anger.

"You can't do this with me...here...please."

"Why's that? Because your brother is a gangster who's trying for politics and because he's gay, so he likes to take you along to these events as his plus one and pretend not to be...?" He looked challenging like that story had better be true.

She had to laugh, which made Reese's eyes darken. "He's not gay."

"Yes, he has to be." Reese growled menacingly.

"Has to be?" The growl that came out of her mouth was challenging to his own.

Reese stepped closer to her, intimidating her with his height. "Yes, otherwise that PDA I just witnessed takes on a whole new light, Quinn, and I saw your reluctance to him touching you like that."

She frowned and looked away knowing this was the end of the lies. "He's not gay." She said quietly.

Reese felt his rage building dangerously. "What the fuck are you saying to me right now?"

Quinn looked back, her expression solemn. "He's not gay and he's not a blood relative, so don't panic...he's my step-brother, that's why I don't have the same name, I was never adopted by Augusto, he just married my mom."

"Step-brother!" Reese was stunned. "So...you're actually fucking him?" He ran a hand over his hair in disbelief. Fuck, it all made sense now.

She shrugged noncommittedly.

His eyes narrowed dangerously on her pale drawn face. "Is that fucker making you?"

"There you are...Antonio wants you back inside so finish whatever the fuck this is quickly." A huge man in a completely black suit with leather gloves and a stern expression walked out and glared at the two of them. Quinn's stomach dropped as Matteo stepped out.

"Yeah, okay..." She replied quickly.

Matteo looked Reese over with a frown. "Who's this?" His voice was harsh and accusing to find Quinn talking to a young man.

Reese was just eyeballing him and sucking on his teeth, his lips twisting in an annoyed grimace.

"This is Reese...he goes to the same college."

"Huh...O'Shea's son...of course." His eyes were intense as he stepped up closer, putting his hands casually in his pockets as he studied Reese, Reese just stared back unafraid. "You were Quinn's little visitor to her door?" Quinn quailed as Matteo's gaze slid to her. "Go inside." He ordered, his voice low and calm.

"He was just talking..." Quinn tried to say, hearing the tone.

"Go inside, Quinn." Matteo ordered again. "Be a good girl."

Reese stiffened as that his hands clenching into fists. Quinn huffed and looked at Reese with a little remorse before leaving the balcony obediently.

Reese leaned back on the balustrade with a cocky grin, taking out his vape and inhaling a long draw before lifting his chin arrogantly and letting the vapor out between them. "What? You going to threaten me to leave the girl alone?"

"If you know what's good for you." Matteo replied in an emotionless voice.

"Ha!" Reese looked away for a moment before looking back at a click sound. He startled to see the guy had drawn a gun. He flinched back in reflex more from the surprise of seeing it than it actually being a threat to him but Matteo grinned.

"You get it now?"

"You're in here armed?"

"Fully licensed to carry and registered as a bodyguard...now take the hint kid...stay the hell away from Miss Quinn."

Reese clucked his tongue at this guy's attitude. "Because she's the sister of a Mafioso and he's ridiculously protective?" Reese scoffed sarcastically.

Matteo scowled at him. "Go with that."

Reese barked a harsh laugh. "You're all delusional...I know what's going on between them."

"Listen you little prick, if you want to live leave the girl alone...you have no idea what Antonio would do to you if he found out you were sniffing around her. Take the damn warning."

"You really think he would risk the peace by going after someone wanting to simply date his *step-sister*?" Reese sneered the last word for effect.

Matteo's jaw clenched, his eyes darkening. "You don't get anything...just back off."

Reese watched the bodyguard pivot and walk back inside. "What don't I get, you asshole?" Reese muttered darkly. "She is actually fucking her step-brother?" He ran a hand over his hair exasperated by the evening's events. "Fuck..."

But why did he get the creeping feeling of dread at Quinn's reaction when he asked if Antonio was making her.

He sucked on his vape with a sour huff. "Fucking hell..."

As he stepped back inside his father's off-sider, Liam, stormed up to him. "There you are! Don't go off on your own...that Ferrante bastard is here, it's not safe."

"Yeah, I saw." Reese flicked a look over to where he could see Quinn standing with a wife of some big wig. "You able to do something for me without telling my father about it?"

Liam eyed Reese with a droll look. "Depends what it is, boyo?"

Reese flicked his head. "See that girl, the one with the long red hair..."

Liam looked over and actually caught the pretty young woman's eye as she was glancing nervously over at Reese every few seconds. He chuckled. "Yeah."

"I want a full background check done on her."

"What for?"

"Let's just say I don't like her circumstances..."

Liam gave Reese a strange look over before taking out his phone. "Okay, what's her name?"

"Quinn Malley."

Liam took a sneaky pic of her and put his phone away. "Alright, I can see she likes you...I'll see what I can find out."

Liam looked back just as Antonio came up behind Quinn and palmed her bottom then slid his hand up around her waist and led her away.

"Hang on, she's with Ferrante?"

"That's the sort of information I want you to try and find out...what's their real connection?"

"Hmm..." Liam looked dubious.

"Please..." Reese breathed out harshly.

"Yeah, okay..." Liam relented.

"Thank you, I'll owe you one."

21

I won't quit on you

Friday was a nervous day for Quinn as she tried to keep her head down and not be found by Reese. She met Cory during her break in classes for lunch and they sat in the café Artifice.

"So you were right about being home late...I saw your message this morning, I fell asleep." Cory said sheepishly. She hadn't been dropped home till Antonio was done with her at 2am.

"I told you..."

"So where did you go, on a date?" He asked coyly.

She laughed. "You're not smooth...I was attending a charity auction with my brother."

"Not the one for Cancer treatments in Africa?"

Quinn startled. "Yeah..."

"Damn, I was supposed to go to that...wait, Reese was there wasn't he?"

Quinn frowned with remorse. "Yeah, I saw him there...but couldn't talk to him."

"Huh? Why's that?"

She gave him a strange look. "Our families don't get on."

"Oh, right...yeah...Ferrante's your brother, scary shit."

Quinn looked him over, he didn't seem to know anything. She smiled in relief, well perhaps she could just pursue a little flirtation with him and leave Reese the hell alone. She really hoped that after last night he intended to do the same with her.

The smile slid off her face as if by thinking about him conjured his appearance as he slipped into the seat next to her at their table. Cory looked up with a strange twinkle in his eye as Reese leaned around into her face.

"Hello Quinn, I've been looking for you." His voice was not pleasant.

"You may have noticed she's not alone, jerk off." Cory muttered.

Reese turned to look at Cory with a smirk. "I can see that, but this is important."

"I don't want to talk to you." Quinn spat, glaring at him.

"I really think you should..." Reese growled.

Cory frowned at the tension in the air and Reese's obnoxious attitude. "What's going on now? Honestly you two are like wild cats stuck in a sack."

Quinn's mouth twisted in discontent while Reese chuckled darkly. "Should I tell him?"

Quinn looked at Reese with a pleading expression. "Can't you just drop it?"

He leaned back in his chair, letting out a sharp breath as he sucked his teeth, his gaze wandering over her. "I really want to...honestly I do...but I can't."

Quinn sighed bitterly looking at her lap.

"Bruises are bruises, Quinn...no denying them."

She grimaced and looked up sideways at him with contempt as Cory sat up, alert. "Bruises, what fucking bruises?"

Quinn stood up and started walking away. "Hurry up then, make this quick."

Reese stood up, pressing a hand to Cory's shoulder. "Stay." He ordered.

Cory's jaw clenched as he watched Reese follow Quinn out of the café and down the walkway. "What the fuck is going on?"

Quinn stopped in a thoroughfare through from building to building. "What do you want me to say?"

"Tell me what the fuck is going on with you and that Italian bastard."

Quinn gave him a haughty look. "That is none of your business...I told you I was seeing someone that wasn't a boyfriend...it's complicated and I'm not discussing it with you."

Reese licked his lips as he chuckled sinisterly. "So why the fuck are you doing this little dance with me? You kissed me back yesterday."

"You remember my answer to the question at bowls about body count?" She folded her arms and settled a benign stare at him.

Reese frowned slightly. "One...that fucker?"

"Yes, one...only one. You pursued me and I liked it."

"You like Cory too..." Reese stated his eyes dark and broody as he just stared at her unwavering to the point she had to look away.

"I think I do..." She dropped her arms and looked back at him. "Look, I haven't led you on...I was pretty clear I wasn't available, but I'm not going to lie anymore. I like you and I'm being selfish 'cause I've never had these kinds of things happen to me before, same with Cory...I'm enjoying the moment, but now you know I get it if you don't want to talk to me anymore."

Reese looked away, shuffling his feet and putting his hands in his pockets. "I won't quit on you."

Quinn gaped at him. "Why the fuck not?"

He breathed in and out a measured breath, settling his gaze back on her. "Because there's something about you, Quinn Malley...and I want to find out what it is."

Quinn's heart thumped in her chest. Was he for real?

"Plus, I don't think you really want me to quit on you, do you?"

Quinn chewed her lip not wanting to admit to that but he smirked in triumph anyway.

"If you want me to save you, Quinn, just say the words..."

Quinn startled, her eyes widening at his poignant statement as his eyes bore a hole into her soul like he could see her screaming out from her gilded cage for help.

He turned then and slowly walked away. "Don't ignore me, babe!" He called back at the top of his voice, waving his hand out.

"Son of a bitch." Another male voice growled.

Quinn turned around to see Cory coming up.

"He saw me coming and literally took off...what's going on? You guys are acting like you have some big secret between you..."

"We do." Quinn dazzled with a huge smile.

Cory pouted. "Well that's not fair..."

"It's nothing worth knowing, trust me." Quinn said.

"Hmm..." Cory's blue eyes held hers for a moment as if he was trying to determine the truth of it. Quinn watched with a sudden flutter in her belly as his expression suddenly changed, she had never seen this expression on Cory's face, she had seen it on Antonio's face and Reese's face but never carefree Cory's...he was looking at her with a possessive heated smolder that made her forget how to breathe.

He grabbed her arm and swung her around, walked her backwards until she hit the wall and planted his hands either side of her. She gaped at him to realize he had been fooling her with his teddy bear act.

"Make it up to me." He said with a hard tone.

"Make what up to you?" She asked meekly, staring at him like she didn't know who he was, her heart thumping in her chest.

"You left our date with another guy, I'm a little pissed off." His gaze was intense as it wandered her face and he grinned roguishly. "A kiss ought to do it."

"W-what?" Quinn's mouth went dry, she couldn't believe the change in this guy.

He lifted one hand and pointed to his cheek. "Right here...come on, you owe me that much."

"A kiss on the cheek?" Quinn asked dubiously.

"You're getting off far too lightly, I know." His eyes twinkled with his playfulness and it made her smile.

No, he was still the same guy. "You scared me for a second..."

"Scared you?" That intensity came back into his eyes for a moment and she again found herself holding her breath. "Not scared, turned on...right? Every girl likes a little bit of manhandling every now and then..." He grinned and turned his face away, pointing to his cheek again. "Now come on...hurry up."

Quinn could feel her cheeks heating up and quickly leaned up to kiss his cheek. He turned his head just at that moment and she found her lips planted firmly on his. She startled for a second, her eyes going wide and seeing his in her vision before she pulled back and saw his smirking smug face.

"Nice..." He commented.

Quinn knew she was blushing now and covered her cheeks with her hands. "Oh my god, stop...this is too much."

Cory chuckled and dropped his hands from the wall, stepping away. "All good, I got what I wanted." He held his hand out to her. "Shall I walk you to class?"

It was going to rain just as Quinn was heading home. She cursed the weather report not telling her that morning as she drew her hood up on her sweatshirt and bowed her head into the wind. She had been walking for a week now, since her car was in the shop...and although she liked the walk as she didn't live too far away days like this made her wish she had her car back.

A V8 engine sounded next to her as a car pulled over to the curb, she turned to look and saw a black Camaro.

She stopped walking as the window on the passenger side opened and Reese leaned over from the driver's side with a big ass smile on his face.

"You don't have your car back yet, do you?"

"Obviously no..." Quinn drawled sarcastically.

"Get in, let me take you home, it's going to rain soon."

Quinn looked at the stormy grey sky feeling the wind whipping up around her and grudgingly got into Reese's car.

"Wow, you really had to think about that, huh?" He chuckled as he pulled back out into traffic. "So, why aren't you being picked up and driven home?"

"I told them I would rather walk."

Reese snorted, amused. "You're really quite savage, aren't you...even in the face of gangsters."

"Sometimes I have to be otherwise I'll never feel even remotely free..." Quinn stated.

Reese frowned to hear the sad tone and focused on the road for a bit as the rain started pelting the windscreen.

"You have it tough, huh?" He said after a while of silence.

Quinn almost jumped out of her skin when he spoke again. He laughed. "Sorry, didn't mean to scare you!"

"I was enjoying the peace and quiet watching the rain on the window..." Quinn's fingers traced the rain tracks on the side window pushed by the slipstream of the car. "As a kid I used to call it water worms, used to freak my mom out, she hated anything worm-like."

Reese chuckled softly. "Sounds like you liked your mom a lot, my condolences, I heard she passed only a few weeks ago."

"Life was good when she was around." Quinn's comment was subdued and Reese glanced at her. She looked sad as she stared out the side window.

Reese caught flashes of light in his eyes and looked into the rear view mirror. "Fuck, you were being followed."

"Me?" Quinn whipped around in her seat to look out the back window. "Are you sure it's me?"

"It wouldn't be me, trust me...if my people wanted me they would ring and I don't have tails to worry about."

Quinn gave him a strange look before they both heard a loud obnoxious beeping from the car behind.

"Do I pull over or keep driving?"

Quinn hugged her bag to her chest, feeling sick from panic and checked her phone. There was a message from Antonio she obviously hadn't heard it while walking.

A - **Rain is expected, I've sent Matteo to you**

"Oh, no, it is for me, you better pull over...I'm sorry." Matteo! Why not Danny the driver, at least then this could all be kept hidden from Antonio, there was no way after last night Matteo will let this go.

Reese clucked his tongue. "We're almost there and if you have to get out to swap cars you'll get wet."

"Please, Reese." She pleaded with him.

"Fine..." He sighed and looked for a place to pull over, turning onto a side street with trees lining the road and parked under the boughs of one. "There, stay under the tree."

The other car screeched to a halt and a guy jumped out, stalking up to the car on the passenger side and throwing the door open violently.

"Quinn! Get out!" Matteo bristled with anger.

Quinn hesitated seeing his unjustified rage.

"Hey, asshole..." Reese called out. "It's raining and she was walking, I was just being a decent human being and giving her a lift!"

Matteo leaned down and peered into the car with a menacing hiss. "You! And after last night...this makes it your third offense, you want to die that much?" He looked at Quinn. "You better make the right decision here, Quinn, otherwise it's going to be really bad for you." He grabbed her by the arm and hauled her out of the car making her squeal in pain and distress.

"Hey! Treat her with some respect, isn't she your boss's sister?" Reese yelled at him.

"Sister?" Matteo scoffed. "She doesn't deserve any more respect than you do you Irish dog!"

Reese laughed manically. "Fucking hell, you Italian piece of shit."

Matteo slammed the door shut and dragged Quinn to his car, opening the passenger door and threw her in. Reese sucked on his teeth to see how roughly Antonio's off-sider treated Quinn, no wonder she had bruises all the time. There was definitely no respect for her being part of the family...what was the deal? Even if they were in a relationship that was more than just step-siblings surely that would make her Antonio's main squeeze which should at least earn some respect from his subordinates?

Reese saw Matteo come back round to his window and Reese huffed as he lowered it a crack. "Come to apologize for your behavior...we do have a peace treaty and I outrank you, asshole."

"I don't know what your game is, bud, but I do know who you are...and Antonio will not like the fact that you know Quinn well enough for her to get in your car knowing the consequences."

Reese frowned. "He doesn't need to know..."

Matteo grinned and leaned his arm on the car, bringing his face closer. "Is there any incentive for me to not tell him?"

Reese clucked his tongue. "You're pure scum...how much?"

"How about five big ones."

"Are you kidding me? One."

"Don't barter with me, Irish dog! You know it won't be you punished for talking to Quinn...it will be her."

Reese grit his teeth. "Fuck...alright." He grabbed his phone as Matteo laughed and held his up to the crack in the window. Reese transferred the money.

"Pleasure doing business with you, Mr O'Shea." The sarcasm was thick as his phone bleeped with the transaction. He stood up and walked back to his car without another word.

"Piece of shit! If you didn't carry a fucking gun and not hesitate to use it, I would kill you where you fucking stand!" Reese muttered as he threw his phone over to the passenger seat.

He watched as Matteo pulled out and drove past him. He saw Quinn smile and give a little wave of thanks, Matteo must have told her that he just paid for his silence on the matter.

"You'll keep."

22

A rainy car ride home gone wrong

Matteo parked up the drive right outside Quinn's apartment and got out, coming around to her door and opening it for her to get out. She gave him a confused look.

"You shouldn't stop here on the drive...I can let myself out."

"No one will dare say anything. I'm coming inside, we need to have a little chat."

Quinn swallowed hard and nodded. "Okay, but Antonio will see you on the cameras..." She got out and walked to the front door.

Matteo chuckled. "No, he won't." He said coming up behind her as she opened the door.

Quinn looked back at him. "How can you sound so sure?"

As they walked in Matteo looked around the lounge room as he took his wet jacket off. Quinn dumped her bag down and did the same, stripping her wet sweatshirt off.

"I know because these cameras run in real time, they don't record unless selected to and Antonio is in a very important meeting right now...he gets an alert and usually by looking at the time he knows it's just you, he'll usually have a quick check on you and that's all...you're really not that important to him, Quinn." He seemed amused.

He looked over Quinn's body in the tight string strapped singlet she was wearing noticing the bra straps as well and the padding from a push up bra, she had quite nice tits, a perfect handful for a man with large hands, probably equated to a C-cup. He also noticed the faint bruising on her wrists and licked his lips.

"Your wrists are still bruised...is that why the sweatshirt in this freakishly warm weather?"

Quinn looked at her wrists startled and hid them behind her back self-consciously. "Y-yeah...I tried makeup like on my neck but it just wears off too fast on my wrists..."

"You don't have to hide them from me since I already know." Matteo smirked at her and sat down in a chair. "Get me a drink."

Quinn's eyes narrowed on him at the bossy tone. "What do you want?"

He smiled as she didn't argue. "A coffee will do, I still have a busy day."

"Alright..." Quinn went over to the kitchen area and started making a coffee. She was nervous having Matteo in her house, alone. She didn't trust him, he saw too much and what he did see he always seemed to watch with a dark excited gaze.

"You obviously don't want Antonio knowing about today?" Matteo leaned back in his chair and commented casually. "On top of the last two offenses you're incurring quite a debt with me."

Quinn felt a little flutter of nerves. "Of course he can't find out...but I thought you said..."

"Just because that boy pays for my silence doesn't mean shit to me, more fool him." Matteo interrupted, his voice sounding annoyed. "You're the one that needs to convince me to not say anything."

Quinn felt her skin crawl. "H-how?"

He looked over to her with a shit-eating grin. "Well now, it's nice to finally have you in this position, Quinn...you know what Antonio would do to you if he found out about you and that kid...are you fucking him?"

She looked mortified. "Of course not!"

"Not yet, huh? He's certainly putting in the ground work though...I wonder why?" Matteo wondered if Quinn was fully aware of who exactly Reese O'Shea was and whether Reese knew Quinn was a possible way in with the Ferrantes.

Quinn chewed her lip as she came over and put Matteo's coffee down on the table. He smirked up at her. "Thanks...now sit down." His voice lowered into an order making Quinn flinch and sink into the seat facing him. "Not there, bitch, on your knees."

"W-what?" Quinn looked up at him with real fear as a knot gripped her stomach.

"You heard, now! I am not fooling around here, Quinn." His deep growl was intimidating.

Quinn pressed her mouth together in a tight line and sank to her knees on the floor beside Matteo, sitting back on her heels and looking at her hands in her lap.

"Yeah, that's the pose..." He chuckled darkly and leaned forward, grabbing his coffee off the table and lifting it to his mouth, he took a tasting sip of it. He smacked his lips and peered sideways at her. "Not bad...now..." He put the cup down but didn't sit back up instead he turned to face her. He was close in this position and she feared to look up at him. "...let's discuss what you're going to do to keep my mouth shut about all these indiscretions." He leaned back and suggestively opened his legs.

Quinn stood up and backed away from him mortified, her cheeks blazing with a shameful heat. "What the fuck are you saying to me?"

"Are you deaf? I'm pretty sure you're not deaf. You heard exactly what I just said, Quinn."

Quinn pulled her phone out of her back pocket. "I'm ringing Antonio about this!"

Matteo collapsed back in his seat with an amused chuckle. "Go right ahead."

Quinn paused, her eyes narrowing suspiciously. "You don't care if I tell him what you're asking me to do?"

He pulled his phone out. "How about I ring him myself, explain this whole situation."

"Why would you?" Quinn was frantic, did Matteo's confidence in what he had blatantly suggested mean Antonio was going to be okay with it?

Matteo paused holding the phone up showing Antonio's number under the name Boss. "You sure about this offer being a no?"

Quinn wiped her hands down her thighs and licked her lips in nervous fright, she had never been put in this predicament by anyone who worked for Antonio before. "You seriously want me to suck your dick so you won't say anything about Reese?"

"Yeah, so what will it be? Is this something you need to keep a secret?"

Quinn frowned and shook her head. "He just offered me a ride in the rain, I swear."

"Alright then..."

"No..." She breathed, feeling a tightening in her stomach as Matteo hit dial and put the phone on speaker.

"What is it?" Antonio's voice answered.

"Problem, sir...Quinn was picked up by someone else before I got there...I managed to flag them down and retrieve her but..."

"Don't bullshit this!" Quinn yelled so Antonio would hear her down the phone. "You clearly wanted me to suck your dick to keep you quiet!"

Matteo chuckled under his breath but Quinn heard the hiss of breath and cluck of tongue from Antonio.

"Whose car?" Antonio asked, ignoring what she had just informed him.

"Excuse me!?" She blinked a little shocked as Matteo smirked at her. "Did you not hear what I just said?"

"I heard...and I asked a question." Antonio's voice was lethal. Quinn clamped her mouth shut, biting her lip nervously.

Something wasn't right here...

"It was Reese O'Shea's car, sir." Matteo said calmly. "Cillian's son."

"What the fuck! Get Quinn and you over to my place, right the fuck now!" Antonio growled fiercely and hung up.

Quinn stared at Matteo as he stood up, put his jacket back on and then put his phone into the inside pocket of his jacket. He calmly regarded her with a small cool smile. "You heard him, are you going to put up a fight and defy his order?"

She let out a insufferable sigh. "No..."

"Then, get up and let's get going, it's an hour's drive at this time of day at least."

The car ride was silent as Quinn opted to sit in the back and pout. She was still concerned at how Antonio just glossed over what she had accused Matteo of like he didn't hear or wasn't bothered by it. That really made her nervous...Matteo was a huge guy and could really seriously hurt her.

Once they entered Antonio's apartment he was there waiting for them. He had removed his suit jacket, tie and vest and rolled his sleeves up and was sitting in his favorite chair in front of the large glass windows with a whisky glass in his hand. His dark broody eyes lifted to Quinn as she entered.

She opened her mouth to speak but he lifted a finger in warning.

"Rules, petalo." He warned in a deep calm tone.

Quinn grimaced and closed her mouth. She was forbidden to speak until spoken to and given permission these days. She watched Matteo as he made his way over to Antonio and stood in front of him with his hands clasped behind his back and his feet a foot apart. Antonio's gaze hadn't left her and his eyebrow rose slightly in question.

"Are you choosing to defy the rules of my house, Quinn?" His voice sent chills through her and she slowly started to undress down to her underwear. She wasn't allowed in his house wearing anything more and she always had to strip off at the door. She had hoped with today's circumstances things would be different. She felt sick, humiliated and angry, was her love for him turning to hate?

Once undressed she padded over and sank down to sit at his feet, glancing at Matteo's shoes next to her.

Antonio tapped his glass as they both waited silently.

"Matteo..." Antonio finally said.

Quinn wanted to scream, he was going to get the story from Matteo and make her stay quiet and wait. That was unfair, she knew he would twist things.

"Sir." Matteo inclined his head in a small bow and let out a little cough to clear his throat.

"Did you really ask Quinn for a blowjob to pay for your silence?" Antonio's voice sounded amused and Quinn couldn't help but look up at him. She saw his smirk as his eyes dropped to hers and held them with an intense dark fire.

"The boy paid me five thousand dollars to keep my mouth shut, I wondered how far she would be willing to go for the same thing."

"So you were merely testing her resolve regarding the O'Shea boy?"

Quinn went to speak but Antonio was quick and lunged forward with one hand clamping it around her throat. He pointed a finger in her face in warning to not speak then pressed that finger to her lips.

"Correct." Matteo answered with confidence.

"But she didn't agree?" Antonio regarded her as she trembled at his mercy. "So what were you doing in the car of Reese O'Shea, petalo?" He tilted his head at her curiously. "Hmm...did the nice boy offer you a ride home to escape the rain? Why would he do that, huh? How do you know him well enough for him to pull over and offer you a fucking ride home? Does he know who you are to me?"

Antonio's voice had slowly escalated in tone to a vicious growl, slowly squeezing her neck tighter and tighter.

He released Quinn's throat as tears fell down her cheeks, and she gasped for breath.

"What are you crying for?" He spat, annoyed.

"Do you not even care that Matteo was trying to...?"

"No...and do you know why?" Antonio asked with a coy grin.

Quinn heard Matteo snort in amusement as Antonio lifted her chin and pushed his thumb into her mouth, pressing down on her tongue and opening her mouth wide.

She tried to shake her head in answer.

"Because if Matteo wanted to actually fuck your pretty little mouth or any of your holes all he would have to do is ask me. He never has so I know he's not interested in you at all and understands that I am the only man that gets to touch you."

Quinn felt her stomach drop and she whimpered as Antonio played his thumb over her tongue. Was that true...what would Antonio actually answer if Matteo did ask?

"So, I know he's telling the truth when he says it was merely a test, but you passed it, petalo...well done." He released her mouth and sat back. "And now here you are and you're going to explain why and how you know Reese O'Shea son of the leader of New York's Irish Mob."

Quinn wiped her face of her drool and felt a piercing jolt in her heart at that revelation, but she had other worries right now. She gave Antonio a blazing glare. "Are you saying you would say yes if Matteo asked?"

Antonio grabbed his whisky and took a sip, swirling the contents as he sucked his teeth with a dark expression. "We've shared many women, petalo...you do know I fuck other women as well as you, right?" He chuckled at the devastated look on her face with no remorse. "You're the only one I've kept to myself...I'm not sure what I would answer if he asked..." He looked up at Matteo with an askance expression. Matteo was the closest person to a friend he had ever had and they had been side by side for years.

Quinn looked up holding her breath with trepidation of Matteo actually framing the question right now. Matteo looked down at her for a long silent pause, enjoying the terrified look in her eyes.

"She's not my type, sir."

Antonio laughed as Quinn let out a gush of breath, relieved. "Now, if you don't start answering my fucking questions, Quinn, I'll order him to fuck you right here on the fucking floor while I watch!" Antonio growled out at the end of his tether.

Quinn jolted in panic. "Sorry, sir...I...I don't really know him and I had no idea what he was, honest. He asked me out in the first week and I said no...then he bumped into me here and there on campus..." She paused as her stomach tightened up and she covered her mouth fighting being sick in fear, hoping her half-truths would be convincing.

Antonio tapped his glass, irritated.

"...he said hi a couple of times around campus, there's been nothing more...he's the president of the student executive, I have to be polite...I swear to you, Antonio...he just offered a ride out of the rain...he knows what happened to my car and took pity on me I guess."

She really hoped Matteo didn't decide to tell Antonio the rest of what he knew. She lifted up onto her knees and placed her hands on his knees. "Please, sir...I beg of you, believe me."

His eyes were intense and cold as he stared at her. He sucked his teeth as he contemplated the truth of her confession.

"She wasn't willing to keep the silence on their encounter, sir, so I don't think there is anything more personal going on." Matteo spoke up like he was defending her now. She didn't want his input, test bullshit, he would have taken that blowjob!

"Hmm..." Antonio stroked her cheek and sat forward so they were only a few inches apart. "Still...I don't like the O'Shea's and I told you not to fraternize with any male students...don't trust him he's probably using you to try and spy on me." He came closer and stared into her fretting eyes. "I'm going to punish you for this...and it's going to hurt."

Quinn's eyes brimmed with tears and her body trembled and sweated in terror.

"And I'm going to gag that popular little mouth of yours so you can't scream your safe word at me!" He sat back with an evil twisted grin. "I'm going to enjoy this weekend..."

Quinn startled and her eyes widened. "I thought..."

Antonio clucked his tongue. "You thought..." He said in a derogatory tone. "Yes, I was supposed to be going to Boston this weekend, but my little bratty pet can't be trusted to behave so I changed the dates."

He stood up, towering over her. "You can crawl on your hands and knees to the playroom now..." He dropped a collar and leash at her feet. "After you've put that around your sweet little neck for me."

He looked up at Matteo. "Go, come back when your duties are complete."

23
As love turns to hate

Matteo entered the apartment four hours later on Friday evening after finally finishing his duties, as instructed to find it eerily quiet. He called out to no response. Usually Antonio was enjoying a drink while Quinn was waiting quietly at his feet or already in bed. The bodyguards were still at the main foyer so he knew Antonio was still here.

"Shit, he's not still going, is he?" Matteo grumbled to himself as he walked up the hallway to the door with the lock pad on it.

He thumped heavily on the door knowing it was a sound proof room, trying to be heard. The door opened to reveal a naked Antonio in an aroused state covered in sweat.

"Matteo? Shit I forgot all about you coming back, is it that late already?"

Matteo stiffened. "Are you still doing her?"

Antonio grinned like a true psychopath, licking his tongue over his teeth, his black eyes glittering. Matteo saw a fleck of red on Antonio's cheek.

"Is that blood? Shit, Antonio...what the hell?"

Antonio stepped away from the door, wiping his cheek. "She's past out at the moment, I was just letting her rest a moment before waking her...have a look, it's a beautiful sight."

Matteo stepped in and his teeth clenched together.

Quinn was tied over a bench, blindfolded and deafened with noise canceling headphones, a ball gag in her mouth as drool pooled on the floor a testament to how long she had been there. Her buttocks, lower back and thighs were covered in large red welts and small bloody cuts and scratches, nothing too deep but it looked horrific as the blood was sprayed everywhere from the use to a whip and cane. Vibrators, anal beads, wands and plugs all discarded and used, thrown on the bed.

"You've never gone this hard on her before, sir...I think you should call it quits for the night."

"Hmm..." Antonio's gaze swept over Quinn's body as his tongue licked out over his teeth. "You're probably right, this will be quite a shock for her to endure. I certainly don't want to break her mind, she's useless to me if that happens...but fuck..." He raked a hand through his sweaty hair, sweeping it off his eyes. "She's fucking amazing, it's true what they say about red-heads having a higher pain threshold...I should have been doing this with her from a while ago, her pride is unquenchable."

Matteo huffed averting his eyes, he knew Quinn was breathing okay, Antonio knew what he was doing. "I know you're pissed off about the boy, but I didn't think you would ever go this far with her?"

"I planned to one day...maybe once we were married and I truly had her for life...but the rage I felt over her talking to another guy without my permission!" Antonio's expression went dark and his eyes settled on Quinn's marked ass. "But for it to be that Irish son of a bitch's son!" He laughed maniacally. "What are the chances? No fucking way she is going to go anywhere near him after this!" He went to pick up the cane again.

"Antonio!" Matteo yelled. "She can't take anymore..."

Antonio sucked his teeth. "No, you're right..." His fist clenched as he stared at the cane within reach, then relaxed, dropping his gaze with a sigh.

"She's going to have to take time off school as it is." Matteo added.

"Hmm...very well." He huffed and moved away from the cane. "But she stays here tonight so why don't you grab the spare room since it's so late. I'll still have to treat her wounds and clean her up nice, tuck her into bed."

Matteo saw the warmth enter Antonio's eyes and knew he had come back to his senses. "Yes, sir."

When Quinn woke the next day it was mid-morning and she found herself lying face down in Antonio's bed still completely naked, her skin feeling tight and her muscles, pussy and ass sore. She lifted her head with a groan, lifting up on one hand to turn over.

"Is my dirty little cannoli hole finally awake? I wouldn't move if I was you." The deep smooth baritone made her body flinch in reaction as she paused and lifted her fearful gaze to where Antonio was just coming out of the bathroom, the water still glistening on his body as he rubbed a towel over his hair.

He clucked his tongue at her. "Don't flinch like that!"

She obediently lay back down on her stomach, feeling a scratchy hoarseness to her throat as she tried to speak. "Why?" Her voice broke as tears fell. "I screamed for you to stop! I kept trying to say my safe word!"

Antonio chuckled darkly. "Yet you came so many times...don't kid yourself or try to guilt trip me, Quinn Malley...and you don't have a safe word any more..."

She lifted her head and looked over at him, seeing the monster that he truly was. "It hurt! It hurt so fucking much!"

She scrambled up off the bed on the opposite side from him, gritting her teeth against the flaring pain it caused to move that suddenly. She stood, trembling before him, tears falling, but her eyes hard with defiance.

"I want to go home."

Antonio wiped his thumb over his bottom lip, chuckling at her. "You are home, petalo...stop being ridiculous and calm down."

"No! I hate you! I don't want to do this anymore...I'm leaving!"

Quinn made a dash for the door managing to get it open and she ran down the hall towards the front door of the apartment where her clothes were.

Antonio sucked his teeth as he casually walked out behind her, not making any effort to actually chase her down but stalked up the hall behind her.

Matteo came out of the spare room and stared in shock at Quinn running naked passed him. He looked up at Antonio who shook his head at him to stay where he was, his jaw clenching at the mistake Quinn was making.

As she grabbed her clothes she looked back and saw Antonio stalking towards her, a maniacal grin upon his face as he stared down his prey.

She hurriedly put her panties on and got halfway through putting her t-shirt on when Antonio grabbed a fistful of her hair, yanking her off her feet and started walking back up the hall dragging her as she screamed and struggled against him, her hands gripping at his wrist, her legs flailing.

"You fucking ungrateful brat! How dare you fucking say you hate me after all I do for you!"

"Antonio..." Matteo went to say something as he past.

Antonio struck out like lightning and grabbed Matteo's throat with his free hand. "Don't you fucking dare say something, you heard what she said to me! It's because of the fucking little Irish prick and I'm going to beat the brat out of her!"

"Please stop! Antonio...sir, please...I can't take anymore..." Quinn's pathetic sobs continued as Antonio dragged her back into the play room and closed the door.

Matteo rubbed his hands over his face. "Fucking hell...I hope he remembers he made plans to meet with Senator Peloski on the golf course this afternoon to make amends for rearranging their trip to Boston..."

Surprising Matteo in the kitchen making a coffee, Antonio appeared only an hour later, dressed in leisurely slacks and polo shirt ready for the golf course.

Antonio saw Matteo's questioning gaze and shrugged. "I didn't forget about my commitments with Senator Peloski but I couldn't let that bitch smart mouth me...I merely spanked her ass till she couldn't breathe for apologizing."

Matteo nodded. "Coffee?"

"Sure..." Antonio straightened his watch. "You sure you don't want to fuck her? Sending you in right now could really put her back in her place..."

Matteo shook his head with a coy smirk. "You know I like them older and you like her untouched."

"Hmm..." Antonio snorted. "You like them bossy."

Matteo chuckled and poured Antonio a black coffee, sliding it over the counter.

"Take her home for me." Antonio said then, taking his phone out and picking up his coffee, walking off to his chair by the windows in the living area. "I'm going to treat Peloski to dinner then a trip to the Black Diamond Club, I'll be gone all night. I'll take Renzo and Pietro with me. Meet up later."

"Yes, sir."

Matteo heard Antonio talk to the Dean of the Business Faculty excusing Quinn from attending classes for the next few days due to contracting covid, it was a good excuse, no one would come calling with that.

Quinn appeared, meek and damaged, picking up her jeans off the floor where they had been dropped in her struggle and hugged them to her chest.

Antonio placed his phone down and sipped his coffee, watching her over the rim of his cup as Matteo leaned back on the kitchen counter and took his phone out to look busy and avoid eye contact.

"Come here." Antonio ordered, placing his cup down.

Quinn reluctantly obeyed, shifting slowly over till she was standing before him.

"What's the problem?" He asked softly.

"I can't put my jeans on...not over the..." Her voice hiccupped and Antonio grinned.

"You don't want to sit down either, I imagine?"

Quinn bit her lip and shook her head, her cheeks blushing with her shame.

"Words, Quinn, come on..." Antonio sighed, flicking her in the stomach with his fingers.

She gasped, flinching and Antonio's gaze darkened. "Sit." He slapped his thigh.

When she hesitated he grabbed the front of her panties and pulled her forward, forcing her down on his left thigh.

"Breathe, petalo..." He instructed calmly, taking up his coffee cup and holding it out to her face. "Drink...then Matteo will take you home." He turned to Matteo as Quinn took the cup in both hands and sipped the strong black coffee, grateful he was sending her home and she didn't have to spend another night with him.

"Go into my closet and grab out a pair of sweat shorts. Quinn can wear those home, they will be loose and soft."

"T-thank you, sir." Quinn said in a subdued hushed tone.

Matteo moved off down the hall as Antonio combed his fingers through Quinn's long chestnut red hair, sweeping it back off her shoulder.

"Don't give me a reason to hurt you, Quinn, learn this lesson. Stay away from Reese O'Shea and every other bastard or I'll pull you out of that school and chain you in my play room permanently."

"I'm sorry, sir...never again."

He smiled and his handsome face lit up. "Good girl."

As Quinn walked into her house she turned and looked back at Matteo as he followed her in, scowling at him. "What do you want?"

"Hey!" He held his hands up. "Calm down, I'm just instructed to do a perimeter search before leaving you here."

"I fucking hate you! This is all your fault!"

He looked stunned. "My fault? How the fuck do you figure that one? If anything you should be thanking me for not mentioning more."

"Do me a favor or I'll tell Antonio..." She mimicked him, pulling a face. "If you hadn't have tried that shit he wouldn't have ever whipped me!" Tears flowed once more down her face.

Matteo's jaw clenched and he rolled back on his heels. "You're an idiot...all you have to do is obey his orders and you'll get to live the high life, but for some reason you just can't."

Quinn glared at him and he shook his head, walking off through the house.

She walked to the kitchen and grabbed a bottle of water and a tissue, wiping her nose. Matteo came back and she turned to face him.

"I'm going...you have this week off because you have covid, rest up because I guarantee Antonio will want an encore of this now he's gone this far with you."

Quinn's eyes widened and her lip quivered. "No..."

Matteo clucked his tongue. "Don't you get it? This is the real him, he's off the nice shit now, just behave yourself from now on and stay away from others, especially rival organizations and their sons."

"I didn't know..."

"Well you do now, do you feel scammed? You should." He walked to the door and left.

Quinn walked slowly to where her jacket was over the arm of a chair where she had dropped it after coming home with Matteo before all this happened. There was no way she was going to take her phone and have Antonio search through it.

She took her phone out and plugged it in to charge.

Later several messages came through, some from the girls, most from Cory and Reese.

She dropped into a chair, hissing in pain as the raw welts rubbed and opened her messages to send her final message to Reese and block him.

"Damn you, Antonio...I fucking hate you!" She screamed as she sent Reese his final message.

Q - **So you're Mob? I get it now how stupid and gullible was I? Leave me alone!**

24
A way to sneak out

Quinn didn't go to college for the next three days. She also messaged both Cory and Reese and told them to stay away. Reese knew something was up, the stirring in his instincts telling him that Matteo had betrayed their deal. If Quinn was hurt it was because of being seen with him and that thought put him in a very foul mood. He knew Antonio would jump to conclusions of him after Quinn because of them being rival crime syndicates, but he didn't care about that...his father was in charge of that for another couple of years at least and there was a peace treaty. Why would he need to use Quinn to get to Antonio, there really wasn't any solid reason, but after Quinn's message he guessed Antonio had definitely persuaded her.

As he stalked the halls of the Business Faculty people saw the dark moody expression on his face and quickly stepped out of his way.

As Monday turned to Tuesday his mood got even darker, by the time Wednesday came around even his own friends were keeping their distance from him prompting Tank and Jacob to seek out Cory in an attempt to try and ease Reese's burning self-anger. Even they noticed that there was a definite calmness about Reese when he was around Cory.

Cory found him in the executive office.

"Hey man, what's eating at you?"

"Antonio found out about me being interested in Quinn..."

"Is that why she's not here? What's happened to her?" Cory was filled with anxiety knowing they were dealing with a gangster with a bloody reputation.

"I don't know, she sent me a message telling me to leave her alone from now on and blocked me." Reese looked up with that intense gaze. "What about you?"

"She said she had covid so was quite sick and wouldn't be online much."

"I think Antonio hurt her."

"What the fuck! Then we should go round there..."

"We can't...neither of us can be seen anywhere near her right now...and don't let her know you know any of this stuff about her."

Cory grimly looked away with a bitter sigh. "Then send a girl...fuck, Reese...I'll kill him myself if he's hurt her!"

Reese sucked on his teeth. "He hurts her all the time...why do you think she hides under those hoodies all the time...her wrists and her neck...he must tie her up or something weird."

Cory looked at him darkly. "What the fuck are you saying?"

"He's her step brother, Cory...they are fucking."

Cory gaped at him like a goldfish.

"But I think Antonio has a few nasty kinks..."

Cory raked a hand through his hair and walked off to the window. "Jesus fucking Christ...it just gets worse..."

"Want to know what's worse?" Reese asked in a sardonic drawl. Cory turned to glare at Reese. "She's not into it...I think he's forcing her."

"Don't..." Cory growled, gritting his teeth as his fists clenched. "I can't hear another word come out of your fucking mouth without you first telling me you're going to kill him...why are you not telling me that, Reese? You're the damn wolf!"

Reese heard the tremors of emotion in Cory's voice and looked away feeling a little ashamed. "It's all conjecture at this point...I'm gathering the full story...don't worry. The main thing is Cory, I need to get Quinn away from that asshole permanently, and I don't think it's going to be easy, I can't be seen to be involved in anything as a direct strike at Antonio, it will start a war...I need to keep to the background."

"What full story are you gathering?"

"Who she is exactly..." Reese's eyes went dark and Cory frowned.

"Who do you think she is?"

Reese shrugged. "Collateral for something...something big."

Cory looked away, his jaw ticking. "This is why I hate you gangster mother fuckers."

Reese just watched him silently with an intense gaze.

Cory closed his eyes and let out a sigh before turning back. "I'll go talk with the girls that she hangs with...get one of them to go over there and check on her."

"Alright...ask Emma Johnson, she owes me."

"Keep me informed..." Cory paused and regarded Reese with a strange expression. "Are we still competing?"

Reese sucked his teeth with a twisted grimace. "Not sure...are we?"

"Is there any point?" Cory asked sarcastically. "Let's just save the girl from the mafia first."

Reese grinned. "Good idea." He watched Cory leave before taking out his phone to check in with Liam about how he was getting on finding out about Quinn's identity. He paused and looked back at the door.

He sighed and closed his eyes for a moment. He didn't want to compete with Cory for Quinn, he wanted to work with Cory to have Quinn...both of them, together. His loins ached at the mere thought of sharing his bed with both of them.

Emma knocked on the door of Quinn's house and was greeted by her cheery face behind a cute pink mask as Quinn swung the door open wide.

"Hey! Come in..." Quinn said cheerfully. "I'm so glad you offered to bring me the work...I really feel like I'm getting behind not being there."

"You know you could have just asked..." Emma said with a quirky lopsided tilt to her head as she walked in. "Gotta say though, you don't look very sick? I wore this mask for nothing, didn't I?"

Quinn looked at her sheepishly. "Yeah..."

"So...who are you avoiding?" Emma asked as she slipped onto a stool at the kitchen counter and took the mask off.

Quinn came round into the kitchen and opened the fridge. "You want an OJ?"

"Sure..."

Quinn busied herself with getting the drinks as Emma tapped the counter with her fingernails. "You're not going to say?"

Quinn gave her a little bemused look. "Thought it would be obvious to you."

Emma rolled her eyes. "Reese or Cory...or both?"

Quinn shrugged. "Kinda both, but definitely Reese."

"Why, did he do something to my precious Quinny-poo?"

Quinn gave Emma a weird look but she just grinned, sticking her tongue between her teeth. "He didn't really do anything, my brother found out about him is all..."

"Ah...that's too bad...you really have to stop seeing him?"

"I wasn't really seeing him...but yeah it's best I just stop whatever it was going on with us."

Quinn put the juice back in the fridge and came around to sit on the stool next to Emma. Emma sipped her orange and looked sideways at Quinn with a curious look.

"Do you want to ask me something, you look like you're bouncing on your seat?" Emma asked with a weird look.

"How was the rave?"

Emma pursed her lips and frowned. "I didn't go...I said my invitation was based on if you went."

"Oh, sorry...are there any parties coming up?"

"You can't live vicariously through me, you know...if you want to know what a rave or college party is like go to one."

Quinn sulked, looking at the counter. "How can I?"

Emma looked around the room looking for cameras. "You just have to be smarter and more devious than the ones watching..."

Quinn gaped at her. "Are you an expert on this stuff?"

"No, but my brother is..."

"Your brother?"

"Yeah, he was a real expert at sneaking out of our house when he was young...knew exactly how to avoid the cameras and stuff, hack the house alarm..." Emma gave Quinn a look that conveyed her enthusiasm. "I've been speaking to him...he's become quite a hacker these days."

Quinn swallowed hard in her excitement. "And?"

"All we need to do is find the blind spot...my brother says there is usually at least one in every home security system..."

"Blind spot?"

"Where aren't there cameras? Wait, firstly, do your cameras have sound?"

Quinn shook her head. "I don't think so, only the one in the door."

"Right, that's good...we can talk freely, so...cameras, where?"

"Outside on the drive, out there on the back patio, and in here." Quinn explained.

"So none on the second floor?"

"None in my bedroom...no point putting any in the second bedroom, it's not used."

"You have a second bedroom? So I could stay over?"

"I guess so..."

"Cool..." Emma grinned.

"You really want to stay over?"

"Yeah...we can sort this out tonight and prepare for the weekend."

"The weekend?"

"There is a party every weekend happening somewhere...I'll find one and then you are going to the ball Cinderella." Emma announced, lifting her glass in a toast.

Quinn giggled. "Should I call you my fairy godmother then?"

They both laughed and Quinn decided right then she was going to this party, Antonio was going to be away in Boston doing what he should have been doing last weekend, and she was over doing what he demanded. He did not own her, and if this worked maybe she could use the same strategy to run away and never come back. It meant leaving college and never finishing her degree but what choice did she have, she was not going to be Antonio's plaything anymore.

Emma bounced up to Reese as he strode across the lawn from the carpark, stopping in front of him and swaying her hips back and forth like a child in her glee.

Reese gave her a dark stare. "What's got you so bouncy so early in the morning?"

"I stayed the night at Quinn's last night."

Reese settled a tight stare on her and licked his lips in a smirk. "That was your little hatchback parked outside?" He had driven past as he did every night...every night just after midnight he could guarantee to see the light upstairs on and know it was her.

"Ah-huh..." Her eyes were twinkling and Reese huffed a little chuckle.

"Alright, you better come with me then." He started walking again and headed for the administration building and his executive office.

Emma bounced alongside him practically humming. He glared down at her. "Do you mind? People will think I've made you that happy."

"Oh? Well, I'll enjoy the momentary attention...you mean they'll think you slept with me, right?"

Reese clucked his tongue. "What would Dean Franks think?"

"Hey!" Emma startled, looking around herself. "Don't be mean."

Reese snorted. "This better be good news for me..."

"Oh, it is..." They walked up the stairs to the second level and to the executive rooms. Reese opened the door and with a flourish of his arm bowed for Emma to enter.

"Good news messengers get to go first."

Emma giggled and walked in, dropping down into a couch. "You're a really good guy underneath all that gangster bravado..."

Reese sat in front of her on the opposite couch, leaning forward with his arms on his thighs and scowled at her. "Did you want your pictures going viral?"

Emma gasped a little startled breath. "Easy, I won't tell anyone."

"Best you don't..." Reese laughed and leaned back into the seat. "So, spill."

"Well, she's not sick with covid for one..."

Reese frowned. That wasn't good news, that meant she had been hurt by Antonio enough that she had to stay home and heal. His jaw ticked as he settled his intense gaze on Emma.

"And we've worked out a way for her to leave her house without being detected by her cameras..."

Reese sat forward again feeling an elation bubbling up inside him. "And?"

"And, it seems she is really wanting to rebel all of a sudden, so I'm going to need you to organize a party for Saturday."

"This Saturday?" That wasn't much notice.

"I'm sure you can do it...she is adamant she wants to sneak out and have some fun all of a sudden, almost like something has happened to change her perspective...best not to wait and pounce on it before she changes her mind and gets timid again."

Reese stood up and walked to the window. He had to laugh, Antonio thought hurting Quinn was going to break her and make her more subservient, but she was rebelling instead, fighting back against his harsh control...and he would be right here to capitalize on it.

He turned back to find Emma smiling at him expectantly.

"Good work...now tell me how exactly."

"It's her cameras...they aren't on the second floor or down the side of the house that is really close to the neighbors...if she sneaks out her bedroom window, crawls across to the neighbors fence line she can get down over their side of the fence using a ladder and she's free..."

Reese rubbed his jaw with a smirk. "You don't say..."

"Just to be sure, I'm going to get a girl to sneak in and stay the night at hers, get up in the dark around midnight and get a glass of water, that should set the alerts off for whoever is tracking it that there was movement, they'll see her there and going back to bed and Quinn will even have evidence she was in all night. The model of her cameras means they are black and white so hair color is meaningless. In the morning the girl will get up and go for a run, meet up with Quinn and Quinn can return home."

Reese's eyes narrowed. "You're actually quite sneaky?"

"Nah, I can't take the credit...it's my brother, he was the Houdini of sneaking out of our house and has taken hacking to an art form."

Reese chuckled. "Well, good for him...if this works I'll buy him a car."

"And delete those pics?" Emma added with a frown.

Reese beamed a very sexy smile at her. "Of course."

He pulled his phone out of his pocket and messaged his group chat.

R - **Party this Saturday at Mac's house**

Mac replied back almost immediately.

M - WTH?

R - **Do it, I have a special guest coming**

M - Okay, boss...spread the word guys

Reese stood up and opened the door for Emma to leave. She pouted as she stood up.

"You're kicking me out?"

Reese smirked. "You want to join my family? Initiation is tough..."

Emma baulked, knowing what he meant. "Ah...no thanks." She stepped out into the hall. "Let me know the details...and I'll get Quinn organized."

Reese frowned and leaned out the door slightly. "Did she say anything about me or Cory?"

"Just that she was avoiding you both...and that her brother found out about you so she felt it better to just stop whatever was going on with you...sorry."

Reese scowled darkly, stood up and closed the door. Emma huffed at it and walked off.

Reese sucked his teeth, raking a hand through his hair as he grabbed his vape and opened the window...this party was make or break for Quinn's feelings regarding him...he couldn't fuck this up.

25
Party time!

Emma had a wide smile of satisfaction on her face as she walked into the party with her arms wrapped around one of Quinn's pulling her inside.

"Come on...don't be shy, this will be fun!"

She searched the room but didn't see Reese anywhere as she dragged Quinn through to the kitchen. "Come on, let's get a drink."

"I don't want alcohol...not yet." Quinn huffed and finally managed to pull her arm from Emma. God, she was strong for someone so skinny. Emma pouted but smiled when Quinn continued to follow her on her own, looking around herself with an awed expression.

In the kitchen was a small crowd around a keg, having their cups filled by one guy managing the filling.

"Hey girls!" He called out causing everyone to turn and look at them. "Party is this way!"

The guys all grinned at seeing the two girls were cute and clearly freshmen. Emma laughed and went over, taking a cup offered by one guy and letting it be filled with frothy beer, beaming in self-confidence.

Quinn hung back, her hands in the front pocket of her hoodie and chewed her bottom lip.

"Are you not partaking?" The guy asked.

"Nah, she's shy...maybe later." Emma answered for her. "We're going out back." She flicked her head to Quinn to follow and Quinn gave a small nervous smile at the guy and followed feeling all the eyes on her.

"Make sure to come back and see me..." The guy called out.

"Fuck man, don't come on to that one, she's Curry and Rice's..." Another guy hissed under his breath.

"What? That's her? Damn...why do they always get the hot ones?"

Quinn frowned at hearing that but decided to ignore it, if it meant other guys left her alone to enjoy herself unfettered then that was good, she only had to avoid Cory and Reese.

As she walked outside she saw Emma walk over to a group of people standing in the dark and tap the shoulder of one.

As he turned his golden stare seemed to glow as his face hit the lights from the house. Quinn met Reese's gaze and felt the heat as he gave her a little smirk.

"Hey, you made it."

'Fuck he's hot!' Quinn couldn't help but admit to herself. 'No! I am not here to fraternize with a Mobster!'

"Hey, Quinn! Over here!" Another voice called out earning her attention and she looked over to see Cory with the football team grouped around a large grill. He waved out enthusiastically with his gorgeous smile turned on full.

'Why are they both so different but both so damn attractive?' Quinn chewed her lip, not sure what to do.

She looked from Cory to Reese several times then turned on her heels and went back inside, retreating. She was going to have to get a drink to deal with those two judging from the dark frowns that had slowly clouded over both their faces at each other when she didn't react to either of them.

"Argh..." She grumbled as she walked into the hall. "What is up with those two? Freaking hell, that was too intense..."

"You don't know?" A voice said beside her, making her jump.

"Know what?" She scowled at the guy leaning on the wall right behind her. He hadn't been there before so must have followed her.

"Their competition...to fuck you." He smirked, his dark eyes watching her face.

"Excuse me?" Quinn felt the bottom of her stomach fall out and her heart thumped painfully.

"They are competing against each other to see which one can get you in bed first, the loser has to pay up...it's a lot of money on the line apparently."

"Are you fucking kidding me?" Quinn looked at the guy horrified.

"Why? Not interested?" He laughed.

"No!" Quinn hissed through gritted teeth.

"They're the two best looking guys on campus...you can take your pick of them, its just a side bet...since they both really want you."

"The main words in that are 'on campus' who do they think they are!" She turned and stalked off leaving Cole looking at her back and laughing.

He felt an arm snake over his shoulder and hook his neck. He turned his head and tensed up to see Reese's deadly gaze right in front of him.

"What was that cozy little conversation?"

"She was asking what your and Curry's deal is with those intense glares you were both giving her out there."

"And? What did you tell her?"

"That you're competing...she's got a right to know what you jerks are doing."

Reese clucked his tongue. "So what did she say?"

"She said she's not interested in either of you."

"What exactly did she say?" Reese growled in Cole's ear, tightening his arm around his neck.

"She said she wasn't interested and when I said that you are the best looking guys on campus she said the main words in that was 'on campus' and she walked off."

Reese let Cole go and rubbed his neck, confused. "What the hell does that mean?"

"I don't know, maybe it means she dates hot older guys?"

"Fuck..." Reese growled, storming off down the hall.

No, it meant something far more dangerous...was she planning to leave college to try and run?

That would be suicide.

Quinn went back to the kitchen and found it empty, the keg had been moved outside. She grabbed a plastic cup and a bottle of white wine, filling the cup half way then topped it with some gin she found on the counter top. She found some raspberry soda in the fridge to fill the cup up then walked through to the lounge taking a couple of big gulps of the concoction trying to numb her brain from the turmoil it was now in.

How dare those bastards bet money on sleeping with her! Is that what this whole month had really been about? She felt duped, she had begun to like them only to find out everything about them was a lie. She was right to decide to block Reese and she would do the same with Cory as soon as she got home and had her phone. She had left it at home knowing it was tracked.

"Quinn!"

She turned and saw Reese coming through the door behind her like he was purposely looking for her. She grimaced and let out a suffering breath.

"Hey? What's the sigh for?" Reese asked a little annoyed. "And why have you blocked me? What did that prick do to you?"

"Nothing..." Quinn growled, looking away and sipped her drink trying to pretend he wasn't there, she wasn't going to start shit here. She saw Cory over Reese's shoulder and rolled her eyes. "You guys need to seriously stop following me!"

She turned and walked away as Reese frowned and looked back to see Cory grin at him. "What the fuck!?" He mouthed to him for being seen and followed Quinn to the next room. He was getting seriously pissed off with the amount of people here and the fact that she now knew about their competition...on top of the fact she knew what he was it was obvious she had decided he was too much trouble to be around, he needed some serious damage control.

He froze when he saw her talking to a group of guys like she knew them. Cory came up to his shoulder and made a weird sound in his throat of disapproval.

"What the hell is going on there?" Cory muttered.

Quinn had decided to teach Curry and Rice a lesson, she was going to show them she wasn't here for anything to do with them, she was here to have fun, fuck them!

Quinn approached a group of guys from her law classes, she was at least familiar with one and had often shared a 'hello, how are you' in class.

He was fairly cute looking and she remembered his name was Troy Buchanan. "Hey there..." She said shyly.

He almost died of shock but recovered quickly as his mates all went quiet and grinned, shuffling round so she could join them and stand next to Troy.

"Hey...what are you drinking?" He asked as he eyed her red colored drink.

"It's a special mix." Quinn said back with a smile, fully aware that Reese and Cory had entered the room and were watching her.

"Special, huh? Can I taste it?" He thought to try and get a sneaky secondary kiss off the cup.

She gave him a strange look and smirked. "You want to taste my drink?"

"Yeah, come on..." He held his hand out for the cup.

"Okay..." She took a big swig of her drink, grabbed him strongly round the neck and planted her lips over his. She stared into his eyes as his were wide with surprise, then he opened his mouth as his arms came around her. She opened her mouth and they kissed as the drink swirled around their mouths. He finally swallowed it and pulled away with a shocked look.

She wiped the dribble from the corner of her mouth. "Hope it was worth it?" She murmured, turned and walked off, heading up the stairs to the second floor.

"What the fuck?" Troy glanced at his friends as he wiped his mouth. "Worth it? What the hell does that mean?"

"Go find out, man...don't let her do that and leave. She's heading for the bedrooms, she wants it!"

His mates pushed him forward encouraging him with suggestive comments.

"Right." He prepped himself and walked off to look for her.

He only got a few paces up the stairs when he was dragged back down by a strong hand on his shoulder, making him stumble back.

"Sit this one out, fucker." Reese growled at him as he let go of his shoulder and walked passed. Cory hot on his heels glared at him too, giving him a shove against the wall.

"Stay in your lane!" Cory warned him with a snarl as he passed.

"What the hell?" Troy watched them completely perplexed and intimidated.

As Reese reached the landing he saw Quinn standing in front of an open doorway looking back. She didn't look surprised to see him followed by Cory instead of Troy, in fact she scowled at him, stuck her tongue out at them both and walked into the room.

"Cheeky little bitch!" Reese hissed.

Cory chuckled. "I think this is it, bro."

When they entered the room Quinn was standing there with her arms folded waiting for them and she did not look happy.

"What do you think you're doing following me, stalkers?"

"You tell us, after that little performance?" Reese accused as Cory closed the door.

Quinn lashed out a hand, gesturing wildly. "I knew you would come in here, I knew you would be the ones to follow!"

"So basically you're telling us you set us up like this to teach us a lesson, make us jealous?" Cory asked as Reese just stared intently at her.

"No. To let you both know that I know everything about your little competition, so you can both just leave me alone and go to hell!"

"You came to the party to see which one of us you like, didn't you?" Reese grumbled.

"So who spilled?" Cory asked, confirming what Cole had told her.

"I actually came because Emma persuaded me to sneak out and come have some fun for once in my life, while I could."

"Sneak out?" Cory scoffed. "You sound like a preppy high schooler, you live alone don't you? Who the hell are you sneaking out from?"

Reese's mouth tightened. "Antonio has security cameras everywhere at her house and tracks her movements. He's that obsessed with his little sister..." He sneered, his top lip lifting on one side.

Quinn gave him a lethal look, daring him to say anything more. "Shut up! You know nothing. Are you just trying to get with me because you're a mobster, using me to get information or something?"

Reese bared his teeth. "Don't be ridiculous, Quinn."

Cory frowned. "I can back him up on that, this has nothing to do with any of that gangster bullshit."

"Then what is it?" Quinn retorted. "Just a game to you guys, do you do this every year, pick a freshman and see who she chooses?"

They saw the tears forming in her eyes as she accused them. Cory sighed and rubbed his neck. "Fuck...no, of course we don't."

"Oh, so it's just me...lucky me!" Quinn spat.

"You already knew we were competing for you, and you didn't have a problem with it...you were enjoying the attention, what does it matter now if money was involved?" Reese's low tone was intimidating and Quinn swallowed hard, stepping back slightly.

"It's humiliating! I thought you genuinely liked me, then I find out you're a gangster and that you're betting on me! How the fuck should I feel?"

Cory hissed, it did sound really bad. "It's not like that...honest."

Reese sucked his teeth, hearing Cory's remorse. "Okay, we apologize for the bet, it still doesn't change anything..."

Quinn chewed her lip realizing her mistake in trying to teach these two egotistical assholes a lesson. "It changes a lot for me!"

She went to step around them and leave but Reese grabbed her around the upper arm and yanked her roughly back to stand in front of them again.

"You don't get to leave so easily, Quinn...you put your lips on another guy's mouth. Was that for our benefit too? Did you really want to provoke us to action?" His voice was menacing and low and Quinn frowned.

Looking at the two of them with concern now as they blocked her escape. “Yeah, okay...that was going too far...” She folded her arms defensively. “But I’m really pissed!”

“Too far?” Cory asked, stumped by her action. “Damn right it was too far.”

Reese chuckled darkly. “Well, I guess we get to both kiss you now too, even the playing field.”

Cory gave him a strange look then looked back at Quinn with a sultry smirk. “Sounds fair...I’m game, gives you a real chance to pick one of us.”

Quinn’s stomach tied in knots, were they not listening to her? “You can’t be serious?”

“I’m pretty much always serious...” Reese said with a cocky tilt to his head, his eyes intensely watching her.

“Yeah, he is...” Cory grinned. “So, who’s going first?” He looked at her for the answer.

“No one!” Quinn scoffed, backing up.

“We can stand in this room all night then, good chance to ask you some pertinent questions.” Reese said, licking his lips.

Quinn’s eyes narrowed on him. “Like what?”

“Your true relationship with your brother...” Reese stated. He knew she probably didn’t want to talk about that stuff in front of Cory since she had no idea how much he already knew.

Cory’s little frown looked to Quinn like he looked confused and she thought maybe he didn’t know what Reese knew so he had effectively backed her into a corner.

“Fine...” She huffed, dropping her arms in resignation. She looked at Cory who at that point in time looked like the safer option. “Come here then...let’s get this over with so I can leave.”

Cory blinked at the sudden change in her decision. “What?”

“Kiss me.”

“Wow, avoidance.” Reese chuckled, wiping a thumb over his bottom lip and smirking on one side of his mouth like he just won big.

“So, we’re doing this?” Cory asked, looking at Reese.

Reese held his hand out towards Quinn who was standing like a deer in headlights. "She clearly gave her consent for you to go first."

Reese folded his arms and leaned back on one leg. His expression was intense, heated and yet amused as he watched Quinn's nervousness.

"Fuck, okay..." Cory looked at Quinn and gave her a roguish grin. He stepped up and ran a hand up her cheek and around her ear as her large eyes locked onto his face. Her heart thumping out of her chest.

This was really happening!?

He leaned in and she instinctively grabbed out at his chest, grabbing handfuls of his shirt as his lips pressed to hers.

She thought that would be it and actually felt a little pang of disappointment.

Cory's other hand came to the other side of her head as he inched his body closer planting his feet, tilting his head as he licked his tongue over her lips for entry, digging it between them to her teeth. She opened her mouth and his tongue rolled around hers languidly as they both enjoyed each other. Quinn forgot all about being pissed off.

He groaned into her mouth as he pushed, backing her up while he kissed her slowly and seductively. A moan escaped her as she clung to him, he was a good kisser.

Her legs hit the bed and she pushed against him hard to stop, startled. He grinned as he lifted his head away slightly turned onto another angle and covered her mouth with his again. His arm circling her waist pulling her hard against him. She felt his erection quite clearly against her lower stomach as he leaned his weight forward to try and tip her over onto the bed behind her.

She started struggling against him and whimpered until he finally pulled back and broke off the kiss, letting her go with a bitter breath.

She gasped in a breath, her hand going to cover her mouth as her eyes blazed and she moved quickly away from the bed.

"What were you trying to do?" She breathed out scared, glancing at the bed behind her.

"Sorry, got carried away...you're fucking delicious and were responding so well..." Cory commented with a smug smirk and he ran a hand through his blond locks.

Reese lurched forward, grabbed Quinn by the arm and spun her around, turning her and throwing her up against the back of the door. He grabbed her by the hand, pinning it to the door as he stepped right into her body. One leg pushed between her thighs as his other hand fisted her hair at the back of her head and he pulled down on it.

Quinn gasped in shock at the fast movements. Dangerous, trained...like Antonio, but quicker.

She found herself suddenly engulfed by Reese's hot mouth, his tongue lashing into hers with full control taking everything and leaving her breathless as her eyes fluttered closed and her muscle memory made her relax in submission.

Her free hand gripped his shoulder as he pressed his body against hers. He felt her surrender to him, melt into him and start to kiss him back. He dropped his hands to her ass and lifted her up, sliding her up the door. Her legs went straight around his waist and her arms came around his neck as he pressed himself into her soft hot body, his thigh sliding in under her, his forearms lifting to the door either side of her head.

She moaned against him and he lifted his face from hers looking at her dazed expression as she blinked back to reality realizing this wasn't Antonio. "That was a really nice reaction, babe."

He smirked at her as Cory groaned behind them. "Ah, fucking hell, Reese..."

Quinn felt shame slam into her and struggled. "Put me down, fuck! Let me go!"

Reese dropped her, stepping back. "Easy babe, relax...we're all adults here."

"No! I can't do this with you...either of you." She glared at them for taking advantage of her. "You're both assholes!"

She spun around and opened the door behind her and took off down the hall. "Stop this stupid game!" Her voice came back angry and full of self-shame and regret.

Reese raked a hand through his hair with a deep breath and looked back at Cory. "Seems this remains unresolved." He said with not a hint of remorse.

"She kisses nice..." Cory sighed as he dropped down to sit on the bed.

"She's sublime..." Reese muttered.

Cory looked at him darkly. "She obviously likes you more..."

"Nah, not sure about that, I think it was all the approach I took." Reese's eyes looked dark as he muttered in thought. She had lost herself for a moment and that raised very dark questions for him.

"Approach? You really think she likes that rough stuff?"

Reese glanced back at Cory and gave him a cheeky look, sticking his tongue out between his teeth. "Only one way to find out..."

"You don't think maybe we should back off, we do look like assholes right now."

"You can...I have something to prove."

"What's going on Reese? I feel like there's something else going on here with you?"

Reese looked at him darkly and sucked his teeth for a moment. "When I have the info I'll let you know...I told you." He growled annoyed before leaving.

Cory huffed a heavy sigh and collapsed back on the bed looking at the ceiling. Damn this girl, he wished he could let his attraction for her go but now he had kissed her and she had beautifully kissed him back before freaking out at him trying to get her to drop to the bed, he couldn't just give her up to Reese or leave her with Antonio.

But man, the way she had reacted to Reese pinning her to the door like that! It was so hot to watch them both.

He chuckled as he sat up. Damn if those two didn't get his blood boiling.

26
Truce

Reese came down the stairs to search for Quinn and saw her talking to another girl, she looked distressed and that annoyed him.

He clucked his tongue and advanced on her location. The other girl was facing him and saw his approach, her eyes going wide and she touched Quinn's arm.

Was Quinn talking nonsense about him?

Quinn turned to see him then fled passed the girl and out the front door. Reese cursed under his breath and ran after her. He wouldn't let panic take her over.

When he got outside he saw her rushing down the driveway. "Quinn! Stop, where are you going?"

She stopped and turned to face him as he approached her. "You can't just run off down the street!" He paused to see her distraught expression, something on her cheek glistened in the light from the house.

"Wait...are you crying?" Fuck, he suddenly felt bad.

He reached out a hand and she tried to turn her face away. "Don't..." She croaked.

"Quinn!" He snapped and she stilled, her large eyes looking up at him with apprehension. He gently held the side of her face while his thumb wiped the tears away. "Don't cry, babe...I didn't mean to scare you...I'm sorry...Cory's sorry, okay? We'll back off." He had no intention of doing that but it was what she needed to hear.

She blinked and looked at the ground as she stepped back from him. "Thanks, I would appreciate that..."

"Why are you so scared?" Reese asked softly, his golden hazel gaze burning into her with an intense heat.

She looked up and quickly looked away from that gaze. "It's not you...it's my life. You don't understand..."

"I want to, please Quinn...if you are in trouble maybe I can help? I'm well connected..."

"You can't help, just let me go home." She turned away and walked to the end of the drive where she stood with nowhere to go. She awkwardly looked back and saw he was still standing there. He was leaning back on one leg, his hands in his jacket pockets as he silently watched her.

He smirked as she turned and glanced back at him. "You don't have your car here and your ride is still inside."

"Yeah, thanks for that..." Quinn folded her arms looking pissy.

"You've basically just got here...come back inside I promise both me and Curry will leave you alone...I want you to enjoy yourself."

"That's what I wanted too, but you guys..."

"Sorry...the competition was a dick move...the kissing..." His mouth twisted in a coy way as his eyes glittered. "I'm not going to apologize for that considering how you kissed me back."

Quinn glared at him and he laughed. "Alright, alright...I'm sorry. You kissed another guy what was I supposed to do...I got jealous and I'm a straight shooter...don't provoke me."

Quinn scowled. "I didn't really kiss him, I transferred my drink..."

"Seriously? You knew exactly what you were doing because we were watching you." Reese interrupted her excuse.

She pouted and rolled her eyes. "Yeah, okay...we've all done stupid shit tonight." She looked away and shuffled her feet.

"Truce then?" Reese asked with a sexy little grin.

Quinn gave him a small shy smile. "Fine, but let me just have some fun with the girls, okay?"

"Sure thing, but answer a question first."

Quinn sighed and looked at the sky. "Do you ever quit bartering?"

He chuckled and shook his head. "Do you actually like me, knowing who I am?"

She looked taken aback by the question and chewed her lip wondering if she should just answer with a firm no, problem was it wasn't the truth.

"I honestly don't know right now...I hoped to get the chance to have a good night and chat and find out about both of you a little."

"Told you." Reese smirked in triumph.

"Yeah, yeah...but you both ruined that!"

Reese sighed and raked a hand through his hair. "Okay...come on, I'll walk you back inside, then I'll go find Curry and tell him about our truce." He paused, his eyes darkening into a glower as he grimaced. "How are you going to deal with that dick, the guy you kissed? Do you want me to speak to him?"

"And say what?"

"I'll tell him you were wasted and trying to make me jealous." He grinned showing his teeth. She noticed the four front teeth on the top were slightly flat, angling back ever so slightly that made his canines look long and pronounced. Sexy teeth too, damn if this guy wasn't a near ten.

"No thanks, I can handle it, it was my mistake, if he comes back at me over it just stay away."

"Well, if you need my help...with anything, Quinn...I'm here, remember that always."

She gave him a weird look. "Why? Why are you saying that?"

He shrugged. "I don't know...I just think you need to hear it and know you have options." He smiled covertly and turned back to the house with a little flap of his jacket for his hand in his pocket, pointing. "Come on..."

Quinn walked up to him and they walked side by side back up the driveway. Quinn was quiet, her eyes to the ground as Reese watched her from the side. She really was attractive, beyond hot or sexy or the usual things he went for...she was sassy yet demure, pretty cute and articulate and what those amazing green eyes did to him when she looked up at him so pitifully.

He wanted to hurt anyone who would hurt her and that included enemy number one, Antonio Ferrante.

"You know how intriguing I find you, Quinn? I don't just find you sexy and attractive...at first maybe, but you know what?"

She looked over at him, a curious glint in her eye that made him actually feel a little thump in his chest. He stopped at the bottom of the steps and she stopped with him. He kept his hands in his pockets and locked eyes with her.

"I have this overwhelming sense that there is something amazingly special about you and I can't look away."

Quinn's heart pounded as she gaped at him in wonder. She had not expected something so genuine and sweet to come out of this guy's mouth. He saw her eyes widen and a small appreciative smile come over her face but it clouded with doubt. "I'm not sure..." She paused and looked away before looking back with a smile back on her face. "Thank you." She said simply.

"No problem." He chuckled a sexy little snort.

"I get the feeling you are very misunderstood." She said causing him to startle then chuckle to himself again.

"I hope you decide to bother to find out, babe."

She looked back at him, her eyes shining with a happy light. "Yeah, I just might." She stepped away and up the steps, going inside.

Reese let out a long breath and raked a hand through his hair before looking away with a small amused chuckle. "Well damn..." That came back around nicely.

"That was sweet, you're almost blushing." Cory's voice came out of the darkness to the side of the house.

Reese looked over with a frown hearing the facetious tone. "I convinced her to stay, don't be a dick."

"Yeah, I saw...nice work."

"I told her we would both back off."

"Did you..." Cory huffed. "Well, that seemed to work for you." His mouth twisted, annoyed.

Reese shrugged and smirked. "What can I say? She likes me."

Cory sucked his teeth, annoyed Reese was scoring all the points and turned away to leave back around the side of the house.

"Hey!" Reese called him and he turned back.

"What?"

"Back off doesn't mean leave alone...we just need to play it cool for now while we sort things out."

"We?" Cory huffed again.

"She admitted she came here to get to know more about *us*. I don't want you to give up just yet."

"Fuck you...what are you really getting out of all this?" Cory grumbled.

Reese just continued to smirk and winked at him. "Get me a drink, twinky boy."

"Shut the fuck up!" Cory turned away while flipping the bird but Reese caught up and hooked an arm around Cory's neck, bringing his mouth close to Cory's ear.

"Come on, babe...I'm sure we can entertain each other if Quinn's not interested." He blew in Cory's ear.

Cory struggled out of his grip and shoved him off. "You reckon, asshole!?"

He walked around the back and up to a cooler full of beer cans, grabbed two out and turned back. He threw one straight at Reese's head as he rounded the corner.

Reese caught it and laughed. "Thanks, Curry babe, I can always count on you."

"Hmm." Cory snorted as he cracked open his beer, looking away with a little smirk.

27

Hot for tatts and tight shirts

After a few beers Reese and Cory were laughing and joking around play fighting in the back yard with the rest of the guys, Reese's gang versus the football team, as several girls were watching and giggling.

Quinn, Emma and Tania came out of the house fanning themselves to cool off from dancing and saw the crowd.

Reese was standing on the opposite side with his mates Jacob and Mac, he had no shirt on, his jeans sitting low on his hips showing his amazing flat abdominal muscles and a well-defined v-line with a little happy trail of dark hair going from below his belly button and disappearing into his pants. He had tattoos on his shoulders coming down his biceps which just added to the dangerous sexy vibe. He was leaning back against a BBQ table and inhaled a drag from his vape sending a great cloud of smoke up into the air. He looked up through his dark bangs as the smoke cleared to see Quinn staring at him.

He gave her a sexy smirk, running his tongue along his teeth.

"Oh, God..." Quinn muttered, looking away from his gaze. He was so damn sexy and dripped such natural sexual charisma and that confident sigma aura, he was hard to look away from, but that cocky grin with the tongue...she felt her core flip and a heat pool deep in her pussy. But as he turned around with his back to her she almost fainted to see the large back tattoo of a huge tiger stalking through bamboo staring at her.

Her gaze dropped to where everyone was looking, tucking some hair nervously behind her ear...maybe it was the alcohol...calm down.

Cory was in a grappling match with one of the wrestling team and was winning. He had the guy pinned on the ground underneath him in a full mount as the guy bucked under him trying to get him off. Cory was laughing and rolling with the guy's attempts but that meant Cory's hips were gyrating like a cowboy on a rodeo bull.

If Reese was a Sigma, alone and confidently dangerous then Cory was an Alpha, natural leader, strong and popular.

"Shit..." Quinn breathed out, feeling hot and bothered. Caught between these two was going to be the death of her. Not to mention being caught between wanting these guys and Antonio Ferrante!

Cory was only wearing a tight white compression shirt that showed every muscle nearly as clearly as Reese being shirtless. He was bulkier with power muscle compared to Reese's lean fighter's type build, but was still more than a feast for the eyes.

She felt her neck and ears getting hot and looked away.

"Fuck, it's getting hotter out here than inside." Tania commented. "We were in the wrong party..."

Quinn had to agree, this was definitely the place to be to watch some amazing sights, no wonder all the girls out here were giggling and gushing.

"I think I need another drink..." Quinn gasped with a dry mouth.

"Over there." Emma pointed to a large cooler packed with ice with a knowing grin. "Just grab one."

Quinn made her way over and grabbed a can, thankfully it was nice and cold and she sipped it gratefully.

"Hey."

She turned to see Cory had finished his fight and was grabbing a beer.

"Oh, hey." She said a little wary.

"Don't worry, Reese and I had a chat."

"Okay..." She sipped her beer and looked away back to the circle of people as two other guys started sparring.

Cory stepped up beside her and cracked his beer open taking a long draft before letting out a loud belch. Quinn gave him a disgusted side-eye. He looked at her and laughed.

"What? Better out than in."

"I guess..." She said non-committed.

"You like watching fights?" He asked.

"Not really..." She answered, looking up at him properly. "I don't really like violence."

"Says a Ferrante." Cory chuckled.

Quinn's frown gave him pause. "I'm not a Ferrante, who told you that, Reese?"

"He mentioned your brother is Antonio Ferrante."

Quinn clucked her tongue annoyed. "We are not related, he's my step-brother if anything."

"Okay..." Cory lifted a hand in surrender. "Sorry..."

She looked away but made no move to walk away so Cory stayed beside her. "You know...Reese has a fight coming up."

Quinn raised an eyebrow and her gaze drifted back across the yard to where he still was. He was talking to one of his mates and she admired his chiseled side profile...all the way down... "Oh, is he next?"

"Not here...a proper fight. In a ring."

Quinn's head snapped around to Cory with surprise.

"What? You didn't know? He's a cage fighter..."

"What the hell?" Quinn felt a little light-headed. She knew by looking at him he was dangerous and obviously trained to handle himself but didn't know he did it professionally.

"Yeah, it's a thing his father has a hand in..."

"His father?" The Mob boss? So was it illegal fighting?

Cory gave her a strange look. "You really need to find out more about us."

"Okay...what about you then? Do you compete in those fights too?"

"Hell no, I can't risk messing up my cute face, Reese is ugly so it doesn't matter about his." He grinned, showing perfect teeth and Quinn couldn't help but laugh.

"So tell me something about yourself, not Reese."

"You really want to know? I figured you would want to know more about our college Prince."

Quinn frowned and gave Cory a serious little pout of discontent. "Not from you, tell me about you. I know you play football but want to be a lawyer?"

"Ha!" Cory snorted. "My parents want me to be a prosecutor...to become a judge."

"A judge! Wow, what do your parents do?"

Cory gave her a strange look. "You don't know?"

"No?"

"I'm surprised no one has told you." He looked away and lifted his beer to his mouth taking a few gulps before lowering it and wiping his mouth. "My step-mother is a prosecutor, my father is Police Commissioner for New York."

"Whoa! I did not see that coming!" She stared at him stunned. How on earth were him and Reese friends? "Is that why you said you were supposed to be at the Charity fundraiser last week?"

Cory gave a surly huff. "Hmm...but I had a game Friday..."

She saw his father, she actually saw his father and didn't even know. "Well, I would much rather spend time talking to you here than at some stuffy charity fundraiser..."

Cory chuckled. "Is that because you wouldn't have been able to talk?" His eyes sparkled with a darkness all of a sudden.

She scowled at him. "Reese told you everything, huh?"

"He told me he had a gun shoved in his face."

"What?" Quinn gaped, mortified and covered her mouth.

"Oh, you didn't know?" Cory's expression was dark and pissed off.

"No! Matteo must have done it after I left...oh god! I need to apologize to Reese."

"Apologize to me for what?" Reese's smooth baritone voice came from behind her and she whipped around, clutching at him but then realizing he was still shirtless as her hands slid over his smooth skin. She jerked her hands back as he smirked at her, one eyebrow rising in amusement.

"Easy tiger..." He chuckled, licking over his teeth.

"Stop! Did Matteo really raise a gun at you?" She asked in a shouted whisper.

Reese's gaze slid up to Cory and he clucked his tongue. "Nothing to worry about, princess..."

"What the hell do you mean by that, you do know how dangerous that man is?"

"He wasn't going to harm me...it would have started a war he can't start, I'm above his pay grade." Reese huffed confidently.

Quinn stared at him. "You remind me of 'him' sometimes, you're frightening." She walked off and joined her friends.

"That went well..." Reese commented dryly.

"Can't help but feel like we're back to square one though..."

"Nah, she interacts nicely. She'll be fine."

"So our competition is a bust, what happens now?"

Reese sucked his teeth. "She likes me, she likes you...I like her, you like her...I like you...you absolutely love me..."

"Fuck up...what's your point muttering all that gibberish...you want a threesome?"

Reese's eyes sparkled in the light and he smirked, winked and walked off. "Watch this space, Curry."

28
A mobster's daughter

Monday morning started for Quinn with a joyful step in her stride, Emma's plan to sneak out had worked a treat, and the girl that was paid a hundred dollars to stay in her house for the night was more than happy to do it again anytime.

Quinn just hoped Antonio going to Boston became a regular thing, or at least him traveling away anywhere for the weekend.

She had, had a ball and now her and Emma and Tania were fast friends. It was exactly what she knew she needed to do to secure those social friendships. Why couldn't Antonio see that? Or was his plan to isolate her from anyone, not just men...although he had mentioned it was okay for her to have girls over to study...

She wondered as she walked if she wanted to spend time studying with a sleep over whether Antonio would allow her to stay home for a weekend instead of going to his? Now that had potential...

She reached her locker and as she opened it she gasped as a pair of hands slid around her waist, crossed over her stomach and pulled her into a hard muscular chest.

"Hey..." The husky voice of Cory sounded in her ear as he nuzzled into her neck. She inclined her head away, pushing at his arms and scrunching her eyes closed.

"What do you think you're doing?" She hissed at him.

"Saying hi to my favorite girl..." He let her go with a chuckle and as she turned around to face him he swept his hair back from his eyes and gave her a cheeky grin. "You have a problem with that?"

She glared up and down the halls. "Yes, actually I do!"

His blue eyes shone with amusement. "Oh, well...that's too bad."

She folded her arms and turned that glare on him. He appraised her mood and could plainly see she wasn't really serious. "Does that mean you'll do it again?"

He grinned wider. "Yeah, that's exactly what it means...you're smart."

"And you're a smart ass! Can you not do that sort of thing please?"

"Why?" He frowned and actually looked confused.

A leather clad arm hooked around his neck and yanked him sideways. Quinn looked up to see Reese's golden gaze glowering at her. "Because we're supposed to be behaving..." He growled into Cory's face.

Cory struggled out of his grip and shoved him off. The Footballers seeing the action immediately came over to back Cory up as Tank and Jacob stood behind Reese chuckling like mad men.

Quinn felt like trying to crawl into her open locker as people started to take their phones out.

"Fuck off, man...are you actually constantly stalking her or what?" Cory hissed. "I can't catch a break with you."

"Why do you want to catch a break?" Reese inquired with a smirk. "I'm telling you to back off like a good boy and do as you're told."

Cory's fists clenched and his mates started egging him on. Reese's eyebrow rose in challenge as he licked across his teeth.

Quinn grabbed her bag and slammed her locker shut gaining everyone's attention. She turned, looking at the two gorgeous men about to throw down with a judgmental look. "Grow up." She said simply and shoved her way through the crowd and walked off.

Reese laughed, raking a hand through his hair. "Well we've both been told. Listen to the girl, Curry." He turned his back on Cory and sauntered off. Tank and Jacob stood in front of Cory for a few more moments then laughed and walked off.

Cory huffed, relaxing his fists and rolled his eyes. "Fuck you." He muttered and turned towards his footballer mates and smirked at them. "Looks like he's whipped for a girl."

They all laughed and wandered off down the halls.

Reese's jaw was clenching as he walked out of the building and took his vape out of his pocket, inhaling heavily and blowing out a massive cloud of smoke to calm down. "I knew he wasn't going to listen..."

Tank and Jacob caught up and Reese turned to them. "Keep an eye on Quinn and make sure that fucking retriever doesn't do anything stupid."

"Stupid like what?" Tank inquired with a stern tone.

Reese huffed on his vape again before answering. "We all know Cory can get a little one track minded...he is a fuck boy after all."

Jacob chuckled. "You guys are really going all out over this chick, huh? She's gorgeous and all but is she worth ruining whatever is left of your friendship at this stage? I kinda thought you were hanging on to hopefully keep that bridge open once you guys were set in your careers."

Reese turned a nasty scowl on Jacob. "Is that what you thought?" He spat and walked off.

Jacob gave Tank a surprised look, Tank shrugged in response and went to follow Reese as he looked like he was heading for the carpark.

As he reached Reese he was just getting in his car. "Are you leaving for the day?"

"I'll be back...Liam called, I have to go meet with him."

"Oh, okay..."

Reese saw that Tank was hovering. "What?" He asked with an eye roll.

"You're serious about that girl?"

Reese sighed and rubbed his eyes, pinching the bridge of his nose. "What if I am?"

"To be honest I figured you would be a lot more possessive and actually threaten Curry off, but you almost seem to be encouraging him to keep trying, I don't get it."

"What's there to get?" Reese smirked. "I want two for the price of one."

Reese chuckled at the surprised look on Tank's face, slipped into the driver's seat of his car and drove off.

Tank scratched his jaw. "Well, fuck...I guess that's to be kept to myself." He barked a harsh amused laugh and walked back inside. He knew Reese was bi-sexual, but he didn't think that Cory was.

Reese walked into the dimly lit club and blinked as his eyes adjusted from the glaring sun outside. He glanced at the doorman and bobbed his head in greeting at him.

"Mr O'Shea." The doorman responded like he was expected.

His gaze moved across the room, there were a couple of early patrons as the girl on the pole lazily moved around it with a bored expression on her face. He always wondered why this place was open so early...but was then reminded of the fact that certain people needed an excuse to walk in there, himself included. He walked to a black door with a huge tattooed man standing in front of it wearing a black suit. He inclined his head respectfully and opened the door.

"Mr O'Shea, you're expected, please go through."

"Thanks." Reese said dryly and walked through to a darkened hallway and made his way down to the end, opening the door and walking into a large office where Liam was sitting to the side on a large L-shaped black leather couch with a coffee cup to his lips. He placed it down as Reese entered and smiled up at him.

"Reese, take a seat...thanks for meeting me here, I thought it was better than at work since you don't want your father finding out about any of this, right?"

"Right, appreciate it..." Reese sat down on the other side of the couch. "So you've got something for me in regards to that research I asked about?"

"Yes and no...regardless I think you have a huge problem, man." Liam leaned forward and picked up a piece of paper sitting in an open folder on the coffee table in front of him and tossed it over to Reese.

"This is her birthdate, yeah?"

Reese looked at the page. "Yeah, that's what her friend said it was...November 23rd."

"Born in Boston?"

"Yes..." Reese frowned with annoyance. "Why?"

"Because there's no record of a Quinn Malley being born in Boston, Massachusetts on that date or any date a week either side of it."

Reese's frown deepened as he collapsed back into the couch with a huff, his gaze steady on Liam seeing by his expression that there was more to say yet.

"Only a Guinevere O'Malley..."

"Huh? That's freaking weird..." Reese grumbled.

"What gets weirder is that Guinevere O'Malley is the daughter of Irish Mob Boss, Patrick O'Malley leader of the Boston syndicate until his untimely death at the hands of his sergeant at arms as a requisite to peace treaty for trying to incite a mob war with the Italian mafia at the time because...get this...his wife was having an affair and trying to get a divorce...with none other than..." Liam looked at Reese expectantly to see if he had figured it out.

Reese sucked his teeth irritably. "Augusto Ferrante." He finished the sentence with a low vile tone.

"Got it in one." Liam smirked.

"Holy fucking Christ!" Reese spat, raking his hands into his hair and holding his head back as he stared at the ceiling.

"I got in touch with a contact over in Boston when I saw who the girl's father was, I recognized the name...my contact knows something extra about this but he didn't want to say anything about it over the phone..."

That was sinister...

Reese dropped his hands with a very penetrating serious look at Liam.

"You know the Boston guys are coming here end of the week, right...my guy wants to catch up on the sly while here, says he'll fill you in on what really went down at the time of Patrick's death."

Reese idly scratched his jaw and looked at his phone. "So your saying hold off on doing anything until I hear what he has to say?"

"Play this really close to your chest, Reese...just until you have the whole picture, you could be stirring up a whole hornet's nest here."

"Yeah..."

Liam looked slightly uncomfortable and Reese's penetrating gaze lifted back to him with an eyebrow raised in question.

"You know your dad is from Boston, yeah?"

"Of course..." Reese rolled his eyes. "Grandad came down from Massachusetts to run Brooklyn after a major gang took out Paulie D back in the fifties."

"Yeah, so it's likely that your dad knows what went on with the O'Malleys and the Ferrantes..."

Reese rubbed his neck as he sighed. "I thought about that...but I came to you instead of him because of that..."

"Yeah, I figured. He will just warn you off."

"Plus, I don't want to rock the boat and start shit if everything about this is above board..."

"Have you just talked to the girl?"

"Can't...she's locked down tighter than a virgin's asshole by Ferrante and I doubt she would be very forthcoming with information anyway...she hasn't been about things up until now."

Liam chuckled.

"Anyway, thanks and set up that meeting. I'll be at the main meeting of course so try and work something to take him and me off the floor at the same time, just for five minutes."

"Got it." Liam paused and gave Reese a strange appreciative smirk. Reese frowned at him slightly concerned. "You're going to do alright, Reese...when you take over."

Reese looked genuinely surprised. "Ah, thanks man. That means a lot coming from you."

"Yeah, your calm and thoughtful about things...take your time, don't rush...all good traits."

Reese cocked his head and grinned. "I'm not going to suck your dick so enough of the praise."

Liam laughed. "Cheeky little shit!"

Reese stood up. "If that's all..."

"Yeah, I'll be in touch..." Liam watched Reese walk out the door. "Go visit your Dad."

Reese rolled his eyes as he walked out of the office. As he walked back down the hall and into the bar a girl rushed up on him, hugging his arm and squealing in delight.

"Reese! It is you..."

"Candice, what's up?" Reese asked of the skinny brunette wearing a leather halter top, black boy leg briefs with garter straps and stocking with four inch heels and not much else.

"I've missed you...how have you been?" She beamed up at him with a slow blink.

"Busy..."

She pouted her bottom lip out. "So you haven't missed me?"

Reese sighed and stopped walking. "What do you want, Candice?"

"Will you visit me again soon?"

Reese clucked his tongue and pulled his arm from Candice's grip. "Not likely, babe, sorry."

"But, I'll be your good girl, you can do more to me..." She seemed suddenly desperate.

Reese saw the owner of Hummingbird come out from the back stage door with the woman that coordinates all the girls' performances. He scowled over at Candice.

"Candice? What are you doing out of the back rooms?"

Reese startled at that. "Wait, you're in the back rooms now?"

Candice looked up at him pitifully. "I have to do extra shifts in there to pay off my debt."

"Your debt? For fuck's sake...for what?"

The club owner wandered over with a sick grin on his face and cupped Candice's bottom giving it a squeeze. "She's developed quite the taste for cocaine, Dom Perignon and partying with a few rich boys on their yacht lately...instead of working, I had to get Simon there to fetch her back."

Reese glanced at the guy that was standing in front of the black door. "What's her debt?"

Candice looked up at him with surprise as the owner lifted his hand to grip into her hair and the back of her head and tossed her to the side making her crash into a table before Simon moved over and hauled her to her feet and through the black door. "It's nothing to do with you, Reese, don't get involved. I know you know the girl from high school but those days are over and her choices are made."

"She can't handle the back rooms...she's too soft." Reese said through gritted teeth.

"I know that, that's why she's there to teach her not to run away again and incur more debt."

Reese stepped up to the fat jerk and got in his face. "The debt?"

"She's in the hole $40,000..."

Reese looked a little shocked. "Forty...?"

"I paid for those tits plus she took the champagne and drugs from here...they probably talked her into it with flowery promises, stupid bitch."

Reese sighed and rubbed his forehead. "I'll give you twenty of it to take her out of the back rooms."

"You're too soft, Reese..."

"I don't agree with that..." Liam said as he came through, his hands in his suit pants pockets. "You know he could kill you with a flick of his wrist and no one is going to lift a finger to him for doing it? Show your boss's son more respect, he's going to be your boss one day, Sonny."

Reese's jaw clenched tight. "I don't need you..."

"Shut it...I'm doing him a favor..." Liam said his gaze burning into Sonny. "I saw your fist clench shut."

Sonny gaped at Reese, glancing down at his hands and Reese chuckled darkly. Everyone knew how lethal Cillian's son was with his fists.

Sonny puffed out a resigned breath. "Fine...I'll remove her from the back rooms..."

Liam flicked his head for Reese to leave.

Reese took the hint and walked out feeling a little irritated by the whole thing, but at least Candice was out of hell. The back rooms were no place for a timid-hearted girl like her, she would be destroyed and probably turn to even heavier drugs to deal with the trauma it all caused for the rest of her short life. He knew she had made her own life decisions leading her to work at Hummingbird, but going into those back rooms where the clients had very niche tastes was never her choice. She liked to dance and strip and feel like she was desired, he got that...and she was popular doing that. She just had to get smarter...

Like a certain other girl he knew...

Ah, Quinn...what the hell was he going to do about this new bit of information? It really did get worse and worse with that girl, but he still felt like there was something worth fighting for.

He got into his car, leaned his head back with his eyes closed and sighed out a long weary breath.

"Fucking hell...who would have guessed my little red haired kitten was actually mob, just like me..."

But it just raised even more questions...mainly, how the fuck was a dead Irish mobster's daughter in the hands of the Italian mafia?

29

Come see Reese fight

Cory was adamant after the party Saturday night that he was going to try and get Quinn to come with him to see Reese fight. He knew it would be in his favor to take her without Reese even knowing, she had said she hated violence...and Cory knew what Reese's matches were like.

Cage fighting was brutal, and being underground fighting the place would be full of gangsters and dangerous vibes that would hopefully scare Quinn off being interested in Reese forever.

It was a nasty trick...

One he really hoped worked.

He wasn't really sure what was going on between the two of them, they seemed to have a connection that he didn't and that pissed him off that he was losing...although the competition was off and he had been warned to back off, all that shit didn't mean jack to him.

He liked Quinn and wanted her.

He found it strange, he had never really had to chase many girls before, as soon as he made it clear he liked them they generally fell to their knees wanting to be with him. Reese was right to call him a fuck boy, he rarely actually dated a girl, just hooked up with them.

But this whole having to chase Quinn down just to spend time with her thing then being told to back off, it made him want her even more.

The whole treat 'em mean, keep 'em keen thing was supposed to work the other way around and it pissed him off that it was working on him.

It was midweek now and as far as he was concerned he had left Quinn alone for long enough. He took his phone out and messaged her.

C - **Hey, I want to ask you something, can we meet up?**

He wondered how long he would have to wait for a response, if it was more than an hour he would message again and then go looking for her.

He was pleasantly surprised when he got her message back after only a few minutes.

Q - ***I guess so, I'm just in study hall with Tania working on our joint assignment***

Okay, this was good...Cory grinned to himself and stood up, leaving his group.

"Hey?" Lucas called out to him.

Cory looked back over his shoulder. "What?"

"Where are you going? We have to head to training shortly...I was going to grab a ride with you?" Cory rolled his eyes, Lucas was such a tight ass on filling his car with gas he hardly ever brought it and always relied on others to chauffeur him around. "Man, stop being such a tight ass and put some gas in your freaking car!"

The other guys snickered and Lucas frowned. "My sister took my car this morning, man..."

"Fuck's sake...alright, meet me at my truck in half an hour."

"Sweet." Lucas grinned as Cory walked off with a huff.

"Hey, he's doing that a lot lately, don't you reckon?" One of the other guys said.

"Doing what?"

"Walking off by himself? You think he's getting sick of footie?"

"Nah, he loves playing...he's off stalking that chick..."

"What?"

"Yeah, I've seen him..." Another laughed. "He's got it really bad for that freshman girl with the long red hair and really nice tits over in the Business Faculty, he keeps drifting over there to find her even when he doesn't have classes there."

Lucas gave the guy a hooded glare. "Yeah, so does Reese so watch your mouth..."

"What? You think he'll get offended for her just because I said she has nice tits?"

"Probably..." Lucas grumbled. "Both of them act really over the top where that girl is concerned..."

Cory stuck his head in to the study hall, a large open room with lots of desks and a huge sign on the door that told people that no noise was permitted inside.

He saw Quinn and waved his hand to try and get her attention. Tania, beside her, looked up and bumped Quinn's shoulder as she smiled at Cory and waved. Cory gave her a huge smile back as Quinn looked up and then stood up, grabbing her phone but leaving her books and walked to the door.

Cory retreated into the hall and waited.

As she came out she gave him a huge smile. "Hey..." She stood there expectantly.

"Hey, want to get coffee or something?"

"Sure, I guess...I'll get one for Tania too..."

They turned and walked down the corridor. Quinn glancing at Cory's side profile several times as they walked. "Is this serious?" She asked a little nervous.

"What? Oh, no...sorry, I didn't mean to give off that vibe...I wanted to ask you, since we were talking about it on Saturday night, if you wanted to come with me to see Reese fight."

Quinn stopped walking. The look on her face was unreadable and seemed to go through several different expressions.

"I..." Her lips pursed and she scratched her neck just below her ear like she was indecisive. "I don't really know to be honest...I've never..."

Cory walked on, laughing a little. "Yeah, I know...it seems scary...but it's exciting to watch him, he's actually quite amazing..."

Quinn walked on, following him to the coffee cart that set up on the corner. He went up and looked back. "What do you want? I'll get them...Tania's too."

"Oh, thank you...I'll have a Chai with spice and I know Tania likes a Mocha."

He placed the order and stepped back to wait next to Quinn.

"He's fighting this Saturday, if you were keen..."

"This Saturday? Oh, no I can't...I've told you before I can't do weekends."

Cory gave her a strange look, pressing his lips together like he was holding something back, Quinn frowned at him. "What?"

"Nothing..." He looked away like he was pissed.

"What?" Quinn asked more insistently.

Cory sighed and glanced back at her. "That damn brother of yours, huh?"

Quinn startled and gaped at him for a second. "If you must know, yes..."

"What exactly does he need you for every weekend?"

She tensed up at the question, her mouth twisting.

"Yeah, none of my business..." Cory grumbled. "Quinn, I know you think I'm just a fuck boy and, yeah, I admit that maybe I am...or was...but I..."

"Whoa, wait up..." Quinn interrupted. "Are you seriously going to try and say you're different with me?" She asked sarcastically. "That's cliché as fuck."

Cory looked at her with surprise and rubbed the back of his neck. "Okay, savage...but nevertheless that is what I was going to say, because I believe it..."

She turned her body to face him directly. "Okay, tell me how it usually goes for you..."

He frowned a little confused. "Usually goes for me?"

"Yeah, how you normally get the girl."

He rubbed the back of his neck awkwardly. "Normally? Ah...usually they'll show interest in me first, you know..."

"Okay, but lots of girls do that, you don't sleep with all of them, so you see one you like, then what?" Quinn folded her arms and stared at him.

He licked his lips. "If I see her at a party I'll approach her...if I see her around campus and like her I'll get her number and invite her to a party or something."

"So you have sex with them..."

"Yeah..." His eyes shifted to her and became intense as his lip lifted in a sexy little smirk on only one side of his mouth. "So you see how you're already different, right?"

"Not really...you can't ask me to a party because I can't normally go out weekends, but the one party I did go to you stalked me, kissed me and tried to get me on the bed."

Cory's face went dark as he scowled at her. Their coffees were called and he looked away, walking off the few steps to collect them and came back. As he handed her the coffees for her and Tania he saw the triumphant little smirk on her lips.

"Alright, I confess..." He leaned in to her ear knowing her hands were full and she couldn't shove him away. "...I want to taste you, all of you." He breathed in her ear in a tantalizing whisper.

He cupped her jaw and buried his face into her neck as she stiffened and looked around at the other people at the coffee cart now looking at them as she was stuck in a weird T-pose while he basically assaulted her. He licked her neck and huffed a sexy little growl in her ear before standing up and looking at her with a huge grin. "Are you happy now, knowing the truth?" He saw her just staring at him, from one eye to the other and then her tongue licked her lips as her eyes dropped to his lips then back to his eyes.

Oh, she did not just give me the triangle?

"Would you like that?" He asked in a low tone that made her go weak at the knees.

Where had the protective teddy bear gone? The guy who gave safe, warm hugs? Quinn blinked a little stunned as her clit actually throbbed.

He chuckled deeply and reached out, wrapped his hand around the back of her head and pulled her into his chest. She had to open her arms out even wider to avoid the coffees from getting crushed but it meant she was crushed instead.

"Fucking hell, Quinn..." Cory muttered. "We need to move..." He started walking, pulling her along with his arm firmly around her waist and headed straight for an alcove and enclosed doorway in the old stone building that was closest. He pushed her up against the wall in the darkened space and took the coffees from her hands, putting them on the ground.

Quinn looked down at him crouching and wondered why she wasn't taking the opportunity to jump away. As he stood up she watched his eyes come up last, taking in every inch of her body in a slow rise that left her holding her breath and heat pooling in her deepest darkest places.

"Holy shit..." She breathed out causing him to chuckle again as he stepped into her and leaned his forearm on the wall next to her head. He lifted her chin with his other hand and melted his lips to hers. She opened her mouth to him obediently, realizing that she had been completely ruined by Antonio to these two enigmatic dominant men that wanted her, as soon as they took control. She wanted them too, so badly. She felt swept up by each of them every time they showed their true colors and desires.

After kissing her nearly breathless Cory moved back to her neck, his hand dropping to caress a breast in a quick little fondle before he pressed his body firmly against hers.

"Fuck, I want you." He growled in her ear making her shiver.

"Cory...please stop..." She panted, fully aware of just where they were.

He lifted his head and the dark look in his eyes as the blue was almost gone behind dilated pupils made her suck in a breath. "Not here..." She breathed.

He looked up and away as he let out a long breath before stepping away from her and raking a hand through his hair. "Go back to your friend..."

Quinn gaped at him. "What?" Did she hear that right?

He looked back at her with a grimace. "You want me to prove I want more than just sex, go now before I drag you to my truck..."

"But?"

"Go!" He dropped his back to the wall adjacent and heaved a heavy breath trying to calm his dick back down as it pressed painfully against his jeans.

Quinn bent and picked up the coffees and moved away, stopping at the archway of the alcove and looking back, chewing apprehensively on her bottom lip.

He looked up to meet her eyes, his still dark and wanting.

"Maybe we could do something on Friday?" Quinn said with a beautiful smile.

He lifted his chin and laughed. "Alright...I'll message you."

He watched as she hurriedly walked off then groaned as he stood up. He was going to have to pit stop in the fucking toilets somewhere to relieve himself...

Fuck! Damn training...what a cock blocker!

Quinn raced back to study hall and collapsed down in her seat next to Tania, putting the coffee cups down, picking up a note book and fanning her heated face.

Tania looked at her strangely. "Did you run all the way back? It's like fifty meters away..."

Quinn gave Tania a weird little pout and shook her head. "No..." She pressed her hands to her cheeks trying to calm them down.

Tania's eyes narrowed suspiciously. "Did something happen with Cory?"

Quinn nodded, a silly little grin coming onto her face. "Ah-huh..."

Tania rolled her eyes. "You bragging bitch." She insulted in good humor making Quinn giggle. "So are you really going to go all the way with each of them before you decide which one you're serious about?"

Quinn paused at the question.

Antonio's words bubbled up out of her intrusive thoughts about her staying pure to him. Her face and good humor fell instantly and she grabbed her coffee cup, hugging her hands around it.

"Whoa! What just happened there?" Tania asked.

Quinn shook her head. "It doesn't matter either way, I shouldn't get excited and need to stop this, I can't lead these guys on any longer...I'm not in a situation to date either one of them."

"Oh!?" Tania's eyes went wide in surprise. "You already have a boyfriend...that's right. He must be super freaking hot to not want to dump him for either Curry or Rice..."

Quinn gave a little awkward shrug of her shoulders. "I used to think so...lately I'm starting to doubt he's good for me."

30

A date with Curry

Friday night and Quinn had managed to successfully sneak out again, feigning not feeling well after studying too hard Antonio had told her to go to bed early and he would send Danny to pick her up in the morning. He knew she had her first assessment coming up on the Fundamentals of Property Law as it pertains to large commercial infrastructure, something that was important to know in his business model.

Now, she was waiting on the corner of her street for Cory's truck. She had to slap her cheeks to make sure she wasn't dreaming this.

A date.

An actual date!

She had never been on one before...and although she had purposely asked for something casual and fun when they had been messaging each other to plan it out she couldn't get the image of what happened on Wednesday out of her head.

As his truck pulled up and she jumped in with a smile, her stomach flipped and her heart thumped at the prospect of kissing this hunk of a man again. His blue eyes sparkled as he looked at her, like she was the most amazing thing he had ever seen and she cherished it. It wasn't like she had dressed up for the occasion, she was still just wearing jeans and an oversized sweatshirt, but her hair was down, cascading in bouncing waves around her and all the way down her back and she had put on mascara to just define her eyes and a little tinted strawberry lip balm.

As she put her seatbelt on he leaned over and peered up at her face through the hair that had fallen forward as she was bending her head down to find the belt clip.

He lifted a finger and pulled her hair back like drawing open a curtain and she lifted her head, grabbing her hair and tucking it behind her ear as she lifted her gaze from the belt clip to his eyes.

"Are you blushing?'" He asked in an amused lilt.

"What?" She asked horrified, clasping her hands over her cheeks and looking away. "No! The wind was cold."

He leaned back in his seat with a coy smirk. "Oh, Quinn...you are so freaking adorable, just like a bunny..."

She frowned at him as he drove off from the curb. "You've said that before..."

"Yeah, I have...bunny." He glanced at her with a wicked grin. "That's you're new nickname."

She twisted her mouth as her eyebrows furrowed for a moment. Did she want to be called Bunny? Would he stop if she didn't like it? As if to answer her unspoken questions he grinned.

"Live with it."

She huffed a little pouty laugh and looked away out the side window. "I guess I have to then." It wasn't so bad, she supposed, she could live with it.

"Yep." He confirmed cheekily.

He drove them to the nearest mall with a movie theatre and a games center, she wanted fun he was going to give her fun...games fun. He wanted to hear her laugh and tease and see how competitive she could be.

As they entered the large open space filled with arcade games he saw the smile on her face and the sparkle in her eyes like a child.

"Have you ever been to one of these places?"

She shook her head. "I've walked past them several times when I'm at the mall..."

"Cool, I'm glad I get to show you how much fun you can have then." Cory beamed that roguish smile and took her hand leading her over to a counter to first buy a card for the machines. He handed her one and pointed to a car racing game that was free. "Race ya."

She looked at the card then to the racing seat, grinning from ear to ear and practically ran over to it. Cory chuckled to himself as he followed and slipped into the race seat next to her and showed her how to start the game up.

"You're like a kid..." He commented at her excited giggling as she steered the game like a demon. She was definitely competitive.

After that they played several other two man racing games and shoot 'em up games and finally ended up on a Foosball table.

Cory watched her face as she frowned in concentration and the way she stuck her tongue out at a funny angle. "Christ, bunny...I feel like just letting you win you're taking this so seriously." He laughed at her. She had been teasing him about losing the games, accusing him of letting her win, so he had won the last two easily and now she was pouting.

She looked up, her eyes bright and smiled showing her teeth. "I'm not serious, I'm having so much fun!"

He walked around the table to her side looking at his watch. "Well, sorry to burst your bubble, but our movie starts in fifteen minutes, we have to go now."

"Aww, can we come back after?"

He leaned over her shoulder and to her ear. "If I can't persuade you to do something else with me after the movie..."

He felt her tense up slightly and look up at him over her shoulder. He leaned back with a smirk, took her hand and turned away. "You're too easy to fluster, bunny...it's adorable."

"Shut up!" She chewed on her lip as he led her out of the arcade and up the stairs to where the movie theatre was above it. She really wanted to find out exactly what Cory meant by something else. She realized that he probably meant sex and that made her a little nervous.

He turned to look at her and grinned. "Calm down...I didn't mean anything by it other than maybe a little make out session...but we can do that during the movie if it's boring."

Quinn pursed her lips, giving him a strange look and stopped walking half way up the stairs. "How serious are you willing to make this?"

Cory startled at the question, letting go of her hand and backing up a step as he raked a hand through his hair. "Well, fuck...straight to the point huh?" He looked away at the other people walking up the stairs around them before taking her hand and pulling her up the stairs to the foyer and moving them to the side out of the way. "Look, I'm trying to prove to you that I am serious, so I'm guessing for you that means sex is off the table for as long as it takes to persuade you that I want more. Does that answer your question?"

She didn't know...being stuck with Antonio she was beginning to feel a bit like a tease leading this guy on. The real question was what was she trying to prove to herself by doing this?

Cory saw her gaze drop to the floor and her expression turn melancholy. He dipped his fingers under her chin and lifted it.

"Hey...look I know all about Antonio, Reese did tell me...I can help you get away from him."

"W-what?" Quinn gaped at him.

He glanced down at her wrists, his jaw flexing. Quinn grabbed her sleeves in an involuntary response. "I can help you report his abuse...you don't have to put up with it."

She grit her teeth. He had no idea what was truly going on, did he? Reese had guessed they were having sex but had he told Cory that much?

Cory clucked his tongue and looked away to the candy bar. "I'll go get popcorn and drinks...just stay there...let's not ruin tonight with conversations about your dickhead step-brother, okay." He wandered off leaving her staring after him.

She breathed in a deep cleansing breath, letting go of her anxiety. There was no way she could ever go to the police and make a report, what a joke...

As they seated themselves in the theater Cory huffed in amusement. "You know I've never brought a girl to the movies before...I usually just come with mates when we're really bored of sitting at home and watching movies...then go out to a bar..."

"Oh, yeah, right, you're twenty one, you get to drink..."

"I'm twenty two next month."

"Really? What date?" Quinn asked, looking straight up at him with full interest. October...

He tilted his head, his eyes narrowing slightly. "I love the way you give your full attention to things, it really makes me think you care about the answers."

Her brow furrowed with a mix of confusion and amusement. "I do care about the answers, otherwise I wouldn't ask the questions."

He chuckled and lifted his arm, putting it around her shoulders and pulled her into his side. 'Geeze, with an answer like that I could fall in love with you.' He thought to himself with a coy smirk on his lips.

She pressed a hand to his chest and tilted her chin up to him. "So?"

"Eighteenth..." He answered.

"Hmm...Libra. No wonder..."

"No wonder what? Don't tell me you're into that astrology rubbish?"

"Well, a Libra is said to be a nice person...don't you want to be a nice person?"

He grinned down at her. "I guess, what else?"

"They like balance in all things, but are known as being people pleasers who try to keep everyone happy."

Cory grit his teeth and looked at the screen. "Yeah, I suppose you could say that's me..."

"I've heard you hate seeing a girl upset, and you've proven that to me before."

Cory huffed and shoved the popcorn at her. "Here...you know who else has a birthday in October?"

"No, who?" Quinn asked as she took the popcorn box and popped a kernel into her mouth.

"Reese...think he's a people pleaser?"

"What date was he born?"

"Twenty eighth."

Quinn giggled and shook her head. "Oh, no...that explains everything about him...he's a Scorpio!"

"And?" He leaned away from her to look at her with a raised eyebrow.

"What can I say about Scorpio...?" Quinn twisted her mouth into a sultry little pout making Cory scowl.

"Oh, let me guess...they're great lovers?" He hissed under his breath as the movie started and the lights went out.

Quinn giggled behind her hand. "Amongst other things...they are pretty narcissistic people, psychopathic almost...possessive and over protective."

"Hmm..." Cory rolled his eyes. "I guess there is something in the star sign thing after all...that's him to a T."

"Ah-huh..."

"So what's yours?"

"Mine? I'm born at the end of November so I'm a Sagittarius..."

"And what does that mean?"

Quinn shrugged with a wistful look. "Not much."

"You're not going to tell me?"

"I'm sure if you were really interested you could find out for yourself..." She gave him a challenging little pout and turned to focus on the movie.

He clucked his tongue and took out his phone, the screen light blazing out in the darkness.

"Hey, you can't do that!" Quinn said.

"Why?" Cory asked. "We're in the back row, whose going to care...besides, you've intrigued me enough to find out why you won't tell me about your star sign..."

Quinn giggled and put some popcorn in her mouth, looking back to the movie. Cory chuckled at the subtle way she just gave him permission to continue and find out. He searched it up and sat reading.

Sagittarius are typically outspokenly optimistic extroverts who elicit respect and affection from everyone they come into contact with. They are loyal, smart, assertive and compassionate. They are one-of-a-kind, talented and have impeccable discernment.

"Holy crap!" Cory muttered, wiping a hand over his face. "Did you pay Google off to write this shit?"

Quinn turned and in the light of the movie playing her grin was too much. He reached out and covered her face with one hand. "Stop gloating."

He couldn't believe how right the description was and the bit about eliciting affection from everyone they come across...that just made him jealous for no reason at all. He suddenly wanted to lock her away from the world and keep her all to himself. Shit! He had never felt like that over anyone...it actually scared him a little.

Quinn grabbed his hand and pulled it into her lap with a small smile. His eyebrow rose but she wasn't looking at him anymore, he stared at her side profile lit by the movie playing...she was beautiful...and that little nose was to die for. He leaned over bringing his other hand up under her chin to turn her face back to him, even as he curled the fingers of his other hand to entwine them with hers and kissed her pert little nose. She blinked at him in surprise.

He grinned. "Your nose is so cute..."

She scowled at him. "Shut up!"

"You shut up." He growled and planted his lips on hers, licking across them even as her eyes fluttered closed and her mouth opened.

His hand drifted around to the back of her head and he dipped his tongue into her mouth and around her tongue. Taking his time, not rushing he savored her taste, slightly salty from the popcorn. He angled his mouth over hers before turning and angling it the other way, leaning over her as his passion for her increased with every languid lick.

She moaned in his mouth, gripping his other hand tightly until he finally pulled back to allow her to take a breath. He swiped her chin and pinched it teasingly. "You're a beautiful kisser, bunny...I love the way you just relax into my lead. Too many girls try to shove their tongues down your throat..."

Quinn couldn't help but giggle a little at that.

He pulled her back to being tucked into his side and grabbed a handful of popcorn from the box she was still holding out to the side. He slipped down in his seat a little so her head could rest on his pec as he threw the popcorn into his mouth.

Quinn nestled in, feeling a glow of happiness.

But how long could this glow realistically last? She was beginning to feel guilt creeping up her spine that perhaps Cory really did genuinely like her for real not just for the score.

When the movie was finished and they were walking out Cory slipped his hand into hers and entwined their fingers together. He leaned over her shoulder.

"So are we going back to the arcade?"

Quinn shook her head. "No, I think maybe I should just go home..."

He frowned slightly, his mouth pressing into a line as he led her silently to the carpark and they got in his truck. He sat there staring at the wheel for a moment before clucking his tongue and turning to face her.

"What happened in your head during the movie, you became slowly more distant and now you just want to go home?"

She hung her head feeling a little ashamed. "I'm so sorry, I didn't mean to ruin the good time, I really did enjoy myself I just..."

Cory rolled his bottom lip under his teeth. "I enjoyed this too and I want to be able to do it again so don't you dare tell me you don't want this or like me anymore."

"I do like you, that's the problem..." Quinn huffed, fidgeting her hands in her lap.

Cory clucked his tongue and looked away into the parking lot, this level was almost empty, only about twenty cars dotted around and another couple were just getting into a car about twenty meters away. "Quinn..." He looked back at her and she lifted her head at him saying her name, her eyes large and shining. "...only you can decide what you want in life...but if you need help in getting it you just need to raise your hand and ask for it. There are people who can help."

"What are you saying?" Quinn looked more like a trapped bunny than ever.

Cory raked a hand through his hair and his mouth twisted as his jaw clenched. "I wasn't meant to say anything, but Reese reckons you're being forced to do shit by that step-brother of yours and well..."

Quinn's stomach dropped through the floor. So he did know! She had really hoped that he didn't. "Just take me home, please."

"I know you don't want to talk about it, but I can't help it...I really want you, Quinn, but I know exactly what's holding you back and it pisses me off." Cory leaned over her and grabbed her chin while he spoke, his voice hoarse with anger building up. "Why...why do you want to be with someone like that?"

Quinn stared at Cory's fine chiseled face, it was broader than both Reese and Antonio's, more square and his lips were full and soft. A tear fell from the corner of her eye and trailed down her cheek as he stared at it, his jaw muscles ticking. He let her go and shifted back into his seat, gripping the steering wheel for dear life. He had squeezed her jaw and hurt her. "Shit sorry."

She dropped her head to stare at her hands. "It's okay, I know you didn't mean it...you would never hurt me."

"No, never intentionally...are you okay?"

She nodded and wiped her cheek.

"Okay, let's get you home then..." He started up his truck and drove out of the parking lot, both of them silent and awkward.

Half way back and Quinn finally spoke up. "I'm afraid..."

Cory's jaw clenched. "Yeah, I get that..."

"I'm afraid for you, not me so much..."

He glanced at her and saw she looked miserable. "Don't worry about me, bunny...but we really need to figure out what to do about getting you out of that fucked up situation."

She nodded, falling silent again.

Cory sighed and reached out a hand, rubbing her thigh as he drove. "It's going to be alright, bunny..."

When he dropped her off and she disappeared into the night he dropped his forehead to the steering wheel. He wanted to talk to Reese, needed to talk to Reese...but Reese was busy, the night before his fight and he was with his father meeting the rival fighter's sponsors for dinner.

He knew that because Reese had messaged him earlier to tell him they needed to talk soon.

They needed to talk now!

31

Dinner with the Boston Mob Boss

"Do I have to go to the dinner?" Reese huffed irritably to his father.

"Of course you do, you'll be expected to make a toast as my heir..." Cillian grumbled back as he adjusted his tie.

"Ah, fuck..." Reese raked a hand through his hair, frustrated he couldn't act on the information burning a hole in his soul.

"Reese..." Cillian growled. "Pack in the macho shit."

"I'm not doing it on purpose, Dad, I just..." He sighed frustrated.

"Yeah, look I don't like the guy either, so I'm glad your perceptions are on the right wave length but you need to learn not to show it."

"Yeah, yeah...enough of the lecture, I get it."

Cillian grinned, then clapped Reese on the shoulder. "Take your grievance out on his fighter tomorrow night."

Reese grinned back, his golden eyes sparkling. "Oh, I intend to, can't fucking wait."

"That's my boy!" Cillian laughed. "Look, do the toast, stay for the main then excuse yourself...you do need to rest for the fight and I'm sure his fighter won't even attend...it's only because who you are is important, you have to show."

"I know, thanks, dad..."

As they walked into the elevator Reese messaged Cory, now he was about to hear all the information on Quinn and what happened in

Boston it was time for the two of them to sit down and have a serious discussion about Quinn Malley or Guinevere O'Malley or whatever the fuck her name is!

Reese cringed shaking hands with Flanagan, boss of the Boston division. Knowing what he knew and was about to find out, he looked at that man with a grim expression. They all seated themselves around a huge table in the middle of the top floor restaurant of the hotel Flanagan and his men were staying in. The waitresses looked nervous, as well they should be, as it was fairly obvious these men that were gathering weren't your normal business men out for dinner.

Reese felt a hand come over his shoulder and he glanced sideways to see Liam lean in discreetly. "Your man is waiting for you."

Reese's gaze went to his father who was watching with a mild interest as he sipped his red wine. Reese stood up, buttoning up his jacket and bowed his head slightly to Cillian. "I'll be back in five minutes..."

Cillian lowered his glass, looking at Liam then back to Reese with the slightest frown of disapproval. "Be sure that you do."

Reese moved back through the restaurant, it would be fine, everyone wasn't even settled yet so it looked like he was just skipping off to the toilet before things got serious.

He followed Liam out into the foyer and Liam hit the elevator button. They went down ten floors and to a hotel room. Entering Reese saw an older man there looking frightfully nervous, pacing the room. He looked up when they entered and he extended his hand.

"Ah, Reese O'Shea? I'm Pat...Docherty."

"Nice to meet you, Pat...I'm sure you know I don't have a lot of time so shall we...?" He indicated the chairs at the small table in the room and pulled one out to sit down. Liam stood behind him as Pat took the other one nervously running a hand over his balding head.

"Okay where should I start?"

"Start at what happened with O'Malley."

Pat nodded and collected his thoughts. "Not sure if you know this but Ferrante rules the whole Northeast Megalopolis so spent a lot of time traveling to Boston especially a decade ago up to this happening. When O'Malley found out about his wife and Ferrante hooking up he went ballistic, as you would...although they were already separated. He sent a hit for Ferrante which wasn't sanctioned and it was luckily intercepted, but during the interception is what caused the car crash that resulted in Augusto's wife's death. Augusto wasn't that aggrieved by it to be honest, their marriage had been one of convenience people say, but Antonio was, he wanted reparation or was going to start a blood war...the boy was already showing himself to be a psychopath and he was running unchecked on the streets in his rage even as a teen. Flanagan though, he saw the opportunity to dethrone O'Malley because of his unruly actions and sanctioned O'Malley's death by execution and agreed that Maria and the daughter would change names and disappear with Ferrante to New York.

Antonio was the one who demanded the girl...everyone could see he just wanted the opportunity to destroy her, although all the while her mother was alive he was kept at bay."

Reese's jaw was ticking with anger. "She was only a kid then?"

"Yeah, and others spoke out about it at the time...they truly wanted her to stay within the family, her uncle was willing to take her in...but Flanagan went ahead and made these agreements without listening, he didn't care about the girl or her lineage. He cooked the books on O'Malley's death and kept the girl's inheritance...ten million dollars...it secured an alliance with the mafia and the leadership of the Boston Mob with him."

"Okay, so let's get this straight..." Reese growled, sitting forward with a finger in the air, pointing. "That fucker that's sitting in the restaurant above us agreed to having O'Malley killed and his daughter go to the Ferrantes under a different name so he could swipe the inheritance for himself as the back-hander?"

"Yeah, basically. He gained support of his leadership after gaining financial control over the docks thanks to that money, his leadership has been quite fruitful ever since." Pat looked at Reese with an expression to say he has power and loyalty.

"That motherfucker! He basically human trafficked the girl straight to her biggest enemy! And no one stopped him!?" Reese was pacing the room now, agitated and wanting to punch something.

"Calm down, Reese, you're going to have to return to that restaurant like nothing's changed." Liam said.

"Yeah, on that, I'm going back..." Pat said standing up and looking at his watch.

"Wait...one more thing...what did Quinn's mother do with all this happening?"

Pat barked a savage laugh. "Never heard or saw her...once that Ferrante bastard had her firmly in his clutches no one saw her, that caused enough of a dilemma being that she was the daughter of our founding father, Will O'Rourke."

"She fucking what?" Reese stared at him stunned.

"He had no sons that's why O'Malley had married her in the first place to become boss after O'Rourke died...he basically got into Will's back pocket and made it happen for himself, he never cared for Maria, was abusive to her, we all knew that..." He hung his head in shame. "She was a beautiful woman, but used to violence...she would have been easy pickings for Ferrante to control because she hated her father and the Mob lifestyle...but I do think Augusto was actually in love with her. However his marriage to her cemented the peace treaty between the Mafia and Mob in Boston because of who she is...or was. That young girl is the golden goose..."

Reese rubbed his eyes, pinching the bridge of his nose. "Thanks, you've made things a lot clearer..." Reese waved him away and watched him leave then looked at Liam with a grim expression. "I need to get Quinn away from the fucker, now her mother is gone he's off the leash where Quinn is concerned. Augusto won't care enough to stop him and he's been grooming her to obey his orders since she was fucking twelve! It's clear he intends to use her somehow due to her bloodline and the peace treaty...did you know he's going into politics?"

Liam frowned at that news. "I think you need to talk to your father...I don't think he knows about this, if he knew then I would too."

Reese nodded, taking in a deep breath to calm himself down. "Yeah...I will but not now, so for now I need you to stay quiet on it."

Liam held his hands out. "Hey, I'm clean in this...this is your deal to stir up."

Reese chuckled. "Yeah, thanks..."

The rest of the night was hard for Reese, he kept finding himself staring at Flanagan and he could only imagine the expression he was giving off. He wanted to expose him as traitorous scum, he wanted to kill him for what he did for his own selfish gain.

As the dinner reached the conclusion of the main Reese made his excuses and gratefully left. His father followed him out and halted him with a hand on his arm in the foyer, pulling his to the side.

"What's your problem with Flanagan?"

Reese clucked his tongue, he had been too obvious. "No problem, just don't like the guy."

"This was your formal introduction, Reese, learn to keep that psycho aura of yours in the cage where it belongs!"

Reese sighed and stuck his hands in his suit pant pockets, sweeping his jacket back behind his elbows. "Yeah...sorry."

"Shit, you were looking at the guy like he murdered your mother! It was putting everyone on edge...lucky I can palm it off as fight angst..."

Reese shrugged and grinned cockily. "That's all it is...I'm ready to kill someone."

Cillian gave Reese a serious look over. "The day you do actually kill someone son you will realize it's not all its jacked up to be..."

Reese sucked his teeth and looked away from his father's serious glare.

"Go, get some sleep..." Cillian ordered.

Sleep was the furthest thing from his mind as Reese walked back to his car, a bodyguard following along behind him to make sure he made it, organized by his father. They may be all from the same crime organization but no one took any chances, rivalry still existed between factions...and Reese was going to be stirring up some real shit between them soon.

32
The fight

Reese was really riled up for this fight, he hadn't slept last night due to the information he had received on top of the fact that he hadn't had a drop of alcohol for the last week or seen or heard from Quinn for the last few days while he prepared for the fight. He tended to close himself off as he prepared for fights, he knew he got moody and was not nice company to be around, fair enough.

He had also received a weird ass message from Cory this morning too, apparently he had gone on a date with Quinn.

Fucking great!

Since when did fuck boy, golden retriever take girls out on dates?

Damn it!

But the message wasn't bragging, something had happened...and Reese instinctively knew it had something to do with Antonio and Quinn's fucked up relationship. Cory must have said something...

But he really couldn't focus on that right now...not today. The mere thought of the fact that Quinn was with Antonio right now was enough for Reese to exude an aura that had everyone ducking to get out of his way.

Reese stepped up onto the platform in front of the fighting cage and lifted his hand, dropping the hood of his sweats and looked up at the large glass window on the left hand side above. There were two mezzanine areas behind glass on each side of the ring where the two camps of each fighter housed their more special guests and sponsors. Reese saw his father and gave him a quick salute. As he turned towards the center of the cage to inspect it he glanced up at the other window. He normally didn't even care to look, but something today had made him.

He wished he hadn't.

Especially knowing what he knew now.

There was Antonio Ferrante shaking hands with Flanagan blatantly without a care in the world. What the fuck was he even doing here, the smug piece of shit? Had Flanagan invited him? Had Cillian okayed this? He looked extra smug as he adjusted his shirt sleeve under his jacket, rattling his very expensive watch.

Reese's blood ran cold when he saw the flash of dark red hair and saw the svelte figure of Quinn as Antonio moved sideways.

What the fuck!

Antonio stepped closer to the glass and seemed to know Reese was staring as he looked down and met his dark gaze with a cocky smirk.

"Son of a bitch!" Reese muttered, turning away to focus on the man in front of him, the ref was speaking to him.

What the hell is he here to try and prove?

Reese jumped down and went to speak to his father's men who were surrounding him. "Does my father know that fucker Ferrante is up there with Flanagan?" He demanded.

From down on this angle you couldn't see him now he had moved away from the viewing window. One of the men moved off to find out what was going on as there was a ripple of concern.

As he stalked back and forth, shrugging his shoulders and listening to his coach before the start he saw the familiar face of Cory hidden under a grey hoodie in among the crowd of betters. Their eyes met and Reese sucked his teeth, scowling at him for sneaking in here.

Cory dropped his gaze.

"Damn it!" Reese spat, now he had two fronts to be concerned about.

Reese looked up at the seven foot tall monster that moved through the crowd, jumped up onto the platform raising his fist to cheering from the Boston crowd before ducking his head as he entered the cage.

"What the fuck is this?" Reese questioned of the referee, this was not the guy he had been scheduled to fight.

"I don't know, sorry Reese...hang tight." The Ref said as he walked up to Flanagan's crew acting as the fighter's corner men to question what was going on.

Reese looked up at the glass window and saw his father's face contorted with rage as he sent some people out of the VIP room to also find out what was going on.

Reese glanced to the other window to see Antonio, his hands in his pockets, giving him a shit-eating grin as Flanagan laughed boisterously beside him.

The Ref came back just as Liam came up beside Reese.

"It seems the Boston fighter had a mishap in his hotel room last night, slipped in the bathroom and has sprained his ankle..."

Reese sucked his teeth, bitterly, realizing what this was...

"And that fucker? Where did he come from?" Liam demanded, pointing at the monster prowling around in the cage chuckling like a psycho.

"It seems rather than calling off the fight they found themselves a replacement..."

"Convenient..." Reese muttered. Just let me guess who he came here with...

Liam swiped a hand through his hair and looked at Reese. "It's up to you if you want to continue the fight."

Reese chuckled darkly. "No, I have no choice, don't you see that fucker up there...this is his fighter."

Liam glanced up to the glass and saw Antonio and Flanagan sparking up cigars like they were already celebrating. His jaw clenched and he looked at Reese seriously. "Don't get sucked into whatever they are trying to do."

Reese's mouth twisted bitterly. "No, I can do this...that fucker isn't a threat to me."

He saw Quinn was being hidden behind Antonio's body but was standing by his side the whole time. He started growling deep in his throat when he saw Flanagan reach out and touch Quinn's shoulder, pulling her in under his arm and hooking it around her neck like some forced hug by a creepy uncle. Quinn was chewing her bottom lip nervously as she stared like a deer in headlights until Antonio dragged her back to his side and they stepped back from the window.

"I'm going to kill him." Reese muttered, jumping up onto the platform before ducking into the cage. He glared at the monster of a guy in front of him, he looked like a wrestler from WWE but Reese wasn't in the mood to fuck around now...this guy wasn't going to be any hindrance.

The Ref made some announcements to the raucous crowd as Reese looked back to where Cory was and his eyes seemed to glow with his ire.

He heard the cage shut and lock.

This was it, no turning back now. He faced the guy in front of him and sucked his teeth around the mouth guard now in his mouth. The big guy grinned back and slapped his chest.

The fight was brutal, Reese was a lot quicker on his feet than the heavy monster and he dealt a lot of damage to the guy in a short space of time, aiming for his tree trunk legs. Hammering them over and over with hard kicks. This fucker was not going to be able to walk tomorrow...

In between the kicks Reese was jabbing at the guy's kidneys and his eyebrows alternatively. One eyebrow opened up nicely, blood pouring down the guy's face and half blinding him. There was no time out or rounds in this cage, this was one long fight to the end, no rules. The Ref on the outside to make sure no one else interfered and when a fighter surrendered or was unconscious the cage was opened up.

The monster wasn't completely useless and he had a hard hit to him. He got Reese a couple of times, throwing him back and making his head groggy. His own left eye swelling closed. But Reese was winning and it wouldn't be too long until the big guy's legs collapsed under him.

Quinn had been shaken to her core when she was led into such a place and then to see what place it actually was, to see Reese locked in that cage with a man that looked like a Minotaur, Quinn really didn't want to be here. Antonio had been laughing with this sleazy old guy about the new fighter Antonio had found for him at short notice.

Bullshit to that, it was all a clear set up and Antonio was doing all this deliberately because of her. He had told her as much. As soon as he had dragged her back from the old guy's groping arm he had whispered in her ear that what ever happened to Reese from here was her fault.

She had also been surprised to learn that the old guy, Flanagan he was introduced as, said he had known her father and he had once bounced her on his knee when she was little. She wanted to ask him about it but seeing the way he grinned at her and licked his lips she really didn't want anything to do with the guy...they were all obviously depraved gangsters.

"Fuck that little prick is winning! He's a real beast!" Flanagan exclaimed.

Antonio turned to the glass with an evil sneer. "Not for long...I have a secret weapon." He stepped over to where Quinn had been seated, grabbed her up out of her seat by her long hair and pulled her to the glass, slamming her up against it and holding her there by her neck as she struggled and Flanagan laughed.

"Oh, does Reese know Quinn? What are the odds of that?"

"Oh, yeah, he knows her...how well I have no idea..." Antonio seethed in Quinn's ear as she flinched back. He pressed himself to her back pinning her to the window and lifted his other hand to grope her breast for everyone below to see, leering over her shoulder as Reese looked up and snarled like a wild beast. He purposely licked her neck his dark eyes dancing with his sick amusement. She was wearing a form fitting short dress that had a high neck so she wasn't actually flashing skin while Antonio squeezed her ample breast but it still got some of the crowd going to look over and see her pressed up and helpless as some dark gangster mauled her and licked her neck making her look like a whore hired for the night's other entertainment.

Reese jumped up onto the cage fencing and scrambled to the top, pointing and yelling at the window.

"You fucking mother fucker piece of shit! What the fuck! Get your hands off her, stop! Let her go!"

Antonio and Flanagan laughed.

Cory pulled his hood further over his face and closed his eyes in bitter regret of coming tonight. He hadn't ever seen Antonio...he had now and he would be forever etched into his brain. He clenched his fists as he shook with rage at what that bastard was doing to Quinn to bait Reese. This was why he hated fucking gangsters!

The fighter behind Reese stood up and turned, looking up at Reese high on the cage and stalked forward. People were screaming at Reese in warning. Cillian was up at the window yelling in fury and concern. Reese turned to look down at the mat just as the monster reached him, grabbed him by the leg and pulled him down enough to grab his arm as well then threw him off the cage, over his head and sent him crashing to the mat, a hefty fall of ten feet.

Quinn sobbed out a 'no' as Reese was dazed by the fall, clutching at his ribs. The monster came up behind him, grabbed him by the hair yanking his head back and punched him full in the face five times before letting him go to walk around the ring with his arms up and celebrating. Reese was lying prone in a pool of his own blood streaming from his nose.

Antonio leaned into Quinn's ear. "See, all your fault...seems he has quite the thing for you."

"Please stop this...I beg of you."

"Oh, you'll be begging me, petalo...you'll be screaming for me to stop later when it's your turn."

Quinn froze as her blood went cold and tears fell down her face. Antonio dragged her away from the window and threw her into a chair.

Flanagan looked at her with a sickening amused interest.

"Quite beautiful..." He murmured making Quinn look at him with a fire etched in her eyes. Antonio chuckled and placed a hand on the top of her head.

"Easy, Flanagan..." Antonio warned with a growl.

A cheer went up in the warehouse making them look back. Antonio hissed as he saw Reese had gained his feet and was shaking his head to clear it, his eyes fixed on the monster that turned to face him with a little surprise.

"Damn it." Antonio said.

"Wow, that boy really is the true monster...you know he reminds me a lot of you." Flanagan said with a laugh. "But you play with guns while he likes to play with his fists and get bloody."

Antonio glared at Flanagan. "You can't punch someone from ten feet away but you sure can shoot them fucking dead."

Flanagan roared with laughter as Quinn felt like she was going to be sick.

Reese did a drop and sweep with his leg taking out the monsters ankle and dropping him to the mat. Reese jumped on him in a full mount, securing his arms under himself and started punching the guy's face over and over, his face getting redder and redder with blood as his eyes rolled back in his head.

Antonio clucked his tongue, his scowl dark and fierce. Quinn couldn't see but knew that Reese must be winning the fight again and felt pleased he was able to do so after being hit like that, but that meant all Antonio's fury was going to be turned on her.

When the cage was unlocked and people ran in to drag Reese off the monster before he killed him Antonio turned and grabbed Quinn up roughly by the arm.

"We're leaving."

Matteo opened the door and they quickly exited the room as Flanagan snorted and sipped his scotch.

In the car Antonio forced Quinn to the floor between his legs and unzipped his pants, pulling his cock out, grabbing her by the back of her head and slamming his cock into her mouth.

"You're little fucker admirer is good...he can obviously take pain well...let's see just how much pain you can withstand."

33
Reese the shadow beast

Quinn was dropped home on Sunday afternoon by Danny. He helped her to the door and she waved him off, not wanting him to come in. They were all complicit in her torture, not doing anything to help her, just doing their jobs and looking the other way.

He handed her a bag full of ointment for her to treat her wounds and bruises. She scowled at him and snatched it from his grasp before slamming the door shut. She heaved a heavy sob and dropped to her knees, gasping for breath as she felt like the walls were closing in on her.

She heard her phone go off and looked with shock over to the kitchen where it was lying on the bench plugged into the charger at the socket.

She stared at it, walking slowly over towards it, her anxiety spiking and her stomach threatening to empty of the late lunch she had been forced by Antonio to eat before he sent her home satisfied in the marks left on her skin.

She had not left her phone there.

She picked it up, unplugging it and saw there was a message from Reese. She opened it quickly, she had been so worried about him after seeing him take that awful fall and get punched by that behemoth of a man in the cage.

R - **Go upstairs**

Quinn stared at it. "Go upstairs?" She murmured. What was that about? Was that message meant for her, and the timing...was he watching her, did he see her get dropped off?

She chewed her lip wondering what she should do.

She put her phone down and made her way to the stairs. As she walked up she noticed her bedroom door was closed.

She paused.

She had left it open, she always did.

Had Reese been in her house and plugged her phone in just so she would get his message?

As she opened the bedroom door and stepped in she saw the curtains were drawn shut and there was a dark figure slouched over sitting on the end of her bed. As the shadow lifted its head she saw from the light behind her, his golden gaze lock on to her with a menacing heat that made her stop breathing.

"Close the door, Quinn."

"How did you..."

"Close the fucking door." He growled out. She could see he was sitting forward his forearms on his knees and his fists were clenched tight.

She chewed her lip feeling like she should run out of the room and close the door on him, but that heated gaze kept her still. Her hand was still on the edge of the door and she pushed it behind her, hearing the click as she was plunged into darkness with the shadow beast slowly rising to his feet.

"R-Reese?" She breathed out, scared.

"Baby, I want you to show me what he did...take your clothes off."

Quinn backed up to the door clutching at her sweatshirt. "W-what?"

"You heard me, baby...now do it. I'm not here to fuck around...no more." He was anger personified as he loomed up out of the gloom in front of her and stood looking down on her with a menace she had never ever felt before.

"No, please don't make me..." She breathed, craning her head up against the door to look at his face in the gloom. His eyes seemed to glow in the darkness. Holy shit there was something so sexy about him right now, she could faintly make out the cuts and bruises from his fight on his face. Quinn licked her lips and she heard Reese chuckle making her body vibrate with the sound.

"I'm not going to ask again, Quinn...then I'll rip that fucking sweatshirt off you myself." His husky growling order made her instantly wet. His hand came to her chin and lifted it, barely touching her, gentle and she was reminded that this was not Antonio. "I'm not going to hurt you, baby...but by Christ you better do what I say from now on."

Her mouth went dry and she dropped her hands to the bottom of her sweatshirt and lifted it up and over her head, as he stepped back, and dumped it on the floor at her feet.

She watched him go to her bedside table and turn the reading lamp on that was over the headboard. It wasn't enough light but he turned and flicked his fingers at her.

"Come here."

She felt her stomach swirling in nerves as she walked slowly over to him. He took her shoulders in his hands and rubbed them gently. He turned her so her back was to the light and she let out a strangled little whimper.

"Easy, baby...it's okay...let me see." His voice dropped to a gentle tone as he grabbed the hem of her singlet and pulled it up over her head, throwing it away. She heard the deadly hiss escape his gritted teeth and he dropped to sit on the bed, pulling her back into him as his legs opened and he pressed his forehead to her back holding onto her around her hips for dear life.

"Fuck, I'm so sorry..." He breathed.

Quinn felt tears stream down her face in her embarrassment.

She startled as his hands undid her jeans and yanked them down. "No..." She wailed as the marks on her buttocks and thighs were bared to him. She heard his rasping breath growl out in anger. She gasped as she felt his lips press to her back.

He turned her around and kissed her stomach before pulling back to look up at her face. He didn't get that far, he didn't look up at all as his eyes focused and slid to the name tattooed on her skin.

He ran his hand over it in disbelief as she panicked and tried to cover it up.

"That fucker did not!" Reese growled. He grabbed her hands by her wrists with one large hand and held them up between her breasts, his other hand rubbing at the inked name hoping it was just written on.

"R-reese...please..."

He looked up into her teary eyes, his were dark against the light. "That fucker tattooed his name on you? How could you let him do that, Quinn?" He sounded devastated.

The accusing tone in his voice made her fire spark. "You think I let him?" She struggled against his grip on her wrists but he tightened it, turned her and had her down on the bed her hands above her head before she could blink. She managed to gasp in a breath before Reese's mouth consumed hers in a desperate passionate kiss as he rumbled an animalistic growl deep in his throat.

His other hand breached her panties and delved into her pussy, she mewled into his mouth as he groaned, feeling her wet.

He was relentless with his tongue not giving her any chance to speak, plead or beg as his fingers played up around her clit then thrust into her pussy. She bucked against him, panting against this unexpected but now completely wanted onslaught.

He let go of her hands and drifted down to between her legs, pulling her panties aside and licking up her folds and around her clit, sucking it into his mouth like his life depended on it as he plunged his fingers into her again.

"Fuck..." He breathed out at the taste of her. "I fucking need you to come for me...think only of me."

His eyes flicked up as she moaned out and arched back into his fingers as he dug them into her pussy, curling them up and stroking over that spot that made her see lights spark behind her eyes. He flicked and licked her clit as he watched her body writhe under him.

He felt her body tighten and her hands dropped to curl into his hair in a desperate need for him to not stop now. His tongue was amazing, but what he was doing with his fingers, he knew a lot about how to please a woman.

As she pulled his head down he engulfed her clit, sucking on it hard then bit down on it. Her climax ripped through her as she threw her head back and cried out in her pleasure, unashamed. He kept his fingers moving as her hands dropped from his head and he lightened up on the licking before he pulled his fingers out, grabbed her hips and tilted her up thrusting his tongue deep inside her to get every morsel of her creamy goodness. She bucked against him, sensitive now, her body still quivering.

"Oh fuck..." She moaned out and knew she was going to come again if he kept this up.

"Say my name...I want you to know whose making you come." He breathed against her wet skin before plunging his tongue into her again, he pinched her clit making her body jolt fiercely.

"R-Reese...fuck...me..."

He chuckled against her and shook his head, lifting his face and sitting up between her legs, one hand playing with her clit and one plunging into her wet hole making obscene noises. "You don't get my dick, baby...not until you tell me you're mine."

She whimpered, her legs thrown open wide for him as he played with her, sending sparks off behind her eyes again as her pressed into the mattress and her butt lifted off trying to get his fingers deeper inside her.

"Fuck, baby, you're fucking beautiful..." Reese groaned as she came for him again, gripping onto the blankets underneath her in her small fists and crying out his name in a heavenly hiss.

He eased her back down before standing up and grabbing his jacket.

He leaned over her, brushing sweaty hair from her face and kissed her roughly but chastely on the lips. She looked up at him with a dreamy smile, her eyes dazed and dropping closed like she was going to fall asleep any minute.

"Have a nice dream, baby...we'll talk soon."

He stepped away from her to the window and crawled out onto the roof and over to the side fence, jumping down onto the fence, holding onto the guttering leaning over the three foot gap before twisting to jump to the ground on the neighbor's side. He grimaced in pain, hissing out a breath as his ribs complained about the movements. He straightened up, leaning on the fence for a second to get his breath back before hurrying out of the neighbor's yard before he was seen and into his car.

He breathed in deeply, still smelling Quinn on himself and smirked as he relaxed his head back and took out his vape.

"Fuck me..." He chuckled. He had never done anything like that before, but he had been so worked up knowing while he was in the hospital getting his ribs and split cheek sorted out she was in the hands of Antonio. Lucky the guy hadn't managed to break his nose, but in the clear light of day his face was a mess.

Not as big of a mess as Quinn's skin was though.

He sighed as his fist clenched around his large vape machine.

And as for the fucker tattooing his name on her fucking skin like she was his fucking slave! That was going to go the second he had Quinn in the clear and away from that psychopath...

He let himself smile.

Hopefully she would be thinking of him for the days she was going to take to heal and not what that fucking Italian bastard did to her.

He was going to pay, but first things first, as much as Reese wanted to just slide a knife between Antonio's ribs and twist it while looking into his eyes while he gasped his final breath, he had to make sure Quinn was going to be safe. He wasn't dealing with a normal Jo Blogs, this was the dangerous Don of the fucking mafia, he had to be diligent if he ever hoped to take that bastard down.

Quinn sat up startled out of her dream by realizing she was asleep within it and jolting awake. Her room was dark with the drapes pulled shut but she knew it was still light outside. She groaned a little at the pain from her back and rolled over onto her stomach. She crawled off the bed seeing her semi naked state and stood up, searching for her phone.

She knew she hadn't dreamed Reese coming into her room and demanding her body come for him...twice. She grabbed the robe off the back of the door and made her way downstairs, grabbing her phone and sending him a message.

Q - ***Why did you leave?***

She crumbled onto a stool at the breakfast counter and buried her face into the crook of her arm. Oh my god...that was...indescribable...and she wanted more. Just the thought of the way his tongue manipulated her body was enough to make her wet again but what he could do with his fingers...he was the devil.

She jumped when her phone pinged and quickly checked the message.

R - **I could no longer trust myself. Hope you have nice dreams about me from now on, babe**

She stared at the message, reading it over and over. Had he done that to make her think of him? Well, congratulations he was the only thing that she was going to think about for days until she could see him again.

34
A pact is made

Reese decided to ride his motorbike to college on Monday, he usually liked to ride it if he knew the weather was going to be good, it was no fun riding in the rain. As it was slowly turning colder it was a risk to take and he would soon be faced with locking his bike away for the winter as he did every year.

He swung his leg over and stood up, pulling his helmet off and placing it on the seat. It was safe there, no one in this college was interested in stealing a bike helmet, especially when they all knew whose bike it was.

He looked up over the grass and saw Vanessa and her crew hanging around the main building. He rolled his eyes...cheerleaders always left him cold, there was something about those fake smiles and the way they always seemed to bounce that just turned him off. Apart from the flexibility he really didn't see anything good in cheerleaders. He knew Vanessa hungered for him, it was like a sport, always evading her interest. One day he was going to have to set her straight, maybe today was the day, that all depended on how she acted and what she said. She was clearly waiting for him.

As he walked closer he noticed Mila wasn't there, good. That girl was a serious pain in the ass, her squeaky voice and bouncing tits, the way she always flicked her bleached hair like she was god's gift to men. He was glad Cory had finally put her in her place, it irked him that the lovable retriever always picked girls like that to fuck, yeah they were easy but easy wasn't always good even in a bind.

Vanessa grinned at him and stepped towards him as he approached. He had to stop himself from rolling his eyes. "Van...are you waiting for me?" He asked in a droll sexy voice.

She scanned his face taking in the cuts and bruises. "What the hell happened to you?"

He chuckled. "Fight...so no wrapping your arms around me, I have cracked ribs."

Her lips pursed and her friends whispered and gasped at his confession. "Oh my god! Are you okay? Is there anything I can do?"

Reese chuffed a little laugh. "No, unless you're secretly a witch and can heal broken bones...but maybe you should go heal the other guy, his face is a lot worse than mine and I doubt he can walk today..."

Her eyes widened and her hand came to her mouth like she was watching a horror movie. "You paralyzed him?"

Reese couldn't help but laugh, swishing his hair from his eyes and licking his lips, making all the girls in front of him swoon and stare fixated on his mouth. "Nah...should have though. So, what do you want, I'm a bit busy this morning..." He had a meeting with Cory.

Vanessa took out her phone and swiped through it then held it up to show him something. He almost didn't want to look, whatever it was, was going to be salacious no doubt, these girls were catty bitches – another reason he didn't like cheerleaders.

He glanced with an uninterested expression at the screen, then frowned to see it was a video. He reached out and hit the play arrow. He squinted at the screen to see Cory and Quinn making out in a movie theater. His jaw clenched tight and so did his hand, right around Vanessa's throat.

She startled and dropped her phone on the grass as Reese pulled her closer to him, squeezing just enough to scare her and control her but not enough to make her choke. His gaze was like molten gold as his bared his teeth at her in a snarl.

"I've warned you before, leave Quinn alone...whatever she's doing is no concern of yours and I don't need you trying to earn brownie points with me that don't fucking exist, got it!"

He threw his arm back, releasing her, making her stumble back with fear in her eyes into her friends as they caught her and stared at him with a mixture of anger and fear.

"I know about the date, I don't care." Especially after having her pussy in my mouth yesterday! He wanted to say.

He stormed off to the admin building and climbed the stairs. He did care, it pissed him off, but after visiting Quinn in her bedroom, he had finally settled on a plan of conquest.

As he entered the Executive room Cory was already waiting for him. Tank and Jacob were there and stood up as he entered.

"Hey Boss, how're you feeling?" Tank asked, scrutinizing Reese's body.

"Bit tender, not too bad..."

"Do you think riding your bike was a good idea with cracked ribs?" Jacob said. "Fuck man, we all know you're tough, no need to prove it."

Reese sucked his teeth and smirked at Jacob's lame attempt to make him laugh, laughing right now hurt. Jacob grinned and waved at Cory.

"Anyway, Curry has an appointment apparently, so we let him in."

"Yeah, he does, thanks...you can go." Reese said it with a distinct lowering of tone.

Jacob and Tank took the hint and made their way to the door, closing it behind them.

Cory had been sitting in a computer chair just watching him, trying to garner his mood. He had messaged to say sorry for turning up to watch the fight and sorry for all the things that transpired there, even though they were nothing to do with him, he felt bad.

Reese glared at him as he took his jacket off and threw it over the back of one of the couches, took his vape out and went to the window. He huffed a long inhale and blew the vapor out before turning back to glare at Cory again.

"Man..." Cory grumbled. "Stop looking at me like that, I'm sorry."

"How many times do I have to fucking say it, Cory...don't be seen with me."

"I'm sorry, Rice, but..."

"No buts, damn it...I don't need you on any of those fuckers radar...and look who was there that night!"

Cory frowned and looked at his feet with a regretful sigh. "Yeah...fucking hell."

"That's exactly what I'm talking about...but, I've called you in here today because I've finally got that information about Quinn and you're going to like it about as much as digging in shit."

Cory's blue ocean gaze came up with an intense fire in them. "I already don't like what I saw on Saturday night..."

"Yeah, I bet after cuddling up to her on Friday...to see that fucker mauling her."

"So what did you find out?"

Reese told Cory all about Quinn being Guinevere O'Malley and how she got sold out by the Boston division of the Mob to try and keep the peace with a psychopath, while pocketing her inheritance.

Cory got up and walked to the window, staring out with a grim expression on his face.

"Can we save her?"

Reese hooked a hand around Cory's neck holding him still as he stared his golden gaze into Cory's blue one, the intensity smoldering.

"W-what are you doing? Why are you so intense all of a sudden?" Cory asked backing up.

Reese stepped closer, both hands coming to cup over Cory's ears making Cory start to fret as he was already backed against the wall now. "Reese, what are you..."

Reese's grip tightened and he pressed his lips to Cory's cutting him off, mushing his lips and licking them. Cory gasped and Reese slid his tongue inside kissing Cory deeply.

Cory gripped Reese's shirt by the shoulders unsure whether to push him away or pull him closer as he groaned out a whimper of reluctance and need. Reese pulled his mouth away and smirked at Cory's challenging expression.

"I want you, Curry...I always have, you know this..."

Cory looked bewildered and a little frightened. "I've told you before I can't bottom for you, Reese." He shoved Reese back but he only moved a step, enough for Cory to be able to get away from the wall and step away from Reese, pacing off raking a hand through his hair, trying to calm his thumping heart.

Reese turned and watched him, a darkness in his eyes. "I'm not asking that of you...I'm asking you to be with me through a three-way relationship with Quinn."

Cory spun around and gaped at him.

"We both really like her, she likes both of us as shown by the way she kisses both of us...and she has the perfect personality for this to work."

"Shit, Reese..." He knew he meant submissive. She would have to be willing to submit to both of their needs and wants for this to work.

"I want both of you." Reese stated. "I feel like I've found my family, my purpose in life and it's always been you but now it's her and everything feels right and in balance."

Cory swallowed hard. How did Reese manage to say all that with a straight face? "You're really serious?"

"Yes."

"You really think this can work this time?"

"Yes."

Cory walked up to Reese and Reese straightened up in anticipation. Cory placed a hand on his chest over his heart feeling his heartbeat was calm and steady. "How can you be so calm about this? My heart is frantic..."

Reese lifted his hand to Cory's chest and pressed it against his heart feeling the thumping. "I'm calm because I know what I want and how to get it."

Cory looked up and met Reese's intense gaze. Reese's hand slipped up Cory's chest and curled around the side of his neck. "I love you, Cory...and I know we've only just met Quinn but I find myself caught up in her so much I believe I love her too. We were meant for this...to protect her from whatever is happening to her right now and to do it together." Reese smirked a sexy little grin at Cory. "My little wolf pack, I want to protect you both."

Cory dipped his head and leaned forward, pressing his forehead to Reese's chest. "You have a way of emasculating me in a way I absolutely love..." Cory breathed in a sigh of surrender. "You're right, we need to help and protect Quinn...I love her too, it's freaking me out!"

Reese pressed his lips to Cory's head but Cory lifted his head to look him in the eye. There was a couple of inches difference in height that Cory always liked when Reese was being all Sigma male to him. Reese exuded this deathly calm possession over him whenever they were around each other...it was partly the reason they had gone their separate ways. He needed to find himself and feel strong and capable and alpha himself. Football had been good for that, hanging with the boys, fucking girls that came to him, in everyone else's eyes he was a strong independent male with a protective aura.

Exactly what he wanted, but to Reese he was always going to be different, the burden of having to be masculine, in control and decisive was deferred. He had a soft spot that melted on contact with Reese, although he wasn't gay the strong affection was closer than brothers. He would always be Reese's golden retriever to his wolf.

He chuckled. "You've always loved using those wolf pack terms...are you sure you're not secretly a werewolf and that's why you're so freakishly strong?"

Reese chuckled and his eyes seemed to sparkle with an amazing golden iridescence. He shrugged in a cocky manner. "Maybe...wouldn't you like a wolf pack with me and our little omega?"

They stared at each other for a long moment then Reese leaned in and pressed his lips chastely to Cory's before pulling back. "I've missed you...come back to me, I can protect you now."

Cory slowly nodded. "I love you too, Reese...let's do this, although I'm not sure how my father is going to react...but I really believe Quinn has brought us together when she could have so easily torn us further apart. I agree, this feels right, let's save her from the mafia and bring her back home."

Reese's grin lit up the entire room as he tugged Cory into his arms and embraced him fiercely.

"Now we just need to convince Quinn..."

35
We're here for you

Quinn knocked on the door to the student executive office with a little trepidation. She really wasn't sure why Reese would send her a slip requiring her to attend a disciplinary meeting. She knew it was probably a farce, but she had been consecutively taking Mondays and Tuesdays off so it could be legit. Regardless she welcomed the opportunity to talk about what happened, especially on Sunday afternoon.

As she opened the door and walked in she saw Reese sitting on a couch with his feet up on a coffee table drinking a can of coffee.

"Nice to see you're punctual." He said with a sultry smirk, his eyes roamed her figure remembering what she tasted like.

She saw the look and instantly felt heat pool deep within. "What's this all about?"

"Sit down...you've got some explaining to do."

"Explaining what?" She asked feeling quite nervous as she sat down on the other couch facing him as Reese dropped his feet to the floor and leaned forward to rest his forearms on his knees, his intense gaze looked serious.

"How about you explain to me how a dead Boston mob boss's daughter is in the hands of the Italian mafia here in New York?"

Quinn's face drained of blood as she started to tremble. "W-what?"

"You heard me Guinevere O'Malley!" He lifted a folder that had been tucked down the side of his couch and tossed it on the table between them. "Your father was Patrick O'Malley, your mother changed your name legally when she married Augusto Ferrante, but not to Ferrante, just enough to hide your connection to the Boston Mob!"

"I..." Quinn stared at the unopened folder. "How do you know this?"

"Do you even know who I am? My father is head of the mob here in New York. I'm to take over when I turn twenty five just like Antonio did."

Quinn just stared at him for a moment, unblinking before lowering her eyes and lifting her hand to her throat. "I think I'm going to be sick...Antonio told me..."

"Quinn, I don't think you understand why you were given over to the Ferrantes...when your mother left you should have been taken from her and given over to the family not given to our enemies to exploit. You were sold out by the guy who now leads the Boston division for his own selfish want and power greedy nature."

Quinn's lip started to quiver.

"Please, Quinn...tell me you're okay? I know you're not, I've seen the things Antonio has done to you, he's warned you off me using pain and fear...I've shown you I want you, but I looked into you...and fuck, baby...Antonio has you as revenge for the death of his mother at the hands of your father...this whole situation is fucked up."

Quinn lifted her gaze to Reese, tears clearly brimming in her pale green eyes and Reese gave her a little reassuring smile. "I can help you."

"Oh God..." Quinn breathed out as a stray tear meandered down her face. "I don't know about any of this. I was twelve, my father was violent and my mother kept trying to leave him from when I was very young then met another man, one she could hide behind when my father tried to come for her and drag her back as he kept doing all those years..." She stopped to breathe in a shaky breath, her eyes lifted to Reese and he saw a dark fire in them. "I was given as a prize?"

His jaw clenched tight as he sat up, raking a hand through his hair. "More like collateral for peace."

"That fucking bastard! He's played me like a toy all along..." She looked mortified and her fists clenched in her lap. She was shaking quite violently now as tears were streaming down her face and she was gasping in short breaths.

Reese stood up and went to the computer desks, grabbing a bottle of water and coming back to sit beside her. He held it out to her after cracking the seal.

"Calm down a bit, baby, it's alright. Sorry, I don't have any tissues...use my sleeve." He pulled his sleeve down over his hand and wiped at her face as she took the water. She pushed him away.

"I can do that..." She used her own sleeves and sniffled.

He tilted around so he was facing her, one arm resting up on the back of the couch. "Quinn, what do you mean used you as a toy? You mean Antonio..." The insinuation in his voice made it crack with bitterness.

She nodded meekly as she sipped her water.

"Fucking hell, I knew something wasn't right in that psycho's head. He's actually a sexual sadist?"

"I crushed hard on him when I first met him and I did, stupidly, for years while we lived in the same house and he came home for weekends and holidays. I was only young and he was like nineteen and so fucking hot...dark eyed and mysterious...full of confidence and swagger..." She cursed. "Ah, that damn swagger..." She looked up from her hands to Reese realizing he had the same cocky swagger about him, was it a gangster thing?

He returned her look with a little grimace. "Don't compare me to that fucking asshole. Did he touch you back then, or is this a recent thing?" He remembered something. "Wait, you said you lost your virginity at fifteen and you've only been with one guy."

She looked away, ashamed now.

"That piece of shit." Reese felt his anger starting to rise and swallowed it down. Quinn didn't need his anger right now frightening her anymore. "Sorry..."

"That's okay...I'm feeling like an absolute fool, to be honest I have been for a little while now...its humiliating to admit."

"Why's that?"

She sighed and closed her eyes, collecting her thoughts. Reese thought she looked so beautiful and raw in that moment, he was feeling quite charmed that she had decided to finally open up to him and share her story. He sat quiet and let her talk all the time she needed.

She started picking at the label on the water bottle and he couldn't help but smile to himself at the secret myth of saying about a person doing that was sexually frustrated.

"I thought he loved me like I loved him, but lately his true colors have been showing. He really did a number on me...for years, I stayed faithful to him when he was away at college – this college! Every time he came home he showed more and more affection, more control, he got more demanding and obsessive...I just thought it was his way of showing love, he's a dangerous man I know that, I know what he is, what he does..."

Reese covered his face to hide his expression.

"But lately..." She paused and took a sip of water. "I'm so scared of him. I know he doesn't care for me...he says I'm his property and will do whatever he orders me to do...it terrifies me what he's going to tell me to do next..."

Reese's jaw was ticking, he had seen the tattoo of that fuckers name on her skin. He saw her thighs clench together and he had to stand up and walk away to look out the window and calm down. What the hell had he been forcing her to do?

"Reese?" She asked in such a small vulnerable voice it literally broke his heart. He turned back and leaned on the windowsill, raking a hand through his hair and fixing her with those amazing golden hazel eyes.

"Sorry...I just had to calm down for a minute."

She smiled at him and he knew right then he would do anything to free her from that Italian psycho.

The door opened and Cory stepped a foot in, looking in apprehensively seeing Reese. Quinn startled and curled up into the couch in fear at the intrusion.

Cory shut the door and looked from Reese to Quinn seeing her fear reaction. "What...you started without me?" He rushed over to Quinn.

"Are you okay, beautiful? Ah, shit...were you right about everything, Reese?"

"Yeah..." Reese said solemnly, glad to have Cory finally here.

Cory grabbed Quinn by the shoulders as he sat down facing her. "Oh my God, I'm so, so sorry." He pulled her into his chest and hugged her strongly. "Don't you worry, sweet girl, we'll sort this out...Reese and I, together."

Quinn felt like her heart was going to burst and she sobbed into his chest as she reached out and clung to him. How could he have possibly turned up right at the moment she needed his amazing protective hugs. He rested his head on top of hers and stroked her hair. He looked up at Reese and saw the dark heated gaze as he watched their natural interaction. He motioned with his eyes to the space on the couch behind Quinn.

Reese stood up and came over, coming in behind her and hugging her from behind. They both heard her gasp and then breathe out in a slow sublime little groan as she melted between them.

Reese kissed her shoulder. "Never fear again...we're here for you, baby."

Quinn stuck her head up and looked over her shoulder at Reese. "I'm so scared of what he might do."

Reese cradled her head and pulled it back to his chest, tucking her under his chin.

"You mean hurt you?" Cory asked, rubbing her arms down to her hands and entwining their fingers. She seemed to hide her face under Reese's hand, burrowing into his arm pit and shook her head. "I'm scared he's going to make me sleep with other people."

"What the actual fuck?" Cory exclaimed.

Reese was scrunching his face up, his teeth grit together so hard his jaw started to ache and a low growl of anger came from his throat, but he couldn't speak for a moment until he managed to calm down a bit.

"I'm going to fucking kill him." He finally managed to hiss out.

Quinn's head snapped up and she looked at him with horror. "No!" She scrambled and struggled out from between them and stood up, confronting the two of them as they looked up startled. "That makes you no better than him!"

She looked at Cory then at Reese and realized the connection. Childhood friends...that meant that Cory's father must be corrupt.

"How do I know you guys aren't exactly the same?"

Reese clucked his tongue while Cory held his hands out in protest. "Whoa, I assure you we are not."

Quinn gave Cory a flat stare. "You maybe...you're going to be a lawyer and a judge..." A lightbulb went off in her head and she backed up, her hand coming to her mouth. "Oh my God! You're becoming a judge to work for the mob?"

"You need to lower your damn voice!" Cory huffed, standing up.

Reese laughed, leaning back in the couch and resting his arms up along the back of it. "Wow, smart girl, but that doesn't mean we are anything like that shit, Antonio Ferrante or any of those mafia bastards."

"You're still criminals, hiding your illegal dealings in the guise of legitimate businesses..."

Reese clucked his tongue, they were getting off topic. "And what's the reason for you doing a business degree?"

That made her take pause.

She sat down in a nearby chair looking pale and fragile. "It was to get out on my own after mom died, I thought Augusto didn't want me in his house any longer so I planned to go to Tuck School of Business in Hanover but..." She looked up, rubbing a palm with the thumb of her other hand and gave a little awkward laugh. "Sorry...you don't want to hear..."

"Yes, we do." Cory interrupted. "When did your mom pass?" He perched on the arm of the couch right in front of her chair.

Reese gave her a little encouraging nod. He couldn't be warm and empathetic as Cory could be but he could be a rock to stand behind. He frowned and glanced at Cory, they made a good team.

"Back in April...I barely made it through exams and graduation with mom being sick so I was glad I managed to pull through with a 5.0."

"What the hell? You're smart!" Cory exclaimed.

Reese glowered at her as she beamed a smile at Cory's compliment. She had allowed herself to get entangled with a psychopath for his sick entertainment, she may be book smart but she was not world smart.

"Can I ask what she died of?" Reese asked.

Quinn met his eyes and he felt like she was looking into his soul. "Cancer...but it was quick, she was gone within three months of her diagnosis."

"And that's when all this with Antonio started?"

Quinn nodded, looking uncomfortable again. "We were always casual but serious at the same time...it's hard to explain, but he had rules...and he was the one who made sure I was sent to an all girl's catholic school...he was gone from the house most of the time for college so we only saw each other every couple of months...it was always nice to see him, but he was always quite dark and broody."

"And now?"

"He says I belong to him...and he takes care of everything for me, he sends food, clothes, pays all my bills, the car, the house..."

"Don't make excuses for him! He's turned you into a compliant little submissive slave, he feels nothing for you beyond his obligations and his own gratifications!" Reese growled through his clenched teeth. "He put his fucking name on you like you're his property for fuck's sake!"

36

We're a throuple, baby

"Hey, take it easy..." Cory whispered to him as Quinn ducked her head, ashamed.

"I know that now, but now he's escalated I'm scared of him and he knows it..."

"Well, we're here now." Reese said firmly.

Quinn's eyes brimmed with tears again as she clutched the sleeves of her hoodie in her hands. That motion caught Reese's attention and he frowned.

"Show Cory your wrists...in fact, take your sweatshirt off." He ordered in a growl.

Quinn baulked and gave him a startled gape.

"Can you be any more scary right now, Rice! Fuck's sake..." Cory hit out at him.

Reese grit his teeth making his jaw flex. "I don't mean to be...babe, please show us...Cory needs to see."

Quinn swallowed hard and then slowly stood up, pulling her sweatshirt off over her head and clutching it to her chest as she turned around to face away from them and pulled her hair over her shoulder. She then pulled the back of her t-shirt up enough to show the remains of the welts and bruising still on her skin from four days ago. She turned back as Cory gasped in shock and Reese growled. "Stand still."

She froze as Cory glanced at Reese to see what his problem was this time. Reese's eyes seemed to almost glow. "Show him that." He pointed at her lower stomach.

Quinn swallowed hard and lifted the front of her shirt and tugged her jeans down slightly to show Cory the tattooed name of Antonio Ferrante blazed across her skin like he had been signing an autograph, she quickly righted her clothes and sat down. His eyes dropped to her wrists and he let out a low whistle under his breath. "Fucking hell..."

Reese merely stared at them then lifted his gaze to Quinn's as she sat there looking vulnerable and ashamed.

"I want you to go home with Cory tonight to his place, show his father and tell him everything about your abuse...just don't tell him who you are...he doesn't need to know that part, just that you need a safe place to hide for the moment while you get your head sorted."

"No, he won't know if I don't use Quinn's name...but he may figure it out on his own, I was talking about the Ferrante's only a couple of weeks ago..."

"Go home with Cory? But why not you?" She asked confused.

Reese gave her a little smile, pleased she wanted to stay with him. He was the one who could protect her from the dark evil, but not out in the open.

"Don't worry babe...I'll look after everything, I just need you to hide out with Cory while I do...I can't afford to start a blood war between us and the Italians, so I can't be seen as the one who has taken you."

He looked at Cory who was staring at him with respect and awe. Cory knew Reese wanted Quinn by his side and still he gave her up to him to hide and look after and be close to at night.

"I need to sort a lot of things out very carefully so I'm counting on you to convince your father it's in his best interest to keep this girl in his house under his protection for as long as possible, whether he knows who she is or not. Antonio won't make a move to get her back from you straight away, he'll sit in the knowledge he's done a fine job of fucking her up mentally enough that she goes back to him on her own. He'll only start to really look for her after about two weeks I would guess..."

Quinn chewed her lip at those harsh words, but it was true...she didn't know if it was Stockholm Syndrome or what but she was already thinking that exact thing to save these guys from the trouble she was causing them.

Cory nodded in understanding. "The opposite if you took her...I get it. He's got no reason to look in my direction."

Reese chuckled. "Yeah, he wouldn't hesitate to start a war with me or my father..." He glanced at Quinn. "...especially over you – you're practically his Irish Mob pet. The significance of your bloodline means a lot."

She frowned at him, meeting his gaze. "Y-you want me to do this today?"

"Yeah...you and me, you alright with that, bunny?" Cory grinned at her.

"I need to go home and get some of my stuff." She looked worried.

"Might be too risky..." Cory said, looking at Reese with a sly grin and clicking his fingers. "Reese will buy anything you need, replace everything...I'll take you shopping."

Reese grumbled causing Quinn to giggle a little and he took out his card with a sexy grin at her. "Does the thought of spending my money cheer you up?"

Quinn's face fell into a mortified expression. "No..."

"I was joking..." Reese said quickly as Cory clucked his tongue and gave him a glare. "Spend as much as you need to but there's one condition..."

Quinn's eyes rounded.

"You need to keep making that noise and smile more..." His eyes smoldered into a heated stare.

Quinn looked relieved and looked away with a shy blush, tucking some hair behind her ear. "Oh...I'll try...thank you, I don't know what to say to you both."

"Nothing." Cory smiled.

"Absolutely nothing, babe." Reese confirmed, holding out the card to Cory.

Cory snatched it up and put it in his pocket.

"Lose the phone and laptop too...tell no one about any of this. You're going to have to stop coming to college for a while, I'll speak to the Dean. Don't you worry, I'm sure you can do the work remotely for a while."

Quinn's gaze had dropped to her hands again, she was feeling so many emotions swirling right now mainly about these two guys banding together to help her, they were both so amazing to want to do that despite their separate affections for her, it felt a little awkward. "You guys realize this is just going to make things extremely complicated between me and choosing one of you?"

"Forget that...we have." Cory beamed a roguish grin at her, his eyes twinkling with promise as he swung his head to look at Reese.

Quinn frowned at the strange look and followed his gaze to find Reese smirking at her. He licked over his teeth in that sexy way of his. "Actually, we've decided to stop working against each other and ruining our friendship over you."

"Good to hear..." Quinn drawled out, she got the feeling there was a huge but coming.

"Yeah, from now on we're going to work together on that front too."

"Huh?" Quinn frowned, looking from one to the other and seeing both of their expressions take a turn to the dark side.

"Neither of us want you with anyone else, so we've agreed to share and go after you together as a united front." Reese's smirk was smug and Cory grinned like a loon.

Quinn's face deadpanned and she said nothing, just stared at them. Her body however was doing several strange things all at once, her heart was hammering in her chest, her blood was suddenly hot and her pussy was literally throbbing as she sized up the two of them. What did they mean share her exactly?

"So...what do you reckon, babe? Think you can handle us together?"

Her mouth went dry at the dirty thought that statement provoked. "I reckon that's got to be the most ridiculous thing I've ever heard?" She gasped out like she was begging for water in the desert. She saw Cory's eyes drop to her chest and she knew, by the tightness her body was suddenly feeling that her nipples had gone hard. She covered them with her sweatshirt still in her hands.

Reese chuckled that damn sexy little condescending laugh that made her literally gush. "You sure about that?"

"You're both insane." She breathed, looking at them like wolves surrounding a hare. She understood the bunny reference now.

Reese looked away, running a thumb over his bottom lip. "Yeah...maybe, but it will work. Anyway let's focus on getting you away from that psycho before he decides to sell you out to the highest bidder."

"Reese!" Cory coughed.

Quinn's bottom lip was quivering now. "He wouldn't actually do that..." She said but her words were hollow.

Cory was looking at Reese telling him with his eyes to shut up. Reese rolled his eyes and sighed, looking away darkly. He stood up and went to stand at the window.

Quinn was chewing on her bottom lip and wringing her hands. "I don't know if I can do this, it puts you guys in so much danger..."

Reese came over and crouched down in front of her chair. "I know your nervous, Quinn, but how much are you going to put up with before you're in a situation that you really can't get out of...fuck, baby, I'm scared for you." Reese said, a hoarseness coming into his voice as he stared up at her and her eyes locked to his, quavering with those unshed tears and apprehension. "I don't think you realize the danger you're in if he decides to cross anymore depraved lines."

He reached up and cupped her cheek, his thumb rubbing tears from under her eye. "You can do this, babe...and you need to do this now."

She nodded slowly, leaning her head slightly into his hand and pressed her hand over his, nuzzling it. Her eyes seemed to suddenly sparkle with need and she licked her lips. The touch of Reese's warmth triggering the memory of Sunday and what he had done with that tongue that licked his teeth just now.

Reese's gaze darkened and intensified immediately. "Quinn..." His voice dropped and Cory stiffened to hear it. "If you do that..."

"What?" She gave a cute little frown and held his hand from moving away. She ran her hand up to his wrist and let her fingers dance over his forearm.

"I need to kiss you." He growled out.

She dropped her hand to his chest. "Okay..."

Reese's hand ran to the back of her head as he leaned up on his knees, pushing between her thighs and their lips pressed together. His fingers gripped firmly to the back of her skull as he felt her mouth open for him and his tongue dipped inside. She gave a breathy little moan, grabbed a fistful of his shirt and pulled him closer.

Cory's face darkened as he watched them making out, slow and sensual, Quinn melting under Reese's expert touch. He saw Reese reach a hand out behind himself and grab at his knee, fisting his sweatpants and tugging for him to join them.

Cory dropped to his knees beside Reese and Reese pulled his head back from Quinn's dazed face, still holding her by the base of her skull he turned her face towards Cory and lifted his other hand to the back of Cory's neck and pulled him down. Quinn blinked and saw Cory leaning in and smiled, kissing him willingly. Reese let them go and stood up, looking down at them with a dark gaze of approval.

"Fuck..." He growled out. This is going to work.

Cory kissed Quinn for a full minute enjoying her taste before finally and regretfully pulling back. Quinn looked flushed and dazed and beautiful as Cory stood up next to Reese and they both looked down at her. Reese suddenly hooked an arm around Cory's neck and kissed him full on the lips.

Quinn blinked, surprised and covered her mouth as Reese licked across Cory's lips seductively and Cory opened his mouth to him. Quinn squeaked out an excited little startle, surprised at the jolting throb she felt in her clit at the sight of the two glorious men making out right in front of her.

"Oh my God! You are a couple!"

Reese broke off the kiss and grinned at her like a predatory beast. "No, we are a throuple, baby." The intense sexy look in his eyes was enough to convince her that was exactly what she wanted.

She smiled up at him as he put his hands on the arms of her chair and leaned in. He stopped only a couple of inches from her face.

"Are we on the same page now, princess?"

She glanced up at Cory looking at her expectantly then looked back at Reese. "Can I think about this?"

"Sure...all the while you're hiding out at Cory's you think about it...no one is going to do anything you don't want...and Cory will not touch you without me."

She glanced back up at Cory and he smiled at her a little tensely like he was obeying some agreement.

"You've discussed how this is going to work?"

Reese shrugged a sexy nonchalant little jerk of the shoulders and came in and kissed her lips softly. He pulled back, lifting a hand to her chin and pinching it playfully as he stood up. "We'll work it out together...when you're ready."

He turned with a deep seated regret and walked off to the window, taking his vape off the sill and looking out as he huffed on it to calm himself down before he literally came in his jeans. This had gone better than he had hoped.

"Get going...leave campus separately." He ordered, clear and concise. "I'll be in touch later."

Cory helped Quinn up and she slipped her sweatshirt back on before Cory took her hand in his and kissed her forehead. "You ready, bunny?"

She gave a nervous little nod of her head. "I think so..."

Reese turned back and lifted his hand to her. She stepped towards him taking his hand and let him pull her in close. Cory didn't let go of her other hand and came with her to press to her back as Reese kissed her forehead too.

"I'm gonna miss you, babe...I'll come see you when I can."

She nodded and licked her lips.

He chuckled and pressed a finger to her lips. "Stop...I'm warning you."

Cory breathed on her neck, moving her hair off and kissing her behind her ear. "Maybe we need to just do this...we're all horny as fuck right now."

Reese growled. "Shut up, fuck boy!"

Quinn startled at Cory's words and turned to scowl at him. Reese chuckled and pulled her face back to look at him. "Now you know what

I mean, he's under strict orders not to do anything inappropriate while you're in his house."

Quinn smiled as Cory clucked his tongue.

"Go...for fuck's sake..." Reese grumbled, covering his eyes from her smile.

"Right, enough!" Cory yanked her away from Reese and to the door. "I'll behave like a good dog...you go be the wolf!"

Reese chuckled and shook his head. "Aye, aye..."

37

From an abusive home

Cory stopped at the mall and they ran in for some quick supplies. Quinn wasn't interested in spending Reese's money or buying fashionable brands so she just grabbed the real basic necessities to see her through the next couple of days; underwear, jeans, t-shirt, sweatshirt, toiletries and a cute pair of shorty pajamas.

It took them two hours and Cory bought them some burgers and fries from the food court before heading home.

As they drove up to the security gate he punched in the access code, waved at the guard and drove through into the private gated community.

Quinn gaped at the huge and lovely homes with their immaculate front lawns. "Wow, is this really where you live?"

Cory grinned. "Yeah, why? The real flash homes are the ones further back...they have like an acre of land around them and are eight to ten bedrooms, swimming pool...I'll take you for a wander around later, we're safe within here."

"We could do a jog?"

"Do you run? Awesome, yeah, we'll do that." He gave her a boyish grin as he turned around a roundabout where a children's playground was, the trees surrounding it laced with fairy lights. Quinn thought the whole place looked idyllic to live in, but expensive, but then Cory's parents would be on good money.

Cory pulled up the driveway and Quinn leaned forward to look up at the two storey brick and tile house. "This is your place?"

He chuckled. "Yep, sure is...see, just a normal four bedroom home. What?" He asked at her twisted expression.

"No, nothing...it's a nice place." Far from normal, but very nice.

As they got out Cory gathered up the shopping bags refusing Quinn's help and moved to the front door. Quinn apprehensively followed feeling a tight knot of anxiety building in the pit of her stomach.

"Have you actually told your parents anything about me coming?"

He looked back as he dropped the shopping bags and dug into his pocket for his keys and unlocked the door. "Nah...it'll be fine."

He stepped in and checked the alarm, it wasn't beeping so that meant someone was home. Quinn picked the bags up off the porch and stepped into the foyer. The front door had a lovely stained glass insert and glass down either side of it with urns on the floor containing long wispy grasses and purple flowers. There was a large oak hall table to one side and coat hooks on the other. Cory kicked his sneakers off and shoved them over underneath the table where a line of shoes were and Quinn quickly did the same.

He closed the front door, flicking the lock shut and took the bags off her, stepping through to the large main living area and towards the stairs. Quinn could see a back yard through large patio doors beyond the cream colored room with grey carpet, accented with light blue and burnt orange. Quinn thought the place looked like it had been decorated by a professional and that made her even more nervous about touching anything.

"Let's get you set up in a spare room upstairs then I'll see if it's Dad or Wendy that's home."

"Wendy? You don't call her mom?" Quinn asked a little surprised.

"I do when I want something." Cory beamed a roguish smile completely unashamed. "She's actually my step-mom."

"Oh, okay..."

They reached the landing and Cory pointed up to the end of the hall in one direction. "That's my parent's room...my room is this way at the other end of the house so I'll put you in the room next to mine, okay?"

She nodded, feeling awkward in this new environment. Cory opened the door to a room and walked in, putting the bags down on the double bed that was in there.

The room was painted in a lovely calming sage green with a white bed and white bedroom suite.

"It's lovely." She breathed, barely audible. There was a couple of blankets folded up on the end of the bed but it was bare, the mattress showing it was fairly new.

Cory saw her falter a little and stepped to her, gathered her in his arms, leaning his head down on hers and closed his eyes. She clung to his shirt, pressing tight into his body and let out a shuddering breath, calming and relaxing against him.

"If you're not okay say so, Quinn...you're trembling."

"I'm okay, really...I'm just a little anxious." She lifted her head and Cory looked down on her with a reassuring smile but he could see panic in her eyes. "Antonio will be realizing I haven't gone home by now."

His eyes widened a little as he realized what was causing her anxiety and he hugged her tighter. "Oh, bunny..." He breathed. "Don't panic, there's nothing he can do."

"Cory! Is that you home, dear?" A female voice called out.

"That's mom, do you want to wait here or come straight down?"

Quinn stepped back and tidied herself up, brushing her hair back from her face and tucking her hands into her sleeves. "I would rather introduce myself."

Cory chuckled, reaching out and giving Quinn's chin a playful little pinch. "There's that strong girl." He took her hand and led her out of the room. "Come on, she's a hardball in court but Wendy is actually really nice."

Cory led Quinn down, through the living area and into the kitchen. She saw a middle aged woman in a classy suit with a sharp blond bob and glasses. She was immaculate, except she had a glass of wine in one hand

and a packet of cigarettes in the other as she was walking back to where the kitchen had a sliding door that led outside to the back patio garden.

She froze in surprise as Cory commented dryly. "Tough day?"

"Oh! Yes, rather...I didn't realize you had company..." She put her cigarettes and glass down and stepped over, extending her hand. "Hello, I'm Wendy."

"Quinn, nice to meet you." She shook hands with a nervous smile.

Cory put his arm around Quinn's shoulders and gave Wendy a serious look. "Quinn needs our help, mom. She needs to stay here for a while, please?"

Wendy looked put on the spot and Quinn's stomach knot tightened. "Oh? What's the problem, is it serious?"

Quinn chewed her bottom lip and practically flinched into Cory's side as his father strode into the room completely oblivious of the situation, briefcase in hand like he had just come in the door.

"Ah-ha! Caught you sneaking out for a cigarette, eh!?" His voice boomed out and he laughed.

He stopped as he realized there was an extra person in the room as Wendy screwed her face up at him and rolled her eyes. "Michael! We have a guest."

"Sorry...I didn't realize, are you Cory's newest girlfriend?" He said it as a dig at Cory who clucked his tongue.

"No, actually, Dad...she's just a friend and needs our help."

"What sort of help?" He came up and gave Quinn the once over with his policeman's gaze, noting the oversized sweatshirt, flighty expression and the way she was being sheltered by Cory's arm. He held his hand out to Quinn. "I'm Michael, how can we help you little lady?"

"I'm Quinn..." She said extending her hand to shake his being careful to not pull her sleeve back.

"Quinn, nice name. So you go to college with our boy?"

"Yes, Sir." Quinn's response was automatic.

Michael grinned at the polite, respectful address. "A girl with manners..."

She blushed and smiled at him as Cory sucked his teeth and glared at his father for daring to give this girl shit.

"And you're in trouble?" Michael said bluntly.

Wendy picked up her glass and leaned her hip on the kitchen counter listening intently, thinking what a beautiful girl this Quinn was, the color of her hair was amazing and it was so long...she was a little envious.

"Yes, Sir." Quinn replied meekly.

"She's being abused by her step-brother." Cory grunted out, grabbing Quinn's arm and pulling her sleeve back. "I've convinced her to come stay here for a while until we can sort something out."

Quinn yanked her arm back and fearfully covered up again, glancing up at Michael to see his scathing look. He narrowed his eyes as Wendy exclaimed in shock covering her mouth.

"Oh, you poor dear, of course you can stay."

Quinn gave her a little smile. "Thank you, I really appreciate it."

Cory and Michael were looking at each other and Quinn could see Michael had a lot of questions.

"Wendy, how about you order in something for dinner while I go have a chat with Quinn and Cory in my study."

"We've already eaten." Cory said. "And not sure what else you need to know, dad...just drop it you're making Quinn uncomfortable, can't you see she's shaking?"

"Are you planning on pressing charges?" Wendy asked.

Quinn baulked and went pale. "No...oh, god...no."

Wendy and Michael looked at each other for a moment with matching frowns. "Okay...we'll discuss it later, but we do need to discuss this, you understand this, don't you, Quinn?"

"Yes, sir...I understand."

"I've put her things in the spare room next to mine..." Cory said, looking over at Wendy. "Can we get some sheets and stuff for the bed?"

"Of course, dear..." Wendy made her way out of the kitchen.

Cory grabbed Quinn's hand and walked her out of the room. "Let's go..."

Michael watched them leave and let out a heavy sigh. "What have you got yourself caught up in, son?"

38

Can't escape the PTSD

Wendy handed Quinn a pile of sheets from the cupboard in the hall. "Are you sure? I can very easily do it."

"No, thank you...I'm perfectly capable of making a bed up for myself, you've done enough just letting me stay."

Wendy gave her a smile and looked at Cory who was leaning on the hall wall, watching with a little loving smile on his lips. As Quinn turned and walked into the bedroom Wendy mouthed to Cory 'She's so cute!' and made a little squishy face as she held her fists up under her chin.

Cory laughed and walked past his step-mother, placing a hand on her shoulder. "Calm down..." He walked into the guest room and closed the door.

He leaned his back on it and let out a sigh, shaking his head. Quinn was just throwing the bottom sheet out over the bed, she looked up with a frown.

"What's wrong?"

His lip curled up. "Nothing...Wendy thinks you're cute."

Quinn startled. "Oh!" She looked away as a little blush crept over her face and she tucked a stray lock of hair behind her ear.

Cory chuckled and walked forward coming up the other side of the bed to help tuck the sheet over the corners. "You are, she's not wrong."

Quinn gave a little giggle. "I suppose it's good that she likes me at least since I'm invading her home."

Cory looked up and saw Quinn's voice didn't match her facial expression, she looked sad. He moved round the bed and swamped her into his arms. "Bunny, what's wrong? Jesus, you're killing me here..."

"Sorry..." Quinn sobbed out, pressing her face into his chest. "I'm just on edge."

"Should I ask Wendy for something to help you sleep?"

Quinn nodded against him. "Could you?" She looked up and pushed away from him, hugging her arms around herself and sitting down on the bed. "I need to stop my mind from working...it just keeps running all these horrible scenes through of what could happen..."

Cory sat down next to her and put his arm around her. "Alright...shit, I didn't realize it was that bad...do you seriously suffer from anxiety?"

She nodded, chewing her lip. "Living with Augusto was bad enough having to keep quiet and never be seen by him...but my father was abusive, I remember the nights he came home drunk and I would hide under my bed while my mom screamed and cried as he hit her around and raped her..."

"Fucking hell..." Cory whispered as Quinn continued.

"But living with Antonio breathing down my neck, tracking my movements forcing me to go to him every weekend just to be..." Her breath caught in her throat and she looked up at Cory like a deer in headlights.

His jaw was flexing as he ground his teeth, he had dropped forward, leaning his forearms on his knees, his head down and shoulders hunched, his legs were bouncing with his agitation.

He looked up when she stopped talking and she saw the dark hatred in his eyes. "I fucking hate the fact that dick is so untouchable, I want to just punch the fuck out of his face until its so smashed in he can't breath and chokes to death."

Quinn paled and backed away from Cory as he suddenly stood up. "I'll be right back, bunny."

He left the room and Quinn let out the breath she had been holding. She dropped off the bed and curled up on the floor beside it, pulled the sheet down off the bed and hid underneath it.

She wasn't frightened of him, but the feelings of anxiety she felt for what could be happening out there in the world because of her just wouldn't stop gnawing away at her.

She knew that Antonio would hurt someone tonight because of her, possibly even kill them.

Cory pulled his phone out as he stepped into his own room and rang Reese.

"What's wrong?" Was the immediate answer.

"Did you know how fucking damaged Quinn actually is?" Cory blasted down the phone. "She's in full anxiety meltdown right now over what she thinks that fucker is going to do because...fuck...he's already tortured her for absolutely no reason! Her father beat her mom up in front of her while she hid under the bed and that fucking Augusto made her be small and invisible just to survive in his household! She needs professional help!"

"Where is she now?"

"In the room next to mine."

"You left her alone with all that going on?"

Cory heard the accusation growl to Reese's voice and gripped his phone hard. "I had to leave before I paid into that fear and anxiety and punched the fucking wall!"

"You need to calm the fuck down and take control of your own emotions for her sake, Cory, that's the reason she's with you...I can't do it, but you have to."

Cory grit his teeth. "Fuck, Rice...you're a real asshole." Cory's shoulders slumped and he dropped his face into his hand.

"You're the one, Cory...be the golden retriever, it's what she needs..."

"I can't..." Cory breathed out, his breaking voice conveying his heartbreak.

"You have to!" Reese yelled through the phone. "Pull yourself together, man! Swallow your own feelings and go be there for her! Don't leave her all alone in that room in a house she's never been in before...fuck!"

Cory lifted his head, his jaw set in determination. "Your right...okay...thanks Rice." He hung up and barreled out of his room, running down the stairs and to the living room where Wendy was watching the news.

"Mom! Have you got any benzos?"

Wendy looked at him with a small frown. "I beg your pardon?"

Cory gave her a snort. "Come on, every middle aged woman in America has a stash of them, don't they?"

Wendy folded her arms and gave him a haughty glare. "Excuse me! I am deeply offended by that statement...what do you want them for?"

"Quinn, she's upstairs in full meltdown...she suffers from anxiety thanks to everyone she's ever been raised by..." Wendy gave a little hiccup of a startle at just how bad this girl's life is. "...she needs something to help stop her brain so she can sleep...come on, you must have something...?"

Wendy nodded, getting up and walked off. "I do, it's not as strong as Valium, I hate that stuff, but it should help take the edge off..." Cory raced into the kitchen and grabbed a bottle of water then followed her up the stairs and into the master bedroom. He waited as she went into the bathroom and came back with a little white bottle. "Here, make sure she doesn't take more than one...if she's feeling like that she might..."

"She's not going to try and unalive herself..."

Wendy gave Cory the bottle with a little concerned pout. "She may need to seek proper help if she has been abused that badly."

Cory looked up at Wendy's concern and half-smiled. "Yeah, I think so too, but one step at a time."

"Are you sure you want to get involved in this...I've seen it many times in my line of work and it can get pretty messy getting involved."

Cory frowned darkly at her. "What do you suggest I do then?" His voice was like gravel and Wendy blinked at him.

He turned and stalked from the room making his way back to Quinn's room and opened the door. He paused as he didn't see her anywhere. "Quinn?"

He went to check if she was in the bathroom across the hall and came back. "Quinn?"

He remembered what she said about hiding under the bed and dropped his gaze. The bed wasn't high enough to get under. He put the bottles down and walked around the bed to the side that was next to the window, it was only a gap of two feet, enough to fit the side table.

As he came around he felt his heart constrict to see a tiny little lump on the floor covered in the sheet she had been putting on the bed looking like a mummy. She was curled up so tight in a ball she looked like a small child.

"Ah, fuck, Quinn...I'm sorry, I shouldn't have left..."

He dropped to his knees then to the floor between her back and the bed, grabbing her into his arms and pulling her tight against him, spooning around her protectively. She flinched and startled like she wasn't even aware he had been there and talking to her.

"Shush, it's okay, bunny...I won't leave again...I'm sorry."

He heard her whimper and curl up tighter. He wasn't sure what to do...so he just held her, silently.

He held her like that for ten minutes and his phone chirped in his pocket and vibrated between them. He felt Quinn flinch and stir.

"Shit, sorry, Bunny." He tucked his hand down between them to retrieve his phone. "It's probably Reese."

He was surprised when she lifted her head and pulled the sheet back to peek out, looking back at him over her shoulder. He gave her a huge smile. "Hey there." He cooed at her in a breathy tone. Her eyes looked huge, like one of those bush baby animals as she had the sheet over her head like a cowl.

"Is he checking up on me?" She asked in barely a whisper.

"Of course he is..."

"Did you tell him?" The little frown that crossed her face at him made Cory's heart melt, fuck she was adorable.

"Of course I did..."

"Is that where you went..." She turned back and dropped into a ball again, but didn't cover her face.

"Hey...I got some pills from mom...do you want them?"

She barely nodded her head.

"Okay...can I pick you up? Put you on the bed?"

"I haven't made it yet..." She murmured back, muffled by her position.

"You're already in the sheet...let me lift you up..."

When she said nothing he got on his knees and slowly scooped his hands under her and lifted her up. He stood up and walked around to the other side of the bed and sat down, dropping her onto his lap. She looked up at him, that little frown back on her face. He smiled at her and brushed some hair from her face. "Here, take one of these..." He reached out and grabbed the pills and the bottle of water. He opened the pill bottle once he had placed the water in her hand and dropped two into her hand. "Mom says to only take one, but she also said these aren't as strong as Valium, so..."

As he dropped the two pills into Quinn's hand she looked at them, nodding. He took the water back and cracked it open then handed it back. Quinn tossed the pills into her mouth and drank some water back. He took the water bottle back and placed everything back on the side table.

"Good girl...can you wait while I make the bed?"

She dropped her head into his chest and shook it. "Don't leave me..."

He curled his arms around her and nodded into her hair. "Okay, bunny..." He stood up, grabbed the large blanket that was on the floor and knelt onto the bed, crawling up with Quinn in his arms so he could lay down with her beside him and then arranged the blanket over them and lay down. Quinn nestled into him and he covered her with the blanket completely.

He took his phone up from where he had tossed it up by the pillows and opened the message from Reese asking how it was going.

He answered truthfully.

C - **Rough, mate...fucking rough...settled now but clinging to me like a koala bear**

R - ***Good, she needs you. Talk tomorrow***

Cory sighed and closed his eyes. As good as she felt curled up into his body he really didn't know if he really had the strength for this. He wanted to caress her, love her, kiss her...fuck her.

How fucking selfish of me!

Antonio was raging, pacing his apartment like a lion in a cage ready to kill the first person he saw. Quinn had not appeared at her scheduled time at home and was now over four hours late. It was dark and she wasn't answering her phone.

Matteo had the laptop open on the kitchen counter and was looking back through the security footage of Quinn's house over the last few hours while they waited for their men to reach the townhouse in real time and search through it. Although he had told Quinn footage wasn't recorded it was but every twenty four hours it was over written.

"She never came home from college today, there's no sign of her after she left this morning. Her car is showing as still in the carpark and her laptop and phone are completely switched off."

Antonio growled, taking his phone out of his pocket and glaring at it, he had already tried her number over a hundred times and like every other time it went straight to answer phone. He gripped his phone as he growled and then threw it against the wall, smashing it.

"That fucking little bitch! Where the hell could she be?"

"You don't think something has actually happened to her, do you?"

"Like what?" Antonio's dark gaze slid to him and Matteo grit his teeth over the murderous look.

"Kidnapped?"

Antonio's jaw flexed and clenched under the strain of his rage. "Get the fucking dean of that damn faculty on the phone, I want the footage from the campus cameras. I'll find out who she went with...and if it's that fucking little Irish prick I'll kill him!"

"You really think she's that stupid after last week?" Matteo asked dubiously.

Antonio stared out the windows at the Manhattan nightscape. "She better hope not."

"Look, maybe she's with some girls and her phone is flat...let's just try to relax, she's in college now these things happen..."

"Not her, she's careful not to incite my rage..."

Matteo rubbed his jaw. "Mistakes can happen."

Antonio rounded on him. "Why the fuck are you defending her?" His gaze settled on Matteo like a cobra. "I said I would let you fuck her in the ass next time she failed me, I thought you would be acting more thrilled."

Matteo chuckled, looking back at the laptop as he saw their men arrive and enter the home. "You would think so, huh."

Antonio drifted over and watched the live camera feed as the men searched the home finding nothing.

He huffed and rubbed his eyes.

Matteo moved to the side and grabbed two glasses and the scotch, pouring it out and handing Antonio one. "You look exhausted, boss, get some rest and let me deal with this as much as we can tonight."

"Hmm..." Antonio grunted. "I have a really bad feeling about this...ever since finding out that O'Shea bastard knew her. If he finds out exactly who she is and what transpired back then we could be in for a war if he wants to make a scene about it."

Matteo was swirling his drink around his glass and sculled it back. "He's not the boss yet...his father won't let anything of the sort happen over a girl."

"Confident of that, are you?" Antonio sneered before draining his drink bitterly.

"Fairly confident, yeah."

Antonio grunted out a derisive laugh. "You have no idea how fucking intoxicating that little bitch is..."

Matteo frowned in surprise at the animalistic way Antonio said it.

Antonio was staring down at his empty glass when he suddenly launched it at the wall where his broken phone had already smashed. Matteo flinched at the sound as the glass shattered.

"I need her back!" Antonio hissed, shaking with something much more than rage.

Matteo swallowed hard, Antonio was obsessed.

39
Missing

Cory walked into the kitchen the next morning to make coffee and found his father waiting for him with a frown of disapproval.

"Son, are you ready to talk now?"

Cory sighed resigned to this conversation. "Sure, I guess..."

"Those bruises on her wrists...have you got a name for the person who did that?" He sounded accusatory and Cory wondered if he had already figured it out.

He gave his father a hard challenging look. "Antonio Ferrante."

Michael wiped a hand over his face as he groaned. "I had a feeling that conversation would have something to do with this, the timing was a dead giveaway...I told you..."

"Those bruises aren't the only ones, Dad." Cory interrupted.

Michael's face deadpanned into his policeman expression at receiving bad news. "Go on."

"She has the remains of lash marks on her back, which I really hope are going to fully heal so she doesn't have to live with them all her life! And he fucking tattooed his name on her skin!"

"Jesus Christ..." Michael breathed out. "You do realize how dangerous this situation could get?"

"He has no idea she is here...and no reason to look in this direction."

"You came out of her room this morning..."

Cory looked at his father with a dark look. “She had an anxiety attack last night, Dad, she didn’t want to be left alone.”

“”Yes, Wendy told me about you asking for tablets. But is that it?”

“I’m not sleeping with her if that’s what you’re asking, she’s a friend.”

“I can see the affection, Cory, you’re not fooling anyone.”

Cory folded his arms, leaning back on the counter and sighed.

“It would be a big mistake to go there knowing how damaged this girl is...”

“I know that...” Cory rolled his eyes.

“Good, I hope you do.” He let out a little breath. “So its obvious now why she won’t press charges...but what’s her long term plan?”

“We haven’t thought that far, Dad...it’s really complicated and things need to get sorted out with that first.”

Michael’s eyes narrowed at him. “You’re not going to share?”

“Not right now...it’s not my story to tell.”

“This involves very dangerous people Cory, I’m worried for you...and her, she seems sweet.”

“She is and she really doesn’t deserve what that bastard is doing to her...”

“How did she get messed up with him?”

Cory chewed his lip for a moment before deciding to answer. “”She’s kind of his step-sister, her mother married Augusto Ferrante.”

“Maria is her mother?” Michael sounded surprised.

Cory rolled his eyes again. “Of course, you would have met her before...”

“No one has ever mentioned a daughter...”

“Just goes to show how much they cared about her then, huh.”

Michael rubbed his cheek. “Hmm...Maria died not so long ago...that’s what prompted Augusto to sell up and move back to Sicily.”

“He’s moving back to Sicily?”

“Apparently...” He looked back up at Cory. “So, what does Antonio think has happened to Quinn?”

Cory shrugged. “Run away...”

“So he will be looking for her...he might even file a police report if he’s confident enough that she won’t speak out against him.”

"She won't, I don't think, she's petrified of him."

Michael nodded, walking over to the sink and rinsing his coffee cup out before putting it on the side. "I'll keep an eye out for one...you take care of her."

"Thanks Dad."

"If you want I can give you the number of your mother's old psychiatrist if she needs to talk to someone."

Cory smiled, but it didn't reach his eyes.

His real mother had suffered from bipolar all her life since getting raped as a young teen at a party. She had managed it well until she had got caught up in the World Trade Center collapse, then she changed, hit the bottle and unfortunately would drift, not knowing where she was or what she was doing. She got caught by some guys in Central Park and raped again. She never recovered and took her own life ten years ago when Michael was still just an Inspector. He had dedicated himself to track down the perpetrators and did so, earning a commendation and starting his track to become police commissioner. It was also why he worked with the organized crime world, it was easier to clean up the streets of the malicious nasty little thugs that way. So he had a real personal thing about female abuse even going so far as to regularly visit the clubs these notorious men owned to make sure everything was legit, as far as the sex industry could be.

Quinn woke up to the smell of freshly brewed coffee and looked around the room she was in with a startle, before her mind caught up with her and she looked up to see the cup on the side with a little note.

"I made the coffee black so hopefully it stays hot for you, I'm going to just let you sleep, but if you want to go for a jog and get some fresh air to maybe clear your head when you wake up let me know, I'll be in the basement...it's my gaming pad, movie theater and gym. No one else is home, just you and me."

Quinn smiled and sat up in bed, plumping the pillows behind her and took up the coffee, sipping it to find it was still hot so it hadn't been sitting there for too long. She noted the bed under her unmade and remembered she had been making it before her mind crashed in on her.

She got out of bed and with coffee in hand walked to the door and out on the landing, she went down the stairs and looked around the back side of them to find there was another set of stairs that went down again. She tread down them and saw the door was open. She peeked in to see the basement had been converted to a boy's hang out. She smiled when she saw Cory sitting at a desk with two large screens on it, headphones on, playing some violent war game.

She knocked loudly on the door to get his attention not wanting to scare him by just appearing beside him when he couldn't hear.

He turned and saw her, taking off the headphones and hooking them round his neck. "Hey! Just a sec...I'll get off..."

He pointed to a couch against the wall and she walked over there and sat down as he turned back to his game and spoke to whoever was on the other end. "Hey, I need to get off, sorry guys...win without me."

He chuckled at something said. "Seriously...gotta go."

He pulled the headphones off and put them down, spinning his chair around to face her and gave her a huge boyish grin.

"You're going to be in trouble for ditching..." Quinn said with a small laugh.

"Meh, probably...especially when they find out I ditched for a hot chick sitting in my room wearing PJs." He swept his hair back and his eyes sparkled. "How are you?"

"Better...thanks for the coffee." She answered shyly then sipped the drink as she held it in both hands. "I had to come find you when I saw it and the note and thank you."

"You really didn't have to, you could have stayed in bed the whole day if you wanted."

Quinn shook her head. "No, you were right in the note, I need to get out and get some fresh air...otherwise I'll just start getting in my head again."

Cory nodded, he understood. "So, are you keen on that jog today then?"

"Yeah..."

"Cool, you want anything to eat? Or I could make you a smoothie..."

"Hmm, that sounds good?"

His mouth twisted. "It's what I have only I mix protein powder in while training...but I can make you a simple berry and banana one." He stood up. "You want to wait here or come up to the kitchen?"

"I'll come with you...I feel a bit weird staying in here by myself."

Cory chuckled. "It's not that masculine..."

She looked at all the gaming gear, the huge TV on the wall, the couch that clearly could be dropped down into a bed and the mini fridge and the home gym set up over the other side of the large space in front of the small area left for the washer and dryer. "Yeah, it is..."

Cory shrugged. "Okay, fair enough, come on then..."

He walked to the door as Quinn stood up and followed him out.

Antonio swept onto campus like a storm in stealth mode. His dark aura making the crowds peel back to give him room as he made his way first to Quinn's car, it was unlocked. The keys, her phone and laptop all inside, then to the administration building and up the stairs heading straight for the Chancellor's office.

He had been on the phone with Chancellor Bayton early that morning demanding a meeting with him and Dean Edwards of the Business faculty with all camera footage of Quinn from the previous day ready for his viewing.

The fact he was accompanied by not only Matteo but three other bodyguards as well made everyone stop and stare at his passing. Within minutes the whole school was chattering about his arrival and most of the girls on campus were swooning at his immaculately dressed dangerous persona.

He sat in the Chancellor's office with a silent death glare as he watched the collated material of Quinn's day. Seeing her going in and out of classes, talking and laughing with other girls nothing seemed out of place to what Antonio would expect, except for the last shot of Quinn leaving campus about 3pm all alone and just walking away like she was indeed heading home, but without her car that she had only just got back.

"Is that it?" He growled darkly.

"I'm afraid so...that's all we have." Chancellor Bayton answered nervously.

"Where is the footage of her in the cafeteria at lunchtime?" Matteo asked.

Antonio's face darkened as his eyes fixed on the Dean and Chancellor. "If I find out you've hidden anything from me..."

“I assure you, Mr Ferrante, this is all we have. Perhaps she didn’t eat lunch yesterday...or just got a coffee from a cart...”

“I want the times collated.” Matteo said all business-like. “I feel like some time is missing...predominantly that time around lunch up to when she left...”

Antonio stood up. “I want you to stay here and get this sorted, Matteo.”

“Yes, sir.”

“How the hell does a high security campus lose one girl?”

“She clearly left, Mr Ferrante...this isn’t our issue.” Chancellor Bayton said through gritted teeth.

Antonio leaned over the man’s desk menacingly, sneering his top lip and showing his teeth. “Not your issue?” The tone of his voice made the room go cold.

Matteo stood up and came to his boss’s side. “Sir, calm down...he’s right, she clearly left. I’m just dotting the I’s”

“Hmm...” Antonio stood up straight and straightened his jacket. “I need to go, keep me informed.”

“Yes, sir.” Matteo answered.

Antonio left with two of the three minders and Matteo gave the two scholarly men a serious look. “I really hope I don’t find anything, for your sake.”

As Antonio walked the hall back towards the stairs he froze in place staring down the opposite hall where Reese was just exiting a room and locking the door with a couple of other people, one of which was a huge tank of a man.

The executive office...he remembered it.

Reese turned and looked up, pausing to see Antonio looking at him with a predatory gaze, licking his lips like Reese was going to be his next meal.

Reese chuckled and sauntered up the hall towards the stairs landing not showing any concern at all. Antonio’s hands twitched at the smug look on the younger man’s face. The two bodyguards stepped in front of Antonio as Reese and his thugs reached them and gave Antonio a grin of pure malice.

"Antonio Ferrante...what brings you back here? Thought you graduated years ago."

"You cocky little shit! Show some respect!" One of the bodyguards hissed.

Antonio put a hand on the man's shoulder and shoved him aside, stepping up to go face to face with Reese. "It's alright, I know this boy..." The way he said boy was clearly condescending even though there was only four years difference in age. "...he's Cillian O'Shea's son...the fighter from last Friday night."

Reese licked his tongue over his teeth as he laughed at the slight. "You sound like an old man, Ferrante, work must be weighing you down."

"Ha!" Antonio barked a derisive laugh, then the fake merriment fell from his face. "Where is she?"

Reese's brows furrowed. "Who?"

"Don't fuck with me, kid...you know who I mean."

"If you're talking about your *sister*, I have no idea, I haven't seen her since your man yanked her out of my car last week and that gaudy display you made of yourself during my beating of your giant."

Antonio stepped closer intimidatingly. Reese just cocked his head to the side completely unafraid and raised an eyebrow in contention. "Don't think you're smart if you're hiding her you little shit."

"Hiding her? She's probably just hiding herself after what you did, sick of all those bruises you like to give her."

Antonio went for his gun that wasn't there as it had been confiscated by the guards at the gate, he growled viciously and struck out with his fist like lightning.

Reese was quicker, dodging his body to the side and chuckling tauntingly. "Seriously?" He scoffed.

"Antonio!" Matteo's voice rang out as he ran over, stepping in front of Antonio and pushing him back, earning his glare. "Not here!"

Antonio looked over Matteo's shoulder. "If I find out you know anything about where she is I'm going to kill your entire family!"

Reese clucked his tongue. "Don't act like you fucking care about her. She's nothing but a toy to you...she's gone, run away. I don't blame her! Move on and go find another bitch to play with." Reese growled back.

"Why you little..." Antonio was fighting against Matteo and his own bodyguards trying to get past them to get to Reese as Reese calmly stood his ground and smirked, oozing confidence.

"Wow, I didn't expect to ever see you so flustered...thought nothing could get through to the unflappable Antonio Ferrante. Don't tell me you actually have feelings for Quinn?"

"You need to shut your mouth!" Matteo warned as he struggled against a swearing Antonio. "Fuck off!"

Reese chuckled and shrugged. "Okay...I'm going...but just so you know, I don't have Quinn, look elsewhere. I wiped my hands of your sloppy seconds the minute I found out about your unsavory relationship."

Antonio straightened and glared at Reese and his mates as they walked off down the stairs, his eyes narrowed in on Reese's back trying to determine the truth of his words.

Reese maintained his poker face until he was safely outside.

He swished his hair back and let out a breath. "Fuck..."

Tank chuckled. "Jesus, boss, that was insane."

Jacob blew a large breath out. "I have new respect for you, boss...you're fucking fearless!"

"Did you see the way that fucker went for his gun?" Tank said, shaking his head.

Reese sucked his teeth. "Damn psycho! Let's just hope that was convincing."

He took his phone out as they walked off towards the business faculty. He had to get a message to Cory that he was definitely going to have to stay well away from him and Quinn for at least the next week.

40
A million miles away

Quinn had a huge smile on her face as she panted easily out her mouth. Cory paced along easily beside her as they jogged around the crescent streets of the closed community. It was a chilly day but the sun was shining so once warmed up it wasn't too bad. They crossed a street and Cory led them down towards where the larger homes were. Quinn's eyes raked over the large mansions behind security gates of their own noting the cameras monitoring everything. They past one particular house that was a dark brown brick with white sash windows, a large circular driveway with a fountain in the middle and armed security guards patrolling it.

"Whoa...who lives there?" She muttered once they were past.

Cory chuckled. "You wouldn't believe me if I told you."

"Who?" She demanded with a huge smile. "Come on...tell me. I can keep a secret, or don't you know..." She teased.

"Oh, I know alright...I've even been inside." Cory boasted.

"Who?" Quinn whined.

"Beg me and I'll tell you." Cory teased right back. Quinn jumped over to him, grabbing his shoulder and dragging it down as she gripped his shirt. "Please come on...I'm begging you, please tell me..."

He laughed and wrapped her up in his arms, picking her up off her feet and spinning her around a couple of times as she squealed and giggled.

He dropped her to her feet and she staggered back, panting and laughing, her long red ponytail swishing out in the wind that was picking up. "Alright I'll tell..." Cory said then sprinted off. "Catch me first."

Quinn stood up and glared at him. "Damn it!"

She ran off after him. "That's cheating! You had a head start...come on...stop out!"

He stopped at an intersection, jogging on the spot and grinned at her as she caught up. She braced her legs and dropped her hands to her knees puffing hard now.

"Crap..." She muttered as she huffed.

Cory chuckled. "I wondered how fit you were..."

She stood up with her hands on her hips, licking her tongue out as she puffed. "You're a competitive dick...typical jock."

He laughed his head off, checking his smart watch and pushing a button as he stopped jogging on the spot. "Alright, you really want to know who lives in that house?"

Quinn gave him a surly look. "Nah, I don't care anymore..." She jogged across the road and off down the street, she turned and jogged backwards for a bit, grinning back at him.

He wiped a hand down his face, feeling sweaty and laughed. "Cheeky bitch..." He jogged off after her.

Once showered Quinn walked down the stairs to the kitchen and got a glass of water from the filtered tap.

Cory walked in behind her. "Just grab a bottle of water out of the fridge..." He said as he came up and did just that, grabbing two and handing her one.

"This isn't my house, I don't feel comfortable doing that."

"It is your house for the time being...just relax, bunny. You can use anything in here, okay."

Her mouth twisted like she had no intention of doing that. "Okay..." They fell silent as Cory drank from his water.

"So...whose house was it, are you going to tell me now?" Quinn piped up with a coy smile.

Cory lowered the bottle, wiping his mouth with the back of his hand. "It's Reese's father's place." He announced leaving Quinn gaping at him.

"Seriously?"

"Would I lie?" Cory grinned roguishly.

"Yeah..."

"Hey! I'm offended by that." Cory huffed with a little frown.

"So it is Reese's parent's house?"

"Just his father, he doesn't have a mother either..."

"Oh..."

"I guess we all have that in common, huh..."

Quinn bowed her head slightly, tucking her damp hair behind her ear. "I guess so..." She wanted to ask what had happened to their mothers but hers was still to raw to talk about it.

"Want some lunch?" He picked up his phone and looked at it seeing a message from Reese. His face dropped as he read it.

Quinn saw his expression go grim and her stomach instantly tied in knots. "What is it?"

"Nothing, don't worry about it." He put his phone in the back pocket of his jeans and went to the fridge.

Quinn folded her arms. "Cory...don't shut me out of what is going on, this is about me, isn't it."

He sighed and straightened up, looking at her surly expression around the fridge door. "I don't want or need you breaking down again, bunny, it's as simple as that."

She chewed her lip, dropping her gaze. "That's unfair." She turned and walked off out of the kitchen and up the stairs to her room and closed the door.

He chased after her for a few steps then stopped, letting her go. Best she was upset at him and not what the message had told him about Antonio and Reese facing off at college.

He went back to the kitchen and concentrated on making a sandwich. He made a turkey on rye for Quinn and took it up to her room, knocking on the door.

"What?" Came the surly reply.

He opened the door and leaned on the doorframe. "If you're going to talk like that to me I'll take the sandwich back and eat it myself." He held the plate out with a smirk.

She looked up at him from where she was sitting on the bed. "Sorry. I just want to know what's going on, I don't want to be sheltered from it..."

"Ever thought about going and talking to someone?" He asked as he stepped in and handed her the plate.

"Thank you." She said with those impeccable manners. "Like who, a shrink?"

"Yeah...at least they might give you something proper to help you sleep or something." Cory leaned against the dresser and folded his arms as Quinn picked up the sandwich and bit into it.

She shrugged as she chewed.

"Antonio went to the college looking for information on where you've gone...that was just Reese telling me to keep you from talking to anyone there for a while."

She looked up at him with large frightened eyes.

"I was going to take you out to buy a new phone and stuff today, since I still have Reese's card...but we better hold off on that. You can use my laptop or tablet if you want to just surf the net or whatever..."

"Thank you..." She said quietly, putting the half eaten sandwich down. "And thank you for telling me, I would have fretted worse not knowing."

"Yeah, I figured." Cory huffed. "Okay, well I'll go get my laptop for you..."

He left the room and went to his own, grabbing the laptop and charger. He paused before exiting and grimaced to himself. Something seemed off, he suddenly felt distant from her, he wanted to put his arms around her and kiss her but suddenly felt awkward at even the thought.

"Damn it." He muttered. She felt a million miles away from him right now.

Later that evening Quinn was called down for dinner by Cory's mother. She tentatively came downstairs and entered the kitchen quietly. She was at least glad his parents didn't sit around a dining table and talk, they had ordered Indian and each scooped out what they wanted at the kitchen counter and moved to the lounge to eat while they watched the news channel. Cory looked at Quinn from under his brows with a grumpy expression, she had stayed in her room all day. He had checked on her in the afternoon and found her asleep so had left quietly.

"I'm going to eat mine down in my games room...if you want to come down, we could watch a movie or something?"

She nodded and gave him a small reserved smile. "Yeah, okay."

She followed him down, careful not to trip down the stairs and sat on the couch with her plate on a cushion on her knees.

Cory grit his teeth. "Are you worried about Reese?"

She nodded. "Yeah, I am..."

He took his phone out and called Reese, putting it on speaker and dropping it on the table in front of them. She looked at Cory a little startled, he seemed brusque in his manner with her like she had done something to piss him off and that made her reluctant to speak, especially given the fact that with Antonio she wasn't allowed to speak.

"Problem?" Came the answer as Reese picked up.

"No problem, Quinn just wanted to talk to you, you're on speaker."

"Hi..." Quinn squeaked out.

"Hey, babe, how are you settling in, okay?"

"Yeah...Cory's parents are really nice."

"And Cory? Is he nice too?" Reese asked with a deep chuckle.

Quinn gave a half laugh as she looked up at Cory to find him looking at her with an unreadable expression. "Yeah, he's nice too..." She smiled at him and was glad when he smiled back. "He took me past your father's house today..."

"What the fuck for?" Reese growled.

"We were out for a run." Cory explained.

"Sorry, it was me who asked who lived there..." Quinn spoke over the top of Cory, a little startled at Reese's response.

"Hmm...don't make a habit of it. Jog somewhere else."

"Ah...okay." Quinn stuttered.

Cory clucked his tongue. "Don't be a dick...we'll jog where we want, it's not like they can do anything, plenty of people in this community jog past the place."

Reese just let out a disgruntled huff. "Did you tell Quinn about our campus visitor?"

"Yes, he did...did you see him?" Quinn asked feeling the fear creep up on her.

Reese chuckled. "No, babe I didn't see him..."

"Thank god..." She shoulders slumped a little as she relaxed. Cory frowned at Reese's lie but knew exactly why he had.

"So whatcha doin?" Reese asked in a chirpier voice.

"Cory has me locked in the basement..." Quinn said, grinning up at Cory as he coughed mid-way through shoving some butter chicken into his mouth.

"Ah, shit..." Reese huffed with a little sexy chuckle. "You better be fully clothed."

Cory swallowed his mouthful and laughed. "What if she wasn't...what could you do about it, you said you were staying away for a week."

"A week?" Quinn asked, sounding a little disappointed.

"It'll fly by, babe, don't worry and don't let that fuck boy talk you into anything naughty."

Cory grumbled under his breath but Quinn giggled and leaned forward, putting her plate down and scooping up the phone. "What's classified as naughty?" Cory's eyes were on her sudden playful little smirk.

"You, by the sounds of that...are you being cheeky, Miss Quinn?" Reese's tone dropped and even made Cory sit up and take notice.

"Not at all, I'm just trying to find out what we are and aren't allowed to do without you..." Quinn drawled her words as her eyes fixed on Cory. His mouth went dry as he stared back at her wicked little grin. He slowly put his plate down and wiped his mouth.

"Are you saying you accept our offer to be a throuple?" Reese's voice had increased in intensity.

"Not quite...I'm still thinking about it." She teased.

"So in the mean time you want to play around on me with Curry?" His voice had lowered in tone and hardened with possessiveness and jealousy.

"You've played around with me..." She quipped back in a teasing tone.

They both heard the cluck of his tongue. "This isn't a chance to even up the odds, Quinn..."

"So you're telling me we can't?"

Cory was speechless and getting a hard on seeing her flirt outrageously with Reese over the phone, just how far had the two of them gone?

"I'm telling you, you can't." Reese growled out like he was losing control of himself.

Cory licked his lips and turned to face Quinn directly on the couch. "Nothing more than what we've already done, right?" He asked as he leaned over the phone, looking up at Quinn's face with a roguish lick over his teeth like what Reese usually did. It had the desired effect as Quinn's eyes dropped to his mouth and she gasped in a little breath at having him so close. He took the phone from her hand and hung up, throwing his phone on to the coffee table before swinging his hand back and straight to Quinn's neck, curling his fingers around to the back and looking her dead in the eyes from only a couple of inches away as her eyes glittered with anticipation.

"I hope you like butter chicken kisses..." He said before smashing his mouth onto hers and lashing his tongue around her tongue as he let out a little groan of satisfaction from finally doing what he had wanted to do all day.

His phone bleeped with a message and Quinn giggled into his mouth as she pulled back slightly from his onslaught. He dug his fingers into the base of her skull and covered her mouth again, not giving her any leeway to talk. She gripped onto him and kissed him back and he easily had her leaning back on the couch as he came up over her until she was lying underneath him. He looked down at her finally giving her a breath.

She met his gaze with a slightly dazed one and smiled at him. "We haven't gone any further..."

He chuckled. "I know...frustrating isn't it."

"What do you think the message says?" She asked coyly, glancing at the phone.

"Something along the lines of don't fucking touch her without me." Cory guessed with a sneer. The look he gave her made her think he didn't give a fuck what the message said.

Until his phone started ringing.

He huffed a sigh of frustration to see it was his coach as he sat up and answered it.

Quinn slowly sat back up trying to still her frantic heart. Had she really been about to go further with Cory, in his parent's house with them just upstairs, directly above them? She glanced sideways at him and saw he was looking at her, he winked and grinned boyishly before turning his attention back to the phone with an abrupt 'yes, coach.'

She wondered how many girls this couch had seen...

She twisted her body to sit up properly with her feet back on the floor and grabbed her dinner, taking up a fork full and putting it in her mouth. She could hear that Cory's coach was going over something to do with a game coming up and so left him to it as she ate. Cory shuffled over and leaned over the coffee table and starting eating while he listened, devouring the plate of food in a couple of minutes. He stood up with the phone by his ear and glanced down at her mouthing the word 'sorry' with a shrug and moved to the computer where he started looking something up as the phone conversation continued. Was it a conference call with the team, it sounded pretty serious?

Quinn finished her plate and picking them both up and took them to the kitchen.

As she passed by the living room Wendy called out. "Just put those in the dishwasher, Quinn, thank you...oh, rinse them a little first."

"Sure, no problem." Quinn called back. She noticed Michael wasn't in the living area anymore and Wendy had a pile of papers in front of her. She guessed Michael had gone to his study, both of them obviously bringing work home. Well they were both important people, no doubt this was a normal occurrence in this house.

"Quinn, do you have a moment?"

She was bending down putting the plates into the dishwasher when she startled at the deep voice of Cory's father coming from behind her. She stood up with a jolt and backed away.

She looked up at him with eyes wide showing her fright. His brows furrowed as he noticed.

"Sorry, I didn't mean to scare you."

"Ah, no...that's okay. What did you want to talk about?"

"Cory tells me that Maria Ferrante was your mother, I wanted to give you my condolences."

"Oh..." Quinn was shocked. "Thank you, did you know my mom?"

"I met her a couple of times at events where the lines are somewhat blurred..."

"So you know who my step-brother is..." She pursed her lips with a tentative drop of her gaze.

"Yes and I won't sugar coat it, having you here puts me in a tight spot...I've worked tirelessly alongside these types of men to maintain a peace on the streets of New York."

She chewed her lip and fiddled with her sleeves, he caught the action and his jaw clenched tight. "However, I intend to keep you safe."

"Th-thank you..."

"Quinn!" Cory raced into the kitchen and stopped, panting and let out a sigh of relief. "Oh, fuck...you're here, I turned around and you were gone, frightened the life out of me." He straightened up and glared at his father. "What's going on here?"

"Quinn is putting your dirty dishes into the dishwasher, what's got you so worked up?" Michael growled.

Quinn got the feeling that father and son were always at loggerheads over something.

"Oh, thanks, bu...ah...yeah, thanks." Cory rubbed the back of his neck, catching his near mistake of calling Quinn 'bunny' in front of his Dad.

It was enough as Michael narrowed his gaze on him and huffed. "Well, just so you know Wendy and I are taking a trip up to Emerson Resort on Saturday overnight, thanks to her winning some work raffle, and I don't want any problems while we're away. Have a good night, I'm off to bed." He walked out of the kitchen glaring at both of them with a warning look. Cory turned to Quinn.

"What did he want?"

She tilted her head at him with a curious squint. "Why are you always so confronting with him?"

"Because he's a hypocrite, work raffle my ass, more like a backhand treat from someone important...what did he say?"

"Oh!" Quinn knew what he meant and couldn't really disagree. "He just gave me his condolences for my mom."

Cory looked surprised and his mouth twisted in chagrin. "Sorry, you snuck out of the room, I thought maybe you might be feeling sad again..."

She gave him a small smile of appreciation. "Thanks but I'm fine, you were in an important talk so I just thought I would get rid of the plates..."

"Hmm, we've got a warm up game tomorrow night. Were you going to come back down?" His eyebrow lifted and so did the corner of his lips. "Continue what we started?"

"Ah...no, I don't think so, not with your parents here, I feel a bit weird...I'm just going to go to bed." Quinn bit her lip and moved past him slowly, like sneaking past a sentinel.

Cory raked a hand through his hair as he grit his teeth. "Fuck..." He had lost his opportunity to get closer to her and she had managed to shut down on him again, all thanks to his father.

41

Hot chocolate and cuddles

Saturday night late had Cory sitting outside wrapped in a blanket and on his phone messaging Reese about how things were going with Quinn in the house.

C - **Its hard, bro I think she's avoiding me**

R - Maybe she's just feeling displaced and unsure, she told me as much when we talked last night while you were at the game

C - **Really? I wonder why she can't tell me She trusts you a lot more**

R - Nah, I just make her talk more

C - **You intimidate her to talk, lol**

R - Yeah, probably, lol

Quinn tiptoed through the dark house quietly, feeling nervous and panicky, it was Saturday night and the thoughts of what should be happening to her right now kept invading her head. She wondered if Cory had gone out, he was moody since his team had lost Friday. She was scared but didn't want to turn any lights on, fearing someone was right outside.

Quinn looked out the kitchen window seeing the patio lights were on and saw Cory sitting on the large circular sun bed with his knees pulled up and a blanket wrapped around his shoulders. He was dressed in sweat shorts and a t-shirt like he was dressed ready for bed and Quinn wondered if she should bother him. He was on his phone looking really intense so maybe he was messaging with a girl...he looked piqued and involved as the light illuminated his face making it extra handsome, like an angel.

She wondered if he liked hot chocolate, she had seen sachets of instant hot chocolate in the cupboard the other morning and had been craving something a little indulgent before bed to help her relax and sleep and so had sneaked down to the kitchen to make one, not expecting to see Cory outside.

She didn't want to disturb him, but she felt unsettled in the large house knowing his parents weren't home and they had no security beyond a few cameras attached to a phone app and a house alarm. She feared constantly that Antonio would come crashing in, gun in hand and kidnap her back to lock her in his playroom forever, or kill everyone. She really felt like sticking close to Cory tonight, her nerves were close to shattering she was so scared.

She took her new phone out that Cory had bought her yesterday and sent him a quick message.

Q - *I noticed hot chocolate in the cupboard, would it be okay if I had one please?*

She sent the message and looked out the kitchen window at him looking at his phone. She felt nervous butterflies waiting for his reply.

She felt a jolt as he suddenly sat up and turned to look in at the kitchen. She covered her mouth at being caught looking at him, feeling her face flush hot. He grinned roguishly and looked back at his phone.

Her phone chirped with a reply.

C - **Of course you can. Come out after**

She smiled through the window as she looked up to see him looking at her again. He waved and beckoned her out. She messaged him.

Q - *Would you like one?*

He looked at his phone and she quickly put hers down to collect the cups and the milk to heat in the microwave suddenly sure he would say yes. As her phone chirped she turned back and looked at it seeing a huge smiley kiss face. She laughed and looked up out the window and waved, holding up her hand to indicate five minutes. He gave her a thumbs up and turned away.

She walked out with both cups of hot chocolate and handed one to Cory. He looked over her wearing her PJs and an open zip-through sweatshirt over the top, his eyes going to her very nice toned legs.

He sat up and took the cup, thanking her as she sat down on the edge of the large circular lounge bed he was on and held her cup in two hands, blowing on it to cool it down. Her back was to him and she looked up at the sky.

"You've been ignoring me." He said pointedly.

She turned to look back at him. "Sorry, I didn't mean to...I just..." She hesitated looking down at the cup in her hands and drinking some. "I'm just feeling a little awkward being here in your home...and I know you're in a bad headspace after losing the game last night..."

"I get that...sorry, I'm a bit of a dick when I lose." Cory said. He gulped down half his drink then put it to the side on a small glass table. He studied Quinn for a moment as she sat awkwardly sipping her drink. She stood up and faced him looking out of sorts and uncomfortable like she wanted to ask something but was too nervous to.

"I'll go now..."

"Wait." He called as she stepped away. "That's not all that's bothering you, is it?"

She looked away to the doors like she just wanted to run away inside.

"Why are you so anxious? You think I'm going to do something to you because my parents aren't here?" He sounded annoyed and Quinn felt herself flinch.

"No, nothing like that..." Her hands were trembling causing her cup to shake. Cory shuffled to the edge of the sun bed, putting his feet on the ground, reached out and took her cup putting it on the table then took her hand.

"Then what is it that's got you so anxious?"

She stared at his hand holding hers, chewing frantically at her lip before lifting her eyes as tears welled up in them. "I'm really scared...it's Saturday night and I can't help thinking Antonio is going to come storming in any minute and you're going to get hurt because of me."

"Oh, bunny!" Cory stood up and pulled her into his arms, holding her strongly. She gripped onto his t-shirt and sobbed. He rubbed her back and hushed her in a comforting tone.

"It's going to be okay, don't cry...he won't come here. He still has no idea where you are, you're safe."

"The house is just so quiet and dark tonight..." She mumbled into his chest.

"Sorry, I should have thought...that's my fault." He rested his chin on top of her head, enjoying the feeling of having her in his arms again, the warmth of her seeping through his skin. "I always like it dark and peaceful when my parents are away, and I'm especially dark because we lost...I didn't even realize what Saturday nights would mean to you...fuck, I'm sorry."

She clung to him, pressing herself closer. "Let me stay next to you...I'll be quiet."

His jaw clenched and his heart pounded at the pleading of her voice. "You want to stay out here and lie under the blanket for a bit?"

She nodded her head and he let her go, sitting down he shuffled his way back and grabbed the blanket, throwing it out over his body and straightening it up then held his hand out to her. "Come on, bunny..."

"Is that okay?" She asked nervously.

He couldn't help but take pause, the difference in personality of this girl from campus to here was huge, she really was quite vulnerable and damaged. It made him feel more for her, he wanted to protect her. "Of course...I won't do anything but give you my company and warmth."

She smiled and in that moment it was the most beautiful thing he had ever seen. She took his hand and clambered up beside him, curling her legs up as he pulled the blanket over her legs and put his arm around her shoulders. She snuggled into the side of his chest and sighed contentedly.

"Thank you...I really needed this."

"It's all good, bunny...just relax, go to sleep if you want I'll stay right here."

She giggled quietly. "Bunny, still makes me laugh..."

He chuckled. "Well, yeah...when I first met you, you seemed like such a wild cat but now I see you were putting up a front, you're really quite gentle and sweet."

She looked up at him with a small shy smile. "My heart was racing so hard that first day."

He lifted his hand from her shoulder to stroke her hair back from her face. "You really shocked me with that lollipop act, I think that made you more attractive."

"And now that I'm just a scared little rabbit?"

He gave her an intense look as a little roguish smirk lifted his lips. His hand came back round her head and his fingers lifted her chin as his thumb stroked down her cheek. Her eyes seemed unnaturally large as she looked up at him from this angle and he pressed his lips to her forehead, closing his eyes for a moment.

She shuffled up under him and her lips connected to his. His eyes opened and met hers as he jerked his head back and smiled warmly at the surprise.

"Thank you." She breathed.

"You'll get yourself in trouble thanking me like that, I'm not the gentleman you think I am. I'm barely holding myself back here."

"I know..." She snuggled back down against his chest. "...but right now I feel warm and safe so thank you." Her voice sounded distant and sleepy.

He curled his arm back around her. "You sleepy?"

"Hmm..." She moaned out like she had almost fallen asleep already.

He chuckled to himself, leaning his head back and closing his eyes, enjoying the presence of her and the faint lingering scent of soapy clean on her skin from showering.

He opened his eyes and looked up at the night sky feeling her relax and her breathing even out. She really had fallen asleep.

He lifted his head and searched out his phone with his free hand, taking a selfie showing her snuggled in asleep against him and him with his tongue out between his teeth in a cocky grin and sent it to Reese.

Even though it was after midnight a message came back immediately.

R - ***I see you managed to patch things up. I was actually thinking about risking heading over before that pic***

Cory laughed to himself, that message was so under rated and passive aggressive. Reese was annoyed and jealous.

So of course he had to reply.

C – **I was just about to carry her up to bed**

Reese's reply was immediate

R – ***Whose bed exactly?***

Cory grinned at the message hearing Reese's demanding tone through it, he answered.

C – **Mine, of course. She said she was scared and didn't want to be alone tonight, Saturday nights mean something bad for her**

R - ***Fuck, yeah they probably do but keep it innocent, asshole!***

Cory couldn't help but snort as he tried to contain his laughter at Reese's raging jealousy.

C - **It was your idea for her to stay here with me**

R - ***Kicking myself now...she looks so fucking adorable***

C - **She is, my new name for her fits her well, my Bunny**

R - ***Shit...***

Reese couldn't help but feel a pang of jealousy at the endearment he knew Cory had given Quinn and almost threw his phone in frustration. Then his phone pinged again. He grimaced at what smartass thing Cory could possibly say next, but startled a bit to read his message.

C - **Come over**

R - ***Are you sure about that?***

C - **We agreed, didn't we...I want you to be here when she's feeling so scared and vulnerable. I think she would like it too, she misses her dark knight**

R - ***Lol! Are you serious right now? Because I'm half way out the damn door!***

C - **Come over, I'm not going to say it again**

Cory threw his phone down as Quinn stirred a little, she lifted her head looking around bleary eyed.

"Shit, I fell asleep...sorry..."

"That's okay, sleep on me whenever you want."

She gave him a strange little smirk as she sat up and rubbed her eyes. His phone chirped and he glanced over at it.

"Who's that at this time of night, your girlfriend?" She asked teasingly. He pulled her back into his side with his arm that was still around her.

"Very funny...but my girlfriend is right here and that message was from her dark side boyfriend to say he was on his way over to help me tuck you into bed."

42
Dark and Light

Quinn gasped in a breath of shock, pushing away from Cory and gaping at him like he was an insane man. "What?"

"Which part are you having trouble with, bunny?" He smirked at her lopsided. "We've already talked and decided on this, remember?"

"I know what you said, but..."

"But what? You like him, you like me, he likes you, I like you...it's a forgone conclusion, stop fighting it."

"But, what about the two of you...how the hell do you think this idea could possibly work?"

Cory shrugged. "I like him and I know he likes me...you saw it." Cory's smile was strange and whimsical.

Quinn sat back away from him and folded her arms. "I haven't agreed to anything..."

She chewed her lip in thought. A part of her thought they had been joking with her, but some little part of her was literally zinging with excitement at the prospect of having both these boys at her side.

Cory saw the little twinkle of excitement in her eyes and chuckled. "Yeah, you agree to all of it."

She stifled a yawn. "I'm too tired for this..."

"Then come back to your light side boyfriend...keep warm."

She blinked at him for a long moment as he held his arm up. He lifted the blanket that she had slipped out of and gave her a cute little questioning and enticing smile, but his eyes looked dark. "Now, bunny." He huffed out in a dominant order. "It's chilly."

She dropped to his side. "I'm going to need this to go really slow..." She breathed out as he tucked the blanket round her grinning at that little acceptance.

"Slow as you like...we're not going to push you into doing anything you don't want." Cory answered quiet and calm. "But you need both of us right now to help you get through tonight."

He surprised himself as he was really fighting with himself not to push her onto her back, spread her legs and have her trembling and moaning under him before Reese arrived. He was rock hard after she had just blindly obeyed him before and he knew then what Reese meant, she was perfect.

Quinn was feeling quite apprehensive about it all but she really did feel attracted to them both, they were like flipsides of the same coin, each one brought different attributes and although both of them were also bad boys in their own different ways as well, one very dangerous, she felt that if she could handle Antonio's intense perversions surely she could handle these two? Light and dark, curry and rice, packaged perfectly together.

Quinn had dropped back to sleep feeling warm and cozy and felt a gentle prod as Cory's phone chimed notifying him of movement inside the gates and he looked at the camera app to see Reese's motorbike come down the drive.

Reese had always had full access to the gated community and to Cory's parent's house, although Cory's parents didn't know that due to them backing off their friendship in the public eye as they got older.

"Hey, bunny...Rice is here."

"Hmm..." Quinn groaned but didn't raise her head.

Cory looked down at her trying to see her face that she had buried into the blanket. "Are you fully asleep?"

She shuffled a little bit but seemed to just snuggle in tighter rather than wake up.

Cory chuckled and looked up to see the black leather clad figure of Reese come through the back patio doors and approach them, his helmet still in hand.

He looked hot, swishing his hair out of his golden eyes as he strode with that full of self-confidence aura of his. Cory couldn't help but give him a low wolf whistle as he reached them and stared down at them with a dark sultry gaze.

"Jesus, could you tone down the sex appeal, Rice..." Cory grumbled. "She's asleep, it's being wasted."

Reese grinned, giving Cory a very sexy smile. "Who says the sexy is all for her, Curry?"

Cory clucked his tongue and looked away, but smiled coyly. "Fuck...what's she going to think if she ever finds out about that?"

Reese chuckled darkly. "Can't wait to find out."

"You can't tell her!" Cory sounded frantic and moved to sit up. That made Quinn stir and groan, lifting her head. She blinked in disorientation as Reese sat down on the lounge bed and leaned over Cory's legs towards her. He flicked her hair back.

"Hey, princess...you want me to carry you up to Cory's room?"

"Reese? You're actually here?"

"Of course, babe...I wouldn't miss an opportunity for us to all bond."

She giggled and buried her face into the blanket. "Oh my god! You guys are actually serious?"

Reese looked up at Cory who shrugged and grinned. "I'm always serious, babe."

He got up, leaving his helmet on the ground and walked around to behind her, wrapped the blanket round her legs and then slipped his arms under her, lifting her up and into his chest.

She whimpered a little and his eyes locked on hers as she looked demurely up at him. "Did I hurt you?"

She shook her head, blushing. This was a little embarrassing but her heart was thumping hard as well as her groin.

"God, you almost weight nothing..." Reese commented as Cory knelt up and started fussing the blanket over her. When he was satisfied he clambered off the lounge bed, grabbed the mugs and Reese's helmet and walked off inside.

"Come on...you know the way, I'll wash these up and follow you up."

"Don't forget to lock up." Reese said as he followed, carrying Quinn like his bride inside. She rested her head against his chest and had her free hand on his far shoulder, her other arm was trapped against him. He walked easily up the stairs carrying her.

"You smell nice..." She said in a dreamy tone.

He chuckled. "I should hope so this cologne is expensive."

He reached Cory's room and kicked the door open as it wasn't latched and walked to the bed. Cory rushed in and pulled the blankets back.

Reese lay Quinn down in the middle, placing one knee on the bed and looked down at her with a grin as Cory shuffled the blanket over her from the other side.

She looked up at the two of them with a little apprehension. "Are we really doing this?"

Reese's gaze lifted to Cory who frowned at him, he looked down at Quinn. "Tonight's all about trusting us to do right by you, so nothing's going to happen."

"But, you're both going to sleep here..." She patted the bed on both sides of her. "...right?"

Cory gave her that roguish grin as Reese smirked and licked his tongue over his teeth. "If that's what you want, princess."

She was blushing and pulled the covers up to her eyes, peering at them and covering her embarrassment. "It is what I want, but I feel like it's weird to ask."

Reese chuckled and stood up, pulling his jacket off and throwing it over on the small couch in Cory's room, then started pulling his t-shirt off revealing those yakuza inspired tattoos that made Quinn's pussy walls clench tight.

"Not weird, babe, natural...but I do sleep only in boxers..." He grabbed the belt to his leather pants and unbuckled it then whipped it out and threaded it though his hand with that sexy grin making Quinn gasp and feel herself ache. She stifled the gasp and excited giggle into the blanket.

Cory huffed. "What the hell sort of dominatrix move is that?" He lifted the blankets on his side and crawled into bed, pressing against Quinn and putting his arm around her, looking over at Reese. "Make a real show of it, we're both watching..."

Reese blinked as he threw his belt away then licked his tongue over his teeth as his eyes seemed to glow with an intense desire at seeing both of them in bed.

Quinn whimpered at the comment, giving Cory a wild look but he just laughed and moved her so her back was pressed to his chest.

"Well, alright then..." Reese breathed and started to kick his boots off.

Quinn's eyes raked over his body as he made a show of unzipping his fly and pushing his pants down his legs to pose in his boxers with a clearly defined and almost peeking out the top semi that made Quinn bite the blanket in her teeth to stop from letting out a groan.

Cory huffed. "Yeah, yeah, that's enough..."

Reese laughed. "Are you sure, Currilicious?" He palmed his cock in his boxers and thrust his hips as they stared at each other. Cory dropped his face into Quinn's neck and closed his eyes. "I prefer this, thanks..."

Quinn giggled as Cory's hot lips pressed to behind her ear, tickling her.

Reese dived into bed and flicked Cory's forehead with his finger. "Hey! Back off, gremlin...we're only sleeping tonight..."

"Cuddles are permitted...Quinn needs them." Cory growled. "Don't you, bunny?"

Quinn was looking at Reese as he lay his head on the pillow right next to her face and locked eyes with her. His eyes were so beautiful and a rare color and his eyelashes were so dark and defined. Reese reached up and cupped her cheek, leaning in and giving her a chaste kiss on the lips.

He groaned, closing his eyes as he pulled back. "Fuck, your lips are so soft..."

Cory reared up over her. "My turn."

She turned her head and looked up at him as he pressed his lips to hers. He pulled back and she blinked in realization that this could be her life from now on.

"Oh god..." She breathed.

"Don't overwhelm her..." Reese grit out, trying hard not to just grab them both in a three way kiss that none of them would forget. "Go to sleep, both of you."

He turned back on himself and turned out the light.

43
Bewitching hour

Reese woke in the early hours at around 3am, blinking in the light of the lamp left on in the room over by Cory's desk. He could sense that Quinn was no longer beside him, he could hear the soft snoring of Cory still there though.

He sat up, his body tensing, raking his hair back out of his eyes as they swept the room. He saw her and his body visibly relaxed. She was curled up in the box window seat, the drapes pulled open and her head resting on the glass as she stared out the window into the darkness. She had a thin blanket over her legs and the hood of her sweatshirt was pulled up over her head, her hair gathered and pulled over one shoulder in a loose braid.

She looked so serene, her side profile beautiful, he almost didn't want to disturb her. "Quinn?"

She turned her head, slightly, not even lifting it from the glass and gave him a small reassuring smile. "Couldn't you sleep?" She whispered softly.

"Shouldn't that be my question? Why are you over there?" Reese put his feet on the floor and stood up, glancing back at the heavily sleeping Cory.

"I got too hot being between you." She answered with a coy smile and lifting her head as he padded across to her and sat on the box seat next to her feet.

He could feel her eyes drift over his body as he came over and he twisted his torso to face her as he sat down, placing a hand on her shin. He remembered her heated gaze at his tattoo reveal too.

"You don't have to wear a thick hoodie to bed, you know..." He took her hand and raised it, catching the sleeve with his other hand and pulling it back. "We both know you have these marks on your wrists and they'll be gone soon, just like the ones on your throat did." His eyes dropped to her wrists and he inspected the fading yellow bruises and burn marks from the vicious ropes Antonio had been using. He clucked his tongue annoyed.

"He really didn't need to mark you like this, the bastard...it's really not necessary."

Reese could feel the tension in Quinn's arm, pulling against him and he let her go allowing her to retreat her arm and hide it once again.

"I know, he never used to..." Quinn said quietly. She wondered how Reese knew that.

Reese placed a finger on her forehead making her look at him with those huge green eyes perplexed. He gave her a sultry grin. "Penny for your thoughts, you looked deep into it when I woke up just now."

She surprised him by taking his finger and cupping his hand into both of hers and nuzzling it under her chin. "I was just trying to figure all this out."

"All this?" Reese shuffled forward and stretched his fingers out getting them inside her hood to brush against her throat. She gasped in a little breath and met his eyes. He pulled her hood down with his other hand as she let go of his and slid her hands up his arm drawing him closer, both of them feeling the pull of sexual attraction.

"How is all this with the two of you really going to work?"

"Just let it happen, princess...we'll take care of the details." He smirked at her wanton expression before pressing his lips slowly to hers and seeing her eyes flutter closed. He could feel her clinging to him and her mouth opened immediately as they kissed passionately. He took his time, languidly enjoying the sweet taste of her mouth before pulling back to watch her open her eyes in a dazed expression. He chuckled and wiped his thumb over her lips.

"You needed that from me, huh? Has Cory not been a good boyfriend these last few days? I'll have to punish him."

Her eyes went wide and she gasped in a breath. Reese rumbled a sexy little chuckle and swiped his own lips. "Kidding...although..." He turned to look over at Cory, but startled when Quinn spoke.

"It's my fault, I've been really on edge and uncomfortable feeling like a victim in a safe house...and Cory's been walking around me on eggshells giving me the space I need...I just didn't know what to do or say to bridge the gap, especially with his parents being so nice to me but keeping a watchful eye."

Reese gave a little amused snort, stood up and moved to the other side of her. "Move down, let me get behind you so I can hold you properly."

She complied and he sat with his back on the wall and Quinn between his legs curled up into his chest. "That's better, huh?"

"Much better..." She purred contently.

"You're so damn sweet...I thought you were a real hard bad ass at first."

"Cory said the same thing, sorry to disappoint you both but it really is just a wall I put up to keep guys away from me...not that either of you took the hint."

"I'm not disappointed...I think it's definitely a true part of you though, we just dug deeper, that's all."

She craned her head back to look up at him. "You guys are really strange."

He couldn't help but laugh. "How so?"

"That you would even want to do this, why would you want to share?"

"We actually tried it once before..."

Quinn sat up instantly, glaring at him. He cocked his head at her with a cheeky grin. "It obviously didn't work out, but not because of us...just the wrong girl. The two of us actually get along really well in working together, but perhaps we were all too immature at the time...we were last year of high school..."

Quinn looked over at Cory's sleeping form, her brow furrowed in thought. "You're like complete opposites but neither of you is a good guy..." The gangster and the bully jock.

Reese huffed a throaty scornful chortle. "Quite right...but he's a lot more attentive on an emotional level, that's why he's such a player, he tugs at girl's heartstrings where as I'm just a cold abrupt thug and that seems to attract them anyway."

"Yeah, but he also gives great hugs." Quinn smiled at the handsome man sleeping soundly before looking back at Reese, her expression turning sultry as she licked her lips. Reese's eyebrow twerked up. "So what are you more attentive too?" She asked leading.

"My girl's needs." Reese said with a smirk as he reached round her neck and pulled her back to his mouth, licking across her lips and into her mouth in full control.

She moaned into his mouth as his hands pulled her into his body, they kissed as her hands rubbed over his chest feeling all the perfect ridges and valleys of his amazing fighter's body. He grabbed her hand stopping her and pulled back when her hand went below the line of his boxers.

"Easy, little beastie..." His voice was husky, his eyes intense.

She looked embarrassed and pulled away to sit up. "I-I'm sorry."

"Don't be sorry, I know this just isn't the right time, babe..." He reached out and hooked some hair behind her ear and stroked her cheek as his eyes drifted over to Cory.

"Right..." Quinn nodded. "We probably shouldn't with him right there." She blushed and looked back at Reese under her lashes.

His smirk was like the devil. "Not what I meant, princess...when we do it, it will be all together...the three of us."

"W-what?" Quinn paled slightly but her blush deepened and a hotness travelled over her skin as her core clamped down hard.

Reese's eyes sparkled with delight. "Sharing doesn't mean one at a time, babe...although once we're all comfortable with this we may have one on one sessions, but for now it's crucial there is no intimacy without the third party."

Quinn had covered her mouth in shock. She had no idea this is what they actually meant. Her mind was going at light speed thinking of all the ways that could possibly happen and it was making her insides quiver with excitement.

Reese watched her eyes and saw that dark sexual desire coming through the more her mind worked on it. She finally looked up at him and met his amused sexy gaze with a glint of fear.

"Are you really that shocked? Did you think we would line up for your pussy, Quinn?" He asked with a sexy smirk.

Quinn slowly shook her head. "I guess...maybe a little, I honestly didn't really think about the possibility of having both of you inside..." She stopped talking and bit her lips, her eyes widening at the thought.

Reese was enjoying her reactions immensely and wished Cory was awake to see how adorable she was, how keen she actually looked. "Should we wake Cory up then?"

Her mouth dropped open and she shook her head as she covered it. "Ah, no...I need to process this..."

Reese chuckled and grabbed out for her. She didn't give any resistance and let him pull her back to lay on his chest, her face coming back to his. He caught her face in his large hands and settled a rather ambiguous stare on her, his eyes deep and dark.

"You understand now? Your whole body, every hole, will be shared by us, together, at the same time...whenever you're ready, Quinn...are you okay with that?"

She nodded numbly, just staring at his lips as her body thrummed with a need she never knew she had.

"Relax, Quinn...it won't be tonight even if Cory does wake up." His smile was warm and strangely protective as he kissed her chastely on the lips and tucked her head under his chin. "You're going to be so perfect...I want the timing to be perfect too."

Quinn closed her eyes and inhaled the intoxicating scent of the man. She could feel his hard erection pressing against her stomach and knew he was raring to go. The fact he was being so considerate and holding himself back made her feel like she could trust him completely, and she had to be able to because she also knew from his intenseness that once her permission was given they would own her body completely, erasing Antonio from her thoughts once and for all.

She lifted her head and looked up at him imploringly. "Can we kiss more, please...you're an amazing kisser."

Reese cupped her face again, regarding her with an intense expression. "I'm nearly at my limit here, Quinn."

"Please, sir?" She slipped into the title subconsciously and gasped, her eyes going wide as she realized.

Reese glared at her with an intensity she hadn't seen before, it looked like rage.

"I-I'm sorry...I..."

As if by instinct Cory groaned and shuffled in the bed turning over and lifting his head. "Hey! If you love birds are done over there can you hurry back to bed, I'm getting cold over here." He grumbled, his voice full of sleep and gritty.

Quinn blinked, but Reese held her head strongly not letting her look around or respond. "I just need to clean this girl's damn mouth first!" Reese growled then kissed her roughly, taking every part of her mouth and ravaging it. She started to struggle for breath and grasp out at his arms as tears filled her scrunched eyes. She mewled and whimpered into his mouth.

"Reese!" Cory said bitterly. "Freezing over here! Bring my bunny back to bed!"

Reese broke the kiss off and stood up, scooping the dazed Quinn up into his arms and carrying her back to bed. He lay her down abruptly next to Cory threw the blanket over her and walked off.

"Rip that damn hoodie off her before she's allowed back to sleep...I'm going to get a glass of water!" He growled out, his fists clenched as he stalked out of the room.

Quinn went to sit up but Cory stopped her.

"Reese!" She called out in distress.

Cory wrapped her up in his arms and legs, spooning into her back and nuzzling his face into her hair. "Leave him to calm down. When he walks away it's for your own good, learn that. Shit, you feel good..." His murmurs were still sleepy and husky. "Relax, he'll be fine, it probably just surprised him."

"You heard?" Quinn asked, mortified. "Just how long have you been awake?"

"Long enough." He chortled and kissed her neck. "But I like my sleep so I wasn't going to wake up just for Reese to say no."

Quinn bit her lip. Being with these two might just end up being as intense as Antonio.

"Now, get that sweatshirt off so you can sleep comfortably...we've got a lot to talk about tomorrow before my parents get back."

Quinn felt Cory's body pull back and she sat up, pulled her hoodie off and threw it to the end of the bed. Cory dragged her instantly back down under the covers back into his body with a gratifying groan. "That's better..." She felt his large hands slide over her stomach and brush over her breasts, it felt good, natural.

"Is he going to be angry?" Quinn asked quietly.

"I'm not angry." Reese's voice came back and Quinn saw him walk around the bed as Cory lifted his head and put his chin on her shoulder protectively. "I'm sorry." Reese breathed.

"Good, glad to hear it." Cory grumbled.

Reese gave him a death glare. "You do realize what actually just happened?"

Quinn felt her heart thumping in her chest again but this time it was laced with fear. Did Reese know she had mentally slipped into the darkness of Antonio's subliminal training?

"Yes, but what are you going to do about it?" Cory's eyes seemed suddenly alert and Reese's jaw clenched as he looked away and dropped his gaze to Quinn who was peeking up at him concerned.

Reese let out an exhausted breath. "Nothing...let's sleep."

He got into bed and lay his head down on the pillow and locked eyes with Quinn as Cory nuzzled into her neck and kissed her behind the ear again.

He reached out and touched her swollen lips. "I'm sorry...did I hurt you?"

Cory lifted his head and looked down over her shoulder at her as she shook her head but didn't answer. He looked at Reese and reached out to touch his face. "Alright, Rice...lets sleep." He made Reese close his eyes by dragging his fingers down over them but Reese grabbed his hand and licked his palm with a sultry expression.

Quinn bit her lip as Cory pulled his hand back with a yelp. Reese's sexy chuckle and Cory's huff into her neck were the last noises of the night before they all fell asleep.

44
Morning flirtations

Reese woke early, he was used to getting up in the mornings and going for a run before a workout, shower and off to college. He sat up, rubbing his face and looked down at Quinn sleeping quietly beside him. Cory had turned over to face away, his feet out of the covers and Quinn was back to back with him with a contented look on her peaceful face. Reese lay back down and just took the moment to gaze at her face. She really was beautiful and without a doubt he knew if she had plastered herself all over social media like most girls her age she would have been snapped up as a model. He reached out and took up the loose braid that she had put her hair in to sleep and ran it through his hand appreciating the unusual color, he looked at his scarred and calloused knuckles through her hair and paused, dropping her hair and pulling his hand away. Did he even deserve to touch something so exquisite with hands like these? Hands trained to maim and kill, rough hands that would only scratch such fine delicate skin.

He sat back up with a little annoyed growl, his hands curling into fists. Damn it!

He got up and went to Cory's drawers pulling out some shorts and pulled them on followed by a t-shirt. He stood at the end of the bed just looking at the two beautiful people in bed for a long moment. Cory stirred and shuffled onto his back, blinking awake with a yawn and looked up startled at the dark figure at the end of his bed.

"Jesus, Reese! What the fuck..."

"Sorry..." Reese grinned at Cory getting a fright. "I was going out for a quick run, but got stuck just staring at the two of you..."

Cory snorted a little amused and looked down at Quinn still fast asleep, she was curled up on her side, the blankets tucked up under her chin. Cory ran a hand down the side of her body earning a little breathy moan of resistance from her as she curled tighter. He dropped down to spoon around her and snuggled back in, not wanting to get up yet.

"She's so fucking cute...come back to bed, do you have to run every morning?" Cory glanced back up to Reese who was watching him like a dark sentinel.

Reese clucked his tongue. "I can't...if I do now, I'm going to have to fuck someone..."

Cory slow blinked and lifted the blanket up over his face. "Goodbye..." Came the muffled reply.

Reese couldn't help but laugh. "Fucker...I need the bathroom now..." He groaned, palming his cock and headed out into the hall.

As if the magic was broken by Reese leaving Quinn stirred and woke just five minutes later. Cory squeezed her into his body, breathing in the faint scent of her hair. "Good morning..."

She opened her eyes with a little smile and reached a hand up to stroke his cheek. "Good morning..." She saw the bed was empty in front of her. "Where's Reese?"

"Gone for a run, that man is dedicated to his craft..."

"Oh, well, I suppose you have to be to be that good at it."

"Yeah, you're making me feel inadequate..." Cory chuckled into her shoulder.

She squirmed around so she was lying on her back as he wouldn't release his arms from around her, she turned her head to look into his eyes as he groaned at her body rubbing against his. He dropped his head back on the pillow and smiled at her. "I didn't mean to infer anything..."

"Nah, I know, I was only joking...I would much rather be lying here with you than working up a sweat any other way because I can't touch you the way I want."

Quinn's eyes widened as she realized what Cory was saying. "Is that really why he's running?"

Cory grinned widely. "Probably..."

Quinn's eyes dropped to his arm across her and she placed her hand upon it. "And you?" Her eyes came back up heated and curious.

Cory lifted up to lean over her on one elbow, grabbing her hand then slowly pressed her hand to his groin. "I'm in pain to be honest..."

Quinn gulped back a gasp to feel the rigid erection under her hand...he had a good length but he was thick. She curled her fingers and pressed harder in fascination, her eyes locked onto Cory's and saw his gaze lose focus as he bit his lip into his mouth.

"Fuck, Quinn, don't do that..."

"Why, you put my hand there..." She squeezed a bit harder through the blanket really trying to determine his size and ground her palm down.

Cory snatched her hand away and slammed it to the mattress, pinning it beside her head as he reared up over her. "Regretting it now, behave before you get into trouble."

"What if I don't want to behave with you?" The flirty little look she gave looking up at him made him close his eyes and drop his face into her neck.

"Fuck...stop it...are you horny in the mornings?"

Quinn giggled and touched his back with her other hand, running it down to the end of his shirt and then up against his hot skin.

"Quinn..." He groaned out, his hips grinding down on instinct as he dug his legs between hers.

She gasped as she felt his erection grind against her pubic bone and she looked into his eyes as he glared down at her.

"Fuck, bunny...we can't do this..." He got up and turned to the door. "What the fuck!"

He startled back to find Reese leaning on the door frame, his arms folded, silently watching them with an angry glaze to his eyes. Quinn sat up with a frightful squeak.

"Reese!"

He sucked his teeth, not in the sexy way and gave them both a deadly glare. "I'm glad you decided to stop on your own, Curry..."

"I thought you went for a run?"

"I did too, but I forgot my phone so headed back..."

Cory huffed, looking back at Quinn who was looking mortified like she had just been caught cheating on her boyfriend. Cory clucked his tongue and looked back at Reese. "She's horny as fuck, what's the problem?"

"You made an agreement, I don't care if she's spread her lips begging you for it..."

"What the hell?" Quinn growled.

Reese gave her a little amused glance, his eyebrow lifting at her indignant little huff. "Get dressed, we need to talk." He looked at Cory, his eyes raking down his body to his cock tenting his shorts and back. "Both of you."

"We're both adults, you know!" Quinn shouted as he left.

Cory turned to her. "Shut up..." He muttered.

Quinn clamped her mouth shut, startled and stared at Cory. He glanced back at her with a dirty look like this was her fault, which it was. She frowned at him. "What's going on?"

"Just do as he says..." He stalked out of the room leaving Quinn in a state of complete confusion.

Cory went downstairs to find Reese in the fridge grabbing a bottle of water, he turned, flicking the fridge door closed and wrenched the cap off the bottle, sculling it back as he watched with that intense golden glow as Cory walked in behind him.

"You could have just joined in?" Cory said sourly, dropping down on to a stool at the kitchen counter.

"Principals, Curry...without them, this won't work, especially with Quinn..."

Quinn came rushing in. "What won't work, exactly?"

Reese put the bottle down and leaned back against the kitchen bench to face the two of them. "Sit down, Quinn."

She glanced at Cory as he grimaced and then obediently sat on the stool next to him. "Is this because you said it has to be the three of us?"

Reese sucked his teeth, composing his words. "In order for this to work, babe, we all need to be on the same page...communication of your needs is going to be paramount considering what you've been though, this may sound harsh but I'm not wanting to get all worked up with you just to have you get triggered like last night. The best way to do that is through discussion and writing your wants and needs, your hard passes and your kinks all down."

"What?" She breathed, her cheeks going red.

Reese looked surly at her reaction. "You should know about NDA's and S and M Contracts around this sort of stuff, Quinn..." He raked a hand through his hair, frustrated by her blank look. "Fuck, that prick!"

"Ah...hang on...you want me to sign a contract agreeing to this...this throuple thing?"

"Not in so many words...but there needs to be an agreement made on certain things." Reese stated. "Cory and I have already spoken in depth about this before...and we have our understandings already in place between us."

She gaped at them both and Cory looked a little regretful as he wiped a hand down his face and looked away. "So that's why you said we couldn't do it...and pulled away?"

"Exactly..." Reese said.

Quinn's mouth twisted at his bossy attitude. "You're talking like a dad just caught us."

Reese smirked. "I'll be your daddy, little girl."

She blinked at him and fidgeted on her seat. "Okay..."

"You're obviously ready to start this conversation with us, yes?" He chuckled.

"I was just horny...I'm sorry for everything." She pouted, folding her arms.

Cory groaned and dropped his forehead to the countertop. "Fuck..." He drawled out. It was clear he wasn't coping.

Quinn grinned at his needy reaction, the moment had past now never to be retrieved. Reese chuckled and swiped a thumb over his lip. "I think we have well established that little truth, baby...are you just teasing us both now?"

"No...I'm intrigued to say the least..." Cory peeked up at her and she smiled down at him. "So we can't do anything with you not here?" Her eyes went back to Reese with a questioning look.

Cory, lifted his face so his chin was on the counter top. "No, he's too damn jealous and possessive to have us play on our own."

Reese chuckled. "Fuck the two of you are so fucking adorable, you're acting like a pair of naughty puppies and I am so here for this."

"Naughty puppies?" Cory groaned, lifting his head and rubbing the heel of his hand into one eye. "Jesus Christ...I'm not awake enough for this conversation."

Quinn was chewing on her lip, looking from one hot guy to the other, back and forth, her pussy literally aching. "What if I want you both right now?"

Reese's gaze went dark instantly. "Not happening, sweet cheeks...I do not want to fuck this up, we need to get all your concerns, all your desires and your full understanding out exposed for all of us to see before anything happens."

"But we've already..." Quinn went to protest, causing Cory to drop his hand and look at Reese darkly.

Reese smirked. "That was before...and if you remember what I said you'll understand what's happening now."

"That was when you were still competing?" Quinn said facetiously.

Cory huffed and stood up, coming around to the kitchen side of the counter and went into a cupboard for coffee. "I need to have a coffee before this..."

Quinn chewed her lip some more in thought while Cory shuffled around making coffee. Reese stood up and moved to Cory's stool and sat down. Quinn looked up at him with a wide innocent expression.

Reese cocked an eyebrow at her. "What's with that look, bambi? You're far from a novice in this sort of thing, just because you haven't been allowed to share your thoughts on what you like and dislike doesn't make you any more innocent of the actions you enjoyed."

Her face went scarlet and she pouted at him. "Excuse me?!"

He reached out and pinched those puffed out cheeks between the fingers and thumb of one hand and gave her a sexy smirk as her lips pouted up further to look like a goldfish. "Just start talking, princess...it's for your benefit in the long run."

"Now?" She squeak out as he leaned in and brushed her nose with his with a smirk.

"It might be your last chance for a while...I can't be seen coming and going from here, and Cory needs to return to college too."

"Oh!" Quinn blinked in surprise and felt a little darkness inside at the prospect of being left alone.

"So, I like to tie girls up and spank them..." Reese said with a smirk, letting her go and sitting back.

She felt a thump deep in her gut and an instant heat bloom. "Oh, really?"

"Yeah, I like to play with them, with toys, fingering, my mouth...I love using my mouth." He tilted his head at her gaping at him as she flushed from the memory. "I like to receive blowjobs from girls on their knees while I grab them by the hair, I like my balls played with and even a finger in my butt sometimes."

She covered her mouth and looked away at that point. "Jesus, okay..."

"You get the gist?"

"Yeah, I think so..."

"Good, you know enough now to start compiling your list."

She looked up at Cory who was watching her like a hawk then back at Reese. "And you guys have both already done this list?"

"Yeah, and you'll get to see our lists as part of being a throuple once your list is done and we have your complete agreement."

"Fuck...okay..." She gave a cute little smile and tucked a stray wisp of hair behind her ear. "I'll work on it today."

Reese grinned. "Good girl, it should keep you busy...I want it thorough...especially your hard nos."

"Hard no's?" She thought about it, what hadn't she done with Antonio already and what had she not liked from what he did. "Like whipping?" She said nervously.

Cory clucked his tongue and turned away. Reese reached out and touched her cheek. "Yeah babe...stuff like that, and other sexual stuff to, like fisting...put it all in there."

"Fisting!" She startled and went bright red again. "Yeah, no..."

He chuckled and patted her on the head. "All good...Cory won't let me fuck his ass, so hey, we all have out limits..."

She heard Cory let out a muttered curse before turning back with a coffee in his hand. "Here, fuckface...I don't see you offering me *your* ass."

She could see he was bright red too, she grinned wickedly and leaned towards Reese. "Has he ever?" She whispered.

Cory gave her a look like he was going to leap over the counter and strangle her. Reese chuckled. "Maybe..."

She rolled her lips in containing a smirk and then covered her face with her hands and giggled. "I'm sorry, I might be a little too immature to take all this quite so bluntly..."

Cory clucked his tongue but Reese licked his lips. "Nah, babe, I can see it excites you...and don't worry, we'll do a review on things after a while...maybe Cory will change his mind when he sees how much you enjoy it."

The widening of her eyes was almost impossible as her hands dropped away from her face and her mouth dropped open. Reese reached out and tipped her mouth closed with one finger, his eyes sparkling with delight.

"I can't...this conversation is..." Quinn got up and walked away on shaky legs. "I'm going to shower...a cold freaking shower...absolutely freezing..."

Reese watched her with a dark gaze then dropped his eyes to the bench and chuckled to himself. Cory let out an amused husky breath. "Fuck, you know she's going to fuck herself in the shower..."

"Yeah...that's fine. No rules against that..."

Reese looked down at Cory's cock and stood up, moving around the bench like the flash and pressing up to Cory, his hand running down his chest. "No rule against us having a little fun, either...we both need it now."

Cory sucked in a breath as Reese's hand ran down his stomach, breached his shorts and his strong fingers wrapped around his hard cock. He gripped the edge of the bench with both hands. "Rice, fuck..."

Reese licked his neck and breathed on it as he stroked Cory's hard cock. "Come on...we're both needy as fuck...this won't take long..." He looked down at the cock in his hand leaking thick sticky precum.

Reese pressed his hips to Cory's taking out his own erection and grabbed them both in his hand together, slicking them with their combined juices. "Help me, Cory..."

Cory wrapped his hand around them both too and they both started stroking their cocks together. Cory grabbed the edge of his shirt and gripped it in his teeth, exposing his stomach and leaning back slightly as Reese just pulled his shirt off.

"Kiss me." Reese ordered with a desperate groan.

Cory lifted his free hand to the back of Reese's neck and pulled Reese to his mouth kissing passionately as they both raced towards climax.

They were both so horny it didn't take more than a few strokes and they were both coming. Reese burying his face in Cory's neck as Cory's head was thrown back, his teeth gritted together and they both grunted out their pleasure between them.

Reese let out a husky satisfied breath. "Fuck..."

Cory panted through clenched teeth, his fingers still on the back of Reese's neck and he clenched them slightly, pulling Reese in close. "That was intense..." He chuckled and Reese lifted his head as Cory dropped his hand back, searching out the paper towel roll, pulling a long line. Reese's hand slammed down on the roll so Cory could rip the sheets off and then he dragged the paper towels to between them, swiping the bunch across his stomach. Reese put his hand over Cory's and guided his hand to rub over his stomach too then stood up and went to the sink, washing his hands. Cory crouched down and wiped the floor of the splashes that had landed there then threw the paper towels in the bin before washing his hands too. Reese had walked back to his seat and was now sipping his coffee with a pleased smile on his face.

"Stop smirking, you bastard." Cory huffed.

"Why? I just had my cake and ate it too...Quinn's coming round and you are all on board with me, baby." He gave Cory a sexy smirk. "I really fucking missed you."

Cory rolled his eyes, grabbing his coffee and walking off. "I'm going to go shower too...use my parents one."

"Any idea when your parents will be home?"

Cory stopped and looked back. "Nah, probably later on this afternoon though."

Reese sculled back his coffee and put the cup in the dishwasher. "Okay, I need to get going before my bike is seen by Dad's guys..."

"Okay, your helmet is there..." Cory pointed over next to the door leading to the garage.

Reese walked over and hooked his arm around Cory's neck planting a kiss on his cheek before pushing past and heading for the stairs. "Let me shower first then I can go. Make sure our little omega knows the rules about homework...the faster it's done..."

45

Rules about Homework

Quinn was quite industrious in compiling her list and Cory didn't need to make sure she did it. He had her sitting in the basement on his laptop searching up some rather riskè shit and he chuckled to think how he would explain it if his parents ever saw his search history.

Quinn dropped back into the couch with a huff at one point on Sunday, scratching her head. Cory looked around from the assignment he was working on for college at that frustrated little huff. "What's the problem?"

"Oh, nothing..."

He swung his chair around to give her a challenging look. "Talk, bunny."

"I'm just not sure what the difference between flogging and whipping is..."

Cory's jaw clenched tight and he swallowed hard. I shouldn't have asked. "Okay...it's just the implement that's used I thought..."

"So it can still hurt and scar?"

He closed his eyes for a moment. "Bunny..." He called through gritted teeth. "What exactly are you trying to work out here?"

She pursed her lips, seeing his reluctance to want to talk about anything to do with Antonio and what happened to her, she had noticed it before, he tended to shut down and withdraw like it angered him immensely. "Can we talk freely about this, Reese said I was supposed to..."

Cory got up and walked over to the couch dropping down on it next to her and tipping the laptop towards himself so he could see what was on the screen. "Of course..."

"Okay, well how do I say I like something when it has such a wide range of pleasure to pain..."

"You like flogging?" Cory's voice sounded strained as he looked at the screen.

She pointed to a photo on the screen of a short black rubber toy with many tails. "I've had that before...it was quite teasing and I liked it, it didn't hurt..."

Cory looked at her seriously. "It can...the person chose not to do it hard enough to cause pain...I guess you're going to have to decide how much pain is good pain." His mouth was dry and he coughed.

Quinn pursed her lips, a pen in her hand coming up to tap against them. He chuckled and leaned over kissing her shoulder then dropped his cheek on it and looked at the screen. "Maybe put you like a sharp sting but nothing that will mark the skin."

Quinn grinned and jotted that down on the pad on her lap. "Okay...but spanking marks the skin?"

He groaned. "You like spanking...fuck, I'm hard, stop...."

She giggled. "Sorry, I didn't mean to tease you or anything."

He lifted his head and leaned away from her. "This is a lot harder than I thought it was going to be...look, if you go into here..." He tapped the mouse pad and moved to some files then opened one up. "Here's my list."

Quinn looked through it, her cheeks rising in redness the more she read. "Oh..."

He chuckled. "Nothing says we're going to do all of that, it's not a list to work though...it's just a way of knowing what your partner wants and can be willing to handle...yours will be important because of what that dick has done to you...we really don't want to hurt you, physically or mentally."

She nodded, a warm fuzzy feeling growing in her as she gave him a shy little smile. "Okay, I get it, thanks..."

She went back to her notepad and frowned at it with a serious pout.

He stood up, placing a hand on her head and messing her hair. "Fucking adorable..." He muttered.

"Hey!" She moved her head away. "I don't mind you guys patting me on the head but don't mess up my hair."

He gave her a strange look. "Put it on the list, I dare you." He laughed and went back to his work.

Quinn was really not looking forward to Monday morning and coming down stairs to find the house empty of all its inhabitants, so she got a little bit of a surprise to find Wendy, Cory's step-mom, doing yoga in the living room when she finally decided she was hungry enough to go downstairs.

Wendy stood up from her warrior pose and turned the relaxing rain music off.

"Oh, Quinn...you're up..."

"Good morning, Mrs McMillan...I didn't know anyone was still here today, I thought I was going to be on my own so was sort of putting off coming down."

"Oh, I see...that's quite alright, I was actually hoping to spend the day with you."

"With me?' Quinn pointed to herself, her fingers curling up into her chest.

"Yes, I need to go dress shopping...want to come?"

Quinn genuinely smiled. "I would love to!"

"Great! Let's both get dressed and I'll buy you breakfast on the way." Wendy walked to the stairs with a coaxing wave and Quinn grinned.

In her room she messaged Cory and Reese through their group chat telling them Wendy was asking her to go dress shopping. Cory just sent back a thumbs up, but Reese sent a message that startled her.

R - **Buy yourself a nice dress too, there's an event coming up that you can attend with Cory, use my card, it's still in Cory's room in his bedside table**

She frowned as Cory replied to the comment.

C - ***You think that's wise, I wasn't going to go?***

Quinn typed into the group chat.

Q - *What event?*

R - **Police Awards and Charity night…it's a big event for Cory's family so he's going…and you can go too. So am I, as my father attends and puts a lot of money up for this event as a major sponsor**

God, Quinn thought, is anything not corrupt?

R - **By the way, I got your list…nice work, babe**

Q - *Cool, so when can I see you both?*

She saw Cory and Reese both typing to that and smiled. It felt nice to have two handsome men hanging off her every word like this, she wondered how long it would last once they both got what they wanted...she definitely wanted them both but a little part of her also wanted to hold back and enjoy the sexual teasing and doting for a while longer.

R - **You need to behave, princess, all your dreams will come true soon enough, be patient…we are!**

She smiled at Reese's reply just as Cory's reply came through.

C - ***Shit, bunny, you're killing me here!***

She had an amazing time with Wendy that afternoon, she was really nice and best of all she had kept their little outing non-personal. Quinn had expected some daunting questions to be thrown at her knowing Wendy was a prosecution lawyer but she hadn't asked Quinn one single personal question beyond what color she liked in dresses and as they walked in the door from the garage into the kitchen laughing and carrying several shopping bags Quinn felt obliged to do something in thanks for the day and to thank both Cory's parents for letting her stay in their home for free.

"I notice you all eat takeout a lot...if you like I would like to cook a meal for everyone, as a thank you."

Wendy gave Quinn a pleased smile. "That would be wonderful, Quinn...the problem is we aren't normally all home at the same time...I work long hours when I have a case and Michael generally has a lot of out of office meetings during the evenings due to his dealings with certain groups." Wendy's mouth twisted sardonically.

Quinn gave her a strange look. "You're on board with all that?"

Wendy shrugged. "It's a balancing act, the top guys in any organized crime syndicate are quite untouchable anyway, I do the work that is put over my desk. I understand how Michael's dealings are beneficial to the city as a whole and believe it or not, but the large syndicates are actually quite helpful in clearing out the petty criminals from their territories."

"Oh..." Quinn was surprised that Wendy saw it that way, it was like she purposely looked the other way, but then she did drive a very nice BMW and lived in a posh gated community. "But...they still deal drugs to kids...and stuff like that..."

Wendy gave a little laugh. "Like I said it's a balancing act and I'll take down as many of those street thugs as I can...but if you were to say that to the likes of Augusto or Cillian...they don't sell drugs to kids...they sell drugs to the lesser gangs, what they do with them is up to them..." She saw Quinn's dubious expression. "I know..."

Michael and Cory both came into the kitchen like they had already been together. Michael grabbed beers from the fridge and handed one to Cory who came up to Quinn and gave her a brief hug.

Wendy looked at the time. "You're home early?"

"Hmm..." Michael huffed. "I heard you played hooky from work today..." He smirked at her hands full of shopping bags.

"I had to get a new dress for Saturday night and I just knew it would be a good chance for Quinn and I to get to know each other."

Cory smiled and sipped his beer happy they were all getting along.

"Well, just remember Quinn isn't Cory's girlfriend and she's only staying for a short time."

"Hey!" Cory huffed at his father's impertinence as Quinn's gaze immediately dropped to the floor. "Don't say it like that..."

"Yes dear, that was a little insensitive..." Wendy berated him too.

Michael coughed. "Sorry, I merely mean that I've actually been looking into a few things for you, Quinn and also, on that note...you've been filed as a missing person by Antonio today."

"Oh..." Quinn felt a digging dread in the pit of her stomach. "Really, so what happens now?"

"I had a few guys on the lookout for this happening, and they took the case file and made it disappear...I'll handle the rest, send Antonio a few false reports and keep him treading water on it."

"I don't know what to say...thank you." Quinn felt a little flushed and Cory stepped over with a hug.

"I was going to talk to you too, dear..." Wendy said. "I think Quinn should come with us on Saturday."

Michael's face clouded. "I just said..."

"Dad!" Cory interrupted. "Quinn and I might not be at a level that we are serious yet, but we like each other and it could be, you know..."

"Hmm..." Michael grunted. "I thought as much..."

"So what were these things you mentioned?" Quinn asked trying to change the conversation.

Michael lifted his beer and took a sip. "Well, for one I've made an appointment for you to have a talk to someone...and I've also spoken to a couple of people who might be able to set you up with a way to complete your degree by correspondence and night classes...since your grades are exceptional...and maybe find you a job placement so you can earn some money."

"Wow! Thank you so much!"

"Wow, dad...yeah, thanks."

Michael gave Cory a little side glance and smirk. "I'm not all bad, son, but before Quinn can go out and do all this something has to be done to smooth things out with Antonio, especially if Quinn is going to stay in New York."

Cory rubbed the back of his neck. “”Yeah...that’s Reese’s field.”

“Perhaps I should speak to him...”

Cory gave his father a worried nod of the head. “You could try, for sure...but I would leave it for now, he seems really busy...”

“Alright, I’ll try and speak to him next week, does Cillian know anything about this?”

“No, nothing.”

Michael frowned. “I hope he tells him soon, if Antonio makes a move I would like to know that Cillian and his men are in the wings with full knowledge of what’s going on.”

Cory squeezed Quinn’s shoulder as he felt her tense up.

46
Mundane Truths

All was quiet over the week, Quinn was able to meet with the psychiatrist on Wednesday and talk about her confused feelings towards Antonio, how he treated her, his escalating violence and control and how that could affect her relationships going forward. The fact that she had been attracted to and consented with Antonio in the years previous and had enjoyed sex, submission and bondage with him under his control but was still of a mind to recognize his increasing violence, control and removal of her right to object as wrong indicated she was perfectly normal. Especially given the fact that she had sought a way out of the relationship at these indicators and left the situation, the shrink praised her for being a brave, intelligent young woman. She didn't mention Reese and Cory but by the sounds of what the shrink had told her the list was a great idea. Had Reese researched things? It made her able to trust that she would be in safer hands with the two of them and that she had a voice, something she had never had with Antonio. And that was the biggest fear that needed to be overcome, that removal of her voice...that slipping into the role that Antonio trained her for. The shrink had gone into how she shouldn't feel embarrassed to admit that the actions around being submissive she enjoyed and there was no shame in continuing to explore such things with a different partner, but communication was the key to everything and she had to be open and honest in explaining her history and her fears before proceeding.

Reese was right on all levels...just how experienced in all this was he?

The more she thought about it the more she just wanted to have the two of them in front of her, her on her knees and just tell them to fuck her...she was so damn ready and wanting, but this rule of being together as a throuple for anything to happen made it awkward to be around Cory. She was masturbating every damn day! Frustrated by just kissing and cuddling.

Aside from that meeting giving her a boost of confidence Quinn had also decided to start being a bit more proactive in other areas that she could affect in her immediate surroundings. She got back into working out in the mornings and even went so far as to start cleaning the house every day, she ordered a whole lot of groceries through the house account that Wendy had given her and started cooking meals every night for everyone. She made sure they were meals that could be heated up easily, or taken out of the fridge, like salads.

Wendy had objected to her doing all these things at first, Michael was of a mind to not say anything and let whoever wanted to clean and cook, clean and cook, as long as it meant it wasn't him he was happy...but they understood Quinn felt the need to contribute and it did make her feel a lot better about freeloading off their hospitality.

She wondered if she should look for a part time job...perhaps something she could do during the day while the house was empty...she hated the house being empty...it was daunting knowing Antonio was out there looking for her, it set her on edge and although the shrink had prescribed some light weight sleeping tablets, and some pills to take the edge off her anxiety if she felt it was escalating, she still couldn't shake the feeling that she was on borrowed time. She needed money to gain freedom...if that meant she was going to have to move away, change her name, whatever it took to escape him, she was willing to do it...even if it meant leaving her loveable throuple boys behind. She had to take control of her life and learn to stand on her own two feet as a strong independent woman.

She wondered how Reese and Cory would feel if she spoke to them about all this, would they be understanding and supportive? She felt like they would be...

When Cory arrived home on Friday, he was rushing to get his gear before heading out to training.

Quinn bounced on her toes as he came in to see her there. He smiled as she came to him and wrapped her arms around him, resting her head on his chest.

"Hi." She said in a breathy tone, enjoying the smell of him.

"Hey..." He brushed her off and made his way to the stairs. "Got to rush, training tonight..." He bounded up the stairs two at a time heading for his room. He glanced back and saw Quinn watching him with a little pout on her face.

He grit his teeth. Damn it! He rushed into his room grabbed his boots and gear bag then came back out. As he raced down the stairs and hooked a left around to go into the basement to grab his laptop and water bottle he saw Quinn still standing there, her arms folded and a demanding little frown on her face. He huffed and went downstairs, gathered his stuff and walked back up. Quinn gave him a little scowl.

"What's wrong?"

"Nothing's wrong, I'm in a hurry." He explained.

He was frustrated at having Quinn so close and not being able to touch her the way he wanted...hugs and kisses weren't cutting it and that just made him feel like a selfish douchbag. She was seeking more time from him, more intimate cuddles and affection and although he loved that she was seeking that from him he was battling his own demons from holding back. He was getting snippy, he hated the fact she was being treated like a housemaid by his parents just accepting her cooking and cleaning their house. He loved coming home to see her smiling face pleased to see him but....

He was so damn conflicted and pent up, something was going to have to give.

"When will you be home?" Quinn asked. "I've made a mac and cheese for tonight and put some bacon in it for you..."

"I don't know...we've got a big game coming up so tonight's practice is going to be long..."

"Oh, okay..."

"I'm sure my parent's will enjoy your efforts...I see you've vacuumed again..." He growled out. He knew he was being unreasonable but he saw his step-mother sitting in the lounge with her nose buried in paperwork.

He got the desired effect as she raised her head and looked through the double doors at him in the foyer. Quinn gave him a startled look.

"What!" He growled.

Quinn backed up a step. "I-I'm sorry you're pissed off about something but..."

"Yeah, I am! I want you as my girlfriend not my parent's fucking maid!" He stormed out the door and slammed it shut.

Quinn stood gaping at the door in disbelief. Wendy came over and touched her shoulder. "Goodness what was that all about?"

"I don't know..." Quinn said, looking at the floor, tears trying to fill her eyes.

"I'm sorry, Quinn...is that how you feel?"

"No!" Quinn shook her head. "I do it to fill the day because I'm bored and the house is too quiet otherwise...I..."

"Perhaps we are taking it for granted a bit...you have cooked and cleaned every day this week."

"I was just helping out, you are all so busy and I'm stuck hiding out here in your house..."

Wendy smiled. "I get that, but perhaps you are doing too much."

"I thought about getting a part time job during the day, but..."

"It's risky, I mean, Mr Ferrante can't search the entirety of New York for you, but having a job means loading your social security number into a database and well...I'm not sure but he can probably get into places to make that sort of thing trigger where you are...I have no idea of the resources available to him, but money talks..."

"Really?" Quinn looked a little surprised.

"I don't know, but I'm always quite surprised by the capabilities these people have at their disposal."

"Oh..." Quinn's mouth twisted. "I really wanted to try and earn some money to be able to move out...get my own place again...start living again. Mr McMillan said something about getting me an internship, but that's only once I at least past first year."

Wendy frowned. "Hmm...I can understand that, but don't think we want you out...this may take months, Quinn, I'm happy to have you here, helping out...it's nice and I like you...don't be too hasty to leave. Let's work something out, like a roster...that might make Cory feel a bit better about it. I really don't know what's got him so riled up all of a sudden."

"Neither do I?" Quinn responded with a hint of sadness.

She went up to her room and took out her phone, messaging Reese directly rather than though the group chat so Cory didn't see.

Q – *Hey, did you see Cory at college today?*

R – **Yeah, for a minute, why, what's up?**

Q – *He came in and yelled at me about wanting me as his girlfriend not his parent's maid and left for training. Now I feel like I've done something wrong, I've just been cleaning and cooking cause I'm bored and to feel like I'm contributing...*

R – **He's got blue balls, ignore him, I'll talk to him**

Q – *Really?*

R – **What do you expect? He's got you right next to him every day...I'm jealous but understand it must be hard not to touch. He's been complaining to me every day about it**

Q – *Can I do something about it?*

R – **Like what?**

Q – *'Something'*

R – **No**

Q – *It's getting hard for me too, you know*

R – **Let's try and talk this out tomorrow night face to face**

Q – *Ok*

Quinn dropped her phone to the bed as she lay back and looked at the ceiling with a huff. It wasn't like she wasn't feeling the same thing...perhaps she should just do it with Cory and be done with it?

What would Reese really be able to do about it?

She curled up and grabbed her pillow, clutching it to her chest. She sighed, troubled, she really wanted Reese too though.

Antonio was finding it hard to focus on the meeting in front of him, Quinn had been missing for a week now with no results. She had just disappeared in a puff of dust. That infuriated Antonio even more because he knew someone out there knew something, he just had to find the person. He was still keeping an eye on the O'Sheas but could only manage that from a distance. He had called an assembly of the freshmen at college under supervision from the Chancellor and asked for any information as to where Quinn might be. He had people go through all the footage of the cameras on campus and singled out those she spoke to in her last day, nothing. Where the hell could she be with no money, no car, no phone...someone had to be sheltering her.

He looked up with a start to find everyone at the table looking at him expectantly. He grimaced to himself as he hadn't heard the whole last part of anything that had been said.

"Fine, proceed with that." He stood up and walked out.

Matteo stood up and followed him out with a sour expression as the executives all looked at each other with unsatisfied shakes of their heads.

They both halted in their steps to find Augusto standing in the assistant's office talking softly to her. Antonio glanced around at Matteo with a deadly look.

"Wasn't me...I don't know why he's here..." Matteo stated.

Augusto looked up as Antonio stepped into the large open space heading for his own office behind.

"Ah! Antonio, just the person..."

"No doubt, come in...get coffee." He growled at the woman assistant.

"What brings you to Manhattan?" Antonio asked sitting down in his large leather chair behind his immaculate desk, looking up at his father with a cocked eyebrow and a smile of pure malice on his lips.

"A little birdy told me you've lost our Irish rose."

"Our?" Antonio sneered. "Don't push it...I heard the house is sold, that was quick work."

Augusto's smile was like a crocodile as he passed a hand over his slicked back hair. "Yes, so I will be leaving soon."

"How soon?"

"I leave on Sunday...do you think you will have Quinn back by then?"

Antonio clucked his tongue at how his father had brought the conversation back around to Quinn. "Not likely, I even reported her as a runaway with the police...I have no idea where she has gone. I've questioned the people at college that appeared to be her friends on the cameras, even the ones that appeared to dislike her, no one knows anything. They are all as surprised as I am that she has disappeared."

"Hmm...perhaps you would like some help?" Augusto smiled sedately.

"Do you know something I don't?" Antonio asked as the assistant brought in the coffee and placed the tray down on the desk. "Leave, we can pour it." He growled out and Matteo closed the door after her.

Matteo came over and poured the coffees black, added a spoon of sugar to Antonio's and a splash of cream to Augusto's and stepped back.

Augusto took his cup up and leaned back in his chair, cradling the cup in the palm of one hand while holding the handle in the other. "There are places I could ask that you are not privy to."

"Why aren't I privy to them? Have I taken over as Don or not?"

"Of course, but there are certain people that have decided to retire along with me and no longer wish to be called upon, I'm sure I could call in a last favor."

Antonio's eyes narrowed at his father's smug grin. "You gave them this clemency, why?"

Augusto shrugged. "After a long and faithful service to me, it goes without saying that some people will die on that hill alongside me, Antonio."

"Hmm..." He snorted. "Alright then, see what your people can drag up that mine can't..."

Augusto grinned behind his coffee cup, took a sip then placed it down on the tray. "Son...is that anyway to ask your father and still head of this family for a favor?"

Antonio's expression went flat, his jaw ticking as he stared at his father darkly for a moment. Augusto merely stared back with that benign smile on his face. He flexed his hand that had a huge signet ring of solid gold that held the family crest and lay it on the chair arm.

Antonio glanced at Matteo who was looking grimly at the floor.

He clucked his tongue and stood up coming around the desk and dropped to his knees at his father's feet and kissed the ring, keeping his head down.

"Please father, I ask you to aid me in finding Quinn."

Augusto lifted the hand and placed it on Antonio's head, patting him condescendingly. "There, you see, you can still be humble...it's a good thing to remember, son...very well, I will contact my guy and see what he can unearth."

Augusto stood up, buttoned up his jacket and walked from the room while Antonio stayed kneeling with his head down.

Antonio stayed that way until he was sure his father had left hearing range then stood up grabbed the coffee cup and hurled it at the back of the door with an animalistic growl.

It smashed into a million pieces, coffee spraying out everywhere and running down the door to pool on the grey carpet. Matteo merely watched, silent and grim.

"Fuck!" Antonio growled. "I thought I was done with that fucking man!"

47
Unwanted guest

Augusto Ferrante sauntered through the entrance doors and into the large marbled foyer of the venue for the Annual Police Awards Dinner and Charity Fundraiser. He stroked his hand down his jacket over the buttons watching the men on the doors to the event hall panic at his unannounced presence.

The fact that he had arrived with a large entourage of ten men with concealed weapons was probably what was causing most of the drama now going on before his eyes but because he was making no move to try and enter the actual event it seemed the people didn't know what to do as the foyer was quite obviously a public space.

He was quite happy to stay right here and wait for the Commissioner to arrive, he wished to speak to him about a certain rumor he had heard.

He watched with little interest, an amused smirk on his face as the guests started to arrive. The police among them knew exactly who he was and seemed agitated by his presence. The other contingent, the mob in their guise of the main business sponsor of the night, hadn't arrived yet.

It wasn't long before Augusto got what he wanted. As Police Commissioner Michael McMillen arrived by Limousine with his family and walked up the steps Augusto saw with his own eyes Quinn Malley walking on the arm of Michael's son, Cory. She looked stunning in an emerald green slip of a dress that clung to every curve and dropped to the floor like ripples on a pond. Her gorgeous chestnut red hair caught up in a dramatic high ponytail, pulled off her face to show off her stunning cheekbones and large green eyes, she was a show stopper.

They all froze and the sweet horrified look on Quinn's face as she gasped in shock and covered her mouth was well worth the wait.

"So here you are with the Police Commissioner's son...you think he can protect you, Quinn?" Augusto asked with an amused, condescending tone.

Michael came forward as Cory took Quinn under his arm protectively. "Augusto, you're not invited here, you should leave."

"I came to prove the truth of some information I received anonymously, it seems to be true..." Augusto turned back to address Quinn. "You really should return to Antonio and stop this nonsense."

"She won't be going anywhere, Augusto." Michael said quite firmly as a few of his fellow police officers started to hang around.

Augusto leveled a snide, confident gaze upon Michael. "Are you daring to back out of our agreements?"

"Of course not, but you know who this event is sponsored by, you can't be here." Michael's voice was firm and unafraid.

"I'm here only to see my step-daughter and advise her as a father should about the bad choices she's making. Antonio thought she was possibly with the O'Shea boy but now I see this, this makes a lot more sense. You need to choose your allies wisely Mr Police Commissioner."

"I've always worked with all of you and maintained peace but let me tell you something, Augusto..." Michael stepped closer, making Augusto's men to tense up. "...I know the truth of Quinn's situation...I know what Antonio has been doing to her."

Augusto snorted. "You're not going to believe a little girl's lies?"

"The bruises I saw with my own eyes were enough to corroborate her story." Michael was starting to get irate.

Augusto sucked his teeth, appraising the situation, wondering if that meant the Mob also knew too much about Quinn's identity.

"Tell Antonio to stop this unhealthy obsession with this girl otherwise I will be given no choice but to re-evaluate our agreements and believe me when I say my wife..." He waved his hand to where Wendy was standing with Cory and Quinn, now surrounded by out of uniform police. "...would like nothing more than to get her hands on your file."

Augusto puffed his chest out and stalked off without another word. As he went down the stairs with his men behind him he saw a young man with black hair, puffing from running. Augusto smirked and gave the boy a cursory glance as he slowly passed him. He recognized the boy, Reese O'Shea.

Arriving alone and looking frantic...knowing that the car carrying Cillian O'Shea and family were being held up by a traffic jam...the boy, Cory, must have messaged him...so they were working together on this.

Augusto stopped on the sidewalk and looked back up through the glass entrance and saw Reese running in and up to Quinn taking her by the chin and stroking her cheek as Cory held her by her shoulders.

Augusto's mouth twisted as he sucked his teeth bitterly. "Well, well...so that's the way it is..."

"Are you alright? What the fuck did he want?" Reese spat, his rage making his hand shake as he touched Quinn's face.

She took his hand into both of hers and pressed it to her mouth too frightened and overwhelmed by what just happened to speak.

"Fuck knows, he spoke to Dad." Cory answered. "He did tell her she needed to return to Antonio, though."

"Mother fuck..." Reese growled but was interrupted by Michael.

"What's going on here with you three?" His voice was suspicious and accusatory.

Reese pulled his hand away from Quinn, stepping back and leveling his golden gaze upon Michael. "I'm the one that got her out, found out everything...I'm just worried."

His gaze glanced at Quinn and Cory in warning then as Michael eyed them all Cory pulled Quinn into his side.

"I think we should go in..." Cory said quietly.

Reese sucked his teeth, appraising Quinn's pale face and trembling shoulders as she clung to Cory's side. "Maybe she should just go home?"

"She's safer here right now surrounded by New York's finest. At least wait until after the main speeches before leaving." Michael coughed, looking over Reese's shoulder. "Your father is finally here." He took Cory by the shoulder and pulled him and Quinn away, taking his wife's hand. "Let's go in, I'll greet your father inside, you fill him in to what's happened."

Reese grit his teeth as the Police Commissioner led his family away and through the doors into the hall.

Quinn looked back at him with a sad little pout. He gave her a roguish smirk as he swept his hair back from his eyes then turned to see his father walking up the steps with his younger girlfriend on his arm, wearing a short sequined dress showing plenty of skin, and two bodyguards. He hadn't even told his father about Quinn yet.

"Reese, you're actually on time for something..." Cillian O'Shea said with an amused chuckle. "What was the hurry?" He asked a little sarcastically, since Reese had jumped out of the limo two blocks away like it was on fire.

Reese's mouth twisted as he took off his coat and handed it off to an attendant to reveal the tux underneath. "Yeah, I need to talk to you about something."

"Hmm, of course you do..." Cillian said cynically. He pierced Reese with a serious gaze. "I'm here with Maya to enjoy a lovely evening, can't it wait?"

He knew what that meant, business wasn't discussed in front of the women or general public. Reese looked at the other people crowding around chatting and showing their invitations to enter. "Not really, I've put it off too long already and now there's been an incident."

Reese saw Liam tense up out of the corner of his eye and flicked him a glance that said volumes. Cillian's eyebrow had risen in question. "Serious?"

"Not yet, but it just happened right here and involved the Police Commissioner and his family." Reese grimaced at the thunderous frown on his father's face. "That road block wasn't an accident."

Cillian rubbed his jaw a moment, glaring at Reese before asking. "Who?"

Reese almost flinched. "Augusto Ferrante was just here."

Cillian hissed. "Fuck's sake, boy." He moved forward to the entrance to the event and walked through heading to their allotted table and seating his girlfriend down.

"I'll be right back, sweetheart."

"Sure thing, babe."

Reese gave her an apologetic smile and they headed to the front of the room and through a door that led behind the stage.

As they passed the Commissioner's table Reese saw Quinn watching him with a nervous gaze. Cory was holding her hand and talking quietly to her but his father and mother were still standing, chatting to people and shaking hands. Reese caught Michael's gaze and gave him a haughty smirk. Michael snorted disapprovingly and looked away.

Quinn saw the interaction.

"Your dad doesn't like Reese very much, is that why he doesn't come around much?"

Cory huffed. "Nah, Reese can't be bothered with the grief, he is who he is and that's not going to change, he likes who he is...of course dad disagrees with it."

"So that's why you drifted apart as friends?"

Cory nodded. "Basically, it just got too hard...but now..." Quinn turned to face him, her eyes lifting with a curious look. He smiled at her. "Neither one of us care what our father's think about our friendship."

"Friendship?" Quinn asked with a cheeky little smirk.

Cory's eyes narrowed and darkened as he chuckled a sexy little rumble and licked his lip. "Yeah well...I guess we have you to thank for bringing us closer together."

Quinn's smile was breath-taking and Cory leaned in and pressed his lips to hers. As he pulled away he playfully pinched her chin. "You're incorrigible, behave, bunny...Reese is going to have to tell his father about you, this is serious."

Quinn's gaze widened then dropped to her lap. "Sorry, I didn't..."

"I know...I'm just feeling really nervous for him right now."

"Perhaps I should just go home." Quinn breathed sadly.

"No, don't do that...I really want you here tonight, you look beautiful."

Quinn looked up with a genuine and truly beautiful smile. Cory leaned over and pecked her lips with his. "God, you're sexy."

Quinn blushed and tilted her head away, grabbing a carafe of water on the table and pouring it into her glass.

Cory chuckled. "Fuck, bunny, you're so damn adorable, I just want to eat you up."

"Cory!" She whispered harshly, glancing at Cory's mother who was now sitting down beside them. Her core felt heated enough just having the two of them in the same room as her, her mind was swirling with the information she now knew about both of them, Reese having sent her his list...now she had given her full consent to be a throuple. This was the first time she had seen Reese in the flesh and having both of them here together in such a public and formal situation just seemed like a tease and she was at her limit.

Wendy gave Quinn a knowing little smile at seeing her dodge away from Cory and berate him. "Don't let that boy talk you into anything you don't feel you're ready for." She patted Cory's arm. "Be nice, this one's a keeper."

"I am always nice." Cory pouted with a roguish side grin.

"Yes, too nice, that's why you always seem to have a different girl every other week."

"Mom!" Cory blushed, his ears reddening as Quinn giggled behind her hand.

Wendy merely gave a little smile and waved over the waitress with the wine tray.

As Michael sat down he gave Cory a serious glance over before he was again interrupted by people approaching him.

Cory's eyes had gone to the side door of the stage where Reese had disappeared with his father, concern heavy in his expression.

Quinn touched his arm. "I hope it's going to be okay?"

Cory snorted. "He has the gift of the gab...don't worry about him, it's you I'm worried about."

"Me?" Quinn gasped, feeling a little sick. "I'm fine."

48

I want you!

Cillian O'Shea was a calm cautious man, but he had a snapping point and when it was reached he was very quick to escalate to violence.

He confronted his son with a patient gaze, golden to match, ready to hear him out before coming to conclusions. Reese grit his teeth, raking a hand through his hair trying to figure out where to start, he glanced at Liam, standing behind his father's left shoulder, and he frowned at him. He had warned Reese to tell his father everything before acting and getting Quinn out of her situation with Antonio.

"Do you know about Augusto Ferrante's second wife?" Reese asked, deciding this might be a good point of entry.

Cillian gave Reese a small frown of thought. "The one that passed just recently?"

"Yeah, well do you know who her first husband was and what happened in Boston?"

Cillian's frown deepened and he coolly folded his arms. "I know enough about the situation, how do you know about it?"

"Because that girl out there with Cory is O'Malley's daughter and she has been abused by that fucker Antonio."

Cillian stared at Reese without comment and Liam gave Reese a little nod to continue.

"Cory and I got her out and away from Antonio, she's been staying with Cory in his parents' home, but Augusto has obviously found out and came here to confirm it and tell Quinn to return to Antonio." Reese's eyes almost seemed to glow golden they were so intense as they challenged his father.

Cillian rubbed his forehead with a tired sigh. "Damn it, Reese...just let the girl go back."

"I can't do that...he's humiliating her as revenge for his own mother's death at Quinn's father's hand. It's not right, she should never have been given to him like that, he's making a mockery of all of us in what he is doing to her."

"Are you sure you have your facts straight?"

"Yes." Reese answered coldly.

"I can confirm, sir." Liam added quietly.

Cillian turned to look at his right hand man, scratching his chin. "Do I even want to know why you know about this?"

"Maybe not tonight, but Ferrante could be a very real threat where this girl is concerned, he seems to be quite obsessed in seeing her destruction."

Cillian let out a long sigh, glancing back at Reese.

"I'm sorry, but I'm not letting her go back to that bastard! There's more to this story." Reese pre-empted his father's words.

Cillian was silent and no one dared speak as he sucked his teeth and thought things over. He nodded. "Fine, let's get some extra men out there and a quiet escort for this girl and the Commissioner's family...let's talk about this tomorrow, since she is obviously staying with Cory under Michael's protection, you can bring her over to my place tomorrow for lunch."

Reese's jaw clenched at the subtle order and nodded.

"Right, let's get back out there...but tell me one thing, Reese?"

Reese's eyes narrowed suspiciously.

"Are you or have you slept with this girl?"

"No." He answered calmly, well he hadn't...yet.

"Is she dating Cory?"

"No."

"So you're both just being concerned citizens?" Cillian's voice was dubious and amused.

"Not quite...but it's not our main concern right now." Reese answered diplomatically.

"Hmm..." Cillian's mouth twisted as he snorted with derision. "Don't complicate things any more than they already are, hear me?"

Reese clucked his tongue. "Yeah, yeah..."

As they walked back out into the main hall things were beginning to settle down and everyone were slowly finding their seats.

Cory and Quinn both looked up with concern as Reese followed his father to their table and sat down. Reese looked up at them and shrugged. Cillian didn't sit down, instead he headed over to their table making Michael and Cory stand up to shake his hand.

"Michael, it's been a while since we had a decent catch up."

"Indeed, seems like the kids are way ahead of us..."

Cillian laughed and looked at Cory. "How are you, Cory? Enjoying college life?"

Cory shook his hand politely. "It's pretty fun."

"Football?"

"Yeah, we're doing okay..." He shrugged.

Cillian turned to Wendy. "Beautiful as ever, Wendy."

"Kind of you to say, I see your lady friends are starting to get towards a decent age gap." Her smile was facetious.

Cillian laughed as Michael coughed. "That's why I like you!"

He turned to Quinn who was sitting quietly trying not to be noticed. "And this must be Quinn..." Her eyes came up to ones that matched Reese's. Cillian was a very handsome older man with silver touches to the sides of his black hair, slicked back, perfectly groomed in an impeccable tux. "...I've just heard a lot about you, my dear...I've never seen my son so animated."

"Ah...thank you?" She wasn't sure.

Cillian appraised her as Cory stood close to her chair, hovering. "You're a real Helen of Troy..."

"Ah..." Quinn frowned not understanding.

"I just hope New York doesn't burn for you as Troy did for Helen's misdeeds..." Cillian turned away, met Michael's eyes for a moment then walked back to his seat.

Michael coughed and took a swallow of wine before tidying his suit. He frowned down at Cory and Quinn as Cory dropped back into his seat before turning away to go and start proceedings with his opening speech.

Quinn shrank back in her seat letting out a huge breath. "That was terrifying!" She breathed, wiping her sweaty palms down her dress, Reese's father had the aura of someone very dangerous.

"Yeah, Mr O'Shea is pretty scary." Cory muttered.

"What do you think he meant about Helen of Troy?"

Cory clucked his tongue. "Not sure..."

"It didn't sound good, it sounded like a threat." Quinn murmured.

Cory grabbed her thigh under the table and gave it a little squeeze for reassurance. "Don't fret about it, Reese won't ever let his father or any of that lot hurt you."

Quinn looked up at Cory, he could see she looked quite pale. "I think he was meaning the possible fallout caused by Antonio."

"Stop, it'll be fine." He patted her leg and rubbed it.

"I'm going to the bathroom before your father starts his speech."

Quinn stood up, grabbing her clutch and walked off.

Cory looked over to the O'Shea's table and saw Reese's gaze tracking her like a laser sight. He smiled to himself, nothing was going to happen to Quinn with the wolf on the prowl.

Reese's gaze slid to him and he twisted his mouth, shrugging back.

Reese stood up and stepped to follow Quinn.

"Sit. Down." Cillian's cold voice ordered.

Reese looked at his father with a challenging glare. "No."

He stalked off after Quinn.

Cillian sucked his teeth and leveled a very angry look at Liam. "What the fuck is really going on with him and that girl?"

"Not sure, you want me to go bring him back?" Liam offered.

"Leave it..." Cillian looked over to where Cory was seated and saw him casually sipping on a drink but his eyes kept going to where the bathrooms were. "I wonder if these boys aren't competing for the girl's affections?" He scoffed a dark chuckle. "You would think she's the only beautiful girl out there...what is it about her?"

"I'm not sure, sir." Liam answered awkwardly.

Maya, Cillian's current girlfriend, stood up and grabbed his shoulder leaning into his ear. "I'll go find out..." She whispered in his ear before sauntering off in her tight dress. Cillian's eyes watched her bottom as he chuckled.

"There's my girl."

Liam frowned and really hoped Maya didn't catch Reese and Quinn in a compromising position.

Maya stepped into the bathroom to find Reese leaning on the door of a cubicle with his arms folded.

"Oh, goodness, Reese...I think you have the wrong bathroom." She exclaimed with fake shock.

Reese's top lip lifted in a derogatory sneer as he stood up. "Yeah, seem to..." He muttered and walked out.

As the door closed Maya turned to face the locked cubicle. "You can come out now, he's gone."

She heard a rather obnoxious sigh and cluck of a tongue. "I'm actually trying to pee if everyone would stop talking to me through the damn door!"

Maya laughed and turned a tap on. "How's that?"

There was silence, just the sound of the rushing water for a bit then the toilet flushed and the door opened.

The stunning young girl that walked out flicked her large green eyes up at Maya as she walked to the vanity and stuck her hands under the flowing water before pumping some soap and washing her hands then turning away as the water stopped automatically.

"Thanks." Quinn said dryly then stuck her hands under the dryer before Maya could say anything back.

The girl was certainly sassy.

Quinn looked over to Maya as she moved her hands under the dryer and raised an eyebrow at the woman who was clearly waiting for her to finish.

As the dryer stopped Quinn didn't move and just blinked at the woman she recognized as Reese's father's date.

"I'm Maya." She introduced herself when it was finally quiet.

"Quinn...did you want something?" She asked directly.

"Why was Reese in here acting like a concerned lover?" Maya asked giving Quinn back the same belligerence.

Quinn scowled at her. "He's a friend." She answered cautiously.

Maya stepped closer looking Quinn up and down. "Who are you trying to kid? I could practically feel the sexual electricity between you as I walked in."

Quinn felt like she was being cornered. "What business is it of yours, you want a piece of father and son?"

Maya grinned, looking away. "You're right, not my business..." Wow! This girl was arrogant.

"Good then...I'm going." Quinn moved sideways to the door as Maya just grinned at her and walked back to the mirror and started touching up her makeup.

Quinn opened the door feeling a little confused and stepped out.

She squealed as a hand clamped her arm and yanked her sideways, pushing her up against the wall in the darkened corridor.

"Quinn." Reese's very annoyed voice growled in her ear as he pressed in on her.

She grabbed out and pushed at his chest. "Reese, stop it...what..."

He smashed his mouth upon hers, forcing his tongue in past her teeth and grabbing the back of her neck.

Quinn felt overwhelmed by him, and her hands on his chest clenched into fists grabbing the fabric of his jacket and turned from pushing to pulling him in as she tilted her head and relaxed into him, kissing him back with a fervent need. She hadn't seen him for days!

He groaned in need and kissed her deeply.

"Goodness, Reese..." Maya's amused voice called as she stepped out of the bathroom.

Reese pulled his head back, placing a hand on Quinn's collarbone to keep her in place as he felt her tense up in fright at being discovered, pinning her like he was an eagle pinning a mouse under his talons. He turned his face and scowled at Maya darkly.

"Go report it to my father, I don't care." His voice was deep and husky and Quinn was panting, still clinging to his jacket.

Maya grinned like a Cheshire Cat and walked off.

Reese pressed his forehead to Quinn's, both hands cupping her neck, his thumbs stroking her cheeks. "Baby, fuck...I just needed to know you were okay..."

"I'm fine...now." Quinn breathed, reaching up a hand to touch his face.

Reese lifted his head and gave her a little smirk. "That's my girl...I told you, you have real strength."

"I want you." Quinn announced, staring into Reese's eyes and seeing them darken as he licked his lips.

"Baby, I told you..."

"Both of you..." She breathed. "I'm sick of waiting for the right time, or for lists or discussions on how this is going to work...I want you both tonight! Don't make me wait any longer...please."

Reese let her go and stepped away, raking a hand through his hair as his hooded golden gaze burned into her. He scoffed a dark laugh. "Fucking hell..." He was rock hard now.

"I'm serious, Reese...we need to sort this thing between the three of us now! I need this, I need you present!"

Reese smirked and reached out to touch her lips. "You're sure about this...have you really thought this through?"

"I've done nothing but think about it for days ever since we all slept in the same bed." Quinn pulled him closer not about to let go of his jacket. He stepped closer and she felt his hands go around her shoulders and he dropped his face into her neck with a breathy groan.

They froze as some waiters walked past them, Quinn's forehead pressed to his shoulder, hiding her face. Reese lifted his head and stepped back, taking her hands off him and holding them in his. "Not here, we need to go back in."

"We can't, not until Mr McMillan's speech is finished, it would be rude."

Reese clucked his tongue. "Fuck..." He looked away regretfully.

Quinn reached out a hand and cupped his cheek, pulling his face back. "Reese..." The breathy way she said his name made his cock twitch. "Can you sort a hotel room for us or something?"

His eyes narrowed and he licked his lips with a coy smirk. "Tonight?"

Quinn's return smile was teasing. "No, for a month from today...of course tonight!"

He scowled at her and raked a hand through his hair. "Jesus, Quinn, you're not making this easy, baby."

"What's not easy?"

His gaze smoldered at her. "Do you have any idea how badly we both want you? If we do this it isn't going to be easy on you."

They heard the applause and knew Michael's speech was over.

Quinn pursed her lips, her expression getting moody. "You think I can't handle it? You have no idea what I can handle."

Reese's dark gaze seared her. "I can well imagine, I've heard about that bastard's kinks..."

"Make me forget." She stated suddenly in a serious tone.

"Forget what?"

They both spun around and Quinn gasped as Cory was standing right behind them. Reese pivoted and leaned his shoulder on the wall next to Quinn, placing his hand back on her collar bone and pressing her to the wall as Cory walked up.

"Your little bunny wants me to book a hotel room tonight so we can make her forget...what exactly was just what she was about to say....good timing." He gave Quinn a smirk as Cory's eyes went wide for a second then he chuckled darkly and leaned on the wall on the opposite side of Quinn and slid his hand to the flat of her stomach, pressing firmly, making her gasp and look up into his heated gaze.

"Please." She grabbed them both by the belts on their pants. "Please make me forget Antonio's touch."

Reese growled and leaned into the crook of her neck. "Fuck, baby, tell me how we do that?"

Cory kissed her temple. "Go on, bunny..."

Quinn bit her lip, she was trembling between them feeling the heat of their bodies, the scent of their colognes and distinct scent of men in arousal mixing into a heady aphrodisiac for her. "I want you both to take me and fuck me into oblivion."

"Jesus Christ, bunny!" Cory exclaimed, hugging her waist tight. Reese just let out a throaty groan and buried his face deeper into her neck, inhaling the sweet smell of her perfume.

"There's a hotel straight across the street..." Reese finally started to murmur into her neck.

"Reese! What the fuck are you two doing?" Liam whisper-yelled as he came around the corner to see them both clinging to Quinn.

Cory jumped as Quinn squeaked in fright and embarrassment. Reese hissed at them both to be quiet and leveled that cool golden gaze at Liam.

"Can't you see? Quinn fainted, we're propping her up...she's having some sort of panic attack, look how red in the face and sweaty she is!"

Cory and Quinn both stared at him in awe at the perfect lie as Liam frowned full of concern. "Shit...okay...ah..." He stammered.

"Tell our Dad's we're taking Quinn home."

Liam scowled at that. "Why do you need to go? Your father wants you back at the table."

Reese felt Quinn's hand clench tight to his belt. He grit his teeth and settled a menacing stare at Liam that actually made him take pause.

"I'm going because these two people here are the most important people in my life to me...and you can direct quote me to dad, I don't give a fuck." He pulled Quinn up from the wall and swept her up in his arms, looking at Cory with a blazing heat in his eyes that made Cory's mouth go dry.

"We're leaving." Reese stated and stalked off down the hall. Cory glanced at Liam who looked a little shell-shocked then followed with a little smirk.

'That's my Rice.'

49
An appetizer

Reese stopped a waiter abruptly, startling him to see Reese carrying a young woman.

"Where's the back entrance?"

"Ah...this way, Sir. Is anything wrong, do you need an ambulance?"

"No, we're fine."

As they crossed the road Reese saw a convenience store two doors down from the hotel and put Quinn down on her feet gently. "Wait here for a sec..."

Cory and Quinn waited as he ran down the street and into the store, Quinn bit her lip as Cory huffed impatiently.

"What the fuck is he doing?"

Quinn glanced at Cory but said nothing. She could guess exactly what he was doing and a nervous excitement started making her skin vibrate and deep inside her start to ache in anticipation.

Cory seemed by instinct or pheromone smell to know and pulled her into his chest, his eyes surveying the street like a possessive serial killer.

Reese reappeared with a smug little grin on his sexy face. He took pause at the feral look on Cory's face as he glowered at Reese hotly.

"About fucking time." He growled out through clenched teeth.

Reese chuckled, licking his tongue over his teeth. "I like this side of you, Cory, it's sexy as fuck...let's go."

In the elevator on the way up Quinn gave Reese an inquisitive sideways glance, he saw it and his eyebrow rose in question. They were all tense and the aura in the closed space was making it hard to breathe.

"I think I know what's in your pocket." She said with a blush.

Cory looked over. "Condoms, right? Good, I've got two in my wallet but I think we're going to need more."

Quinn met Reese's eyes that looked dark and sultry as he smirked. "I've got some of them too, but no, not condoms."

Reese backed Quinn to the wall and kissed her, running a hand up the inside of her dress pressed to the inside of her thigh. He stared into her eyes. "Are you okay with it? You're trembling...."

"Calm down, Rice." Cory beseeched. "You're being too aggressive."

Reese backed off and looked at Quinn's dazed expression. "Fine, it was Quinn who wanted this."

She looked up at him and met his hungry gaze, he licked his lips. "You can lead this...okay?"

She gave a small smile as the elevator doors opened and they followed Reese to the room and entered watching Reese strip his jacket, bowtie and shirt off and kick off his shoes.

He looked back at them and saw them both admiring his lethal body. He smirked at them both.

"Did you mean what you said to that guy?" Quinn asked as she tentatively stepped closer to him, seeing him shirtless with those tattoos made him look dangerous to approach.

"Of course I did, Cory has always been important to me, but you..." Reese stepped up and met her in the middle of the room. "You're like the missing piece of the puzzle."

He stroked the side of her neck and looked over at Cory with a strange smile. "I'm not sure if Cory feels the same way or if he's just here because of his want for you, but I'm all in on this, you know that Curry."

Cory nodded with a coy smirk. "Yeah, I figured."

Quinn could feel the tension between them about how they were going to do this. "I don't want to lead this..." She announced. "I want to be swept up and taken by you. You seem like you guys have some sort of history at this..."

"Yeah, we sure do." Reese chuckled.

"Rice!" Cory hissed.

"What? She's a part of us now..." Reese lifted his hand to the back of her neck, threading his fingers into her hair, looking down on her like a hungry beast.

Quinn's mouth dropped open as she looked up at him. "You...Reese, you seem to be the one who should be in control here..."

Reese and Cory glanced at each other then back to Quinn. "Are you sure?"

"I think in all things to do with our little trio, for this to work you need to be our leader...if Cory agrees, we should both defer to you..." She tipped her head back against Reese's fist in her hair and looked at Cory, her eyes slightly unfocused as he was right there behind her. "And I defer to you too..."

Reese's hand slipped from her hair, down her throat and over her chest. "Fuck..." He breathed, he was barely containing himself right now.

Quinn dropped to her knees before him and his eyes darkened instantly with the lustful heat of desire.

Cory felt Quinn's hand touch his thigh and he dropped to his knees beside her, he looked at her and met her eyes, giving her one of his roguish little grins and winked before looking up at Reese.

"I agree...be our Alpha, Reese." He grinned at him.

"Holy fuck..." Reese muttered, raking a hand through his hair. He found himself unable to move, not wanting to do anything to break this moment in case it was a dream. This was his absolute fantasy.

Quinn reached out and grabbed his hand and placed it on her head. She had recognized the similar needs and desires in Reese to control and she wanted to be controlled by him, she was happy Cory was in love with Reese enough to let him take the lead too, although she needed him to be above her. They both seemed to understand what she wanted. Cory followed her lead and grabbed Reese's other hand and placed it on his head, but also put his hand on top of Reese's on Quinn's head.

Reese licked his lips, threading his fingers in their hair and pulling them forward to press their foreheads on his thighs as he stared darkly down at them.

"Thank you for giving me your trust to take care of you both." He bent slightly and took Cory by the arm and lifted him to his feet as Quinn looked up with a flush to her face. "Tonight is about Quinn, Curry, don't worry...she needs both of us to focus on her tonight."

They both looked down at her kneeling before them as she looked up with those large green eyes. The hungry look on both their faces made butterflies churn in her stomach and a deep warmth spread through her pussy. She licked her lips nervously, she knew if either of them was to touch her down there right now they would find her dripping wet. Reese clapped Cory on the shoulder as he licked his tongue over his teeth sexily.

"I think it's about time Quinn lost that dress...take it off her."

The deep heated gaze Quinn's expression dropped into made Reese smirk even wider as she turned to meet Cory's gaze as he stepped behind her, pulled her to her feet and swept her hair out of the way. He then grabbed the zip at the back and slowly unzipped it then ran his hands up her back making her shudder at his full hands sliding over her skin, up to her shoulders and swept the dress from her shoulders making it drop and pool around her waist. Reese had his tongue bit between his teeth as he watched the slow reveal of Quinn's body. Her breasts her bare except for a couple of nipple pads covering them from showing through her dress. Cory pressed his lips to her shoulder as he slid his hands down the sides of her body to drop the dress from her hips to the floor. Reese reached out and touched his first two fingers to one of the nipple pads. "Take them off." He ordered in a husky little growl.

Quinn peeled them off and held them out to Reese with a quirky little grin.

His eyes blazed at her as he took them between those two fingers and then tossed them away. "Are you going to be cheeky, baby?"

Her eyes shined but she shook her head. "No, I'll be good."

"Fuck..." Cory groaned as his hands rubbed her waist. She was wearing a nice black lace thong and suspenders with stockings. Reese looked her up and down.

"She looks good like this, doesn't she?" He asked Cory. Cory turned her around and looked at her breasts, down her flat stomach to her panties and her thighs. "Fucking beautiful, Bunny."

Reese stepped in behind her and grabbed her ponytail and started braiding it up. Quinn bit her lip at the connotation of him doing that. He peered around at her face and chuckled deeply. "Do what you want with her breasts while I do this, Curry."

Quinn gasped in a breath as Cory's hands enclosed her breasts and his mouth closed over one nipple, his tongue doing a dance around it, making it swell and harden even more than it was already.

Reese's hands dropped and curled around her waist as he looked over her shoulder to watch as Cory kissed and sucked her nipple, playing with the other, moving back and forth.

Quinn's head dropped back onto Reese's chest and he breathed in her ear. "Do you like that, baby?"

"Yes..." She panted out.

"Are you wet?" He asked with a sexy little rumble that sent shivers through her.

"Yes..."

His hand slid over her hip to the front and dipped under her panties and his fingers slid into her folds making her let out a needy moan and reach out to grab hold of Cory's shoulders. Cory looked up and then his mouth was on hers, lashing his tongue into her mouth as he pinched and rolled a nipple in his fingers.

Reese pulled his fingers out of Quinn's pussy and lifted them to beside Cory's face. "You might want to taste this...."

Cory stopped kissing Quinn and wrapped his mouth around Reese's fingers, letting out a groan of satisfaction at her taste. She looked up at Reese with a slightly embarrassed glance. He just smirked at her and pulled his fingers back. Cory dropped to his knees removing Quinn's shoes and unhooked the suspender clips from her stockings removing them slowly one by one, running his fingers up and down her legs making her squirm in impatient need. He then hooked Quinn's panties with his fingers, pulling them down her legs. "You sure you don't want to taste her first?"

"I've already tasted our little Quinn, why do you think she's here now craving more? But she needs to crave your touch too, so go for it...taste your little bunny." Reese reached out and unclipped the suspender belt letting it fall to the floor, the last piece of clothing she had on.

"Hmm..." Cory huffed before he dug his hands between Quinn's thighs and pulled making her step her legs apart and step out of her panties. Reese bent to pick them up and held them to his face for a second before tossing them away as Cory's tongue licked up her pussy and she dropped her head back with a breathy moan.

Reese pressed to her back, palming her breasts and rolling her nipples. He dropped one hand down to Cory's head and buried his fingers into Cory's hair, making him groan and look up as he flicked his tongue around Quinn's clit.

"Lift your leg up over Cory's shoulder, babe...let him devour you."

Cory grinned up at Reese as Quinn lifted her leg shakily and Cory guided her leg up over his shoulder, he looked down at her pussy dripping wet and glistening in front of him and dragged his fingers through it, spreading it open before he covered it with his mouth.

Quinn's body dropped as his tongue entered her, her weight leaning back into Reese as he played with her breasts. "Good girl, that's better, isn't it..."

"Yes..." She breathed out. "Ah...amazing..."

Reese chuckled, his hand pulled Cory tight to Quinn's pussy, holding him there and making him go even deeper with his tongue. They both groaned illicitly.

"Make her come, Curry." Reese stepped away from behind her and Cory, lifted his head, standing up he pushed Quinn back to the couch, making her sit then dropped to his knees lifting her legs high and spreading them out wide, he looked up into her hooded gaze before dropping his mouth back to her pussy, his fingers pushing inside her. She arched in pleasure as his fingers felt so good and her eyes dropped closed and she panted in need.

"She tastes so sweet." Cory growled out against her clit.

"I know..." Reese grinned, standing behind them and watching with a dark lustful gaze.

"Fuck, Quinn...you're addictive." Cory looked up at her face. She opened her eyes for a second meeting his before he curled his fingers up and dragged them back over her front wall. Her body jolted and she groaned out.

"Fuck...Cory...more, I need more..."

He thrust his fingers into her and twisted them round, making her body convulse then started a thrusting as he sucked on her clit. Her body writhed to match his rhythm and Reese had to pull his cock out of his pants to stroke it and try to relieve some of the pressure. He went to the hotel phone and picked it up calling to room service.

"I want a bottle of Veuve Clicquot delivered to Room 2606, three glasses and ice..." He hung up and turned back to gaze at Cory eating Quinn out, she looked close. He walked back and put one knee up on the couch next to her, her eyes opened and she startled a little to see his cock in front of her. She looked up at his smug little smirk before licking out with her tongue to lap at the precum dripping from his cock. He thrummed deep in his throat making Cory look up. He lifted his head and brought his other hand up to press and rub Quinn's clit. She opened her mouth to let out a moan then grabbed Reese's cock in one hand and sucked the head into her mouth. He wrapped her braid around his hand and held her on his cock as he thrust into her mouth.

Cory hissed out a breath through his teeth to see her taking Reese's fat cock all the way down her throat. His own cock was throbbing with the need of release. Quinn's body was tightening and he knew she wasn't far off coming.

"Fuck, she's getting off on your cock..." He muttered, rubbing and flicking her clit mercilessly while thrusting his fingers in her. "She's so fucking wet...she's soaking the leather."

"Fuck, you're a good girl, Quinn...come for us...make me come...then make Cory come too."

Quinn started moaning in needy little pants around Reese's cock then let out a little squeal as her eyes rolled back in her head and her body convulsed and trembled. Cory dived his mouth down and lapped at her creamy goodness as Reese grunted and came in her mouth.

"Drink it all down, baby..."

Cory looked up with a lick of his lips watching Quinn swallow, her eyes opening and looking up at Reese with a dreamy cast to them. Reese pulled out, yanked Quinn forward by her braid so she was face to face with Cory.

"Cory stand up...give her your cock."

She reached out as he stood up, pulling his cock free of his pants eagerly and sucked it into her mouth with a needy little moan of pleasure.

"Fuck..." Cory breathed out, gritting his teeth and grabbed the back of her head as Reese unraveled her braid from his hand and stepped back.

There was a knock at the door and Reese went to answer it as Cory groaned out in orgasm into Quinn's mouth. Reese opened the door as Cory stepped back from Quinn and looked around to see the service waiter staring at them. He tore the tux jacket from his body and threw it over Quinn as she flopped back on the couch with a dazed little grin on her face. Reese had a smug grin on his face as the waiter came in with the champagne bucket full of ice, gawking at Reese with his gangster looking tattoos then at Cory in his tux and then to Quinn, naked, covered by a jacket looking flushed. She startled at seeing a strange face and sat up, grabbing the jacket tight around herself.

"Reese!" She squealed. "What the hell?"

"Calm down, I'm sure he sees this every day..." Reese laughed. "Eh, mate?"

"Ah...sure...maybe not quite like this..."

"Well, I'm sure you know where to keep your eyes so you don't lose them."

"Reese." Cory growled out as the waiter seemed shocked.

Reese chuckled and put his arm around the waiter's neck and led him back to the door, taking his wallet out of his pants pocket he opened it, took out a fifty and handed it to the guy before closing the door on him.

Cory was already pouring the champagne and handed one to Quinn. She smiled and took it, sipping it and looking up at Reese.

"Don't look at me like that, baby...we aren't finished, don't worry..."

She blushed and looked away as Cory chuckled. "That was a nice appetizer..."

"Hmm..." Reese thrummed as he took up his glass and held it aloft. "To our little omega baby, Quinn, for bringing us all together tonight and for always."

Quinn startled, her heart thumping in her chest. Always?

Reese sipped his drink then put it down. "Now, let's not break momentum...I'm already hard again...how about we move this to the bedroom and Quinn gets in the shower."

"Shower?" She asked, as she stood up with no protest to moving things to the next stage. After having them both in her mouth she wanted both of them inside her.

Reese's head tilted as he appraised her. "How ready are you to take two of us at once, baby?"

She got what he meant immediately. "Oh, that...okay..." She moved off to the bathroom immediately.

Reese chuckled. "Good girl."

Cory watched her then saw Reese go to his jacket and take out the condoms and a bottle of lube. "So that's what you mean..."

Reese looked over his shoulder at Cory then turned with a grin. "I don't think Quinn can take us both in one hole, do you?" They were both of good girth and length.

"Yeah, probably not..."

"I'm more than happy to take the back hole..."

"Dirty fucker, of course you are." Cory chuckled. "So that's what she is doing in the shower?"

Reese's eyes sparkled. "I certainly hope so."

Cory laughed.

"Are you going to keep that suit on?" Reese asked, curiously.

Cory looked down at the white shirt and touched the bow tie. "Take it off me."

Reese dropped the things in his hands and came over, his fingers around Cory's neck, in an instant. His mouth closing over Cory's in a heated kiss as Cory groaned. Reese's fingers flicked the bow tie undone and it dropped to the floor as he unbuttoned Cory's shirt, yanking it down over his shoulders and pulled him closer, dipping his head down to lick Cory's neck and chest.

"Easy..." Cory breathed out.

Reese lifted his head and dropped the shirt, grabbing Cory's open pants and dragging them down over his buttocks so they dropped to his ankles. Reese smacked Cory's tight ass in his black boxers. "Get your ass in that bedroom before I take it!"

Cory chuckled and grabbed the champagne bucket. "I assume you have plans for this..."

Reese's eyes gleamed wickedly. "I sure do..."

50
Take us at your pleasure

When Quinn exited the bathroom, one of those small white hotel towels wrapped around her as she clasped it closed, she saw Reese and Cory were waiting for her. She took a moment to just take them both in, standing in their naked glory, erect and wanting. Fucking glorious!

Their eyes raked her body as she dropped the towel and walked towards them. Problem was she didn't know which one she wanted to walk towards the most. Reese solved that problem by reaching out and hooking her neck with one large controlling hand and pulled her towards him, his mouth covering hers as his tongue lashed around her tongue taking her breath, taking her everything.

Cory came up behind her, his hands rubbing her hips before slipping up to cup her breasts. Reese gripped her chin with his other hand and angled her face back over her shoulder, pulling his own mouth away but only enough so Cory could slip his tongue inside too.

Quinn whimpered as both their tongues controlled her mouth, it wasn't a whimper of dislike, it was a whimper of need. Her hands lifted to cup both of their faces, not wanting this three-way kiss to end. Reese pulled away with a smirk though and dropped to his knees, lifting one of her legs and placing her foot on the bed before licking up between her legs from butthole to clit.

"Ah...fuck..." Quinn groaned out as Reese's tongue did wild things to her. His face getting right up in there as he tasted every part.

Cory pinched her nipples making her shriek and he chuckled into her mouth, dragging his lips down her neck. Reese pushed two fingers inside her pussy and curled them forward seeking her weak spot. She jolted when he found it and he looked up with a chuckle, his face glistening with her juices. "Come baby, then I'll let my cock taste your pussy."

"Oh, fuck..." Quinn breathed, reaching back and clinging onto Cory's shoulders for dare life as Reese started pressing his thrusting fingers to that spot again and again, his tongue flicking and teasing her clit. She let out another gasping moan as Cory pinched her nipples again rolling them and pulling them with expert hands that felt so good she didn't know which way was up anymore. She felt Reese's other hand slide up the inside of her thigh and a finger swipe through her dripping pussy then press to her ass.

"Relax a little, baby..." He breathed.

She was holding herself tense as her leg was trembling, Cory pulled her back into his chest. "Hook your arms around my neck, bunny...lean on me."

Quinn did what he said and earned a little whisper into her ear. "Good girl."

She groaned out in pleasure as Reese's finger slid inside. Cory dropped one hand and placed it under the thigh of her leg that was bent up and pushed his hips into the small of her back, lifting her as he ground into her with a groan. "Come, bunny..." He breathed and licked the shell of her ear.

"Oh, fuck...yes...I'm gonna..."

She heard Reese rumble a throaty growl of pleasure as she tipped over the edge and came hard, seeing stars behind her closed eyes.

Midway through her orgasm she felt Reese move away and gasped out a startled. 'No.'

Suddenly he was standing in front of her, scooped her other leg up and out and thrust into her hard, pushing his entire length into her in one go. Her body clenched around him and she cried out as her orgasm intensified. She bucked against his cock as he thrust into her through her orgasm slow but hard until she finally opened her eyes to find him smirking at her. He dropped his mouth to hers and kissed her. She let go of Cory's neck and wrapped them around Reese's, kissing him back with a fervor that was still not quenched.

Cory chuckled behind her. "Jesus, this girl is insatiable..."

Quinn pulled away from kissing Reese and turned her head, giving Cory a blatantly cheeky look. Reese laughed and thrust up into her hard making her cry out. "Behave princess...you'll get us both...I just wanted to feel your pussy climaxing around me first."

She looked back at him with a little frown as he pulled out of her and dropped her to her feet. He gave her a sexy amused smile. "What's wrong, baby? We're just swapping sides..."

He spun her round with a hand on her shoulder to face Cory. Cory's grin was manic, his eyes burning with a strong need as he grabbed her around the buttocks, lifted one of her legs and slid his cock into her then lifted her other leg and she wrapped them around his waist. Curling her arms around his neck she groaned as his cock sank deep into her.

Reese had stepped away to get the lube, running it over his cock then returned. Her head was thrown back and she cried out as Reese put a hand on the small of her back and pressed her down even more onto Cory's cock as Cory thrust up. She felt him hit her cervix, her body jolting.

"Fuck..." She groaned as they relented, Reese chuckling darkly as he came up grabbed her braid in his hand and yanked her head back.

"Take all of him, baby..." He ordered as they did it again, getting a long gritty moan out of her. "Good girl." He kissed the back of her neck and not letting go of her braid he lined his cock up to her ass and slowly pushed in.

Her eyes opened wide, unfocused as she gasped at the feeling of being stretched and filled by his big cock while already filled with Cory's in her pussy. "Oh my god...I don't..." She gasped out.

"Relax, bunny..." Cory breathed huskily, kissing her jaw as Reese held her head.

"Take me...princess, all of me...you want this..." Reese whisper-growled in her ear.

"Oh, fuck...it feels so...different...from toys...this is intense..." She gasped out, blinking at Cory who was watching her with a fire burning in his eyes, his jaw clenched tight. She realized he wasn't moving, just holding himself inside her while holding her up as Reese pushed in the back.

"Kiss me." She breathed.

Cory's top lip twerked up in the corners as his jaw relax and he licked his tongue out over her lips before kissing her slow and languid. She moaned, panting through the kiss as Reese bottomed out in her and she felt his teeth clamp down on her shoulder, not enough to hurt but enough to make her feel like she was being taken by two pure animals.

"Fuck..." He growled out in a husky breath through his teeth.

Cory leaned back to take her weight better, drool dripping between them and landing on her breasts already wet with a sheen of sweat. She squirmed a little as they both moved inside her.

"Oh my god...I don't think...I can...it's too intense..."

"Easy, baby...take us at your pleasure...we only need you to focus on four words right now...listen to me...harder, softer, faster, slower...we'll do whatever you need..." Reese's voice was deep, calm and commanding and in that moment it was exactly what she needed, as his and Cory's cocks pulsed inside her.

She licked her lips and closed her eyes, dropping her head back onto Reese's chest. Both of them had their hands under her thighs supporting her as they both started to move.

"Fucking hell..." Cory grunted at the tight feel of her, feeling Reese's cock through her walls. "You feel amazing, Quinn."

"Slower!" Quinn breathed out.

She felt them both comply and slowed their thrusts together, keeping a steady rhythm. "Good?" Reese asked, nuzzling into her neck.

"Yes..."

"You're fucking addictive, baby..." He groaned.

"Harder...please...I need..." Quinn felt like she was losing her mind.

As they started to thrust hard and slow Reese groaned into her neck, sucking on it as Cory dipped his head down to bite a nipple into his teeth. Quinn gasped, her eyes flying open to stare at Cory. He was grinning at her with her nipple held in his teeth, he shook his head like a dog with a toy. Reese chuckled behind her as she mewled in pleasure when Cory sucked the nipple into his mouth.

"Fuck, I'm going to come soon..." Cory groaned, licking up her chest to where Reese was looking over her shoulder. He licked out over Reese's lips and Reese pressed Quinn tight between them to get closer to Cory as their tongues twined around each other's. They felt Quinn's body tighten as she moaned out watching them.

"I think she likes to watch us make out..." Reese chuckled.

"Pervert..." Cory grinned then kissed her. "Come, Quinn...I'm going to come..."

"Fuck..." Reese groaned, feeling Quinn clamp down on him hard.

"Faster...harder..." Quinn demanded in a breathy groan, reaching her hands out to grab them both by the hair.

"Fuck..." Cory hissed as his head was yanked down.

Reese thrummed that little pleased growl in his throat. "Yank my fucking hair out, Quinn, if you have to...fuck...come baby..."

She cried out as she came, both of them thrusting hard and fast into her, her whole body convulsing between them. Cory came fast behind her and Reese followed soon after that.

They were a standing pile of panting sweaty bodies, all pressed into each other, both boys heads were on each of Quinn's shoulders, her hands still threaded in their hair, gripping tight as she rode out the last of her orgasm, her own hips moving between them as their cocks pulsed inside her.

She felt like she was going to pass out as her hands relaxed and dropped away, her body completely slack.

She felt Reese pull out and step away and let out a little groan at the emptiness she felt, wrapping her arms around Cory's neck and holding on to him like a koala bear. Cory walked her to the bed and dropped to his knees then lowered her down on her back before pulling out of her and laying down beside her. He cupped her breast as she turned to look at him with a sated smile on her face. He brushed some sweat drenched hair from her face then kissed her, slow and doting as Reese came to her other side and sat down on the bed by her hip.

Cory pulled back and Quinn looked up at Reese to see he had one of the champagne flutes in his hand and a few ice cubes in the other. She went to sit up.

"Wait...what are..."

Cory pushed her back with a hand on her chest. "Easy, bunny..."

Reese grinned like the devil, his golden eyes iridescent. "You think we've finished, baby? That was just to get our mad lust out of the way...now we play!"

"Oh, fuck..." Quinn breathed, her insides already squirming.

51
Afterglow

Quinn woke Sunday morning to find herself between her two new lovers. She looked from one side to the other a small pleased smile creeping over her lips as she gazed upon their sleeping peaceful faces. They were both facing her, their free arms over her. She didn't remember getting under the covers or falling asleep, only insane pleasure again and again as they played with her body and made her orgasm reach a plateau that she thought she would never come down from.

Did she finally pass out?

There were plenty of times she thought she was going to...maybe that's what happened?

She stifled a little giggle as she realized someone had obviously wiped her clean before putting her in the bed, these guys had fucked her into oblivion just like she had begged them to, but then cared for her and cleaned her up when she was passed out and gone.

Cory stirred and she looked up at him as his eyes slowly drifted open, she saw them come into focus and look at her, his lips creeping up into a beautiful smile at seeing her.

"Hey..." He called in a husky morning voice.

"Hey..." She answered, smiling back at him. She lifted her fingers to swipe his lips and he kissed them, squeezing his arm around her and pulling her closer.

That movement made Reese's arm tighten and yank back in reaction. They both looked over to him and saw his golden gaze, like a sun rising, appear from under his thick black lashes and glare at them for a moment, then soften as his brain caught up to what was happening. He shuffled closer as Cory chuckled.

"What are you two playing at so early in the morning?" Reese growled out, his voice also husky with sleep and so deep.

"Nothing..." Quinn giggled. "Well, not yet..."

Reese's attention alerted instantly and he leaned up on his elbow. "Are you still not satisfied?"

"Jesus Christ give me strength..." Cory muttered amused. "I think maybe we bit off more than we can chew with this one..."

Quinn giggled more and dug her hands under the blanket to find their cocks. Reese groaned and grabbed her wrist. "Fuck..."

Cory hissed through his teeth but did nothing to stop her.

"I see you both wake up with morning wood..." She teased.

Reese gave her an intensely dark look. "If you're going to confess to knowing that you better be prepared to do something about it."

"I worried you would be sore after last night." Cory groaned as she stroked him.

Quinn shook her head. "No, I'm good...maybe a little muscle sore, but I think the lube helped..."

Reese snorted and let her wrist go so she could touch him too and collapsed back onto his back. "Well who am I to stand in the way of what our princess wants. I can't stay long though I have to get back to see my father at midday..."

Cory collapsed back on his back and reached back to grab his phone off the bedside table, looking at the time.

"It's 9am...what time do we have to check out?"

"I paid for late check out, so twelve noon." Reese grumbled out, his eyes closed as he enjoyed Quinn's hand stroking him.

Cory huffed and put his phone back then sat up making Quinn look up at him and Reese crack an eye open his eyebrow raised in question.

Cory grinned and threw the blankets off them all getting on his knees, grabbed Quinn by the waist and flipped her over onto her stomach then lifted her up onto her knees as she squealed a little at the manhandling. He grabbed into her hair, turning her around so her face was facing Reese's cock and her ass was off the bed as he dropped to his feet on the floor and rubbed his cock against her pussy.

"Suck Rice off while I fuck you."

Reese chuckled as Quinn startled at Cory giving the orders for a moment before he tightened his grip on her hair and shoved her face down. She took Reese's cock in her hands and sucked the head into her mouth obediently.

"Good girl, bunny." Cory growled as he thrust into her.

Reese put his hands behind his head, chuckling to himself. "You're a real horny fuck boy in the mornings, huh?"

"You complaining?" Cory grunted as he was thrusting hard into Quinn's pussy. "I know she's not, she's fucking wet."

Reese grinned. "Nope. I like it."

"Is she sucking you good?"

Reese looked down with a cocky smirk as he felt Quinn angle slightly to look up at him. Her eyes were full of tears but a hunger to hear him praise her. "Could be better." His eyes twinkled at her little frown then her eyes went wide as Cory spanked her ass.

"You heard him..." She reached up with one hand and tapped his hand that was holding her head.

"I think she wants you to stop shoving her mouth down on me...she can't get any movement." Reese said amused.

Cory grunted and let go of her hair, grabbing her hips and thrusting up into her as he pulled her back. He hit the end of her and she let out a loud moan as she tried to finally take a breath.

"Fuck..." She cried out, looking over her shoulder at Cory.

Reese took her chin and turned her to look at him. "Does it feel good or not?"

She frowned, if she said it didn't would he stop Cory? She didn't want him to stop Cory...just...

"Slow down a little..." She breathed.

She was surprised when Cory actually did what she said and she smiled through her panting as the heat coiled inside her better.

"Better, baby?" Reese asked.

She nodded. "Yeah...much..."

"Good, then get back to sucking." He growled out with a twisted grin.

Her eyes blazed at him for a moment but she dropped her head to look at his rigid cock before she wrapped her hands around it again and started licking and sucking the head.

Reese's eyes closed with a contented groan. "Fuck...that's better..."

"I'm going to come!" Cory announced.

Reese clucked his tongue. "Come and I'll spank you as punishment...Quinn comes first, got it?"

"Ah, fuck, Rice..." Cory dropped a hand underneath Quinn and found her clit as he started grinding into her deep with every thrust.

Quinn's moan was decadent and she sucked Reese's cock down her throat in response. Reese dropped a hand to her head and his body bucked up.

"Holy fuck! Her mouth gets demanding when she's being fucked good."

Cory chuckled as he could feel her pussy tightening around him "Oh, yeah...here we go...Jesus..."

Quinn was moaning around Reese's cock stuffed into her mouth with every thrust Cory took as he rubbed her clit. She started lifting her ass up and back to meet his thrusts as she came undone, her body tremoring like an earthquake. Cory came behind her with a throaty growl.

Reese's fingers twined around her hair and cupped her head as she continued to moan and slurp his cock, taking it deep then licking around the head. Cory stayed behind her, rubbing her back as he watched.

Reese finally came with a hearty groan, thrusting his hips up and pressing his head back in the pillow. "Fuuuccckk!"

"Swallow it..." Cory ordered her as he wrapped his arms around her and pressed to her back. She swallowed and licked around the head as she pulled back. "Good girl..."

He lifted her up, sat down on the bed and put her between his legs, his arms still wrapped around her, his face buried into her neck. She was panting and puffing for breath but grinned, wiping her mouth and reached back to stroke a hand over Cory's hair.

Reese stood up looking at the two of them and laughed. "You're fucking adorable...I want a picture." He grabbed his phone and stood at the end of the bed, picking up the blanket and throwing it up so Quinn could cover her body then snapped a pick of the two of them cuddling and grinning at the camera with their sweaty afterglow grins.

"You really are amazing." Reese said to her.

Quinn beamed with pride and felt a thump in her heart, she really did love these two. She wanted to stay here and fuck them forever...they were both so awesome at it.

"Right, breakfast...what do you both want?" Reese asked, pulling his pants on.

"Do we really have to go?" Quinn pouted a little as she sat in the living area of the hotel suite looking up at Cory as Reese was on his phone and putting on his jacket at the same time already running late.

His father had told him to bring Quinn to his house for lunch, but he had no intention of doing what his father wanted...he would speak to Cillian O'Shea himself first.

"Yeah, we have to go...well at least I have to, I have somewhere to be."

"Where is that?" Cory asked a little suspicious.

"Dad wants to talk." Reese muttered, his expressionless face saying far more than the words.

"Oh...okay..." Cory gave Quinn a reassuring smile. "We can do something instead of going home, I've already answered my parent's messages asking where we are."

"Go home." Reese growled. "Augusto would have told Antonio by now...Dad has put men on the street in the community, you're safest there."

He walked up to Quinn as she looked suddenly scared and crouched down in front of her, sweeping her hair back and curling his hand around the back of her neck. "You'll be okay, I promise...just make sure Michael doesn't find out about this..." He kissed her forehead then her lips and stood up. "I have to go...text later."

He walked to the door and left.

"Well, we might as well go too..." Cory said with a smile holding out his hand to her. "Do you have everything?"

She stood up, picking up her clutch and smoothing down her dress. "Yeah..." She took his hand and he pulled her closer, kissing her softly.

"Have I told you how amazing you are?"

Quinn looked up at him and smiled beautifully, her eyes sparkling with that afterglow from great sex. "Yes, you did...thank you."

"Alright then, let's go."

As they walked in the house Wendy came rushing from upstairs. "Oh, thank goodness...I was worried."

Cory's mouth twisted. "I told you we were both fine...Quinn just had an anxiety attack from seeing Mr Ferrante and what he said to her...Reese took us back to his and we spent the night there making Quinn feel safe behind a wall of people."

Wendy frowned but accepted it as true. Michael appeared from the direction of his office with a grumpy look on his face.

"She would have been safer here...Cillian has told me he's putting some men to watch over our place and double check who's coming and going from the community."

Cory nodded. "Yeah, Reese told me that this morning...look we were up all night playing games and keeping Quinn in a happy mood so..." He looked at Quinn for support.

She smiled, tucking her long hair behind her ear. "Yeah, these guys were the best support, I'm sorry if I caused any inconvenience or unnecessary worrying..."

Michael's jaw was clenched tight and ticking as Wendy touched Quinn's arm and pulled her towards the stairs. "No, of course not, dear...you go and rest...do you need anything?"

"I might grab a water if that's okay...I'm a little thirsty..."

"I'll get it, bring it up." Cory said.

"Okay, thanks." Quinn gave him a little smile then retreated up the stairs. Wendy looked from Michael to Cory.

"I'll go get the water..." She made her way quickly to the kitchen.

Michael rubbed his jaw. "So what really happened last night?"

"Why, do you think I'm lying?" Cory answered with a challenging tone.

Michael sighed and looked away. "Fine, I won't push it...but we need to do something we can't have this situation affecting our family."

"Yeah...I get it." Cory grumbled and looked over as Wendy came back with the water. He took it from her and made his way up the stairs to Quinn's room and knocked on the door.

"Yeah..." She called out and he went in.

"Water..."

"Thanks, you want to stay?"

"I better not, dad's suspicious as hell."

"Oh, okay..." Quinn sat down on the bed and grabbed the pillow, cuddling it to her chest.

"Fuck, don't look like I just kicked you..." Cory strode to the bed and sat down next to her, putting his arm around her shoulders and pulling her in to his side. He kissed her hair and rubbed his cheek against her head.

"Sorry, it's just after everything I feel a little lost not having you both there all of a sudden, it was really intense and then nothing...and we don't know when we'll see Reese again...this is going to be hard."

"Yeah, I know...but think of the positives...with great sex like that it's something to look forward to..."

She giggled a little and stroked his chest. "Yeah I guess so."

"Besides, now we've all done it together I'm sure we'll be allowed to play more without Reese..."

She looked up, pulling away from him slightly to get a better look at his face. "Like what exactly?" Her eyes were already lit with that insatiable desire.

Cory chuckled and covered her eyes. "Settle down, bunny, or I might have to spank you..."

"Oh..." She didn't look opposed to that idea either.

"Fucking hell...you're too dangerous...I'm going to go for a run and then shower..."

She squinted at him suspiciously as he stood up. "You're going to run passed the O'Shea place, aren't you?"

He laughed, rubbing his neck. "You got me, and you're not coming...have a rest, I know you need it." He looked at her coyly with a smirk as she clearly stifled a yawn.

Quinn pouted at him. "And that makes you feel smug, huh?"

"Yeah, a little to be honest..." He laughed and bopped her on the nose. "I'll let you know when I'm back, okay."

"Okay..."

52
Cillian O'Shea

Cillian O'Shea sat out the back of his large home by the pool sipping a strong black coffee and enjoying the fine autumn day. His lovely lady was swimming, doing laps in the heated pool and he loved to watch her fluid motions as she free-stroked back and forth, slicing through the water with almost no splash...she had grown up in California so loved to swim as her way of exercise.

He looked up at the men in suits standing on either side of the pool area at the two different exits from the house, sometimes he couldn't wait to give up this lifestyle and retire away somewhere where the world was a safer place for the likes of a gangster like him. Having to be constantly watched over got a little tiring after a while, that's why he tried so hard to give his son, Reese, as much freedom to live as he could right now. Once he was in this cage there was no leaving it until you were prepared to change your identity and disappear.

He sighed, leaning his head back against the lounge chair and closed his eyes, dreaming of a time he could lie on a foreign beach with no threat and no guards.

He heard a little commotion and opened his eyes to see the leader of his security crew coming through the patio doors from the main lounge. Cillian sat up with a grunt of age as the man came to stand in front of him.

"Reese is here, sir."

"Good...is he alone?" He asked with a grumble.

"Ah, yes, sir."

Cillian huffed amused, he knew Reese wouldn't bring the girl over. He got to his feet just as Reese walked casually through from the other direction, glancing down to the pool where Maya had stopped swimming and was looking up at him with a coy smile. Reese's top lip lifted on one side in a sneer before looking over to his father.

"Reese, I see you came alone."

Reese barked a laugh. "You didn't seriously expect me to bring Quinn into this lion's den, did you?"

Cillian chuckled. "Let's head inside..."

Reese heard a splash and looked back to see Maya stepping out of the pool and grabbing her towel, she pressed it to the side of her head rather than cover up. She looked up at Reese from under her lashes and gave him a smoky little smirk. "Aren't you going to say hello?"

Reese sucked his teeth. "Why should I do that?" He turned away and walked off, following his father.

He heard Cillian cluck his tongue as they stepped inside. "What? Don't blame me..."

Cillian huffed. "You know, she even had the audacity to ask me if we would ever consider doing her together..."

"I think it's time to show the skank the door, Dad, honestly eww." Reese cringed and shivered.

Cillian chuckled as he walked into a small private reception lounge and sat down into a soft grey couch, hooking his ankle over the thigh of his other leg.

Reese sat down in an armchair facing him as a petite little maid came in. "Sir, Pedro would like to know if you want him to start lunch?"

Reese's eyes gave the maid a once over as Cillian answered in the affirmative and watched her leave. "Why not just fuck her and get rid of Maya?"

"Who says I'm not fucking Lucia?" Cillian looked at Reese's revolted look and laughed.

"Fuck, I was joking..." Reese muttered.

"Anyway, you're not here to spend quality time with family..." Cillian said a little sarcastically making Reese sneer. "Explain yourself."

Reese explained the situation with Quinn, Antonio and Flanagan. Cillian listened showing no emotion and never interrupting until Reese was done. He chewed over the information for a minute before looking up at Reese with a serious intense stare.

"You have evidence of all this?"

"What evidence do I need? Quinn was obviously living with Augusto up until just over a month ago...she was moved down to here to start college and be under the control of Antonio since he took over as Don. There are people in Boston who know exactly what happened. I was told her uncle tried to stop it, he wanted to take her in but Flanagan is the one that agreed to give her to Ferrante without any consultation. Can we not contact him?"

Cillian walked off and stood looking out the window, his hands in the pockets of his casual slacks.

"He needs to be held accountable." Reese stated with an impatient growl. "He's acting like he's untouchable! Look at what they did to her the other fucking night!"

"Hmm...you know it's not that easy, this has to be approached carefully." Cillian muttered then turned around. "Augusto apparently flies out to Italy today."

That surprised Reese. "Really...shit?"

"Hmm...it worries me...that means Antonio is off the leash. The one and only man that could control that psycho was his father." Cillian rubbed his chin, his mood dropping by the second. "I'm going to have to look into this...what you've accused Flanagan of is serious, he took funds to enable his own leadership and had the previous leader executed for something that really wasn't that major..."

Reese glowered at his father. "He tried to have Augusto killed but instead ended up killing his wife. It's a gentleman's agreement that families aren't to be involved in our 'business dealings' so how the fuck was this even allowed to happen to Quinn? Huh? Fucking explain that to me, dad, before you start trying to tell me just to give her back for peace and the greater good or whatever you're thinking right now. I don't see a problem with the execution, but to basically sell the daughter...who is the granddaughter of Will O'Rourke to the enemy, take her inheritance and treat her as some sort of collateral...I have a huge problem with that! Did you know Antonio is going into politics? He's going to use her connection to one of our founding fathers to broker our compliance. He's going to marry her and produce an heir with Irish blood."

Cillian frowned, deeply concerned at that. "He's not going into politics here that I know of?" He wiped a hand over his face and let out an agitated sigh. "You're right son, this does all need to be questioned...I can't shake the feeling that there is something deeper and more sinister actually going on between Antonio and Flanagan."

"He was with Senator Peloski at the charity auction you made me go to...thick as thieves."

"Hmm...let me look into that further...the fact that Quinn is no longer with him, he's been pretty quiet...I would have expected to hear of his anger by now."

Reese grimaced. "Give him time...it was only Wednesday before last we took her and hid her at Cory's place...now he knows where she is and his father is gone..." Reese's jaw clenched tight as well as his fists.

"Calm down...let me talk to Flanagan..."

"You think that's wise? If there is evidence he'll destroy it...he won't risk being caught out by you."

Cillian chuckled. "Don't worry...I know how to handle Flanagan, and after that stunt he pulled allowing Antonio into our territory like that, I haven't begun to give him the trouble he deserves."

Reese huffed. "Tread carefully, when we need to oust him we need the evidence."

Cillian appraised his son with a tilt to his head. "You're going to be a good leader, son. Step back now though, you still have a few years to enjoy yourself...perhaps Quinn should come under my roof and relieve you and the McMillans of the danger and stress. I can protect her as the main piece of evidence against Flanagan. Antonio will not make a move against me."

Reese grit his teeth. "Right now she stays where she is. She's not connected to us at all and that keeps her safer."

Cillian nodded. "Alright...how much does Liam know of this?"

"It was his man that I spoke to from Boston that filled me in to everything."

Cillian gave a little smile. "Right...he likes you a lot." He sat up with a sigh. "Okay, let me go through that channel first, hear all this first hand and decide on a course of action where Flanagan is concerned, right now though we need to keep our eye on Antonio, what's your plan to get him to let go of Quinn?"

Reese sucked his teeth. "I'm not sure anything will get him to let go of her, he's completely obsessed, it actually scares me how quiet he's been up till now, he went to college and asked around, viewed camera footage and held an assembly of the business faculty about her disappearance, but he hasn't come at me directly since I encountered him on the stairs from Chancellor Bayton's office on day one."

"Hmm..." Cillian thrummed in concern. "He now knows where she is too..."

His head of security walked in and up to his ear, whispered to him and then stood waiting. Cillian pinched the bridge of his nose and rubbed his eyes. "Apparently Cory is at the gate..."

"What?" Reese spat, then shook his head. "That little brat!"

"Go let him in..." Cillian said to the man.

He bowed his head. "Yes, sir."

Reese wiped a hand over his face, exasperated by his golden retriever's actions. "I told him to stay at home."

Cillian gave his son a very worldly look. "Just what is your plan involving those two?"

Reese's piercing gaze hit Cillian like a freight train. "Why?"

Cillian chuckled. "Just remember...although we have a moral code others do not. Weakness is weakness...if you can't keep them safe get rid of them if they mean that much to you. It's safer for them in the long run."

Reese leaned forward, his elbows on his knees and covered his face with a bitter growl. "Fuck..."

Cillian frowned, concerned. "Who means that much to you? The boy or the girl?"

Reese dropped his hands, staring at the floor feeling exposed. "I love them both, dad."

Cillian's jaw clenched tight but he was unable to respond as Cory was led into the room looking remorseful and pitiful in his shorts and t-shirt.

Reese looked up with a dark penetrating gaze making Cory drop his head and not look at him. "Did you run here?"

"Yeah, I had to make it look like I was just going for a run to my parents."

Cillian chuckled and waved to a guard that was standing by the door. "Get Lucia to bring some coffee and tell Pedro to serve Maya her lunch in the north wing."

"Yes, sir."

Cillian flicked his fingers to a seat next to Reese's. "Sit down, young man...we have much to discuss, I assume you know everything that Reese does about what's going on with that delightful red haired girl."

"Quinn...her name is Quinn." Cory said with a grumble as he took his seat. Cillian's eyes narrowed on him at that response and then he chuckled madly to himself.

Reese sucked his teeth and gave Cory a lethal glare. "Why did you come here?"

"This concerns Quinn so it concerns me too..."

"No it really doesn't, this concerns our business...nothing more than that." Reese growled making Cory give him an angry glare back.

"Don't compartmentalize this, Reese...it affects me too no matter which way you try to bend it."

"He's right." Cillian interrupted. "He should be here...you boys have taken it upon yourselves to take something of great value to the Don of the Northeast Mafia, hide it at the Police Commissioner's house with no recourse as to what could happen when he found out." Cillian spoke calmly but his message was harsh. "I wasn't joking when I called her a Helen of Troy."

Cory looked up at Cillian. "To be honest, we didn't perhaps think this all the way through but to see those marks on Quinn's body was enough to just get her the hell out of there and fuck the consequences!"

Cillian chuckled as Reese whacked Cory's arm. Cory glared at him and rubbed his arm. "Oww, what? It's true...we focused on the hurt she was in and prioritized her safety in the short term. I don't see anything wrong with that?"

Reese sighed and patted Cory's shoulder. "Yeah, okay...I love you for it...but..."

"He's going to be a great lawyer..." Cillian commented, amused. "Cory, you know a lot more than you should about our dealings and I'm always willing to overlook it due to your friendship with Reese, but this may be over your heads."

Cory grit his teeth and dropped his gaze. "Yeah..."

"Good at least one of you can admit that."

Reese clucked his tongue. "I can deal with Antonio...he doesn't scare me."

"And therein lies the problem, you're not mature enough to realize the impact such foolish actions would make...my biggest concern is this move into politics you mentioned, that could compromise a lot of our business dealings."

"Is that why you want Quinn here?" Reese spat.

Cillian's gaze slid up to lock with his son's as the maid brought in a tray of coffees. "I brought in black coffee, but if anyone prefers something like a latte or cappuccino I can change it." She said with a small smile.

"Thank you, Lucia, black will be fine." Cillian dismissed her.

Cory looked at Reese and Cillian. "You want to move Quinn here?"

"I believe she will be safest within the fold...we are her actual family after all."

"Actual family?" Cory scoffed. "That's not..."

"Family is family." Cillian said firmly. "It's not a blood relative benefit to be called family. She has clear ties to one of our founding fathers..."

Cory bit his tongue and glanced at Reese, Reese dropped back in his seat with a huff. "Leave it, Cory, she's not moving anywhere." His gaze was intense at his father.

"Well..." Cillian shrugged. "The offer will stand..."

Reese walked Cory to the gate, his hands in his pockets as he looked at the ground at his feet.

"Sorry...I shouldn't have come here...but I was worried."

Reese's burning gaze came up. "Worried about what?"

"That your father was going to order you to hand Quinn back to that monster."

Reese chuckled and reached out a hand to put around Cory's neck, stepping in close to him. "He would never do that...she's Will O'Rourke's granddaughter. That gives her unquestioned immunity whenever she needs it."

Cory nodded, gripping Reese's forearm. "Okay..." He lightly pressed his lips to the inside of Reese's elbow. "I'll get going...when will we see you again, Quinn is already asking?"

Reese chuckled. "She needs to settle down...once she commits she gives her all." He lifted his hand from Cory's neck and raked it though his hair looking off up the drive to where the security minders were watching. "Look, I don't know when I can be seen around here again...I'll message her tonight and I'll see you at college..."

"Okay..." Cory looked at his smart watch. "We can play though, right?"

Reese sucked his teeth, giving Cory a deep glowing gaze. "Yeah...I have no right to say no, it's my own reasons I have to stay away..."

"Cool..." Cory looked up at Reese's mouth as Reese licked over his teeth. Reese chuckled. "Stop or I'll kiss you right here and you know I don't care a fuck who sees."

"Yep, going...bye." Cory moved quickly through the side gate as a guard opened it for him. Reese chuckled to himself.

He watched Cory jog off down the street then let out a bitter sigh. Things were only going to get messy from here.

53
Fallout

Michael was sitting in on a meeting with the prosecution team of a serious murder case on Monday when an assistant entered the board room looking extremely flustered.

"Sir...an Antonio Ferrante is in the building demanding to talk to you."

Michael sighed, passing a weary hand over his face. "Damn it, I knew this would happen."

"Is this something to do with why his father turned up to the awards night, Saturday?" One prosecution lawyer asked. Luckily everyone in this meeting were in his pocket about such things like the Ferrantes.

Michael appraised him. "Yeah, unfortunately it's of a personal matter concerning my son...make that arrogant SOB wait." He ordered to the assistant.

"Ah, sir...what if he gets violent?" The assistant asked literally trembling in fear of the man and his reputation.

"He's not going to come in here in the middle of Police Headquarters acting a fool...he won't even be armed, he's not a complete lunatic. Just guide him to my office, give him coffee..."

"Yes, sir." The assistant left looking pale and sick.

"Perhaps you should go and attend to this matter, Michael?" The chief prosecutor said with a scathing frown.

"No, like I said it's a personal matter and I'm at work, he's got a cheek thinking he can come at me because of some stupid disagreement he's having with his step-sister concerning my son." Michael decided some half-truths may quell the curiosity in everyone's eyes.

"Wait, are you saying your son is dating Antonio's sister?"

"Step-sister...and she doesn't have anything to do with the Ferrante family, she walked away from them and asked my son for aid after her mother passed." Feasible.

"Shit, that red-haired girl at the award's dinner?"

"Yes, that's the one."

Michael entered his office half an hour later to find Antonio standing in front of the window and looking out with his off-sider Matteo standing by the door. Michael had heard there were more men standing down in the lobby and outside the building and the police were in attendance keeping a low but clear profile.

Antonio turned and glared at Michael with those cold black eyes as he entered. "It's about time."

"I'm busy, Mr Ferrante, this is an office and it is Monday. I would prefer if you wanted to discuss personal matters you should be more discreet."

"More discreet? How about I come over to your house then to discuss the fact that your son has my step-sister." Antonio snarled sarcastically.

Michael chuckled and took off his uniform jacket, making out like he was calm and comfortable and not at all intimidated by Antonio's presence. "I think it's a bit on the nose to start calling her your step-sister, don't you think?" He waved his hand at the seats in front of his desk as he sat down behind it. "Please sit down...and you." He glanced at the intimidating form of Matteo.

Antonio sat with a cluck of his tongue while Matteo never moved.

"Look, I'll call her my little whore if that's what you want to hear, I thought to be polite. Either way I want to know why you're holding on to her and not sending her back. Shouldn't a runaway be sent back home when picked up like a stray?"

Michael assessed Antonio's vile sarcastic attitude and leaned back in his chair. "The legal age of majority is eighteen in the state of New York, Mr Ferrante...she doesn't require to be sent back to anywhere she doesn't want to go."

Antonio's expression deadened. "This is a special case, Police Commissioner, don't you think it's worth your extra effort to keep your family from making stupid decisions that could end up life threatening?"

Michael's jaw clenched tight as he locked eyes with the young Ferrante. He could see the cold heartless killer behind them. "I'm sure you have plenty of whores at your disposal, I'm not sure I really understand why you would dare to go to such lengths as to start throwing idle threats around."

Antonio chuckled sinisterly. "Idle threats? Look, the girl is a bit confused right now, she has led a somewhat sheltered life under my father and now she's at college she's obviously let a fuck-boy like your jock son talk her into being a bit rebellious, but she is mine, Mr McMillan and I want her back. I came here to do this the right way through the family head, but I won't continue to be patient."

Matteo stepped over hearing the strain of holding back in Antonio's voice and placed a calming hand on Antonio's shoulder.

Michael could see Antonio was like a pressure cooker ready to blow.

"Like I told your father, I've seen the evidence of how you treat your step-sister, Mr Ferrante and as you know what you're saying right now could be taken as a confession for those things, so I would be very careful about how you describe your relationship with Miss Malley to me." He needed to get Antonio out of the building. "Now, like I said, Quinn is an adult and has made her intentions concerning returning to your family quite clear...she's happy with Cory."

"You think your son is going to be able to keep her satisfied? Unless he has at least eight inches she's gonna be getting bored of him pretty soon, she's a slut for a big cock." Antonio hissed, getting riled up.

Matteo whispered to Antonio to calm down as Michael glared at him in distaste.

"Why does everything have to be turned sexual and vulgar with you, Antonio...you're immature! You need to seriously grow up before you think you can head anything, your father seriously needs to give you another ten years at least with that attitude, before he retires."

Antonio was on his feet and punching the desk as Matteo held him back. "Don't mention my father, he's long gone! And I don't see you complaining when you come to meetings held in my club?"

Michael wasn't going to be baited. "You're going to lose everything over one girl? Seriously, Antonio, what is so important about this one girl...let her go. You never know, she may come back on her own when she gets bored, like you say...or misses the money or even you..."

Antonio sucked his teeth, straightening up and shirking Matteo off his shoulder. He calmed himself and stared at Michael for a moment.

Michael returned his gaze patiently.

"Fine...I'll let her have some space to figure herself out and realize where she belongs."

"Does that mean she can return to college without interference from you or your men?" Michael's gaze flicked to Matteo.

Antonio glared at him darkly then chuckled. "Sure, the college is a neutral zone as agreed...but if I catch her outside...well..." He shrugged. "It's all fair out on the streets, right?"

Michael grimaced, he was going to have to concede this one. "Right..."

Antonio smirked and licked his lips. "Be sure to let Quinn and your son know I dropped by for a chat and remind Quinn of our little chat about keeping herself pure and to take a long hard look at herself in a mirror...naked, if she needs reminding where she belongs."

He turned and walked out with the grim faced Matteo behind him.

Michael let out a relieved breath and wiped a hand over his face not sure what any of that last statement was about.

His assistant came in along with the Senior Police Inspector. "Are you okay, sir? What happened?"

"I'm fine, that jumped up little shit thought he could throw his weight around...just flexing his muscles now he's stepped up..."

"So where does that leave everything in regards to the peace alliance?"

"I'm not sure..." Michael sighed.

That night at home Michael called Cory up from the basement to his study for a private chat.

"What's happening?" Cory asked as he entered to find his father sitting in his chair nursing a large whisky.

Michael sighed, rubbing his eyes. "Close the door I don't want your mother or Quinn hearing this."

Cory frowned and backed up to close the door before walking over and taking a seat.

"Antonio Ferrante paid me a visit at work today." He announced.

"What the hell?" Cory exclaimed. "Why can't he just let Quinn do what she wants?"

"That's what I said to him."

"And?"

"He pretty much said if he sees her out on the street she's fair game...but he won't stop her continuing to attend lectures."

"As if..." Cory grumbled. "All he'll do is wait outside the campus gates for her, then what?"

Michael's gaze was intense. "So you need to get smarter if she wants to continue to attend, otherwise she leaves, goes far away and hides."

"Runaway? That's your answer?"

"No." Michael huffed. "It's not, you know how I feel about running scared in the face of intimidation from these people."

"So how do we do things smarter?"

"There's two options...one, I get boys from NYPD to drive her to and from...but I can't be sure who can be trusted and if it was to get found out could cause an inquiry we don't want or need from a state senator level."

Cory scowled. "And two?"

"Ask Reese O'Shea to deal with it and her."

Cory frowned. "What do you mean by 'and her'?"

Michael grit his teeth. "Let the girl go to him, Cory."

"I thought she was safer here with us rather than another group of gangsters, did you want to start a gang war, Dad?"

"No, of course I don't, but I have to think of *our* safety!"

"Really?" Cory spat. "Reese already said to keep her here."

Michael's expression went flat. "Are you boys just playing with the girl or what?"

"No." Cory stated. "But there are things about her you don't know that Reese is trying to deal with and its best if she's kept away from being seen with him."

"You better tell me everything, son!" Michael demanded.

Quinn backed away from the door, tears in her eyes and sprinted back to her room. She grabbed her phone and pressed the button to video call the only person she trusted right now.

"Hey babe." He answered with a surprised tone.

Quinn burst into tears, sobbing down the phone as emotions overwhelmed her. Damn if this didn't teach her not to eavesdrop on private conversations.

"Hey, hey....what's wrong? Fuck, what's going on Quinn?" Reese sat up trying to get something out of her other than tears, staring at his phone screen.

"I...I'm screwing up everything...I'm so sorry...both of you are..." She descended into crying again.

Reese's jaw clenched.

He stood up and grabbed the keys to his car and walked outside. His minder known only as Bulletproof stood up and Tank did as well, Bulletproof had been sent over by Cillian after Sunday's chat and followed Reese everywhere, he was just as tall as Reese with a swole figure strapped tight into a bulletproof vest ready to sacrifice himself for Reese's safety.

"Where are you going?" Tank asked, concerned by the look on Reese's face. He heard the sobbing and stuttering of a woman on the phone still gripped in Reese's hand. "What's going on?"

Reese threw the keys at him. "Drive me to Cory's place."

"Yes, boss." Tank answered immediately. Bulletproof moved too, sensing something bad was happening.

They made their way to the car and they all got in. "Babe..." Reese spoke into the phone. "Babe, listen to me...I'm not sure what's happened..."

Tank started to drive.

"I'm so sorry to be such a burden to everyone..." She blurted out. "Both your father's hate me for what's happening...I think I should just go..."

"Don't you fucking dare say it, Quinn Malley!" Reese growled at her vehemently. He could see by the video call that she was pacing around like she was packing a bag.

"Fuck!" He shouted. "Don't you dare go back to that bastard!"

Quinn stopped, her breathing stopped too as she gaped down the phone at Reese's angry face, mortified. "No!" She quailed. "Never! Away...go away...I can't stay here."

Reese felt a little relief but wondered what the hell had happened at Cory's house. "Babe, please calm down and talk to me."

She snuffled in a few breaths wiping her face. "I overheard Cory's dad...he doesn't want me here. Antonio..." She sobbed and seemed to choke on her words as her anxiety started to shut her down.

Reese's jaw ticked, he felt fucking helpless. "I'm coming to get you, babe." He whacked Tank's arm to hurry up.

"No, that will cause more trouble." Quinn sobbed.

"I don't fucking care...you're crying, Quinn, I'm coming! Just stay there!"

Quinn sat down on the floor, leaning back against the bed and nodded. "Okay..." She breathed, calming down a bit, trying to get her breathing under control.

She had felt quite devastated to overhear the fact that Antonio had gone to Michael's work, the Police Commissioner and with no recourse had strolled in and made threats. If he was that powerful no one near her was going to be safe. She certainly shouldn't have slept with Reese and Cory Saturday night. Now, if Antonio found out, they were all dead.

It was best to do what she heard Michael say, run away and hide.

"Quinn...breathe, baby girl." Reese said, startling her as she forgot in her reverie that he was still on the phone. She looked at his gorgeous face and smiled.

"Please hurry."

"Quinn? What's going on?" Cory came into her room seeing the bag half full of her stuff, her sitting on the floor with her phone in front of her, her face red and ravaged.

"Cory?" Reese's voice came to him as he dropped to his knees in front of Quinn and cupped her face with both hands.

"Reese?" He searched down and saw the phone in Quinn's hand.

"What the fuck is going on, Quinn wants to leave!" Reese yelled at him.

"What?" Cory looked into Quinn's watery green eyes as she chewed her bottom lip. He looked devastated. "Why?" He asked her.

"Your father doesn't want me here."

"You heard?" Cory gasped, frowning bewildered. "Ah, fuck, bunny..."

He took the phone from her hand and pulled her into himself, kissing her head before lifting the phone to see Reese's lethal face.

"Antonio went to see Dad at his work today, basically threatened that Quinn would be taken off the streets if he sees her." Cory explained.

"Fucking hell, he's a fucking psycho!" Reese spat.

Cory frowned at the phone. "Where are you?"

Reese showed Tank driving. "Coming to yours."

"Shit...okay..." Cory swallowed hard. He didn't try and talk him out of it, he didn't want to and knew no one could ever talk him out of anything anyway.

"Be ready, I'll pick you both up."

"No, come in and talk to Dad...I told him some stuff...but not everything."

"Are you sure?" Reese's voice went flat, business like.

Cory nodded. He felt Quinn clinging to him and shaking her head. "Fuck, I don't know..." He groaned.

"I'll come to the door, if he wants to talk I'll tell him everything."

"Yeah, okay." Cory said and hung up, squeezing Quinn to him tightly. "I'm sorry, bunny...Dad's just worried this might all blow up into something really serious...Ferrante is a loose unit apparently."

"He is..." She muttered.

Cory nodded his head against hers. "I don't want you to leave."

"But your dad..."

"He's not telling you to leave, bunny...you didn't hear the whole conversation. Fuck, why did you have to do that and upset yourself?"

"I knew if your dad wanted to talk to you it would be about me. I want to know what's going on...was anyone going to tell me Antonio went to your Dad's work?"

"Probably not, we don't want you to worry yourself...we'll keep you safe."

"I don't want anyone to get hurt, if he's threatening your family..."

"Then we involve Reese's family...it will probably be enough to make that psycho back off..."

She lifted her head and wiped her hair back. "You seriously think that?"

Cory touched her face with a sad look to see how distraught she was. "We'll do what we have to..."

They heard the V8 of Reese's Camaro pull up a few minutes later and Quinn got to her feet quickly practically running from the room.

Cory stood up and wiped a hand over his face. "Damn it."

54

The three of us

Reese was just stepping up onto the path heading to the front door when Quinn went flying past Cory's dad, opened the door and bolted out into Reese's arms.

He caught her strongly, pressing her cheek to his chest with one large hand on her head the other curled around her waist.

"Hey, hey...it's okay."

He looked up and met Michael's gaze. It was cool and serious, his expression grim. Reese saw Cory step up behind him looking despondent.

"Mr McMillan." Reese said, cold but polite.

"Reese..." He looked up at the two big men standing by the car looking menacing. "You better come in...tell them to sit in the car we don't like thugs here."

Reese licked his tongue over his teeth in a mocking way. "No? Just a couple of blocks away is fine though, eh?"

Michael's mouth twisted and he turned away to walk back inside. Reese knew Michael chose this community because of the mob being close by, his relationship with them being the closest and most trusted.

Cory hovered in the doorway, his eyes fixed on Reese and Quinn. Reese met his gaze and frowned before looking away and bending his height down to bring his head down next to Quinn's.

"Babe, come on now..."

"I hate this...why do you have to stay away?" She lifted her face and stared, big eyed at him. "I miss you."

He smirked and lifted her chin, stroking her cheek with his thumb. "I miss you too, babe...I've thought of nothing else since Saturday night."

She lifted her face more and planted her lips on his. He grabbed the back of her head and lashed his tongue into her mouth suddenly desperate to taste her. She clung to him, opening her mouth and melting her body into his.

"Reese..." Cory called out hoarsely.

Reese and Quinn pulled apart and Reese looked up at Cory. He had walked up behind them and he had glassy eyes and a miserable expression. Reese reached out, hooked his neck and pulled him in.

"Fuck, Curry..." Reese rested his forehead against Cory's and they just breathed.

Cory felt Quinn's arm curl around his waist and they were in a three-way hug. Cory put his arms around them both, all taking soul energy from each other. Tank and Bulletproof both looked at each other with a curious glance.

"What the fuck are we going to do about this?" Cory breathed.

Reese let out a little growl in his throat that made Quinn shudder. He was so animalistically alpha in his possessiveness wanting to protect them both it made her heady.

"I'm not letting either of you go...I don't give a fuck what your father says, I'll tell him straight...we're not kids anymore."

Reese pulled away from them both and stepped around them making his way to the house. "Both of you stay out here."

Cory pulled Quinn into himself and she whimpered. "He's going to be alright, bunny."

Reese walked into the house and saw Cory's mother standing nervously in the foyer by the door that led to the kitchen and dining room. "Mrs McMillan." He greeted with a slight dip of his head.

"Reese...it's been a while."

"Sure has..."

"Reese, this way." Michael said sternly coming out of his office.

Reese grit his teeth and followed Michael into his office and closed the door.

"Cory has told me that Quinn is actually the daughter of the mob boss in Boston that killed Antonio's mother."

"That's correct...he tried to have Augusto killed but only succeeded in killing his wife and injuring Antonio...it's what made Antonio the psycho that he is today...and he wanted that man's daughter to make sure she never had a happy life but he got to slowly destroy her mind, body and soul as reparation."

Michael sighed bitterly. "The poor girl...don't get me wrong here, Reese...I do feel sorry for the girl, that's why she is in my house now, but is it Cory or you actually in a relationship with her? I've seen them hugging and being over-friendly but they always sleep in their own rooms and never cross the line."

Reese smirked to know they had been following the rules so carefully. "Actually, we are all in a relationship...together, the three of us."

Michael's face contorted. "Three of you?"

"You've known since high school I'm bisexual...and that I've always been attracted to Cory."

Michael's disgust showed clearly on his face.

"I backed away like you wanted, we've been separate from each other for nearly five years...keeping our distance from each other and I agree with you it was the best thing for Cory."

Michael grimaced.

"But Quinn has managed to unite us through our mutual love of her and rediscovered our deep affection for each other. We are a throuple...and I will not let either of them go." His intense stare held his conviction and Michael had to look away.

He sighed, rubbing his eyes. He opened the bottom drawer in his desk and lifted out a bottle of Glenfiddich and two glasses. He filled them both with a fingers width of whiskey and slid one over the desk to Reese who was watching with an amused smirk on his face. Was this him conceding to the relationship?

"So what do you intend to do about Antonio, it's pretty clear he wants her back...I don't need trouble in the streets over some girl."

Reese sucked his teeth, taking the glass and leaning back in his chair. "He doesn't know about my involvement...and I'll try to keep my name out of it for as long as possible. It's unfortunate he found out she is staying with you, Cory really is her best bet to stay with right now."

"Right now?" Michael stated, displeased. "That tells me at some point you'll move her to your camp...so how do you intend to keep your name out of things then?"

"I won't need to because the account with Antonio will be settled." Reese stared at Michael with a complete stone-like expression that made his blood run cold.

Michael frowned deeply concerned. "I don't know whether to ask or stay in denial, but if anything rocks the foundations of peace between all you lot that I monitor and maintain you will be the first one I take down, Reese."

"How can you say that?" Reese scoffed with a derisive grin. "Cory and I are trying to do the right thing here...it's basically sex trafficking and slavery that is happening to Quinn under that bastard's control! The one thing I thought you were passionate about stopping?"

Michael rubbed his forehead. "Do you think she would testify against him?"

"No." Reese said firmly.

Michael shrugged. "Think it over...in jail for at least ten years is one way of taking Antonio out of this equation."

Reese appraised Michael's idea as solving only Michael's issues, Reese knew Michael was against Antonio taking over as Don of New York, a lot of people were apprehensive about it. "His men would still seek retribution."

"Then what do you have planned?"

"Best to stay in denial..." Reese said, downing his shot of whiskey and standing up as he placed the glass down on the desk. He gave Michael a little sneer. "So am I taking them both away tonight, because if Quinn has to go, Cory goes too?"

Michael wiped a hand down his face and let out a sufferable sigh. "No...leave them here...please. I'm really not ready to let go of my son just yet."

Reese nodded, smiling as he was pleased Michael had calmed down enough to realize Quinn was safest in his household.

Antonio wouldn't move against the Police Commissioner, especially a corrupt one that kept the balance between all the organized crime syndicates in the city. Michael was one of the main powerhouses in the city because of who and what he knew. He might not have the same income as the Don's and Leaders of the underworld but he held very similar power and was well respected by them all.

"How about I take them for tonight, they need me for a while and I'll bring them back tomorrow once I've settled Quinn."

Michael gave Reese a strange look. He was going to be a very formidable leader in the future when he matured...if he survived that long.

Antonio was pacing back and forth in the VIP room at the back of Diamond Club, Matteo trying to calm him down as two other men kneeled in the room, one bleeding from a nasty gash on his head and glass shattered everywhere. Two girls were also in the room huddled into the couch trying to avoid Antonio's attention. Everyone knew when he was in a foul mood to keep clear, unfortunate for the two men they had to give him the bad news that led to him throwing his glass at the one who spoke's head.

"Why the fuck can't we get someone inside that fucking community?" Antonio growled.

"Sir, please calm down." Matteo tried to placate him back, he had been wound tighter than a coiled spring all day since talking to Michael McMillan and now these idiots decided it was the perfect time to tell him that they had been turned away from the gated community where Quinn was hiding out by not just security guards but chased in a car and threatened to not return by mobsters saying it was their territory. They had then tried to get a guy in posing as a pizza delivery man, but he had been followed through the streets to the house he said he was delivering to and then once he had finished he was escorted out with no chance of deviating to the police commissioner's house even for a quick glance at it.

Antonio glanced at one of the girls as she covered her head in fear. He growled viciously through clenched teeth, kicked the low table out of the way scattering glasses and bottles and grabbed the girl by the hair, dragging her off the couch to the floor and then placing his foot on her naked ass he shoved her towards the door, making her sprawl and face plant at the strength of his attack.

"Get this bitch out of my sight! Fire her ass, she's useless and ugly!" The other girl sat up hoping to be kicked out too, Antonio's eyes slid to her and she froze, petrified in place. "You stay here." His tone made her almost wet herself in fright. He turned to the two men, raking his hair back from his cold black eyes and hissed out a long breath. "Solutions!?"

"Antonio! Cillian has obviously moved to protect the Police Commissioner and his family, it's not unexpected..." Matteo tried to explain.

Antonio lifted his gaze to his right hand man. "That means he knows about Quinn...are you saying his son has had something to do with this all along?"

"Perhaps so...we need to tread lightly, we can't go in guns blazing we'll have half of New York on our tail and it will douse any chance of you moving into politics..."

Antonio's jaw was ticking as he snorted through his nose. "If Cillian knows about Quinn let's try going through another avenue to get them to make her return to me...contact Flanagan..."

"Yes, Sir..." Matteo bowed his head.

"And take these two...they're making my eyes hurt." Antonio flicked a finger at the two men as he turned his full focus on the trembling girl.

Matteo tapped the men's shoulders. "Go..."

They stood up and bowed their heads. "Thank you, Sir." They left as Antonio stalked towards the girl, his eyes blazing with cruel intent. Matteo swallowed hard and closed the door behind him just as Antonio reached the girl.

He heard her scream through the door, begging for Antonio to stop whatever deranged thing he was doing to her. Matteo closed his eyes and shook his head before walking away, leaving the two guards on the door to look at each other bleakly.

55
Gangster pad

Quinn was curled up on Cory's lap, dozing, when they finally reached Reese's place. He reached into the car and gently took her from Cory so he could get out. She opened her eyes and looked up at his face with a little smile.

"Are we here?"

"Yeah, babe...welcome to my pad." He put her down on her feet, keeping a steadying arm around her.

"Will we be safe here?" Cory asked as he stretched his legs.

"Of course." Bulletproof said casually. "We have our men watching the place..."

Reese rolled his eyes, he hated being under his father's men's watch but what choice did he have now he had Quinn here, he certainly couldn't risk a front on confrontation with the mafia right here.

Cory squinted at the guy. "And who are you, I haven't seen you around here before?"

"This is Bulletproof...he's basically just a human shield." Reese hissed snidely, taking Quinn's hand and walking in through the back gate to the pool area.

Quinn looked back at the sour look on Bulletproof's face as Cory grimaced at Reese's cold words. Quinn gazed around the pool area, seeing four men sitting on the loungers even in this cold weather, smoking and drinking...chatting casually. She clung close to Reese at the dangerous vibe these gang members radiated out. Reese felt her tenseness and rubbed her arm as he put his around her shoulders claiming her as untouchable to the men present.

"It's okay, these guys are pussycats, their faces should be familiar..." He pointed to two who were sitting close to the apartment that Reese was heading towards. Quinn smiled at them as she recognized seeing them often with Reese. Mac smiled at her in greeting.

"Hi...I'm Jacob, nice to finally meet you." Jacob grinned at her then lifted his eyes to Cory coming in through the gate, his face furrowed into a frown and he looked from Cory back to Quinn and Reese then back to Cory.

Reese caught the look and clucked his tongue. "Shut up." He warned.

Jacob looked surprised and held his hands out. "I said nothing?"

"Keep it that way." Reese growled and moved through to inside the condo. Cory glared at Jacob as he passed and followed.

Jacob raked a hand through his hair looking confused. "What the hell...?"

Tank came up and chuckled. "Seems the competition is over..."

"So Rice won? Why's Curry here then?"

Tank's eyes sparkled with amusement. "Seems Rice got the girl and the boy."

Jacob's eyes went wide. "You're shitting me?" He looked at the now closed door of the condo then back. "So...like...all three of them are..." He lifted his hands and curled one in a circle and poked the fingers of the other through.

Tank shrugged. "I guess so..."

"How the fuck does that work?" Mac asked from beside Jacob where he had been listening with a shocked look on his face.

"Shuuussshhh!" Tank hissed. "Keep your voice down."

Jacob gave Mac a side-eye. "You know Rice is bi, right? Didn't realize Curry was too...I always wondered what it was between those two, now we know..." He waggled his eyebrows.

Mac rubbed the back of his neck. "Jesus...the three of *them*...that's a porno I would pay to watch."

"Shut the fuck up!" Tank growled, closing his fist and holding it up.

"Can't blame him..." Jacob laughed. "Hot, hot and hotter stirring it up."

"Well, no one is going in that apartment tonight." Tank insisted. "So you better either fuck off or make yourselves comfortable out here."

"Aww, man...you are no fun!" Jacob moaned, getting to his feet.

Quinn walked through the open plan living and kitchen area, looking around with a curious gaze at all Reese's stuff, learning a bit more about him as she saw things that were obviously his interests. She saw a couple of guitars, one acoustic and one electric, sitting on stands, his bike was parked inside and the coffee table in front of the couch was covered in empty beer cans and bottles with a couple of hard liquor bottles as well as even a bong and a piece of glass with white residue on it and a flick knife to round things out. The couch faced a massive TV screen and a PlayStation was sitting on the floor with the controllers next to it charging up.

"Holy moly..." She breathed. "This is like an actual gang pad, huh?"

Reese looked down at her with a sheepish grin. "I wasn't expecting your company, princess."

Cory chuckled. "Now you see why I choose to still live at home...this is normal for college guys, the football team that live in the frat house all live like this too..."

Reese gave him a filthy look. "Yeah, thanks for that...I love being lumped in with those idiots."

Cory shrugged grinning as he pulled Quinn out from underneath Reese's arm and hugged around her collarbone with both arms. "Don't worry, bunny...I'll protect you from the germs."

"Oh, haha! It may be a bit messy but you know it's clean!" Reese scoffed as Quinn giggled. "Come upstairs...its better up there."

He made his way to the stairs and Cory pushed Quinn to follow as he followed her. They went up to find a short hallway with only one bedroom and a bathroom. The bedroom was definitely Reese's room and as Quinn stepped in she was awash with his scent, his cologne and the musky smell of sweat and sex. The bed was a queen size, unmade with the duvet half lying on the floor. Reese stepped over and flicked it up onto the bed, hastily making it while grumbling that the sheets are clean, before sitting down on it with an awkward little smile. The rest of the room was actually tidy and Quinn gave an approving little smile to Reese as she took in the black on black décor.

He lifted his hand and beckoned her to him.

She stepped obediently to him, coming in between his legs and as he put his arms around her hips he pressed his face to her stomach, breathing in deeply. She embraced his head and Cory sat down next to him, wiping a hand over his face, drained of emotion.

"What a night."

Quinn held a hand out to him and he shuffled closer putting his head on Reese's shoulder and taking her hand, putting it on his other cheek. He smiled up at her. "How are you feeling, bunny?"

"Overwhelmed...scared...I just want normal..."

Reese lifted his head and gave her a strange look. "You'll never get normal if you stay with us, princess."

Her hand was hooked around the back of his neck and she leaned down to kiss him. He grabbed her and fell back on the bed as their lips connected, making her straddle him as they kissed.

Cory lay down on his side and ran his hand up Quinn's back as he kissed Reese's shoulder. "Who the fuck wants normal, bunny...this is our normal."

Quinn pulled back from Reese's mouth and looked at Cory. "This is not what I meant..."

She was cut off by Cory grabbing her around the back of the neck and covering her mouth with his, his tongue dancing around hers in full command of her mouth before pulling back leaving her breathless.

Reese turned sideways and dropped her gently down to lie between them. She looked up at the two of them as they both looked down on her sitting up on their elbows and grinning wickedly. Her stomach swirled with nervous excited butterflies at the hungry looks they were both giving her.

"I think I'm in trouble with you two..."

Reese chuckled darkly as his hand went to undo her jeans. Cory gave her that roguish smirk. "Says you that managed to exhaust the both of us that first night."

"I did not! I'm the one who passed out..." Quinn complained then bit her lip into her mouth, her eyes unfocusing as Reese's fingers breached her clothes and found her clit.

"You're wet, baby...that's all we need to know." He breathed in a husky tone, his eyes blazing at her from under his hair. He slid down to the edge of the bed and onto his knees, pulling her sneakers off her feet, grabbing her jeans and pulling them off.

Cory sat up, grabbing her sweatshirt and making her squirm out of it before pulling her t-shirt off as well.

She found herself lying completely naked in seconds between the two gorgeous men as their hands started exploring and rubbing every part of her body.

"I'm going to book you into a laser tattoo removal place tomorrow." Reese growled as his tongue licked over her stomach, his eyes focusing on the tattoo of Antonio's name.

"Maybe we should replace it with ours?" Cory murmured darkly, causing her to startle and glare at him.

Reese shook his head. "Nothing should ever be allowed to mar this perfect skin."

She closed her eyes, her lip clenched in her teeth as Reese opened her legs wide and delved his tongue deep inside her pussy.

"Let your moans out." Cory grumbled, a nipple in his mouth. He reached up and dragged her lip out of her teeth just as Reese rolled her hips up and licked over her ass. She yelped and squirmed.

"Wait...I haven't..."

Reese chuckled. "You come first...then we can all shower...the one perk of this place is the shower is huge..."

"Oh..." Quinn exclaimed in a breathy sigh as Reese's tongue went back to her clit.

Cory sat up and lifting her under her arms he dragged her up onto his lap and caressed her breasts as she lay languid upon his chest as Reese lapped at her pussy with expert skill. She had her arms up around Cory's neck and threaded her fingers into his hair, playing with it as she closed her eyes in ecstasy and lifted her hips to get more of Reese inside her.

He plunged his fingers into her needy pussy and she came after only a couple of strokes of his fingers against her G-spot. Now he knew exactly where to find it he managed to hit it perfect every time.

Cory sucked on her neck as he thrummed deep in his throat, watching her body spasm. She clenched hard into his hair lifted her face and he covered her wanting mouth with his. Reese lifted his face and watched the two of them kiss through Quinn's orgasm and smirked. He really had found his happy place and he would be damned if he was going to let it go.

In the shower the two of them enjoyed soaping up every crevice of Quinn's body as she grabbed the wall for dare life on shaky legs. They were both on their knees on either side of her, fingering her with the water jetting straight up between her legs, kissing her thighs making sure she was nice and clean before returning to the bedroom.

Quinn turned and dropped down to her knees to face Reese. They both looked at her with curiosity and amusement, they both knew she was close to coming again and wondered at what she was going to say.

She cupped Reese's cheek tenderly making him grab her hand and kiss the palm. "I want to ride you..." She breathed out then turned to Cory and cupped his cheek. "...then you, I want to be on top of both of you..."

Reese chuckled a husky deep rumble as Cory thrummed and bit his lip. "Sounds like a great idea..." Reese admitted smugly as he stood up and turned the water off. Cory agreed and stood up, lifting Quinn up to her feet by her arms and steadying her.

"Are you going to be able to?" He asked amused at her legs trembling.

She looked up at him with a cheeky fire in her eyes. "Let me try."

Reese laughed, returning with a towel that he wrapped around her and pulled her into his chest, swiping her wet hair back from her face. "Okay, little brat...let's just get you a bit dry first, okay, you got your hair wet when you knelt down."

Cory grabbed another towel and dropped it over her head, rubbing at her hair. "Hey!" She growled, fighting him off and glaring at him. "Easy on the hair..."

Reese laughed as Cory glared back. "You really don't like your hair messed with, huh?" He tapped her bottom with a flat palm making her squeal. "Hurry up and do it yourself then."

She flattened her hair down pressing the towel into it several times before throwing it over the rail, grabbing a comb and quickly running it through getting the knots out.

"Braid it up." Reese ordered, his voice smooth and commanding as he leaned on the wall with his arms folded just watching her naked body.

She gave him a look of understanding and pulled it back, putting it into a braid at the back of her neck. He smiled at her pleased before standing up and walking out. "I'll be waiting for you, princess."

Cory grinned and followed Quinn out and across the hall to Reese's bedroom.

As she entered Reese was lying on the bed, completely naked and stroking his hard cock. He had his other arm nestled up behind his head and he was propped up on the pillows looking relaxed and sexy as hell.

He grinned at her looking over his body and waggled his cock at her. "Get on board."

She giggled and crawled up on top of him, straddling his hips and he ran the head of his cock through her pussy, stroking it as he looked up into her fascinating green eyes that were lit with a lustful fire. He watched those eyes lose focus and then drop closed as her face took on a look of pure pleasure as she sank down on his cock. He lifted his hand out of the way and put it behind his head and just stared at her face.

"Fuck, you are breathtaking..." He breathed out. "Ah...fuck..." He gritted out as she started to move on him, undulating her hips, her own hands lifting to her breasts as she moaned decadently.

"Holy hell, I like this porno..." Cory said from the side.

"So do I..." Reese managed to grit out, his voice hoarse and husky. He dropped a hand to her hip and pushed her down more. "Take me deeper, princess..."

She dropped down, moaning out a long breath. "Ah...Reese...you feel so good."

"How much of me do you want before you switch to Cory?"

She opened her eyes and they were heavy lidded and smoky looking. She licked her lips as she leaned forward and grabbed his hands, pinning them to the mattress. "I want a bit more..." She started to ride him fast, lifting up and grinding back like a demon. Her eyes sparkled with a dark light as her tongue was caught in her teeth. She had never topped before, Antonio would never allow her this sort of control, and she loved it!

Reese grabbed her hips with both hands. "Fuck...easy, baby...I'll come if you do that!"

"Don't you want to?" Cory asked. He was stroking his own cock while watching. "I think I'm going to just watching her..."

"Nah...not yet..." Reese grit out and lifted Quinn up, making his cock come out of her. She whimpered as he rolled her over and pinned her under him. He smirked down at her and licked his teeth, breathing hard. "You want to play hard, baby?"

Her eyes dazzled him with her glee. "Yeah."

"Cory...get on the bed...it's your turn." Reese ordered before getting up and pulling Quinn up to her feet, turning her to face the bed and smacking her ass hard as Cory lay down. "Now take Cory like a good girl and I'll reward you."

She looked back at Reese with a little cheeky smile before climbing up on Cory and sinking his hard cock into her. She moaned as he groaned out, he cupped her head with his hands and pulled her to his mouth, making her bend right over.

She yelped into Cory's mouth as Reese smacked her ass hard. "You'll take this...then I'll take your ass while you ride Curry, got it, princess?"

"Yes..." She breathed out as Cory held her by the neck and grinned up at her. Their eyes locked as Reese smacked her ass again. She bit her lip to stifle her moan but Cory pulled it out and shook his head.

"Nah-ah...we want to hear how much you like being spanked, bunny."

"Ah...fuck..." She cried out as Reese smacked her ass again.

"Move your hips..." Cory demanded, thrusting up into her and making her body spasm.

Her eyes rolled back in her head and she gripped his shoulders as Reese's hand started rubbing circles on her butt cheeks. Her focus returned as she started riding Cory, slow and controlled with his hands now on her hips, pushing her down to take all of him on every thrust up.

"Oh god..." She mewled as Reese's finger slid into her ass.

"Your reward is my cock too, baby...do you want it?"

"Yes...oh fuck...yes..."

Reese moved so he was behind her as Cory spread his legs out. He coiled her braid around his hand and pulled it taunt making her whimper as her head was pulled back making her arch her back and lift her ass as he sank into her slowly, not stopping until he bottomed out.

Cory hissed through gritted teeth as she tightened around him and could feel Reese's cock enter behind her. "Fuck...I'm gonna come."

"Don't you fucking dare!" Reese growled, taking Quinn's hip in one hand as he pulled back on her hair with the other and started moving like he was riding her.

The loud desperate groan that exited Quinn's mouth was illicit and Cory grabbed her face covering her mouth with his, invading it with his tongue and making her lose her mind as they both found their rhythm inside her and fucked her into a mindless oblivion of pleasure as she careened into an orgasm so powerful she literally passed out for a second as lights flashed behind her eyes and her body shook like it was being electrocuted.

She dully heard through her haze of unstopping pleasure the shouts of her two men coming but they kept thrusting and didn't stop until she came again, lost in a delirium of pleasure not even knowing how to breathe anymore as she completely lost her mind.

She finally came to her senses when she was laid down on the bed, hands caressing her gently and someone was calling her name in a dulcet tone.

She blinked and looked up to see Cory brushing her hair from her face and smiling at her, his eyes looking in awe and sparkled with amazement.

"There you are...fuck that was incredible, bunny."

She felt a hot body press to her side and a heated kiss on her shoulder. "You should drink some water after that, princess..." Reese breathed on her hot sweaty skin. "Then I'll carry you back to the shower to clean up."

"Just let me sleep..." She breathed, closing her eyes and drifting off in her bliss.

56

Antonio is the past

"I have the start of my night classes at Columbia tomorrow evening." Quinn announced as she came downstairs the next morning after checking an email on her phone to find Reese and Cory both on their phones and sipping coffee. She noticed the living room had been cleaned up and blushed a little to realize that whoever cleaned up last night would have heard the three of them having sex...they had made her cry out quite loudly a few times in orgasm. She looked left from the stairs and saw Tank standing behind the kitchen counter pulling subway out of an Uber delivered bag.

"Did you clean up?" She asked a little demurely.

Tank just grinned as he lifted his sandwich and bit into it.

Reese clicked his fingers. "Babe...come here...what do you mean night classes, first I'm hearing about it?"

"Dad set it up with the Board, it coincides with my training nights so I can take her to training go to classes then bring her home, safe." Cory explained.

Reese looked up at Quinn as she stood in front of him and he grabbed her hips dragging her down onto his lap, making her straddle his thighs, pressing her knees down either side of him. He grinned at her glancing to the kitchen towards Tank who was clearly too busy eating to worry about what they were doing.

"Are you okay with doing that, babe?" Reese asked her.

She gave him a beautiful smile that looked a little patient. "Yes, I want to return to school, I'm so far behind and although I've been sent the class stuff from Emma there's just some things I really need to be in class to learn...so there are other adults learning in night classes too, it's not the full Diploma course but it still gives credit towards it so I can carry on with it later rather than just dropping out and having to reapply which looks bad and chances of getting back in are slim to none."

"Okay..."

Quinn frowned a little at Reese's casual attitude about her study. "Look, we're not all genius sons of fathers that already have established businesses, whether legal or not...some of us, like me, are going to have to work hard to find a good job after all this and hope to live a normal life."

"Is that what you meant last night?" Cory asked.

"Yeah..." Quinn huffed. "I have nothing...no money, no family..."

"You have us, baby." Reese said, running a hand through her hair.

She gave him that look again and he frowned. "I can't just let you guys look after me..."

"Why not?" Reese asked, his tone dropping.

"I need to feel like I'm contributing something a little more substantial than my body...otherwise what am I but a whore or whatever I was to Antonio?"

Reese's jaw clenched tight as his eyes went flat. Cory sat up, putting a hand on Reese's shoulder. "Shit, bunny...we don't see you like that..."

"I know that...but this is about me and what I want for myself."

Reese let out his breath, relaxing under her. "I get it...that's cool...make your way in life, but we'll be there to support you, don't you dare think you're all alone just because you don't have family."

"Yeah, we're your family now." Cory said with that golden retriever grin.

Tank looked on in fascination at the three of them in their own world. They really did seem perfectly comfortable as a three instead of a two, it was a little weird but he could see they all seemed to hold a genuine affection for each other.

He coughed, reminding them he was there. "Quinn, do you want coffee?"

She turned, twisting her body to drop off Reese's lap and onto the couch beside him. "Yes, please..."

Reese lifted his phone showing the screen to her. "I've made an appointment for you this afternoon to get that tattoo removed."

"Oh! Okay..." Quinn peered at the screen to see where the place was. "That was fast."

"I'm paying them double to fit you in...they reckon it will be a fairly easy and quick treatment as it's quite small, maybe four treatments, Cory can take you..."

She glanced at Cory and he beamed a smile at her and winked. "Better off than on, he's in the past now."

She smiled back and nodded.

The other large menacing man opened the sliding door and walked in with a bolshie stride, his gaze dropping over the three young adults on the couch before lifting his hand that was holding another Uber eats bag like he was going to throw it. He handed it out to Reese.

"Here..." He seemed a little surly and Quinn lifted her legs onto the couch, bending them up in front of her subconsciously in defense mode, flinching at the brusque action.

Reese's head snapped up, his eyes looking sideways at her then slid up to Bulletproof. "Change your attitude." He snapped as he took the bag from the guy. Everyone in the room looked up as Bulletproof's jaw clenched tight for a second. He dropped his gaze to the floor and bowed his head in deference. "Sorry, Mr O'Shea...I'm just not used to doing this sort of thing."

"Baby sitting, you mean?" Reese snarled. "Fuck off then."

"Hey, Rice..." Tank went to interrupt but Bulletproof bowed his head even lower.

"I'm sorry...but you know I can't do that even if I wanted to. I will endeavor to adapt my behavior to whatever you need me to be while I am assigned to you. I'm not used to being out of the shadows, sir."

Quinn blinked in astonishment as Cory just gaped, so this was the power of the crime boss's son.

Reese sucked his teeth, appraising the man in front of him. "Just do what I ask...it's not like I ordered you to go and get it, I just said can you grab it for me cause I was busy making Quinn her appointment, shit..." Reese clucked his tongue.

"You're right, again I apologize."

Quinn elbowed Reese in the side causing him to look round at her with an eyebrow raised. "What? Am I too hard on the guy?" He sneered then chuckled and dropped the bag of food on top of her knees. "Perhaps I did overreact, but I saw you react to his aggression."

Quinn startled and dropped her knees, grabbing the bag in both hands as Bulletproof gave her a sudden look of understanding and bowed his head to her. "Sorry for scaring you."

Cory huffed, looking at Quinn around Reese's back. "Are you okay?"

"I'm fine...let's not cause a fuss, eh?" She gave a small embarrassed smile then opened the bag wanting to hide her head in it as she peered inside.

Reese lifted a hand and waved the guy away. He moved off and went outside to stand by the door.

"Oh! Is this for me?" Quinn looked back up at Reese after seeing a bagel and cream cheese spread.

"Hmm...eat before you go. I'll get Jacob to take you guys back to Cory's place soon."

"Oh..." Quinn pouted up at him.

He grinned, licking his tongue over his teeth. "Behave, princess...you need to get your things for your classes together and I promised Michael I would give you guys back."

Cory coughed. "You did?"

Reese turned the other way and saw him looking up with a bit of a disappointed look on his face too. "Jesus, what am I gonna do with the two of you?" He chuckled, leaning back into the couch and hooking his arms over both of them, pulling them in. "Do I need to start looking for a bigger place?"

"Maybe just one not so...play boy like." Quinn grinned at him.

Reese let out a breathy laugh and leaned down to kiss her cheek while playfully strangling her with his arm. "That's enough out of you, brat."

Cory was making his way up from the nearby café at Colombia University with two coffees in his hands when Mila and a couple of other cheerleaders walked around from their training heading to that café.

She stopped a little shocked to see Cory, it had been a couple of weeks since his brutal dumping of her at the house and she hadn't really seen him on his own to be able to talk to him since. Now seemed like her chance.

She dropped her friends and started following him, wondering where he was going. She followed him through the campus, across the side street and to the Department of Business Studies. She stopped as he went into the foyer and sat down on a bench seat like he was waiting for someone.

She knew a few classes went on at night but wasn't aware of Cory knowing anyone that took those classes before. She hung back peering around the corner of the large sign out the front of the building and watched as the class let out.

Her teeth clenched and ground together as she saw the red head come out of class, see Cory, smile like the goddamn sun and hug her arms around him as he stood up and handed her a coffee cup.

"You fucking bitch." Mila breathed. "Aren't you supposed to be missing, what the fuck is going on here?"

She stepped away and hid in the darkness of the buildings as Cory led Quinn hand in hand to his truck and they both got in.

"No fucking way..." Mila growled under her breath.

She raced back to her car and got in and drove as fast as she could to where she knew she would intercept Cory's truck at a set of lights. As she watched the truck drive passed she pulled out into traffic and followed at a distance, already knowing the way to Cory's place but surely he had to head to where Quinn was staying first...right?

Wrong.

Mila pulled over as she watched Cory's truck stop at the gated community's security gate as it slowly swung open before it drove on through.

"She's living with him!?" Mila screamed inside her car. "No! No fucking way!"

She turned her car around, her fingers tapping the steering wheel with agitation and she drove home.

"Missing my ass! Hiding from her brother more like it!" Mila smiled to herself. "Well, not for much longer, bitch!"

Who did he work for again?

57
A cruel vendetta

Mila stood outside the skyscraper of a building of Zortex Industries, nibbling on her fingernail nervously as she watched the suited people come and go through the tight security. She suddenly had the creeping feeling that these guys might not just be businessmen. A few of them had neck tattoos and tattoos peeking out from their shirt sleeves, the men in black suits that seemed to just hover around were menacing. When she got a glimpse of one open his jacket and flutter it showing the butt of a gun strapped to his side was enough to make her change her mind about going in.

Whoever these guys were it really wasn't worth it. She had hoped to go in and talk to someone to identify Quinn's brother and let him know she had information concerning his sister and hopefully get something out of it, like the money to buy a new pair of shoes or handbag.

The thought of getting Cory and Quinn found out and possibly broken up by the brother was all she was really after, after him embarrassing her in front of her sorority girls there was no way she wanted him back.

She pivoted around and went to walk away, her mind made up...this place looked too dangerous.

She collided with something solid and looked up to see a black clothed man standing in front of her. She quailed at the size of him and jerked back, but he clamped a hand around her bicep.

"I'm sorry...I didn't see you..." She struggled in his grip as he glared down at her menacingly.

"Really? Well I've seen you for the last ten minutes pacing back and forth passed this building like you have something on your mind..."

"Oh...ah...it's nothing...can you let me go, please?"

The guy grinned perversely at the pretty little blond. "I don't think so...come on." He dragged her to the doors and inside.

"Wait! Let me go..." She tried to struggle against him as he pulled her into the large foyer and deposited her down on a leather couch.

He leered at her with interest. "So, what is it? Someone not returning your calls, sweetheart?"

"What? No...I..." She swallowed hard as she saw more of these black suited men were standing around watching her. She looked through the foyer and saw a face she recognized.

She had seen Quinn's brother the day he had come to talk to the students Quinn had classes with, she had also seen the man that had accompanied him. That man was just stepping out of the elevator behind the security fence.

She pointed over to him, yelling. "Him! I need to talk to him, over there..."

The guy turned and looked, going pale. "Are you sure?"

"Yes! I came to talk to him!"

One of the suits moved and walked up to Matteo, whispering in his ear. He turned his head and his gaze hit Mila like a snake eyeing up a mouse. He moved from the reception desk and started walking over.

Mila swallowed hard, fidgeting in her seat as the guy still in front of her grimaced. "I hope you're being truthful little girl."

She looked up at him and saw the strange expression on his face. He stepped back with a deferring bow to his head as Matteo approached, scowling down at her.

"Do I know you?" He asked in a deep resonate voice. Looking at the girl with the tight as fuck jeans and even tighter top showing a good size pair of tits. She wasn't more than twenty years old and looked fuckable and ready for it.

Mila licked her lips trying to moisten her mouth. Holy heck, what a scary dude. "Ah, no...but I saw you at college...with Quinn's brother..."

Matteo's brow furrowed as his eyes narrowed at her. "Is that right...and?" A college student.

"And..." Mila straightened up a bit feeling her confidence returning slightly. "...is Quinn still missing?"

"No." Matteo grunted, turning away dismissively.

"Wait!" She stood up and grabbed his sleeve. He froze and looked down at her tiny hand on him with her perfect pink nails, then lifted his eyes to hers.

"You're a brave girl touching me...what do you want?"

She pulled her hand back like she had been burnt and clutched it with her other hand. Wow, the alpha vibes on this man made her giddy. She smiled up at him, blinking her eyelashes. "You came to Scarsdale campus wanting information on Quinn's whereabouts or movements...do you not need that information anymore?"

Matteo turned back, appraising the girl, seeing her need to exact some sort of vengeance. "What's your name?"

"Mila...Mila Buick."

Matteo chuckled to himself, was this the girl that had vandalized Quinn's car? "What sort of information can you possibly give me when we already know she's staying with Cory McMillan?"

She pouted coyly. "But you can't get to her there, can you?"

Matteo's eyes darkened, the girl was obviously not stupid and had worked out something wasn't right with everything here.

"I know where she is going that is public and open..." She said as a tidbit.

Matteo's jaw clenched as he stared at her for a moment. If he brought her in front of Antonio only knowing this much and her information was no good he could kill her in his present mood knowing who she is, but she was cute, a bit fake looking, but knew she was appealing. Antonio might even fuck her to pay him back for the car...Matteo knew he was going through girls like water through a sieve at the moment.

He turned away and started heading to the elevators, passing through the security gates again. "Follow me." He commanded deeply.

Mila panicked a moment, was he talking to her?

He looked back over his shoulder, his eyes intense. "Now."

She jumped and trotted after him obediently, passing through the security gates as the men in black suits all grinned at her pet like behavior. She felt like she was walking into Satan's lair.

Matteo stopped before the elevator and looked down at her as she came to stand beside him nervously chewing her lip. "This had better not be a waste of my time or you might find you're the one that goes missing."

She baulked as the doors opened and he stepped into the lift, turning to face back at her with a grin of amusement on his face. He reached out and held the doors open. "Well? What's it going to be, pet?"

She felt a shudder go through her at the deep smooth way he called her that and on shaky legs she stepped into the elevator. She heard him chuckle deeply. "Good girl."

"Excuse me?" She asked rather tartly at that.

The doors closed and he turned to lean on the wall, his eyes travelling the length of her with a heat that left her mouth dry again. She backed up a little fearful.

He smirked as he put his hands in the pockets of his pants. "It's not me you have to worry about, pet? Do you like to be taken by force?"

"What the hell are you saying?" She backed herself tight into the corner, fearing she had made a terrible mistake.

"If you want money for information, tell me now what it is and I'll send you back down free to go on your way..."

She chewed her lip. "Or...?"

His grin was like the devil. "You like to play with fire? If I get you in front of Quinn's brother and your information isn't good enough to appease his mood, he'll appease his mood by using your body...Miss Mila Buick that had Quinn's car vandalized...you came here already owing a debt you foolish girl."

"Oh god..." Mila felt her stomach drop through the floor as she covered her mouth, her eyes bleary with tears. "Please, don't...I...I know that Quinn is taking night classes at Colombia."

Matteo inhaled smoothly, grinning from ear to ear. He stepped up to her and stroked her cheek as a tear ran down it. He swiped it up onto his fingers and then put it to his lips. "Well okay then, that's good information...got proof?"

"I saw it with my own eyes...Cory was picking her up."

"Good..." He placed a hand on the wall and leaned down into her face making her press herself into the corner as hard as she could. "That's good information...what do you want for it?"

"Please let me go?" Mila scrunched her eyes shut as his fingers pressed to her lips and rubbed them.

He chuckled. "Is that all you want now, pet? Does it make us all square?"

The doors opened on the elevator and Matteo moved swiftly to close them again and pushed the button the return to the ground floor.

"Tell me everything you know before we reach the bottom." He demanded, going into his jacket and pulling out a wad of cash. He pulled notes out and threw them at her. "Hurry now."

She gaped at him as the notes fell to the floor.

"There are night classes for adults that work to pass Business level one and two...she's doing them instead of returning to full time study at Scarsdale, obviously to stay hidden from you lot. It's four nights a week Tuesday to Friday at seven to nine p.m."

"Thank you...that's handy information, do you hate Quinn that much?" Matteo chuckled as Mila looked at the money on the floor.

She looked up and he could see it in her eyes. "She's a bitch for stealing my man from me."

Matteo's grin dropped from his face. "Get on your knees and pick that money up."

She baulked at the sudden change in this menacing man and got on her knees, reaching out to the fallen notes. "Sorry...I just..."

"Who's the bitch here I wonder..." Matteo said darkly as he put his boot under her chin and lifted her face to look at him. "You could do with a lesson on manners from Quinn's brother but I fear you wouldn't survive it...so just take this warning, pet...never return here."

The doors of the elevator opened and Matteo calmly put his foot down. "Pick up the money and drag your whore ass out of this building."

Mila grabbed what money she could see got to her feet and ran, tears running down her face. Matteo stepped out of the elevator, watching her, lifting his hand to wave his fingers at the men to let her through. He chuckled to himself and looked back to see a couple of notes still on the floor of the elevator. He reached around the elevator door and pushed the button to keep the doors open.

He looked up at the reception desk. "Miss Emily...come here."

One of the receptionist girls looked up with a worrying glance, licking her lips with nervous energy as she came over.

"Yes, Mr Perrelli?"

"Get in the elevator, pick up those notes."

She glanced in and nodded. "Yes, Sir."

As she stepped in and crouched down, careful not to let her skirt ride up, Matteo walked in, pushed the button and the doors closed. Emily looked up with fear sparking in her eyes as Matteo casually leaned back on the wall and started undoing his belt.

"You need to earn that money before you pick it up..."

As the elevator doors opened once again to the top floor Antonio was standing there, his eagle gaze falling on Matteo with the receptionist on her knees and his cock in her throat.

"I heard you were playing elevators with some blond girl..." He chuckled snidely. "Is there a reason for it?"

"I'm celebrating...I have wonderful news concerning Quinn."

"Really?" Antonio stepped into the elevator with his minders with him. Emily felt the shame as Matteo held her head refusing to let her stop and get up until the deed was completed. She pulled in a shaky breath and continued to suck him off in front of the big boss and his men. She was just another whore in their eyes anyway, dragged over from paying her debt in the club to play receptionist here when the last one fell pregnant.

Matteo grunted in pleasure as he felt her resume her sucking. "Yeah, I think we have the perfect way to snatch her back."

Antonio licked his lips in anticipation, grinning like the devil. "Is that so? Well it's about damn time something went my way..."

58
Accidents happen

It was Friday when it went down, it took two days of organizing and diligent surveillance to work out the path Cory took in his truck and how to make the obstruction. Antonio had first sent in an undercover guy as a student into the classroom to try and get to Quinn that way but Cory was vigilant and stayed by the door for the whole lesson every night.

They got coffee then headed home, always the same route, always the same intersection.

Cory sat at the red light taking the opportunity to take a sip of his coffee as Quinn played with the radio to find a decent tune.

"Why is every station DJ talking right now?" She said frustrated.

Cory looked at the time. "It's on the hour, you got out a bit early today from class...they do the news and then talk for like five minutes and play ads before they ever get around to playing music again."

Quinn rolled her eyes as the light turned green.

Cory put his cup in the cup holder as he eased his foot off the brake and his truck started to roll forward as the car in front of them pulled away through the intersection. Cory applied some acceleration just as Quinn finally found some music playing that wasn't classical or country and she looked up at him with a huge grin.

Her face dropped into a silent O of terror as her eyes went to the blazing headlights of a truck slightly bigger than Cory's careening straight for them through the intersection with a massive steel grate on the front of it.

"Cory!" Quinn managed to get out the quick warning before the truck slammed into the side of theirs with enough force that it shunted their truck sideways several feet, the windows on Cory's side blowing out and the airbags inflating. The other truck continued with its acceleration, tyres squealing in protest until Cory's truck tyres dug in the opposite side from the pressure of sliding sideways causing the truck to flip over onto the roof. The other truck reversed up, turned and accelerated away leaving bystanders to the accident speechless.

Quinn felt groggy, blinking in a dazed fog trying to figure out what just happened. She heard the screech of brakes to her right and the slamming of car doors. She was upside down, the seatbelt digging into her shoulder. She looked to her left and saw Cory unconscious, bleeding from a wound in his head. She stared at it not comprehending for several seconds that felt like a life time watching the blood trail drip slowly down through his hair.

"Cory?" She breathed, her voice shaking in trepidation.

"Cory!" She reached out and gripped his shoulder shaking it.

He groaned and moved his head making her breathe a sigh of relief he was alive. Her door was suddenly wrenched open and hands came in grabbing and pulling. Someone had a knife and cut her belt from her shoulder and waist and she was dragged from the truck.

She protested at the roughness and looked up to see who it was helping them. Several people were gathered around and as she was yanked up to her feet she saw people on the other side tending to Cory. She was suddenly lifted off her feet spun around and dumped on someone's shoulder.

"Wait? What are you doing?" She complained, trying to look up, brushing her hair out of her face. Her head pounded and she felt shaky and nauseous. She heard sirens, good someone must have called an ambulance.

"Let's get out of here!" A gruff voice growled to her right and the man who had her on his shoulder grunted in reply.

"Yes, Sir."

Her blood went cold hearing that formal address. The man stepped over to the car parked in the middle of the intersection right next to their rolled truck as the other guy opened the back door. She was dumped down on the back seat, rolled onto her stomach and someone crawled in over the top of her to grab her hands and pull them behind her as the car doors all slammed shut and the car jerked to sudden acceleration. With a brief squeal of tyres the car roared off.

Quinn's heart was racing, what was going on? Something wasn't right here!?

"No! What are you doing? Let me go!" She struggled against the guy as he cable tied her wrists together behind her back. He grabbed a fistful of her hair and yanked her head back viciously.

"Shut the fuck up bitch!" He slammed her face down hard into the seat, pressed so she couldn't breathe. His other hand swishing her ponytail away from the back of her neck. She struggled for breath for a few seconds before going deathly still at what she heard the guy say next.

"The boss is going to be really happy to see you again."

"Would you just hurry up with the damn shot!" The guy from the passenger seat yelled leaning around and through the gap between the seats. Quinn wondered what they meant, were they going to shoot her?

She gasped as she felt a sharp prick on her neck and a sudden rush of cold fluid.

"No..." She groaned out before everything went black.

Cory was pulled from the mangled wreckage of his side of the truck, going in and out of consciousness, as the ambulance pulled up and the paramedics raced over to tend to him. He struggled to see as blood started to drip in his eyes and he kept trying to sit up but kept being pushed back down.

"Lay down please sir, you could have neck or spine injuries...we're just going to strap a collar around your neck to make sure before we move you any further...sir, please stop moving."

"Quinn! Where is she...where's Quinn!"

"I don't know who you're talking about, sir..."

"She was in the truck with me! Where is she?"

"We didn't see anyone in the truck other than you, sir." The paramedic said with a confused frown. The one strapping him to the stretcher looked up at the watching crowd.

"Did anyone see a girl get out of the truck?"

Someone in the crowd shouted. "Yeah, some guys rushed her to hospital I think."

Cory's stomach lurched. "No! They kidnapped her! Let me go..." He started struggling against the paramedics as they lifted him into the ambulance.

"Sir, we're going to have to get you to lie still..."

"No, don't you get it! This was all set up, this wasn't an accident! Quinn's been taken by those fuckers!"

The paramedics looked at each other perplexed. "Let's give him something to calm him down..."

"No!" Cory fought against the restraints, screaming for someone to listen to him. "My phone, please get my phone...call Reese...we need to get her back!"

"I'm sure she was just taken to the hospital by some concerned citizens, it happens sometimes...the nearest hospital is the one back at the university, it's not too far away and I'm sure that's where she has been taken...don't panic."

Cory grit his teeth. How did he get through to these bastards? While every second Quinn gets further and further away.

He seethed through his clenched teeth as the paramedic gave him a shot of something to calm him down. "I don't need this, I just need my damn phone! I need to call Reese!"

"Sir, your ankle is smashed and you have a serious laceration on your head, do you not remember?" The paramedic shined a torch into his eyes to check his pupils for concussion. "The people who got you out had to prize the metal back from your leg...you need to focus on yourself right now, relax..." The paramedic managed to get a needle into his arm.

Cory started to feel lightheaded and drowsy. His head dropped back onto the stretcher and he shook it as his eyes rolled back.

"No...Quinn...fuck...no..."

As Cory regained consciousness he heard the distraught calling of his name from his step-mother, Wendy and blinked seeing her holding his hand in a hospital room. His foot was in plaster and being held up by a sling. He saw his father standing on the opposite side of the bed looking relieved but troubled.

Cory sat up with a grimace of pain. "Dad! Where's Quinn?"

Michael heaved a sigh and sadly shook his head. "We don't know...when the cops arrived on scene and collected your belongings as the paramedics were dealing with you they realized who you were and contacted me immediately. We've swept the scene for witnesses and they said the Dodge truck came out of nowhere, with a huge bullbar on the front of it and rammed the side of your truck to make it roll. A black sedan that could have been anything from a BMW to a Honda came screaming up, braked, three guys got out and opened the passenger side door, cut the belt off Quinn, picked her up and threw her in the back seat, screaming and took off."

Cory stared at his father in disbelief. "How the fuck does this happen? Where were the guys that were supposed to be keeping a watch?"

Michael coughed and seemed on edge. "We had another report of shots fired only a street away straight after the accident...I haven't been in touch with Cillian to see if it was them possibly trying to stop the fleeing vehicle..."

"Why the fuck not! Call Reese right now! He needs to know."

"We were more worried about you, Cory." Wendy said quietly next to him.

He turned and gave her a savage glare. "If Quinn is in the hands of that fucking monster he could be torturing her before putting a bullet in her head, mom! What the fuck are you guys so worried about me for? I'm alive!"

"You've been in surgery...your ankle..." Wendy covered her mouth and tears threatened to fall.

Cory frowned in confusion and glanced at his ankle in a cast. It throbbed a bit but what of it?

Michael stepped closer to the bed and placed a hand on Cory's arm. "It took three metal plates and several screws to get your ankle right, son...you're not going to be able to play football again."

Cory swallowed hard at the news, he enjoyed playing, he enjoyed the team, the camaraderie, the little bit of fame that went with it...it was still only football to him though.

"Who fucking cares! We need to find Quinn, she's in mortal danger!"

"The police are on it, Cory, you need to not get yourself worked up. As far as I know Cillian's men may have her..."

Cory grit his teeth, glaring at his dad. "Where's my phone?"

"Cory..."

"Where's the damn phone, dad!?"

Wendy got up out of her chair and stepped to the cabinet next to the bed, opened it and pulled a paper bag out. "Your personal things were brought in and placed in there..."

Cory snatched the bag, tearing it open and grabbed his phone. He saw it still had charge and phoned Reese immediately. His eyes lifted to stare at his father almost accusing him of not giving a shit.

Reese answered on the first ring.

"Cory? Shit, thank god you're awake...I'm outside, your Dad won't let me in..."

Cory glared at his dad as Michael clucked his tongue and went to the door of the room, opened it and spoke to the officer standing outside. "Let him in."

"Sir." The policeman walked off to the far end of the corridor past the nurse's station and flicked his hand. Reese came barreling around the corner, the phone still at his ear and was pushing past Michael and up to the bed before anyone could even say anything. He dropped his phone and embraced Cory in his arms, dropping his face to Cory's neck and pressing his lips to his hot skin.

"Fuck...we're doing everything we can to find her, Curry." He breathed.

"Someone rammed my truck at an intersection...I was knocked unconscious..." Cory lifted his free hand to his head and felt the bandage and knew he had stitches as he winced. Reese pulled back to look at his face with concern. "It's bad, Reese...really bad..." He teared up, sobbing the words out as the full implications fell like a dead weight onto his chest. He gripped his chest over his heart feeling an unbelievable cramping ache. "They took her...Rice...I couldn't stop them!"

Reese cupped Cory's cheek, swiping under his eye with his thumb to remove the wet tears. "It'll be alright, she'll be alright."

He grit his teeth as the nurse came in with an angry frown at the disturbance they were causing so late at night. Cory looked at his phone and startled to see it was 3am.

Reese clucked his tongue. "I'm glad you're awake Curry...now I have to go."

He pressed his lips to Cory's for a brief second then backed away so the nurse could get close, turned to glare at Michael for a second then left the room.

Michael followed with a grim expression into the hall. "Was it Cillian's men that fired those shots?"

Reese stopped and turned back looking fraught, raking a hand through his hair. "Yeah, I got a call just after 9pm to say that the car following Curry's truck had been cut off and surrounded by Antonio's people firing at them.

"How do you know it was Antonio's people?" Michael asked cautiously.

"Who else would it be? They must have been following Cory and Quinn for days to put this plan together." Reese spat, his eyes blazing.

"You need to calm down and not go and do something reckless that could end up with you in jail for a very long time." Michael grumbled.

Reese clucked his tongue. "Besides taking some of his men off the street and interrogating them as to where they have Quinn, we have nothing to go on."

"Nothing?" Michael frowned deeply concerned. He did not need this to explode into a street war.

"We have people watching Zortex and Antonio's home building, the docks...his favorite club...there are no sightings of him or his top man, Matteo...wherever he has Quinn its not anywhere we can find."

"Shit..."

"Keep this from Curry...tell him we are doing everything we can." Reese paused and looked away, swishing his hair from his eyes before sliding his gaze back to Michael with a regrettable depth of sadness. "How is he, really?"

"He's never going to play football again." Michael stated calmly.

Reese nodded, dropping his gaze, turned and walked away.

59
Reese's worst nightmare

As Reese walked to the main foyer in absolute despair, his boy was injured in the hospital and his girl was gone, in the hands of a psychopathic killer and probably injured as well going through hell. He had first found out when he had received a call from Liam, straight after the attack on his men in the car that was supposed to follow Cory at all times.

Antonio had somehow found out about Quinn's night classes and had meticulously planned this. Reese felt like a fool, he should have forbid her to go, but she had been adamant in her stubbornness that she had to be able to be who she wanted to be. He wished he had just locked her up like he wanted to do every time he looked at her exotic appearance.

Now she was locked up, but by the wrong monster. She was in the hands of the monster that would hurt her, and right now there was nothing he could do about it, and he knew that time was everything and it was ticking...ticking...he had to get his father's permission to be able to go rogue.

He saw Tank and Bulletproof stand up from the chairs in the waiting area by the main desk and approach him.

Tank moved up to stand beside him. "How is he, boss?"

Reese sighed bitterly. "He's never going to play again apparently..."

"Fuck." Tank breathed. "Sorry."

Reese's glare lifted to him. "Why the fuck are you sorry?" He growled out loudly making everyone in the near vicinity turn to look.

"Hey...calm it down a bit." Bulletproof warned, holding his hand up.

"You think I give a fuck!" Reese yelled and stormed from the building.

He stood out on the curb and took his vape out, huffing on it to try and calm down. He saw the blacked out hummer enter the drive, come up to the doors and stop directly in front of him. The passenger door opened and a man jumped out wearing black combat clothing. He grinned at Reese as he opened the back door.

"Good timing, is everything here settled?"

"Yeah, he's out of surgery and awake." Reese confirmed with a narrowed gaze, was his father keeping tabs?

"Excellent...get in, Mr O'Shea, your father wants to talk to you."

"No doubt." Reese spat and looked back as Bulletproof came up with Tank behind him. "Drive home...I won't need you where I'm going."

"Sure thing." Bulletproof looked at the guy holding the back door open and flicked his head up in greeting. "Hey Max."

"Hey Bronty...go get some sleep, Mr O'Shea will stay at the main house for the rest of the night."

Reese looked back at Bulletproof with an eyebrow raised and a little amused smirk on his lips. "Bronty? Shit, no wonder you get called Bulletproof."

Bulletproof shrugged and looked away. "I hope you have a productive rest of your evening, Mr O'Shea."

"Hmm." Reese grunted and climbed in the back of the Hummer.

Reese was shown into Cillian's dark and broody drawing room and as he took a seat in one of the Chesterfield chairs he glanced over at his father who was seated waiting for him. "What are you doing up at this time of night, old man?" He huffed belligerently.

"My men were shot at and the thing they were supposed to be protecting was taken...what do you think I should be doing right now, napping?"

Reese snorted and settled his gaze on his hands. "What the fuck do we do now, Dad?"

Cillian leaned back in his chair and crossed his legs. "I have other news that might shed some light on just how serious this situation is, beyond the girl being taken back by Antonio."

Reese's dark gaze lifted to his father, his jaw ticking under the strain of clenching.

"I doubt it was coincidence that Flanagan rang me this evening."

"Fuck...coincidence my ass." Reese grumbled. "What time was this?"

"A bit earlier than the fiasco on the streets, around 7pm." Cillian motioned for the guard to pour a drink for him and Reese. "He didn't hide the facts about Quinn being O'Malley's daughter or Maria being our founding father's daughter and Quinn his granddaughter...in fact he seemed rather proud of the fact that he made this alliance agreement with the Ferrantes."

Reese was glaring at the table, his right leg bouncing in agitation. He glanced up as the guard put a glass of whiskey on the table in front of him.

"In fact..." Cillian continued. "He seemed rather put out that we would dare get involved on the wrong side and actually tried to persuade me to take the girl from Michael McMillan's place and give her back. That got me wondering why the concern in his voice about it when I refused."

Reese looked up at his father to see a smug smirk on his face. "So you refusing to step in and get her back for Ferrante resulted in this kidnapping?"

"I'm not sure if Flanagan knew exactly what Antonio had planned but I think it was a warning that came too late, yes."

"They fired the first shot." Reese growled.

"Indeed they have...but it was fired long ago..." Cillian replied cryptically.

Reese scowled at him. "What aren't you saying...you're being mighty coy right now?"

Cillian chuckled. "Right, I am..." He leaned forward and grabbed his glass up, tipping it back to his mouth and taking a hefty sip before placing it back with a satisfied sigh. Reese's leg was bouncing again waiting for his father to hurry up and get to the point.

"It seems this has all been planned out by the Ferrantes from the beginning...the affair to get Maria certainly...to get Quinn to enter a marriage alliance with Antonio. It seems fortuitous that they managed to manipulate her to their side because of O'Malley's stupid error in judgment."

Reese frowned and shook his head. "What the hell are you trying to say, spit it out!"

"Ferrante is planning on producing an heir with Quinn, a combined heir of old families of both Mafia and Mob, with the intent of taking over the Mob territories in Boston and ruling the whole importing side of things from there, all while being mayor of the city...it's a brave plan...a long game plan with rich results. Those docks Flanagan bought with Quinn's inheritance has become Imperial Shipping and he will give it all back to her through her new husband as soon as they are married, which means as Mayor he'll control the port and a major shipping company that uses it in Boston as well as his interests in the ports here in New York."

"And Flanagan was just going to let this happen? The port is worth billions."

"Yes, that's the rub...he has been on board with their plan all along, that's why he used Quinn's inheritance to secure the docks for the Mob specifically...and planned to sit on it for a decade, build it up and then just hand it over. Including all our imports and exports as well."

Reese wiped a hand down his face. "Fucking brazen...how the hell did Flanagan think this was going to be allowed to happen?"

"I have it on good authority that his top lieutenants are all in on it..."

"How the hell did you get someone to talk about this then?"

Cillian chuckled. "I have my ways, son. I've actually been working on this since your last visit."

Reese chuffed in amusement. "So what's going to happen now?"

"Quinn is the key...if she carries the heir to the original founder of the Boston mob and marries into the Mafia it gives Antonio the right to be invited to our table and to her inheritance."

Reese collapsed back into his chair. "Fuck me...is everyone stupid or what?"

"Now we as an outside faction know about it, we can put a stop to it...Flanagan has sold out, he's been in the Ferrante pocket for nearly a decade and I have the proof...I intend, now that Quinn is gone, to present it to our board and deal with this from our side."

"Wait..." Reese sat up with a worried frown. "If you do that now Quinn becomes expendable...Antonio will kill her. I won't let that happen!"

"Hmm..." Cillian looked away with a grim repose. "Helen of Troy indeed."

Reese clucked his tongue.

"She'll be a pariah, son...you won't be able to bring her back into the fold after all this."

"What the fuck?" Reese sounded devastated.

"I'm sorry, son, but this is going to cause a huge disruption within the whole organization, we've been in peace for nearly a decade, this will be war."

"Yeah, thanks to Quinn being sold off!"

"Regardless, this is a messy situation that she is not going to come out of pristine, you need to understand that and I will not let your path deviate because of her."

"Deviate?"

Cillian looked around and locked eyes with Reese. "I will not have you thinking stupidly that you can leave the Mob and your family to go off and have a life with that girl and boy out there."

Reese sucked his teeth, glaring at his father.

"I won't give them up and I have no intention of giving up your seat that's coming my way either. I was born and bred to lead this organization and I intend to, to the best of my ability."

Cillian's mouth twisted up into a one sided smirk as he snorted a little chuckle. "That's my boy."

"I'll work it out, dad, I can have both." Reese's fists were clenched tight. "And I'll kill any one that opposes me on it."

"Of that I have no doubt, your conviction is clear and comforting to see, but just make sure it's in the background and not something easily found out and exploited."

"So are you giving me permission to go rogue?"

Cillian smiled with an evil caste to it. "If we can destroy the Ferrante's here and Flanagan in Boston it opens the world up for us to capitalize."

Reese grinned and licked his tongue over his teeth, lifting his glass and holding it out. "I'll get Antonio, you get Flanagan."

Cillian raised his glass and clinked it with Reese's. "Bring on the mayhem."

They both drained their glasses and put them on the table. "Now go get some sleep, Reese." Cillian ordered with a smile.

Reese nodded and left, going to his own room in Cillian's mansion, closing the door, turning slowly around and leaning his back against it. He covered his face with his hands as he slowly slid down the door, hiding the tears that threatened to fall and wiped them away angrily.

He took in a shuddering breath, closing his eyes against the pain he was feeling in his heart that he couldn't show the world.

60
Quinn's worst nightmare

"Cory!" A scream from her dream tore through her throat and Quinn woke to find herself lying semi-naked on a mattress on the floor of a gloomy, dingy room with a boarded up window, peeling wallpaper and bare wooden floor boards. It looked part of some abandoned house and had her sitting up in a panic trying hard to breathe as her mouth was gagged with a strip of tape. Her hands were still cable tied behind her back, her feet were also bound and she had somehow been stripped down to her underwear. It was cold but that was not why her body trembled uncontrollably as shock settled in. It was daylight as she could see clearly the light shining in through the gaps in the boards on the window. Tears fell like rain as she scrambled on her bottom into the darkest corner of the room trying to hide as best she could from whatever or whoever was on the other side of the door as she heard heavy booted footsteps approaching.

The door unlocked and Quinn watched completely petrified as three men stepped into the room. The front one grinned at her evilly, casting his eyes over her body as she curled up trying her best to cover herself.

"You're awake...good, it's about time." The first guy said as he entered, chuckling as he walked to the side of her and crouched down, removing the tape from her mouth with a savage rip. She flinched in pain and gasped in a decent breath as she noticed he had a bottle of water in his hand. She saw the second guy come in and stay by the door as the third entered silently and ominously.

Quinn's head was grabbed and yanked up so her face was catching the light as the first guy tipped the water bottle up and squeezed her cheeks, filling her open mouth with the water. She choked and coughed as he laughed. She shook her head free and blinked up to see the third man standing above her.

"That's her...good job."

"Matteo?" She trembled almost inaudibly.

"Hello, Quinn." He said back in an unemotional tone.

"H-help me...please." She pleaded causing the guy holding her to change holds and grab a fistful of her hair and chuckle, breathing close to her ear.

"Not sure I can..." Matteo answered casually. "You're the one who ran away straight into the arms of another guy, despite Antonio's constant warnings to you...this is your hell, Quinn."

"What did you do with Cory?" She asked deeply concerned. "Is he okay...what have you done..."

"You need to worry about yourself right now, Quinn!" Matteo growled, interrupting her.

The guy crouching beside her stood up, hauling her up by putting his forearms under her arm pits and dragged her back over to the mattress, dumping her down on it.

Matteo clucked his tongue as the guy leered and chuckled, brushing Quinn's hair back from her face as she struggled to sit up and get away from him. This went on for several seconds as he kept pushing her back down until she relented and stayed laying on her side.

"She's a real struggler...pretty girl, just relax." He crooned creepily as he stroked a hand down her breasts making her scrunch her eyes closed and tremble in fear and trepidation.

"Get your fucking hands off, you moron." Matteo growled causing the guy to stand up with a grimace.

Quinn glanced up at Matteo gratefully but saw his eyes fixed on the tattoo of Antonio's name. He hissed through his teeth, raking a hand through his hair. "Fuck's sake, Quinn, you couldn't wait to get his name off, huh?"

After the first treatment the tattoo had been faded out a lot and Matteo knew Antonio was not going to like it one bit.

"W-where is he? What's he going to do to me?" Quinn asked nervously.

Matteo sighed, looking away at the boarded up window. "I don't know...I really don't know." His eyes came back to her. "You can be one hundred percent sure it's not going to be pleasant though..." He shook his head in pity looking sour. "I'm sorry, Quinn...but if you've been fucking that boy...Jesus...I hate to think what he's going to do to you."

"You're his reasoning, Matteo...please talk to him!"

Matteo chuckled and scoffed. "You think I'm his reasoning?" He shook his head. "You don't get it at all..."

"What don't I get?" Quinn's lip quivered in nervous fear.

"Doesn't really matter, I guess."

A knock sounded on the door and a gruff voice called out from the other side. "He's here!"

Quinn's stomach lurched and she curled up into a tight ball. Matteo's jaw clenched as he gave the two guys in the room a once over. "Get out of here."

They both left and Matteo just stared at Quinn with a grim expression. "Remember his rules."

Antonio stepped into the room dressed as impeccably as always in a dark charcoal three piece suit. He stood a yard away from Quinn as she peeked up at him pitifully while Matteo closed the door and stood in front of it.

His dark gaze just penetrated her as he stood silently staring at her, his jaw was ticking as he casually adjusted the cuffs of his shirt sleeves. Quinn jostled up onto her shins and bowed her head forward in submission.

Antonio stepped forward and lifted his foot dropping it on her head, pressing her forehead to the mattress. She heard him hiss out a breath through his gritted teeth and she whimpered in fear. The silence was oppressive, she would rather he screamed and yelled at her.

He removed his foot and stepped back again. "Look at me." He commanded.

She lifted her head and met his terrifying gaze, looking pitiful and remorseful as possible hoping he would take pity on her but she knew by the cold hard expression he was giving her that her hope went in vain.

"You're a slut, Quinn..." He breathed out, his fist clenching like he was going to hit her. "...just like all the rest."

She flinched just at the hard words, closing her eyes and tilting her head away.

"Look at me!" He growled vehemently.

"Sorry, sir." She blurted out. When she looked back he let fly with a back handed slap so strong it knocked her off her knees, split her lip and made her see stars.

"Who the fuck gave you permission to speak?" He stepped to the edge of the mattress and crouched down, grabbing her by her hair and lifting her head back viciously. "Looks like someone needs to be retrained..." He stared into her petrified eyes then dropped his gaze to her lip. His eyes seemed to fire with an intense heat to see the blood and he leaned down and licked her lip, sucking it into his mouth as she gasped at the sting. He pulled back and chuckled darkly. "You've lost all value in my eyes, Guinevere O'Malley."

She startled to hear him call her that and in such a sadistic tone. "You are no longer pure, but tell me, have you fucked one, two or more?"

She looked up at him with doubt in her eyes whether she should even answer him. He chuckled and his tongue licked out over his top lip in the corner. "Fuck...I know it's at least two, right?"

Her eyes widened in shock. How did he know?

He leaned in closer to her face, his looking cruel and sinister as his gaze flitted over her face taking in every detail. "You're a disappointment...but still useful." He grinned and it made her heart thump in her chest in real fear and the contents of her stomach start to rise up in her throat. "From now on you will fuck whoever I tell you to."

He threw her down on the mattress and stood up, towering over her and put his hands in his pant pockets, sweeping his jacket back. "You're going to be my little trophy wife whore from now on."

Quinn swallowed hard and struggled back onto her knees. "Please, Antonio..."

"Don't fucking speak!" He yelled, holding up his hand in warning.

She flinched back and whimpered.

"Matteo, come here." He lifted his hand and motioned for Matteo to come up next to him. Matteo frowned deeply concerned at Antonio's words and actions but obeyed. Once he was standing in front of Quinn Antonio grinned like the devil. "Suck him off." He ordered of her.

Quinn's face dropped into a disbelieving gape as Matteo turned to give Antonio a disapproving glare. He looked at the two of them and laughed. He pulled his gun out and waved it between the two of them. "If neither of you move to do what I ordered someone is going to die."

"Sir..." Matteo went to object, he knew Antonio would never shoot him or Quinn.

Quinn squealed and crouched into a ball and even Matteo flinched when Antonio fired a shot into the floor right between them both.

Quinn sobbed in true terror. "Please, sir...please don't..."

"Quinn." Matteo's deep voice called her and she looked up with tears in her eyes and shook her head at him, pleadingly. "Just do it."

Antonio chuckled, still waving the gun at them. "You have two minutes to make my boy come..." He lifted his other hand and looked at his watch. "Hurry up!" He growled.

Matteo frowned deeply, he wasn't sure he could even get it up for this girl let alone come in two minutes. He pulled his zipper down and pulled his flaccid cock out in front of Quinn's face, reaching out with his other hand and pressing his hand down to the back of her head to guide her closer.

Quinn sobbed in a shaky breath. "Let my hands go..."

Matteo paused and looked at Antonio. It was a fair request...

Antonio clucked his tongue, putting the gun away and pulled a flick knife out of his pocket. He stepped around behind Quinn and cut the cable tie. She sighed in relief, rubbing her wrists and seeing blood where the plastic had started to cut her skin.

"Your time is running out." Antonio chuckled, standing up behind her and leering down at her. She swallowed her pride and leaned up on her knees, taking Matteo's cock in her hand and licking up underneath, around the head, flicking the tip before it started to come to life. She repeated the actions with more pressure, swirling her tongue around the head then digging the tip of her tongue into the eye as she grabbed the hardened phallus in both hands. He groaned out through clenched teeth and gripped harder into her hair.

God, he had a big cock...

When she sucked it in and swirled her tongue Matteo let out a deep groan of pleasure. "Fuck..."

Antonio chuckled darkly. "She's good, huh? I trained her good...not for just anyone's dick."

She took him to the back of her throat and thrummed. His hips bucked and he gasped out. "Fucking hell...yeah, she's fucking good boss...shit..." He really didn't want to do this, he really didn't want to enjoy it, but fucking hell she was doing her best that was for sure.

"Fuck her throat good, she can take it. She's waiting for it, aren't you, petalo?" Antonio was mocking and condescending, humiliating her even more.

Matteo felt her open her throat up by tilting her head up more and he grabbed her head in both hands and started thrusting hard. Antonio sucked his teeth, looking away and walked off to lean against a wall, watching with a dark detachment as Matteo came in Quinn's mouth as tears fell from her eyes.

He checked his watch as Matteo held Quinn in position until she swallowed before stepping back and zipping his cock away. Quinn looked at the floor, ashamed, humiliated and sore as she wiped her mouth and breathed in a few ragged coughs of breath.

Matteo looked up at Antonio and met his dark gaze with a solemn one. "Happy now?"

"Oh, I think you should be the happy one...rate her skills."

"What?" Matteo glowered at him, displeased.

Antonio glared at him. "You heard me...rate her, out of ten."

"An eight."

"Hmm...above average...not too bad. I'm sure it wasn't her best effort either...was it, petalo?" His voice dropped when he spoke to her and she felt her skin crawl.

"No, sir..."

"Hmm." He grunted. "You better do your best with your next challenge, since you went over the allotted time."

She looked up at him with shock as he walked to the door and opened it, calling out through the abandoned house to the other men. "Hey you lot, come in here."

Quinn started babbling in fear. "Please, Antonio...I'm sorry, please don't do this...I so sorry...I..."

Matteo stepped up to Antonio. "What the hell are you doing?"

Antonio gave him a look with absolutely no expression as the men appeared in the hall. "Quinn is now going to fuck you all...at once and until you are all satisfied."

Matteo growled. "Antonio! What the hell?"

"You too, Matteo...you will stay here and you will fuck her too, and I mean until you are all satisfied...then tomorrow you can bring her over to the Black Diamond where I'm going to have a few guests waiting for her..." Antonio gripped Matteo's tie and pulled him up face to face. "And if you don't obey me, I'll have every single one of these men including you shot and killed and it won't change her fate."

Quinn was screaming and crying in fear as she saw the men through the door. Antonio looked back once and sucked his teeth, his top lip lifting on one side before he dropped his hand from Matteo and stalked off down the hall. "Enjoy my gift."

The men pushed into the room as Quinn backed up into the far corner, petrified and crying. There were six of them and with Matteo that was seven.

Two of them rushed up and grabbed her ankles dragging her out of the corner as she struggled against them, snapping the cable tie and bringing her back to the mattress as they laughed and slapped her around a little, toying with her, enjoying her fear.

More hands pinned her arms down as her legs were pulled apart and someone stuffed something into her mouth to stop her screaming.

Matteo raced after Antonio and followed him doggedly to the car trying to persuade him not to allow this. "Sir, you really don't want to do this, you'll regret making this decision, just calm down before deciding something like this..."

Antonio turned as Danny opened the back door of the Bentley for him, his face a mask of pure calmness. "Don't you get it, Matteo? I don't want her anymore, she defiled herself...she only has herself to blame for becoming a whore."

"But, you still have to marry her?"

"So what? I can still get her knocked up too...I don't need to touch her for that...and right now she is still on the injection..." He turned away and got in the car, Danny closed the door with a pained look at Matteo before getting in the front.

Antonio wound his window down. "You better get back in there...I want photos of you in particular fucking her ass..." He gave a vile grin and wound the window back up.

Matteo raked a hand through his hair and spat on the ground. "Fucking hell..." He turned and raced back into the house as the car drove off, he could hear laughter and a muffled distressed squealing and when he got to the room he saw that no one had penetrated Quinn yet, they were having their fun and taking it slow, dragging out the humiliation.

He pulled his gun out and shot three shots into the roof.

"Back the fuck away from her now!"

She was completely naked now, her underwear having been ripped away and still being held down as hands groped her everywhere.

61
Matteo's morals

"What the fuck, Matteo, the boss said she was ours to do with as we want? You gonna take her all for yourself?" One guy stood up, objecting.

Matteo shot him in the head. He fell where he stood, his eyes still open and staring blankly. "You guys seriously believe that? If he suddenly changes his mind, what the fuck do you think happens to all of you?" The rest of the guys quickly backed off from Quinn and Matteo motioned to her.

"Come here, Quinn."

She scrambled up and ran to him, pressing her naked body against him as he put an arm around her and pulled her close. He backed out of the room closing and locking the door.

He dropped his arm and quickly took his suit jacket off handing it to Quinn to put on and cover her nakedness.

"Thank you, Matteo...thank you...fuck...I..." Quinn was shaking uncontrollably as Matteo put his arm back around her shoulders and started moving her down the hall.

"Enough, let's just get you out of here...I'm going to move you to somewhere safe and deal with this...this isn't right. Antonio has lost it."

He bundled Quinn into his car and when he got in he looked at her in the passenger seat looking crumpled and terrified. He sighed bitterly as she looked up at him with large watery eyes, her lip quivering as tears streaked her face.

"You're going to be killed for doing this." She said quietly.

He snorted. "Maybe...but probably not...once Antonio calms down and sees sense he'll probably thank me. I kinda have the feeling he told me to fuck you knowing I wouldn't...I'm sorry for the forced blowie."

She looked away with a sour pout. "I doubt that, he hates me...and I'm sorry that you were put in that position." She looked away with her face red with embarrassment.

He shook his head clearing his mind of how fucking good it was. He liked his women older, curvier and demanding.

He started up his car and left the abandoned house, driving through the streets of the broken down neighborhood. Quinn saw there were several abandoned houses in this area and shivered to think she would probably never have been found if killed and left there.

"I can't believe he did this to me..." Quinn murmured softly. She glanced up at Matteo's side profile to see his jaw tight and his eyes fixed hard on the road. "What's the big deal about me being touched only by him...he still visits whores, I know he does."

Matteo grumbled and his hands clenched the steering wheel in frustration. "I'm fucked if I know, he's always been unhinged where you are concerned."

She blinked and chewed her lip before asking. "Is it because my father killed his mother?"

Matteo glanced at her with shock then grimaced. "Shit, you know everything, huh?"

"I know enough...was I really sold to him?"

Matteo's jaw was grinding as he went through a busy intersection before turning down a relatively quiet street. "Yeah, you really were, sorry."

Quinn fell silent for the rest of the trip, hugging Matteo's suit jacket tight around her body as best she could. He noticed she kept pulling on the bottom of his jacket to keep her bottom half covered and sighed out bitterly. He noticed a place to pull over and got out of the car, going to the trunk and opening it up. He returned to the driver's seat and dropped something into Quinn's lap.

"Here, it's not much but it will at least cover you better until we get you inside my apartment."

Quinn looked down and saw it was a pair of shorts and a t-shirt in a men's XL. "Are these your workout clothes?"

He smiled. "Yeah, but they're clean, don't worry."

"Okay...but how do I?" She looked at the clothes wondering how to get them on without flashing her naked body to Matteo.

He clucked his tongue, focusing on the road once more. "I've seen everything you have to offer, Quinn...just put them on in the back seat."

Quinn grimaced to realize that was probably quite true. She unhooked her seatbelt and clambered through to the back seat, safe in the knowledge the dark tint on the windows wouldn't show her to any other drivers. She quickly put the clothes on and sat back looking out the windows not wanting to go back to the front.

Matteo looked back at her when stopped at a red light. "Lie down if you want, use my jacket as a blanket...with this traffic we could be another hour to get back across the city."

"Are you really taking me to your place?"

"Where else can I take you?"

"To Reese O'Shea."

Matteo clucked his tongue. "You know I can't do that, Quinn..."

She looked down at her hands, picking her thumb nails with apprehension. "So what are you going to do with me?"

Matteo sighed irritably. "The only thing I can do is appeal to Augusto."

Quinn's head snapped up with her eyes large and pleading. "Do you have to do that?"

Matteo glared at her in the rearview mirror. "Yes, Quinn." His tone was final.

Matteo had a loft apartment on the seventh floor of a brown brick building in the middle of NoHo. It was neat, perfectly neat and minimalist with polished wood floors and a separate bedroom. He walked in and threw his keys down with Quinn following him in like a little lost puppy, clutching the clothes to her like someone might try to take them away. He pointed over to the dark grey couch and ordered her to sit.

She did as she was told and sat nervously watching him as he went into the kitchen area and put a kettle on the gas stove top to boil. He took out two mugs from the cupboard and set them on the bench then took some tea bags from a container and put them into the mugs.

He looked up and saw Quinn pouting at him with a curious little frown on her face. "What? Can't believe a big guy like me drinks herbal tea?"

"No." She replied honestly.

He chuckled and shrugged. "I guess it is a little out of character, but it helps me relax...I usually take it to help me sleep, because I never know what time of the day or night I'll get sleep."

"You really devote your time to him..." Quinn muttered.

Matteo's eyes hardened slightly. "Yeah, I really do."

The kettle boiled and he filled the mugs, bringing one over to her and placing it down on the glass coffee table before going back to stand in the kitchen and take his phone out. She watched as he dialed someone and waited for them to pick up. His eyes went to her across the room as the other person answered.

"Sir, it's Matteo Perrelli, can I have a minute of your time?"

Quinn quailed to realize he was talking to Augusto.

He turned away and walked off to the bedroom as he switched to Italian but didn't close the door and every so often he would look out the door at her.

Was he making sure I don't run away?

Quinn had picked up her mug and sipped on it, enjoying the taste of the chamomile and passionflower tea. She sat back into the couch feeling herself relax finally and feel, if not safe, secure for the moment.

She wondered how she was going to get away from Matteo or maybe convince him to let her go.

Her eyelids dropped closed for a second and she jerked awake, spilling the tea that almost fell from her hands. She looked up as she leaned forward to put the mug down and saw Matteo watching her, standing in the doorway, no longer on the phone. His face was expressionless as he spoke two words to her before her eyes dropped closed again and she slumped back on the couch.

"I'm sorry."

Matteo sighed and walked across the room, scooped Quinn's legs up and onto the couch so she was lying down. He looked down at her sleeping face and brushed some hair away feeling sorry for the young girl. He straightened up and sent a message to someone.

M - **She's ready**

It was only twenty minutes later that there was a knock at the door and two men entered. They gave Matteo a brief greeting before looking over at Quinn. They were dressed as paramedics and had a stretcher, but they weren't.

"Wow, she's a pretty one...are you sure Antonio is going to be okay with this?"

"Just do what you're ordered, these orders come from Don Augusto...you've got exactly one hour to get her to the airport. Here's some extra pills dissolved in water to keep her out when she gets there. Force her to swallow it before the flight."

The guy took the bottle of water and nodded before they took Quinn away strapped to the stretcher and covered by a sheet.

Matteo sighed heavily and sat down, wiping a hand over his face. He looked at his phone and waited...as soon as he knew the plane had left he would inform Antonio.

It was only another half an hour later that Matteo got a message from Antonio.

A - **Where are my photos?**

Matteo grimaced, he knew Antonio would have been informed by the other men by now about what happened. He was probably just outside the damn building.

He went to the window that looked down at the street and saw the Bentley and two other blacked out cars. He sighed and went to get his jacket, putting it on he placed his gun on the kitchen counter and stood in the middle of the room taking in a deep breath and waited.

They didn't even bother knocking, a deep booming sounded up on the door and it broke in to show two men with a police doorbreaker. They walked in as Matteo dropped to his knees with his hands behind his head, resigned to his fate. He looked up as Antonio walked in with several others and they all searched the apartment coming back to say Quinn wasn't there.

Antonio stood in front of Matteo, a gun in his hand as he rubbed the barrel up and down the side of his head, licking his tongue out over his teeth and chuckling like a true psycho.

"Of every person on the face of the planet, why you, Matteo?" He asked like this had to be a joke.

Matteo dropped his gaze to the floor at Antonio's feet. He had to stall for time. "I have no idea what you're talking about."

The crack to his head came from behind and dropped him to the floor, he was dragged back to his knees and his hands were then bound behind his back. Antonio had never moved and his eyes pierced Matteo with their vehemence.

"You want me to kill you?"

"I would rather you didn't." Matteo chuckled deeply, feeling blood run down the side of his neck.

"Where is she?" Antonio hissed.

"Who?" Matteo answered with a grin.

This time he got more of a beating, the guys standing around him all getting either a fist or a boot into him as he was held up from falling, men he knew, men he had previously led for years. He looked up at Antonio, licking blood from his split and swollen lip after they finally stopped at a barked order from Antonio after several minutes.

"Can I get the time?" He asked as he coughed.

Antonio's eyes narrowed suspiciously and he crouched down, putting the barrel of his gun to Matteo's cheek. "Why is the time important to you right now?"

Matteo shrugged, not perturbed by the gun in his face.

Antonio sucked his teeth for a second then glanced at his watch. "It's twenty to eleven."

Matteo grimaced, only another five minutes, should he risk it and reveal it yet?

Antonio's intense gaze studied his face and he looked into those dead black eyes and coughed, spilling some blood out of his mouth.

"What have you done, Matteo?" Antonio growled at him as he saw a slight smirk lift Matteo's lips.

Antonio stood up and aimed the gun at him.

"She's out of your reach for now, Antonio...I had to stop this, you know it wasn't right, she's no whore. You love her, you would have regretted it."

Antonio grit his teeth and hissed in a breath then started laughing like a lunatic. "Is that what you think, you poor deluded romantic..."

"She's on her way to Italy." Matteo announced, stopping Antonio's rant mid-sentence. He glared at Matteo stunned for a second before slowly lifting the gun back up, his eyes piercing in their hatred.

"You betrayed me to my father?"

"I had to. I know you would end up regretting what you were going to do to her."

Antonio's phone chirped and he breathed in a calming breath, taking it out to check it, keeping his gun trained on Matteo.

His face went from calm and curious to demented rage in a second. "What the fuck! There's been an explosion at the shipping yards!"

Matteo gained his feet. "Sir...it will be the O'Shea boy."

Antonio glared at him. "Typical Irish fucking mongrels!" He looked down at Matteo's leg and shot him in the thigh making him collapse back to his knees with a shout of pain. "Get yourself to a hospital then back to

HQ. You four with me, you two...make sure he makes it there..." Antonio turned around and swept from the room.

Matteo chuckled, grimacing in pain as one of the men helped him back to his feet and cut the bonds holding his hands. "You lucky son of a bitch..." The guy said impressed.

Matteo nodded. He should buy a lottery ticket.

62

Reese goes rogue

Reese had no intention of playing with Antonio any longer, he had to draw him out and what better way to do that than by destroying all his assets. Starting with the shipping yards he organized to blow at just before 11am the next day, then he stormed into the Black Diamond Club with twenty men.

At this time of the morning there wasn't anyone here besides the manager and a few men as he came in to do the cash. They usually had a couple of girls there as well and made it a time for 'auditions'. It wasn't hard to get that sort of information and the Mob had known it for a long time, sitting on it for just this occasion.

As Reese strolled in, his men fanning out through the main bar area and jumping up on the stage to get through to the back, the men there all looked at them gob-smacked and it took them a moment of disbelief to realize what was happening. They quickly came to their senses when some serious hardware in the form of semi-automatic guns were shoved in their faces and they were made to sit back down in their seats in front of the stage and some other men started smashing everything up behind the bar.

"What the fuck do you think you're doing? Do you know who owns this club?" The Manager screamed, holding his head in despair as he watched the guys behind the bar using the butts of their rifles to smash all the bottles and glasses by sweeping them off the shelves.

Reese walked casually up and stood in front of him. "Get up and take me to the office..."

"Why the hell should I do that?" The manager yelled at him.

Reese took out a butterfly knife, handling it with astounding skill to flick it open and jammed it into the Manager's leg. The Manager screamed, grabbing his thigh as Reese pulled the blade out and grabbed the manager around the back of the neck and stuck the blade into his mouth. The manager froze in fear at the golden stare that bore into his soul. "Want me to widen that smile of yours, joker?"

"Who the fuck...?" The Manager breathed out as Reese pulled away and one of his men pulled the Manager to his feet.

"Reese O'Shea...I want you to tell that fucking boss of yours exactly who I am." He nodded his head and the manager was dragged off to his office to open the safe. "He has something of mine I want returned."

Reese looked around and saw the girls crouching in fright in one corner with a guy keeping them quiet, holding a gun over their heads. He sucked his teeth for a second, thinking.

"Get those bitches out of here..."

The guy jabbed the gun in their direction getting them on their feet and escorting them out. Reese then turned to the other men on their knees before him. There was no emotion in his eyes as he looked up at the two men standing behind them and nodded before pivoting and walking off to the office.

The sound of the bullet spray filled the floor, men screaming and dying then silence.

He stepped into the office and the manager stared at him in horror to realize all his men had just been executed.

"Why are you doing this?"

"Like I said, Antonio took something from me...so I intend to take everything from him until he faces me and gives it back."

The next day at the precise same time several men stormed up to the front of the Zortex Headquarters, lined up out the front of the glass entrance and started shooting their machine guns into the building, they wore all black combat clothing, motorbike helmets and bulletproof vests, looking like a special ops swat team. In and gone in under two minutes.

Another explosion went up at a large warehouse complex in New Jersey not half an hour later where Antonio's construction business stored their equipment worth millions.

Another hour after that and a group of men playing cards and drinking at a storage warehouse business in Queens were disturbed from their entertainment by a huge truck ramming through the chain link gates and screeching to a halt with several men jumping out the back and shooting at them, yelling for them to get on their knees and surrender, also all dressed in blacked out combat gear.

After a brief shoot out where the men from the storage facility were drastically out gunned Reese jumped out of the truck and wandered up to them once they were on their knees and lined up. "Who's going to open the lucky container?"

"Who the fuck are you?" One guy asked, looking at the young punk in the leather jacket.

"Reese O'Shea...I've come to collect what it is that Antonio Ferrante hides here."

The men paled and blanched. They had been sent word of something happening in Manhattan at the Black Diamond club and an explosion at Zortex Shipping was already on the news, but how did the mob know about this place?

As Reese got back in the truck, wiping his hands of the blood from having to get a bit rough with the guys at the storage facility, he heard his phone ringing. He glanced at it on the truck dash and rolled his eyes to see it was Michael McMillan. No surprises there, it was fairly obvious to anyone by now that he was on a rampage. Still no call from Antonio however...and he was pretty sure Antonio would know his number.

Oh well, on to the next plant...

He would keep going until he was either stopped or Antonio came out to talk.

Cillian got out of the car after the four hour drive to Boston and straightened up with a little relief, looking up at the ten story building in front of him. He checked his watch and saw the time was perfect for checking in, walking up to the front entrance as the porter opened the door for him with a polite greeting. The valet stared at him with a little awe wondering who this handsome older man was to pull up in a car with a chauffeur, not needing him at all, and two body guards. Another car pulled up behind him and they all got out and followed him in as well. Who the hell was this guy, he dressed like a casual playboy type, did that make him a gangster? It was rumored this hotel was owned by gangsters.

Cillian walked into the lobby and let Liam sort his booking for him, walking through to the hotel bar and taking a seat at the bar, looking at the petite young blond behind it with a congenial smile.

"What will you have, sir?"

"Nothing for the moment, I'm waiting for someone..."

Liam walked in and stood behind him, leaning down slightly. "I saw the receptionist make a phone call as soon as my back was turned..."

"Good, we shouldn't have to wait long then..." He looked up at the girl behind the bar. "Perhaps just a coffee then, doll."

"Certainly, sir." She smiled and walked off to get one ordered from the café side.

It wasn't long until Flanagan flanked by two men walked in and sat down next to Cillian as the two men took up places standing either side of the door while Liam stood facing them. Cillian calmly sipped his coffee, looking up at the female bartender. "Perhaps it's time for your break, darlin'?" She looked nervously at the new arrivals and nodded, leaving quickly.

"I heard that you called a meeting of the Council...now you turn up here? Is this about the fight because I seem to remember your boy won...and I've already cleared the issue with you in regards to Antonio being there, at least I thought I had...so why are you here, Cillian? Surely it's not about that red haired slut?"

"This isn't about a fight. I've simply moved out of New York for a few days, I hope you can be accommodating...and as soon as the Council are together I'll say what I have to say to all of you."

Flanagan's jaw flexed at Cillian superior tone. "You're needing an alibi? What's this about, Cillian?"

Cillian sighed and looked up with a small smile. He took a long slow sip of his coffee before turning to look at Flanagan who was grinding his teeth in his impatience.

"I hear Antonio Ferrante is moving into local politics in Boston...that of course concerns us and I wonder why you didn't make mention of it when you were down, but instead invited him to our little friendly contest and made it into some farce of a demonstration of power and control and then have the audacity to ring me on behalf of that Italian bastard to say to me, of all people, to not get involved in his business and make sure the girl gets returned to him...right before the son of the Police Commissioner gets rammed in a truck and sent to the hospital and the girl kidnapped back."

Flanagan grit his teeth and stood up. "Why are you here?" His men tensed up but Liam shook his head at them in warning.

Cillian appraised Flanagan with a calm smirk. "I've already spoken to the Council and explained everything to them about your betrayal to our cause, your defection to the mafia and the plan to hand over all our port assets in Boston to Antonio Ferrante once he marries Guinevere O'Malley who has a stake in our holdings here due to her inheritance which you stole from her when you sold her."

Flanagan blustered and stepped away as his men were forced back from the door by several men crashing in with guns held up and swat vests on looking like police doing a raid. Only they all knew it wasn't the police, but it would stop any public witnesses from calling the police.

Cillian watched as Flanagan and his men were forced to lie on the ground and then rose to his feet to stand over them. "As we speak your top lieutenants have all been visited in a similar fashion to you and told the same things...it's over, Sean..."

Flanagan chuckled into the floor before looking up. "Wait until the mafia get news of this, Antonio won't just lie down and take this set back."

"Set back?" Cillian's chuckle was chilling. "Antonio has his hands full back in New York right now, his own businesses are going up in flames." Cillian had Flanagan dragged up to his knees. "Antonio runs the ports in New York, how dare you think to hand over our biggest asset of the ports here in Boston to him as well...what the hell were you getting out of it to risk your life like this? If we didn't kill you the Triads certainly would...you know our agreements with them go back decades."

Flanagan's eyes narrowed suspiciously. "What do you mean, Antonio's businesses are up in flames?"

Cillian smiled and tilted his head as he went back to the bar and sat down, lifting his coffee and taking a sip. As he placed it back down he looked back at Flanagan who was looking sweaty and worried now.

"It seems my son has a personal vendetta with Antonio over this girl now that Antonio kidnapped her back, he has some stupid crazy idea that he's in love with her...so I let him off the leash."

Flanagan paled as Liam stepped in front of him and showed him the news reports on his phone.

"This is the end for Antonio...or my son, whichever one comes out of this dead at the end...we've even spoken to the mafia in the south and west, they agree to stand back as long as we don't actually take over any of the territories destroyed, we'll let them rebuild...the triads are behind our actions and the local gangs will adapt."

Flanagan sighed. "You've done your homework...so when and where?"

Cillian snorted in amusement. He knew that Flanagan meant his execution. "Don't be so quick to die, old friend...you have a lot of paperwork to sort out and put right first."

Matteo hobbled into Antonio's apartment to find him sitting in his armchair, his shoulders slumped forward, his forearms resting on his knees, his eyes closed and his fists clenched.

"Sir." Matteo said quietly.

Antonio's head lifted and he glared at Matteo as Matteo struggled down onto his knees with a grimace of pain from the stitched wound in his leg. He sat up and dropped back into the seat with an amused huff of breath as he looked at Matteo struggling.

"You've heard about what's going on?"

"Yes, sir."

"And I don't even have the bitch to be able to negotiate...thanks to you."

Matteo flinched a bit but looked up at Antonio with a raised eyebrow. "Would you have negotiated?"

Antonio's smirk told his answer. "I'm going to kill the little fucker! He thinks he can come storming in and destroy everything our Family has built and not suffer any consequences, he's gone fucking mad! I can't believe Cillian has allowed this, over a fucking girl! That wasn't even his to begin with..."

Antonio wiped a hand over his face as he laughed insanely.

"Do we retaliate?"

"Yeah, we fucking retaliate...I would say we go after Michael McMillan's son, but he's pulled him out of the hospital and put him in hiding...his police are now centered at every known site of ours so we can't even mobilize..."

"So he's supporting the Irish in this?" Matteo frowned deeply.

Antonio's fingers tapped the arm of the chair. "He rang me, he's pissed about his son getting injured, apparently he needed pins in his ankle and he won't play football anymore..." He cackled. "Like I give a shit! He said the only involvement he will have is to stop any more action from both sides and cover it up, so I can only assume that he has police blocking the Irish sites as well..." Antonio stood up and walked to stare out the large windows down at Manhattan harbor. "Fuck...that little shit. The Irish sure do like to blow things up, luckily the explosives used were clearly just a warning and not too much damage was done, but he's killing a lot of my people..."

He turned and gave Matteo a smirk to see him still kneeling. "Get the fuck up, there's work to do!"

Matteo struggled to his feet, gritting his teeth. "Yes, sir...what first?"

"I had a call from my father...Quinn arrived safe and sound, he sounded most amused...and you know what that means. My head is on the line for this fuck up..."

Matteo drew in a breath before speaking. "Perhaps a meeting with Reese O'Shea would be the best course to stop this rampage of his."

"And then what?" Antonio sneered. "Give him what he asks for? Fuck that...Quinn is mine."

Matteo's brows furrowed deeply, if neither side gave up on the girl this would escalate further. Another man came running in with a phone in his hand.

"Sir, we have a huge problem."

Antonio sucked his teeth and rolled his eyes. "What the fuck now?"

"Cillian O'Shea is in Boston and has executed Sean Flanagan."

Antonio glared at him for a long moment, no one daring to say anything, then he started laughing like an insane person.

63
Quinn in Sicily

Quinn woke to bright sunshine streaming into a strange room as someone pulled the heavy drapes back. She nervously lifted her head to peer at the person, her heart beating frantically as visions of her last few memories flashed in her head. She saw it was an elderly woman with a gentle face and lifted her head slightly.

The woman glanced at Quinn and smiled. "You are awake...how do you feel? How is your head?"

Her accent was thick Italian but her English was good. Quinn held her head as she sat up with a groan. The room spun a bit and made her feel nauseous. "My head feels thick and my body heavy..." Quinn looked at her hand, it felt like it was moving through water.

"It will be like that for a little while, it is the drug they use."

The matter-of-fact way the woman said it made Quinn startle and remember everything about the kidnapping, Antonio, the assault and Matteo in clear detail.

"Where am I?" Quinn asked with a desperation. She tried to get out of bed and realized two things that disturbed her greatly.

One; her clothes had been changed from Matteo's workout gear to a simple white satin chemise and underwear.

Two; her ankle was chained and shackled to the end of the heavy iron bed.

"What is this?!" She panicked, grabbing the chain and yanking desperately at it to try and get it off somehow.

"Stop, you will hurt yourself." The woman berated her. "I will go and tell the master of the house that you are awake and get you something to eat and drink, you must be thirsty. Please, for your own sake, keep quiet."

Quinn swallowed hard as tears rolled down her cheeks. "Please, tell me where I am."

The old lady gave a small emotionless smile like she was used to tending to girls chained to beds pleading at her. "Welcome to Sicily."

Quinn gaped at her as she left the room.

Sicily?

As in Italy?!

How could she be in a different country...a different continent?

She didn't even have a passport!

Did this mean she was smuggled here, trapped here?

Why would Antonio do this? Wait, it wasn't Antonio...Matteo had sent her here.

The door opened and Quinn startled to see Augusto walk in with a grim expression. He looked well, relaxed, wearing a patterned silk shirt and leisurely slacks. The smile he gave her was languid and almost serene. "Quinn...I can't say I'm happy to see you."

"What am I doing here? Let me go, you can't keep me here!"

"Well, I can and I will." He stated with no emotion. "Antonio is clearly needing time to calm down and not kill you, so I had you flown here in a private plane while unconscious to save you from him. You are probably aware that Matteo contacted me. Antonio was about to send you to his BDSM club and have you gang raped apparently, so you have Matteo to thank for saving your life."

Quinn covered her mouth thinking she was going to throw up at the memories of all those men in that dirty abandoned house stripping her naked, their hands all over her.

Quinn wiped the tears from her face. "Why?" She breathed out timidly.

"In his eyes you're soiled now, he doesn't want you but like I told you, you're part of an alliance agreement and I will not allow you to ruin it."

"I can't be with Antonio, I can't marry him! He doesn't love me, he hates me. He hurts me!" Quinn screamed in distress.

Augusto hardly even blinked. "That may be out of the question now, but let me explain something to you that has been in the works for seven years. I have been planning and negotiating the takeover of Sean Flanagan's mob territories since the first day I met your mother and found my way in to infiltrate their ranks and find a weakness. I found it in Flanagan...and his hatred and jealousy for your father, who I also hated for his abuse of Maria."

Quinn didn't care, she just wanted to go home. How was anyone going to find her if she was thousands of miles away and across an ocean!?

"I'm sure you also know your mother was the daughter of Will O'Rourke, your father only married her to take over the Boston territories before O'Rourke mysteriously died of food poisoning. Your father was a cruel husband and when I found her she had already left him and was in hiding looking for a savior."

Augusto stepped forward making Quinn look up at him wary. "She came to me, Quinn...or should I say Guinevere...she held the key to everything and right now you do the same."

"I don't care! You can't do this to me!"

"You will stay here until Antonio calms down...he just needs time to realize it doesn't matter if you've slept with other people what matters is getting Boston in every which way, legally and illegally."

"Every which way, legally...how?"

"As you know Antonio is breaking into politics with the intention of becoming mayor...but it's not going to be of New York."

"Boston?" Quinn breathed, it all made sense now.

Augusto smiled like he was pleased she got it. "Yes of Boston but the larger goal is becoming governor of Massachusetts...and with our territories and the mobs hold on the port we'll have a fist hold over both sides of the fence...all of it."

"So he's moving to Boston?"

"Indeed he is and setting his sights on the election next year, he has a lot of legwork and net-working to do, he's going to be busy and stressed...he's going to need his little pet to keep him calm and focused."

The smile he gave Quinn made her feel sick again as she felt bile rise in her throat.

"His little pet? What if I refuse? I'm not here as some stress relief toy!"

"That's exactly what you are, if he takes you back. If he doesn't then you'll be impregnated artificially and the mob will listen to Flanagan about Antonio merging the families and that your inheritance transfers to your husband."

Quinn frowned. "My inheritance?"

Augusto smirked. "Ah, you don't know that much I see...oh well it will all make sense once it happens..."

"I hate him! And I hate you!" Quinn screamed at him.

Augusto looked at her with no remorse. "This is business, little girl. You will do what I want and have Antonio's baby or I will put you in a coma to have one and then Antonio can put a bullet in your head and a lot more people will die bloody...your choice."

Quinn stared at him mortified.

The old lady came back in with a tray of food and water. Augusto gave her a solemn glance. "This is Margareta, make sure you treat her with respect. If you are able to prove you can behave I will allow you to walk around the grounds, they are well guarded, forget escape."

A man in a suit came to the open door puffing and panting. "Don, we just got word from New York, I think you better come..."

Augusto glared at the man who glanced in the room and stared wide eyed at the red haired beauty for a second, she looked disheveled, roughed up and sexy as hell.

"What's the problem exactly?" Augusto growled, turning to the door.

"The mob...they've bombed the shipping yards and..."

Augusto cut the man off with a slice of his hand as he glanced fiercely at Quinn who was staring at them in shock. He stormed from the room and slammed the door shut.

Quinn looked up at the old lady as she put the tray down, then looked out the window with a little smirk of her own. Reese was fighting back, was he fighting to find her?

64

Confrontation, Murder and Settlement

Reese was just getting out of his car with Tank and Bulletproof in the carpark of his condo when a Bentley raced up behind his car and blocked him in. He stood up, looking over at the Bentley knowing exactly who it was.

"Stay here." He said to Bulletproof and Tank, putting his hands in his jacket pockets and leaning on the back of his car, staring at the back of the Bentley as the driver got out and opened the door.

Matteo got out of the passenger side quickly coming around as Antonio barreled out of the back storming up to Reese and getting in his face as Matteo tried to hold him back.

"You fucking little shit, what the hell do you think you're doing? We've had years of peace that you've managed to ruin in a matter of days! Who is going to compensate me for business losses! And now your father has executed Sean Flanagan? Have you Irish dogs all gone rabid?"

Reese sucked his teeth at the verbal onslaught, side eyeing Bulletproof to stand down as he tensed up at Antonio Ferrante being right in front of him.

"I seem to remember you played the first hand in this..."

Antonio sneered a cruel laugh. "That little bitch is mine, I only took back what you refused to give up."

Reese stood up off the car bumper. "You put my friend in the hospital! And fuck knows what sort of state Quinn is in."

Antonio smirked. "She's perfectly fine...not what I had planned for her after her betrayal, but here we are..." He shrugged nonchalantly as Matteo managed to look a little guilty.

Reese frowned at that. "Betrayal? Don't make me laugh...you really think she should have just lived under your abuse?"

Antonio licked his lips, his eyes shining. "Were you fucking her, or was it that other little boy, the cop's son?"

Reese grinned teasingly. "Does it matter, really? She doesn't want you, that's all that's really important for you to get through your thick head."

"No reason to start a fucking war and blow up half my business assets, you little fucker."

"Your business is over from what I hear...Boston is done, so go crawl under a rock and hide from the ones who will take it out on you, like your father." Reese's smirk was cruel.

Antonio seethed, clenching his fists, then let out a little bleak laugh. "Where ever I go to hide, Quinn comes with me."

"Why hold on to someone who is useless to your plans now?" Reese spat bitterly. "Let her go."

Antonio grinned in triumph. "You think you love her, is that it?" He raked a hand through his hair, chuckling madly. "I have one way for things to be put right..."

Reese's brows furrowed in suspicion. "I guessed you had some sort of proposal for me to turn up here like this with no back up...what do you want?"

"How about we fight for her?"

"Are you fucking serious?" Reese had to laugh at the absurdity of it. "Yeah, I'm dying to beat the shit out of you, break a few bones."

"Boss..." Matteo warned but was silenced by a finger held up by Antonio.

"I was clearly thinking more of a duel, like the old days...meeting at noon, with only a second as witness..." Antonio grinned.

"Guns? Of course you would resort to guns, you coward." Reese scoffed.

"No, no, hear me out...let's meet half way, clearly guns is too easy and I'm never going to bare knuckle fight with you..."

Reese frowned. "So what's half way?"

"How about a nasty little knife fight...just you and me and nowhere to hide."

"Boss..." Matteo interrupted again.

"Shut it, Matteo!"

Reese sucked his teeth, his mouth twisting and contorting as he thought it over. "Alright, when?"

"Ah, Rice...?" Tank asked nervously.

"No, this is good, it will settle everything...yes?" He looked at Antonio. "You'll sign an agreement stating the winner takes all with no repercussions?"

"Sure..." Antonio smirked. "There is one other condition I would like added though."

Reese knew it and rolled his eyes. "What?"

"This isn't a sport anymore, kid, this won't be first blood rules or anything like that...I mean to kill you...in order to restore my pride."

Reese hissed through his gritted teeth as Tank stepped forward to protest to him. "You can't agree to this, Rice, your father would never..."

"Quiet, you think I don't know what people would say?" He clucked his tongue and lifted his eyes back to Antonio who was waiting with a cocky smirk on his face, leaning back casually on one leg, so confident.

"Alright, I agree...you try to kill me in a knife fight, mother fucker and we'll see who ends up bleeding out on the concrete!"

Antonio laughed. "Good, let's go then."

"Wait! Now?"

"I don't like this." Tank said, grabbing Reese's arm and pulling him back.

"Choose a second and let's go somewhere private...I'm sure we can write up something on a piece of scrap paper somewhere...as long as it has our signatures and witnesses its legal and binding enough." Antonio was so smug as he turned away.

"I want to see her first." Reese stated coolly.

Antonio paused in his steps and looked back. The look on Matteo's face was cautious and worried. "I can't let you see her, I'm afraid...she's being held in a secret location out of state." It wasn't a lie.

Reese's eyes narrowed suspiciously. "Ever heard of a video call, asshole."

Antonio's mouth twisted. "Thanks to the accident she doesn't have a phone."

"Are you keeping her prisoner or something? If you've hurt her!" Reese stepped forward but Tank clamped a hand around his arm.

Antonio rolled his eyes. "Follow us, I'll make sure to get you at least a photo to prove she's alive and well..."

Antonio sauntered back to his car and got in the back as Matteo got in the driver's seat leaving Danny stranded. He watched as Reese went to get in his car with the really large guy wearing a bulletproof vest that had stood silent and calm, his eyes just watching intently. Antonio rolled his lips and licked them in thought.

"Watch that guy that is coming with Reese O'Shea." He said to Matteo.

"Yeah, I noticed him...he looks like he's special ops trained. He's definitely packing."

Reese approached Jacob and leaned into him close. "Give me your knife." He whispered to him.

Jacob gave him a bewildered look. "Are you sure?"

"Give it...that way I'll have two, get it?" Reese smirked and Jacob took his knife sheath off the back of his belt and handed it to him.

Reese gripped the large hunting knife in his fist and glanced at Tank. "I'm taking Bronty..." He smirked at using Bulletproof's name as Bulletproof rolled his eyes but immediately got in the car.

Tank grabbed his phone as he watched Reese drive away. "This is bad..." He muttered as he turned to look at Jacob and Mac watching from the gate. "This is really bad."

"Who are you calling?" Jacob asked.

"I have Mr O'Shea's number..."

Jacob and Mac stared at him a little in awe. "You have the big boss's direct number?" Jacob asked.

Tank rolled his eyes. "Before that special ops guy came along to be his bodyguard, I was Reese's bodyguard..."

"Right, yeah...of course, no offense buddy." Jacob looked away awkwardly. "But what is he going to be able to do to stop this, he's in Boston."

"I know, but I think he should at least be told what Reese is agreeing to...."

Bulletproof looked at Reese as he drove out of the lot and followed along behind Antonio's car.

"Do you think you can win?" He asked simply.

Reese sucked his teeth. "I'm way better at knives than what that bastard thinks I am..."

"If you lose?"

"Start shooting and get me to a fucking hospital."

Bulletproof chuckled. "You're a fucking legend."

Reese glanced at the guy a little surprised then grinned. "Yeah...I'm going down in history one way or another..."

65
A fight to end all fights

Antonio drove them to an old disused warehouse that he owned the land of and sometimes used the warehouse to store pallets of goods he would rather authorities didn't see. He stepped out of the back of the car with an air of confidence as Matteo went into the trunk and pulled out a briefcase, he placed it down on the bonnet of the car and opened it up, pulling out a document and placing it next to the briefcase.

Reese got out of his car and looked at Matteo and Antonio dubiously.

"You already have a contract?"

"No, that is a standard NDA contract, we can write on the back of it." Matteo explained.

"Huh..." Reese snorted. "Alright then...conditions."

"Winner gets the girl...it's his responsibility to go and pick her up." Antonio sneered.

Matteo gave him a raised eyebrow, smirking while he wrote it down.

Reese clucked his tongue, not getting the amusement. "I still want that photo..."

"Sure, here it is..." He lifted his phone and showed Reese a photo of Quinn sitting on a bed in a room flooded with lovely sunshine. He squinted at it trying to work out where it would be. Antonio showed him the time stamp on the image and then threw his phone in through the car window onto the back seat.

"No phones from here on...this is between the four of us."

Reese consented and handed his phone back to Bulletproof who put both their phones back in Reese's car. Reese took his jacket off, checking his knife was in his back pocket and walked back over. Matteo noticed the large hunting knife strapped to the back of Reese's belt.

"You planning on fighting with that?"

Antonio looked over and snorted derisively. "Yeah, problem?" Reese asked.

"No problem...is it a Bowie?"

"Yeah, I think so...so I can even light a fire and burn your body after." Reese smirked, knowing there was a flint inside the handle.

Matteo couldn't help but chuckle. Antonio clucked his tongue. "Get on with this."

Matteo wrote a few sentences then looked up. "Any other conditions?"

"No recourse from any other parties on the outcome of this...no punishment or recompense can be sort from the losing sides 'family.'" Antonio added.

"For anything leading up to this either...this is to sort everything out from the last few days." Reese also added.

"Fine..." Antonio agreed and Matteo wrote it down.

When Matteo was finished he slowly pulled a pair of handcuffs from his pocket and placed them down on the paper with the pen. "Time to sign."

Reese looked at the handcuffs with a slight frown. "What the hell are those for?"

"Read the agreement..." Antonio grinned as he stepped over and signed it without even reading it.

Reese sucked his teeth as he stepped closer and leaned over to read. "Fuck, your handwriting is terrible..." He commented as he grimaced reading the conditions. "No one said anything to me about being handcuffed to each other?"

"I said no escape..." Antonio sneered. "This fight ends when one of us stands attached to a dead body."

Reese glanced at Bulletproof who was boring holes in the side of his head with his angst against this happening. He gave the guy a little sideways smirk then signed the paper.

Antonio chuckled. "Now your witness..."

Bulletproof sighed and stepped over to sign, shaking his head.

"Alright, let's get this party started." Antonio announced, stripping his suit jacket off and rolling up his shirt sleeves, taking off his watch and taking out his flick knife that had a cruel six inch blade on it. He held his left wrist out and Matteo clicked the handcuff around it.

Reese glared at him for a moment as Antonio merely settled a cold stare at him, daring him to step forward and get handcuffed together. Reese let out a hefty sigh and removed his watch then stepped up facing Antonio, his left hand aligned next to Antonio's left hand, picked up the cuff and snapped it shut around his own left wrist. It meant they had to face away from each other.

Antonio chuckled and Reese huffed. "Yeah, no way I'm letting you handcuff my right hand asshole, you think I'm stupid?"

"I think you're dead." Antonio lifted his right hand in a flash, slashing out to try and get Reese's face. Reese moved quick, stepping around to come into Antonio's back, pulling the large hunting knife from its sheath and going to the kidney's but Antonio managed to swivel away and yank Reese forward making him stumble and the handcuff to tighten on his wrist.

Antonio laughed. "You quick little fucker, but are you quick enough..." He stepped back in with another slashing attempt this time aimed for Reese's chest. He managed to lean back to avoid it but it snagged his t-shirt, ripping a large gash in it.

Reese wiped the back of his hand over his mouth. "Fuck, this was my favorite shirt..."

Antonio hissed as he stabbed in towards Reese's stomach. Reese slashed out with his own knife catching Antonio's hand and cutting across the top of it as he jerked it back.

"Wow, so you're really trying to kill me, huh?" Reese laughed as he yanked their hands up into the air and stepped behind Antonio like he was dancing with him and stabbed into the back of Antonio's thigh.

A ripping growl of pain came from Antonio's throat as he tried to suppress it, his leg folding on him but he was still being held up by Reese's arm being held in the air. Reese grinned like the devil as Antonio looked back at him, his eyes cold.

Matteo took a step forward but Bulletproof pulled his gun and pointed it at him. "No you don't." He stated calmly.

Matteo glared at Bulletproof but stood down, folding his arms. "We could stop this."

"Why would I do that?" Bulletproof said like he was genuinely confused by the statement.

Matteo clucked his tongue. "You know you die if your ward dies..."

Bulletproof shrugged looking at the two combatants. "Reese said to me he will win, that's good enough for me."

Matteo's teeth grit together as he looked back at the two fighting just as they fell to the ground. Antonio had yanked his hand down curling in on Reese, back to chest and lifting him up and over to crash on his back, but the fact they were connected made Antonio overbalance and crash down with him, landing heavily on Reese's already injured ribs. They had both lost their knives in the fall, scattered away to the left and right.

"Fuck!" Reese grit out, trying to push Antonio off him.

Antonio saw the pain flit across Reese's face and punched him in the ribs again making Reese almost black out.

"You fucker!" He hissed.

Antonio stretched out away from Reese trying to reach his knife to end this while Reese was down. Reese rolled to his side away from where Antonio wanted to go, hauling him back. Antonio glared back at him and lunged at him, kneeing him in the ribs once more making Reese see stars.

Antonio laughed. "You agreed to a fight when you're already injured?"

Antonio gained his knees and crawled, dragging Reese by his cuffed hand, to reach the knife still lying a yard away out of reach.

Reese relaxed, letting him try and drag dead weight while he reached around into his back pocket and drew his butterfly knife. He lifted it as he feigned trying to get up, dancing it around his hand to open it and clenched it in his fist. He yanked Antonio's hand back.

Antonio growled in frustration, turning back to deal with Reese once more, lunging over him to punch him in the face this time. He froze as his eyes met Reese's and he felt the biting pain of a knife sliding into his side, angled up and underneath his ribs. Reese grinned up at him as Antonio put his hands around Reese's throat and put his whole weight behind trying to throttle him. Reese just laughed, a strange maniacal sound as it hissed from his mouth while he twisted the blade and shoved it deeper.

Antonio's body convulsed and blood dripped out of his mouth. He hands lost strength and Reese was able to roll them over. He straddled Antonio, pulling the knife free as Antonio coughed, striving for breath, bubbly foam and blood coming out of his mouth and spraying Reese in the face.

Matteo went to rush over to stop the fight but Bulletproof grabbed him and took him to the ground, pinning his arms behind his back. Matteo cried out to Antonio, his boss and friend, as he watched Reese lift the knife and ram it into Antonio's chest.

"Die you mother fucker!" Reese hissed out through clenched teeth as he put his weight on the knife and drove it deeper.

Antonio's body convulsed again, blood spraying up from his mouth before it all stopped and his eyes stared unseeing at the roof and his hands fell lifeless to his sides.

"No!" Matteo fought against Bulletproof in his despair as Reese collapsed down on his back next to the body and breathed heavily to get his breath back, not wanting to move and cause extra pain from his ribs.

Bulletproof took Matteo's gun from him and took the key making his way over to Reese. He knelt in front of him and uncuffed him from Antonio's dead body, seeing that Reese's hands were shaking slightly.

He looked down at Reese's eyes and saw him watching him. Bulletproof placed a hand on his shoulder. "You did well, Boss. Can you move?"

Reese dropped his head to the side and looked at Matteo who was just kneeling in silent shock. "Where is she?" He asked loudly causing a coughing fit and grimace of pain.

Reese held his hand out to Bulletproof and he helped Reese to his feet as he grabbed his ribs tight and hissed in pain. He hobbled over to Matteo and glared at him with that intense golden gaze.

"Where is she?"

Matteo looked up and just glared at him.

"Bronty, shoot him if he won't answer."

"If he's dead he can't answer..."

"Did I say shoot him dead?" Reese spat, looking at Matteo like he was dirt on his shoe.

Matteo chuckled, shaking his head. "You bosses are all the same...unfortunately knowing where she is won't help you...you see, Antonio gets the last laugh because she isn't being held by him..."

Reese crouched down and grabbed the front of Matteo's shirt getting in his face. "Where the fuck is she, asshole!"

Matteo looked up into Reese's menacing glare and smirked. "She's with Augusto in Sicily."

Reese dropped Matteo's shirt and stood up, staggering back a step at the news. "What the fuck?"

Matteo gained his feet, straightening his jacket. "Yeah, so good luck with getting her back..." He took out the piece of paper with the signed agreement on it and dropped it at Reese's feet. "Here, you'll be needing this to prove you had a contract to kill Antonio with no repercussions...you'll need that in the coming days."

Matteo walked past him and up to Antonio's body, getting his phone out and calling someone.

Reese picked up the paper, his jaw clenching tight in bitterness and stumbled to his car. He opened the door and sat down heavily on the passenger seat.

His phone chirped and he grabbed it off the driver's seat to see a strange number messaged him an address. He looked up over to Matteo.

"Give it at least a week of mourning...Antonio's body will be sent back to the home country...that is the address where Quinn is in Sicily." Matteo informed him.

Reese sucked his teeth and turned into the seat properly with a grimace of pain and closed the door. Bulletproof came around and got in the driver's seat.

"Get me to Doc Xavier..."

"Alright, boss."

As Reese's car left Matteo heaved a mournful sigh and looked down at Antonio's body. "You stupid reckless fuck, I knew one day you would meet your match."

He dialed Augusto to tell him the news. He really hoped Augusto didn't take this out on Quinn or him, but he had just lost his only son.

That night Reese walked up the front steps of a nice house in the Hamptons, as he approached the door it opened to reveal Cory standing there, his lower leg in a cast with a hospital moonboot over it.

"Reese! What the fuck, man!?"

Reese enveloped him in a huge embrace, dropping his face into the side of Cory's neck and breathing in deeply. Cory reached around him and embraced him too, clinging on to fistfuls of Reese's jacket. That made Reese gasp in pain and Cory dropped his arms, retreating a step as he gripped Reese's shoulders and looked into his eyes.

"What the fuck have you done to yourself? You better come in."

Cory helped Reese into the main living area and down onto the couch. He looked up as Michael walked in looking not very pleased.

Reese looked up through his hair at the Police Commissioner and smirked as Cory sat beside him and grabbed his hand. Cory looked up with a grimace at his father.

"Not right now, Dad!"

Michael's jaw clenched for a moment then he closed his eyes and sighed, turning away and walking off to leave the two lovebirds alone.

"Wait." Reese called out to him.

He turned and glared back at Reese. "If you're after a favor, I think I'm done."

Reese nodded, he knew he owed Michael a lot for covering up what he had done as accidental gas explosions, petty gang street thugs and extremist oil protesters where the shooting of Zortex Head Office was concerned. "I need advice."

"Advice would have been invaluable before you went on a damn rampage, kid!" Michael growled but came to stand in front of him. "What the hell do you need advice for?"

"Augusto Ferrante...how best to deal with him?"

"Deal with him? Are you planning on killing him too?"

Reese sucked his teeth. "How do you know about that already?"

Cory looked perplexed. "What? What are you saying...Reese?"

"Reese killed Antonio this afternoon...Matteo has been in touch about getting his body taken back to Italy without any paperwork as soon as possible."

"Huh..." Reese nodded.

"You killed Antonio!" Cory breathed, stunned. He put his arms around Reese's neck and as Reese turned to look at him Cory planted his lips over Reese's. "Fuck I love you!"

Reese chuckled and patted Cory's cheek. "You're adorable, retriever...but you're killing me here..." He grimaced in pain.

"Oh, sorry..." Cory let him go with a look of concern.

"Get to the advice, but I'm not helping you to kill any more people." Michael gritted out.

"Nah, nothing like that...I need to know how to approach him after all that's happened."

"You plan to go to Sicily, why?" Michael folded his arms seriously.

"He has Quinn."

Cory jumped in shock. "What the hell? How the fuck are we meant to get her back from there?"

Reese pulled a piece of paper out of his jacket and held it up to Michael. "I have this signed by Antonio, it clears me of any repercussions and states I won Quinn fair and square...the idea was all his."

Michael took the paper and read the scrawling writing. He wiped a hand over his brow. "Shit...well, best as I can help is to tell you to just go to him face to face...no appointment, no talking first...I can give you the address since I helped organize Antonio's body...you're best to wait a few days after the funeral...do you have a passport?"

"Yeah...and I know the address already."

"I'm coming too!" Cory announced.

"No." Reese and Michael both growled.

Cory clucked his tongue. "Neither of you get to say that to me...this is about Quinn and I'm going to go and get her back!"

Quinn was looking out her prison window at all the people milling around out on the back lawn of Augusto's villa, they were all dressed in black and appeared somber.

It was obviously a funeral, but who's? She hadn't seen or heard from Augusto in days.

She squinted as she thought she saw a familiar face.

She did, Matteo!

She pulled the wispy curtain back from the window and banged on it, knowing Margareta had told her to not be seen by anyone today and that she was confined to her room...hell she had actually been chained in her room by Augusto's instruction just to make sure she behaved. She could still reach the window though and as she banged on it several heads turned to look up.

She was aware of her undressed state, only allowed underwear, a couple of white satin chemise and a white satin robe to match. Augusto refused to allow her clothes knowing it meant she would stay within the compound walls and keep away from the men guarding them. He was cruel and mocking of her, allowing her out to walk the grounds and get some sunshine every day, and it made her skin crawl the way the guards eyes followed her around everywhere.

She heard a few people comment. "Is that her?" "That's the one!" "She's here?" While she waved out at Matteo and flicked her fingers asking him to come and see her.

Matteo's face fell into a dark scowl and he stormed from the patio.

Quinn turned from the window to wait for his inevitable arrival.

She heard a commotion in the hall and then the door was unlocked and opened by the old lady, she stood to one side as Matteo strode in looking displeased.

"Quinn, what the hell are you doing? You were told to stay quiet!"

"Matteo! What's going on, why are you here..." She felt a sinking feeling in her stomach that if he was here for a funeral then...

His jaw clenched tight as he sighed out, looking at the floor for a moment before looking back up at her to see her apprehensive and fidgeting her hands.

"I'm sure you can guess why I'm here, why all these people are here, Quinn...it's fairly obvious when you think about it...Antonio is dead."

"D-dead?" She dropped to the floor as her legs gave way underneath her in shock. "H-how?"

Matteo grimaced, putting his hands in his pockets. "He fought with Reese O'Shea and came out second best."

Quinn looked up at him with a wide eyed look of complete disbelief. Matteo clucked his tongue and glared at her like it was all her fault. "So going to the window was a stupid thing to do today of all days, Quinn! There are a hundred people down there that would gladly drag you out of here by your fucking hair and put a bullet in the back of your head."

Quinn started trembling and Matteo sighed bitterly, trying to calm down.

"W-what's going to happen to me?" She looked back up at him with tears of fear and grief running down her face.

Matteo gave her a serious stern look. "I really don't know, Quinn, I'm sorry..."

66

A trip into enemy territory

Ten days later Reese and Cory got out of the Fiat taxi in front of the gates of a villa a mile from the main city of Palermo. They had arrived in Italy the day before catching a boat across that morning and now they stood before the house of the man that had Quinn, Don Augusto Ferrante.

The fact that there were several armed guards standing on the other side of the gates told them their visit had already been informed to Augusto. It had been obvious when they told the taxi driver the address it was well known and the taxi driver had spoken to his comrades at the ferry terminal park in Italian, they had all bristled and shouted at them. Reese had pulled a wallet full of cash and told the driver he could have it all. One had made a phone call as the driver herded them into his car laughing and nodding. He probably thought to just drop them off to their deaths and go about his day.

Reese looked through the wrought iron gate at the guards and sucked his teeth. He was still in no shape to fight, and Cory was still hobbling around on one leg. He walked up and fell to his knees, holding his hands up behind his head.

"What the hell are you doing?" Cory hissed under his breath.

"Do it...they'll demand it of us anyway...we're in enemy territory so let's just play the game, it's like your Dad said, just turning up unannounced will peak Augusto's curiosity...hopefully."

"Hopefully?" Cory hissed.

"You insisted on coming..."

"I could hardly let you come alone!"

The guards were talking among themselves and one was talking through a radio, they opened the gate and surrounded them, tying their hands behind their backs and hauling them to their feet before doing a thorough pat down search of them both, removing their wallets, ID, phones and the paper contract Reese had brought with him then making them walk in front as they prodded rifle barrels into their backs up to the beautiful Italian villa.

They were led into a room that was intricately tiled on the floor with a mosaic pattern in terracotta, white and black. The walls were lined with books and behind the huge desk sat Augusto. Large white French doors were standing open letting in a gentle breeze. Reese could see they led out to a patio that stepped down to an immaculate lawn with a couple of orange trees before sweeping off down a gentle slope to a private white sand beach with glorious crystal clear water.

They were forced to their knees in front of the desk as Augusto glared at them. The guy who took their stuff placed the paper down on the desk with their passports, phones and wallets. Antonio took a moment in silence to read the agreement written by Matteo and signed by them all before dropping it with a sigh and looking up at Reese.

"You have a real nerve coming here, boy...and bringing the Police Commissioner's son?"

"Please, Don...you know why we are here, to plead for Quinn's release. Now that Antonio and Sean Flanagan are gone and your plan to take over Boston has been revealed and quashed you have no reason to keep her here."

Augusto clucked his tongue. "You're lucky I don't just shoot you right here! You're the murderer of my only son, do you really expect me to give you clemency to request anything of me because of some stupid scrawled agreement." He picked up the paper and tossed it over the desk.

Reese's gaze was boring into Augusto's skull. One of his men saw it and cuffed him around the head with the butt of his pistol. "Eyes down, boy!"

Reese turned to glare at him, licking his tongue over his teeth. "You're all tough with a gun in your hand."

"Quiet!" Augusto ordered, rising to his feet. He walked around the desk and to the open doors to the patio. He stood looking out, deliberately turning his back to the room and one of his men opened a cigarette case offering it to him. He took one and the same man lit it for him.

Reese glanced at Cory to make sure he was okay and saw his fists were clenched tight. "Relax..." Reese whispered to him. If they were going to be killed Augusto would have done it by now, he wasn't one to fuck around.

Cory glanced up and Reese saw the emotional worry in his eyes. Reese's jaw clenched tight. "Don Ferrante..." Reese called in a clear voice.

Augusto blew some smoke out and inclined his head slightly for Reese to continue.

"Do with me what you will but let Quinn go back with Cory...she did nothing wrong but fell in love with someone that wasn't your son."

Augusto took another slow drag of his cigarette obviously listening but not reacting.

"You fell in love...regardless of your first intentions regarding Quinn's mother, but Patrick O'Malley couldn't give her up and made rash dangerous decisions that resulted in his death...unfortunately events seem to have repeated themselves. Would you have blamed Maria back then?"

Augusto chuckled deeply, flicking his cigarette away and turned back to give Reese an appraising scrutiny. "Are you suggesting all this is somehow my fault?" He looked around at his men, laughing. "The balls on this kid!"

Reese glowered at the mocking laughter around him. "No, sir, I'm not saying that..."

"But you're saying my son deserved his death at your hands." Augusto's voice had cracked with raw emotion. He wiped a hand down his face and looked away. He sighed after a long pause. "Perhaps all this is my fault..." He muttered to himself. "Do you know why I chose Boston instead of New York?" He turned back and levelled his gaze at Reese.

Reese frowned. "No, sir."

"Because of you O'Shea's...your father is ballsy, strong, fearless and his men are steadfastly loyal to him...I couldn't find a weakness to penetrate."

Reese looked a little surprised to hear the compliment of his father.

"And you..." Augusto chuckled. "You're just like him, but smarter more devious."

"Thank you, sir."

Augusto looked up at his men, with a strange smile. "He takes it as a compliment."

They all chuckled mockingly making Reese's jaw tick with anger.

"So what to do with you? You offer yourself as apology for killing my son?"

"No. I make no apology for killing your son, he was a psychopath on a road to destruction, he was never going to get far on the path you chose for him he was far too reckless. I'm willing to do whatever I have to, to get you to agree to send Quinn home with the man that she loves, Cory McMillan."

Cory looked at Reese, startled, then looked up at Augusto's intense glare. "I'm not leaving here without Reese!"

"Shut up, moron!" Reese hissed.

"No! Reese, you can't do this...I won't let you sacrifice yourself to these men for me and Quinn wouldn't let you either! You're the moron for even saying that shit!"

Augusto chuckled sinisterly as he watched them bicker.

Cory looked back at him as Reese growled. "Shut up, Cory!"

"I won't let anything happen to Reese or Quinn. You have no right to hold her here against her will! And you can't do anything to us so stop with the stupid gangster fucking shit! My father knows we came here and he will notify the authorities here if I don't call him tonight and tell him everything is fine!"

Reese grit his teeth. "What the fuck did you do?"

"I secured your life...I knew you would try this shit! I won't let you die."

Augusto was stunned, the police boy was ferocious. "Just who is in love with who here?" He asked amused.

"I love him and I love Quinn...I want them both to go home with me to New York!" Cory confessed.

Augusto's mouth twisted a little in victory as he saw Reese's face drop and he let out a surrendering sigh. "You idiot..." Reese breathed to Cory.

"Reese, come over here." Augusto ordered as he turned to look out the patio doors once more.

Reese frowned, glancing at Cory as he stood up and stepped over to the doors. One of the guards cut his hands free and he glanced sideways at Augusto with a frown.

"Hold the other one still." Augusto said and his men grabbed Cory by the arms, hauling him to his feet and stuffed his mouth with a cloth as he tried to yell out.

Reese stiffened, turning back to Cory but Augusto pointed out over the lawn at something, grabbing Reese's arm and pushing him out.

Reese looked up, blinking as he saw the sight he feared never to see again.

Quinn was sitting on a garden seat under a pergola, guarded by four armed men. She had seen Augusto standing in the doorway smoking and something told her that something was going on. She had been led out here in her white chemise and matching robe – still the only clothing she had been allowed to wear for two weeks, not including underwear - and told to sit quietly and wait.

Wait for what?

She looked up at a commotion over at Augusto's study and saw Reese stumble out the door and lift his head to look in her direction. She stood up in surprise. "Reese?" She breathed.

One of the men guarding her growled. "Go!"

She blinked up at him thinking he was ordering her back to her room but he was pointing towards Reese. She was scared it was a trap and not Reese at all.

"Quinn!" His voice rang out and she wailed as she was running.

He went to run towards her but Augusto clamped a hand on his shoulder preventing him. He watched her fly towards him, her red hair flying out behind her, wearing that short white chemise and a robe of the same fabric and color, showing her bare thighs and clinging to her breasts. He grit his teeth at what she was made to wear around all these armed men.

As she reached him she crashed into him with full force, her arms clutching around him tightly, her body trembling as she sobbed.

"Reese! It is you...oh my god! I missed you so much, are you here to take me home? Please tell me you're taking me home?" She lifted her head as he held her tight to his chest and kissed her head gently. He looked down into her tear filled green eyes and gave her a small smile. He wiped her face of hair and tears.

"Hey, babe..."

He looked up as Augusto chuckled and clucked his tongue at the snide sound.

"I wonder who it is she really loves?" Augusto said sarcastically.

Reese grimaced as Quinn looked up at them confused. He turned his body so he was side on to the doors and grabbed Quinn's head, turning it to look into the room beyond.

"Cory!" Reese growled. Cory was struggling like a demon against the men holding him back.

Quinn gasped. "Cory? Oh my god!" She ran into the room as the men let him go with a wave from Augusto.

He spat the cloth out as one guard cut his hands free and he opened his arms to catch Quinn as she darted into them.

"Bunny! Thank god!" He embraced her in a smothering embrace as Reese looked back at Augusto, stripping his jacket off.

"I don't know? Who do you think she loves?" Reese walked back inside and up to behind Quinn, covering her with his jacket and then turned back to Augusto standing in front of Cory and Quinn as they cuddled and kissed each other and then looked on apprehensively. The tension was thick in the air between Augusto and Reese as they stared at each other.

Augusto laughed as he wandered back in and sat down. "Well, I have to say I'm shocked. What a fascinating display. So she fucks both of you?"

Reese rolled his eyes, breathing to keep calm and raised a hand back to silence Cory as he heard him take a breath about to snap back.

"What's your decision, Don?" Reese asked coldly.

Quinn looked up at Cory in confusion. "What's happening?" She whispered.

Cory's mouth twisted as his arms tightened around her protectively. "Reese is trying to swap himself for you and let us return to America."

"No!" Quinn wailed in protest.

Reese hissed in annoyed disapproval as he glanced back at Cory with a feral glare. Augusto sighed, collapsing back in his chair and wiped a hand over his face. He dropped his hand to the desk and tapped his fingers as he gave Reese a measured look.

He lifted his other hand, clicking his fingers. "Get Mr O'Shea a chair and someone pour us both a drink."

Reese frowned at the civilized turn in proceedings, this was how he should have been treated in the first place, but now it seemed a little condescending and suspicious.

One man dropped a chair down in front of Augusto's desk and Reese glanced back at Cory and Quinn to see they were being directed over to a couch at the far wall.

Reese sat down once Cory and Quinn were seated, Quinn clinging to Cory for dear life.

Another man brought over a bottle of Amaro Averna and two glasses, pouring a finger nip into each glass and sliding them over the desk to Augusto and Reese.

"This is a special drink of my fair country, produced right here in Sicily." Augusto said picking his up and swirling the brown liqueur. "Let negotiations begin on a fair playing field." He sculled his back and looked Reese in the eye. Reese picked his drink up and gulped it back, slamming the glass down with a fierce sucking in of breath at the fiery, but sweet alcohol. Augusto chuckled.

"Why the sudden change?" Reese asked, genuinely interested.

Augusto leaned forward, placing his forearms on the desk. "I realize it was my son who challenged you to a street fight...you won fair and square. I cannot bare ill will...I always knew Antonio's mental state...especially after his mother was killed. I had doctor's diagnose him psychopathic. Quinn seemed to temper his fire..."

He saw Reese's jaw lock tight and sighed. "I know it wasn't right but in order for Antonio to succeed in the plans I had made he really did need her by his side."

They heard a little gasp come from Quinn and a hushing soothing cooing from Cory. Reese sat unmoving, just holding Augusto's gaze.

"Quinn is rather useless to you now then." He said when it was clear Augusto wished him to say something in response. "So what do you want? Are you planning on returning to the US to take back control again?"

Augusto smirked as he leaned back into his chair once again, taking comfort from holding all the cards. "No, I have no plans to return to the US, I have a nephew there that will step up to clear things up in Boston...and Matteo Perrelli will control New York, the cartel are happy with that as they mainly dealt with Matteo anyway. As for what I want...the only thing you have that I could possibly want is a slice of your import and export licenses in and out of Boston."

Reese grit his teeth, giving Augusto a cold hard glare.

Augusto gave him a benign smile. "Is acceptance of that above your pay grade? Do you need to phone home to get the permission needed?"

"Not at all." Reese answered coldly. "I just can't help but think that was all you were after all along..."

Augusto shrugged and smirked.

Reese studied the look and clucked his tongue. "If I didn't know better I would think you knew your son would fail this outlandish plan from the start."

Augusto chuckled deeply. "Nothing of the sort, I'm just trying to salvage what I can at this point for the good of the family."

"Very well...I'll organize a ten percent share if you give us the same in New York."

Augusto scoffed. "You're supposed to be paying me off for the girl...and recompense for the damages you caused."

"Okay...if you agree to ten percent, I'll offer you five percent of our arms trade, that's fifty million a year for a five percent share of Zortex Shipping's rights in New York."

Augusto tapped his fingers on the desk, staring at Reese as Reese stared back for a tense few moments before Augusto beamed a toothy smile. "Agreed."

He held his hand out and Reese shook it with a grin.

67
Reunion

As Reese led Quinn and Cory into a hotel room back on mainland Italy in the city of Genoa Quinn wrapped her arms around his waist, burying her face into his back and squeezing him tightly.

He grimaced, grabbing her hands and pulling them apart. "Jesus, take it easy, baby..."

"He's got fractured ribs, bunny..." Cory came up behind her and took her arms, making her step back away from Reese as Reese smiled down at her and pinched her chin.

"I'm sorry, I just...I missed you so much..."

"We both missed you too, babe..." Reese said before turning away and clearing his pockets of his phone, wallet and passport, taking off his jacket and dropping down into the small couch in the room.

Quinn could see they had already been staying here before going over to Sicily as their suitcases were still on the floor by the bureau.

"Come here." Reese called for her, tapping his lap.

Quinn practically ran to him, straddling his lap and hugging her arms around his neck as their mouths collided. He threaded his fingers into her hair and melded his mouth to hers as he dropped back into the couch, resting his head back on the top. She kissed him with a desperate need her hands coming up to grip into his hair as well as she ground down on him.

Cory had given her his sweatshirt to cover up a bit better and she had got some strange looks on the ferry dressed the way she was, but she was well protected now by her boys so didn't care. She felt Cory come up behind her and pull the sweatshirt up. It meant she had to break away from Reese's mouth and when she shook her head free and gazed back down at him she saw him smiling up at her with such a tender look her heart melted.

Cory stripped the satin robe from her and kissed her shoulders, pulling her hair back and running his hands through it. "God I love your hair. Never cut it."

She grinned back at him and as she looked up he leaned forward and kissed her gently. She twisted her torso and reached out a hand to his cheek as he cupped her face and they kissed deeper. Quinn felt Reese's hands stroke up her body to her breasts, pulling the chemise up, his fingers trailing up her stomach to cup her breasts as he watched her and Cory kiss passionately.

As Cory pulled back he grabbed the chemise and pulled that from her body too, then unfastened her bra and Reese helped her discard that before licking and sucking a nipple into his mouth.

Cory dropped to his knees and Reese spread his legs apart, giving Cory access to Quinn's pussy from behind. She gripped Reese's shoulders and let out an illicit moan of need as Cory pulled her panties aside and slipped two fingers inside her.

"Babe, you're really needy..." Reese breathed as he lifted his head, grabbed her by the back of her skull and lashed his tongue back into her mouth, his other hand pinching a nipple hard making her gasp into his mouth. Cory dropped his hands to the back of Quinn's thighs and made her lift her bottom up before pushing his face into her pussy and making a meal of her. She had to move above Reese and he clamped a nipple into his mouth as her breasts came up to his face and she had to lean her forearms on his shoulders.

She groaned at the feeling of Cory's tongue teasing her from clit to ass as Reese lavished her breasts. One of Reese's hands dropped to her pussy and he thrust his fingers in, curling them up to hit the front making her body spasm in need.

"Ah...you're so wet, babe..." He breathed on her neck, lifting up slightly to nip at the soft part above her clavicle. "You think you can take us both right now?"

Cory's fingers invaded her ass right on cue and she trembled as she mewled, her eyes rolling back, unable to form words.

Reese chuckled as he brushed her hair back so he could see her face. "Babe...I need an answer..."

"F-fuck me...hurry..." She managed to huff out.

Cory kissed her hip, grating his teeth over her skin as he groaned. "I'm so fucking hard it hurts..."

Reese pulled his cock out of his jeans and rubbed it over Quinn's entrance, lining it up and then tapped her hip. "Sink down on me, baby."

She dropped down slowly, guided by Reese's hands and moaned out a long breath of pleasure as she did, closing her eyes and biting her lip into her mouth. Reese watched her slowly open her eyes as he brushed her hair back, holding it back with his fingers buried in it. She focused on him looking at her and smiled.

"Good?" He asked amused.

"So good..." She breathed.

"Good girl...relax a bit..." He gathered her hair over one shoulder to the front and plaited it up as best he could to keep it out of the way. She closed her eyes, moving her hips in a slight swaying at what Cory was doing behind her with his fingers.

"She's so fucking wet I can use her own juices as lube..." Cory chuckled as he kissed and licked her back, his fingers thrusting in her ass, twisting and stretching her to take him.

"I never got to clean..." She murmured in a pant.

"Don't worry..." Reese breathed, pulling her forward to kiss him.

"You're wonderfully clean, bunny..." Cory said as he stood up, taking his cock in hand and moving to press his chest to her back.

She felt his cock line up with her hole and she turned her head from Reese to seek out Cory's mouth. He obliged and kissed her as he sunk his hard cock deep into her in one thrust.

Her body jolted as she cried out and Reese grabbed her hips and thrust up into her hard as well making her body tighten immediately and dive straight over into a shattering orgasm.

"Oh, fuck!" Cory grit out as she clamped tight on him.

Reese hissed at the feeling of her pussy convulsing around him and as he kept thrusting he knew it wasn't going to take much for him to come. He slipped a hand through Quinn's legs and cupped Cory's balls, squeezing them and rolling them in his fingers.

"Ah, fucking hell, Reese...what the fuck..." Cory gasped out, grabbing hold of Quinn's hips as his body bucked.

"Come with me!" Reese growled with dominant authority. He looked up at Quinn's face as she gasped through her orgasm, gripping her throat and holding her prone as the two of them fucked hard into her making her insides quiver continually. Her throaty moans through the forced panting of their thrusts turned him on even more and he grit his teeth as he came hard into her.

Cory wasn't far behind and pressed his forehead between Quinn's shoulder blades as he panted after his release, wiping the sweat from his brow onto her skin.

"Fuck..." She finally managed to breathe as the two men finally relaxed in their sated afterglow. Cory slipped out of her and collapsed down onto the couch next to Reese as Reese pulled Quinn to lie on his chest. She nuzzled into his neck and breathed out a contented sigh.

"I love you guys so much." She murmured quietly.

Reese tightened his arms around her as Cory curled into Reese's side and stroked her back. "We love you too, bunny."

"Let's go home..." She said solemnly.

Reese chuckled and stroked her head. "We will, babe...in a couple of days..."

She shot up to sitting, grimacing to feel Reese's cock still quite hard inside her. He grinned like the devil at her reaction as her eyes met his. She almost forgot what she was going to say and shook her head.

"Wait...how am I going to get home, I don't even have a passport."

"Of course you do..." Cory scoffed. "I got my father to get one for you, we brought it with us...you'll be fine."

"We're to go to the US Embassy and check in before our flight, they will make sure we get back to New York...don't worry, babe."

She smiled down on them both and then leaned over giving Cory a kiss on the cheek then gave Reese one before snuggling back in under his chin.

"You guys are the best thing to ever happen to me."

68

Home, safe and sound

Michael and Wendy were waiting at the airport as they got off the plane. Cory went up to his dad and they embraced as Reese and Quinn watched. Wendy came up to Quinn and took her into her arms for a hug.

"We're so glad you're all safe and sound..."

"Let's make sure this is the end of all the drama." Michael said, glancing at Reese.

Reese sucked his teeth and looked away, not giving any promises. He saw a group of men wearing black making their way over. He stiffened as he saw his father in the middle of them.

"Wait here." He said and walked off to meet with him.

"Dad, what are you doing here?" Reese asked.

"I've come to take you home." Cillian's eyes lifted to where Quinn was standing with the McMillan family. "I need to talk to her."

Reese's eyes clouded and narrowed. "Why right now?"

"Reese, just do what I ask for once." Cillian turned away and started walking off. "This is non-negotiable, bring them both..."

Reese grit his teeth, seething then let out a sigh of resignation and walked back to Cory and Quinn. Michael's face was stern as Reese looked at him. "Thanks for coming out here, but looks like we're going to get a lift back with dad."

"Everything okay?" Michael asked.

Reese wiped a hand over his face. "Yeah, fine...I'll get it sorted but I needed to talk to you as well..."

Michael gave Reese a little knowing smile. "I know...Cory has already spoken to me about it. I can't say I'm happy about it, but he's an adult and he promises to not let his studies slide...same goes for you Reese, this is your final year."

Reese chuckled at Michael's fatherly berating. "I'm already graduating...I'm a genius remember, but don't worry, if he lives with me I'll make sure he keeps his grades up." Behind them Cory rolled his eyes but smiled happily.

Michael nodded and held his hand out, Reese shook it. "I'm looking for a new place so I'll let you know once we're moving."

Quinn looked at Cory with surprise as he squeezed her shoulders, pulling her closer into him walking off in the direction that Cillian O'Shea went. "We're going to all live together?"

"Yep, apparently Reese can't let either of us out of his sight after the car and kidnapping incident."

Behind them Reese clucked his tongue. "Neither of you are obviously very observant to not see people following you around for days..."

"Hey!" Cory sounded insulted.

Quinn giggled. "I don't care what brought us to this point, I'm just happy we're going to be able to be together."

She held a hand out and Reese took it, entwining their fingers.

Michael sighed as he watched them all walk away together. Wendy curled a hand around his arm and smiled up at him. "They are doing what makes them happy, love."

As Cillian walked in to his house Maya was waiting for him. She embraced him and kissed his cheek before looking back at the girl with the glorious red hair being led in hand in hand by Reese while Cory followed behind looking nervously around.

Maya grinned at Reese's scowl, ignoring him and welcomed Quinn into the house. She swept Quinn's hand from Reese's and held both her hands as she kissed the air by Quinn's cheeks.

"It's so nice to see you again, Quinn...I do hope we can get along."

"Why would you get along?" Reese growled.

Cillian frowned at him. "Because Maya and I are getting married."

"Fuck's sake." Reese rolled his eyes. "Was that what you wanted to say?"

"Of course not, who I marry doesn't really concern you...but let's sit down first...I wish to discuss your future plans concerning these two and keeping them safe...I have an idea."

"Great." Reese clucked his tongue, looking at Cory with a sulky glance before following his father into the living area.

Cory's mouth twisted as he looked at Quinn and Maya, not wanting to go without Quinn. Maya smiled and started leading Quinn to the living room as she gawked around the gorgeous house. "I can't wait for us to go shopping...and you can help me pick a wedding dress if you like...I want us to be friends." Maya was saying as she walked into the living area. Reese looked up at her with a glare that could stop tides.

She faltered and giggled nervously, letting Quinn's hand go.

Reese lifted his hand. "Quinn, come here."

Quinn gave Maya a congenial smile and quickly made her way to Reese, gasping hold of his hand and he pulled her down to the couch next to him. Cory dropped into the couch on the other side of her. Cillian was sitting in a chair facing them and chuckled to see they were both protective of her.

He looked up at Maya as she came to stand beside his chair and placed her hand on his shoulder. He picked her hand up and kissed it. "How about some refreshments, dear."

"Of course...coffee alright?" She looked at everyone for consensus before leaving the room.

Reese gave his father a heavy look. "Are you seriously going to marry that porn star gold digger?"

Cillian frowned in disapproval. "You know she's not a porn star, besides she's willing to sign a pre-nup...I really don't think she's as bad as you make out, Reese."

"Hmm..." He conceded. "I guess she's better than most of them have been, but marriage, I didn't think I would ever see you married?"

Cillian shrugged. "I'm not getting any younger...it's nice to come home knowing there is someone waiting for you...which brings me to you lot."

He turned to look at Quinn making her drop her gaze and chew her lip. "Helen of Troy...the beautiful maiden that caused a decade long war ending in the complete destruction of an entire race of people..." He murmured, making Quinn fidget in embarrassment.

"Knock it off, dad." Reese growled. "None of this was her fault."

Cillian chuckled. "I'm sure it wasn't Helen's fault either...men will do strange things when women and pride are involved."

"Get to the point of this." Reese huffed, placing a hand on Quinn's thigh to try and calm her nerves, he could feel her anxiety building. Cory put his arm around her and tucked her into his side.

"My point, son, is with the story of what happened running rampant through both sides it's like I warned you...you need to have some sort of distance between you and the girl in that story."

"How do I do that? I'm not giving her up."

Quinn grabbed his hand and squeezed it. "Please, Mr O'Shea...I love Reese, there has to be a way..."

"There is one...in the public eye you are in love with Cory McMillan...you live with Cory McMillian and you will marry Cory McMillian."

"What?" All three of them exclaimed.

"If you are all serious about this throuple relationship, then Cory and Quinn will marry in a spectacular wedding covered by the press...you, my boy, will have to play the third in the shadows..."

Cory and Quinn looked horrified but Reese nodded solemnly. "Got it....yeah, it makes sense."

"How the hell does that make sense to you, Rice?" Cory yelled.

Reese turned in his seat to face Quinn and Cory. "To be honest I was going to suggest something pretty similar anyway...you're going to be a lawyer, you're son of the Police Commissioner, you're record is clean and Quinn is going to pass her college degree and get a good job...meanwhile I am about to take over from Dad when I graduate...I'll have eyes on me wherever I go."

"I don't care about that..." Quinn piped up. "I've lived with the mafia, I know how these things work..."

"Reese's reputation took a hammering in how he handled this situation concerning you, Quinn..." Cillian interrupted. "The Boston arm of our organization is in disarray...now I know that's not your fault but some will see it that way. You can't be seen on Reese's arm as his woman without a serious backlash...but if you are seen on Cory's arm we can at least play this off as a heroic act of my son to unite his best friend with the woman he loves...while getting rid of a traitor and our biggest rival."

Quinn and Cory both looked confused and dejected.

"Don't you want to marry each other?"

Quinn looked back at Cory and he smiled at her. "I don't really get why we have to do it this way?" Quinn said perplexed.

"Because it will stop people coming for you..." Reese said firmly.

Cillian smiled to know at least Reese understood.

"I was going to buy a building...a nice one somewhere in Manhattan and I was going to have it so that it looked like we were neighbors..."

Cory frowned. "Neighbors?"

Reese scratched the back of his neck. "Yeah, but it was just going to be an illusion...two apartments in the same building...but we can all just live in one."

Cillian scratched his jaw. "Be careful...I didn't say you couldn't live together but what is presented to the public must be a couple and not you."

Quinn felt terrible and was looking at Reese's hand playing with a large silver ring that he wore on his thumb. Maya came in with coffee and placed it down on the table.

"Well, things look positively depressing in here." She commented sarcastically.

Reese clucked his tongue and looked away as Cillian chuckled. "Why don't you tell Quinn your good news...?"

Reese looked back with suspicion as Cory tightened his arm around her. Quinn looked up with curiosity at Maya as Maya clasped her hands together in front of her chest and bounced on the balls of her feet.

"Oh, yes...absolutely..." She darted off to a cabinet and opened a drawer taking out a business card and handing it to Quinn.

Quinn looked at it with a frown.

"I might have been talking to a talent scout friend of mine..."

"Hell no!" Reese growled whipping the business card out of Quinn's hand and scrunching it in his fist.

"It's a proper legit modeling agency she works for..." Maya pouted. "I have changed my life around, you know..."

Reese huffed, folding his arms. "Anyone wants to come anywhere near Quinn they go through me!"

"And me." Cory added.

Quinn frowned a little but said nothing, she knew these two had only her best interests at heart, but still. "I don't think I have the right personality for modeling..."

"You don't even need a personality..." Maya said with a grin. "You have a distinctive and very attractive look...that's all that's needed, you don't even have to smile most of the time these days."

Reese's mouth twisted, he always thought she had model potential. "We'll talk it over later, there's plenty of time, Quinn hasn't even turned twenty yet." He looked at his father. "And that goes for the whole marriage idea too..."

Cillian sighed and shrugged. "Just as long as you realize."

"We all realize, thanks." Reese growled and stood up. "Time to go, if that's all you had to say?"

"Sit down, Reese...we are far from done." Cillian growled.

Quinn could see so much of Cillian in Reese, they were so alike and acted like two alpha males vying for dominance all the time. She glanced around the room at the men standing guard. Was this what life with

Reese was going to be like? She remembered Tank, Jacob and Mac plus that other guy that Cillian had as Reese's bodyguard and supposed it already was like that.

Cillian dipped into the pocket of his suit jacket and pulled out an envelope. "Here, this is for Quinn."

Quinn looked back at Cillian and glanced down at the envelope as Reese reached out and grabbed it, looked at it front and back noting there was nothing written on it. "What is it?"

"Just give it to her and find out." Cillian muttered darkly.

Reese handed it to Quinn and she nervously opened the envelope and pulled the document from inside, opened it and read it, Reese and Cory both read it over her shoulder and they all stared at the paper with disbelief.

"Holy shit..." Cory breathed.

Reese thrummed in his throat, pleased and rubbed her thigh.

Quinn just stared at the document stating she now had twenty five million dollars, a shareholder payout on investment of her inheritance by Rourke and Murphy Global Shipping and Worldwide Distribution, the Mob holding company that had their controlling interest in the Port that solely owned Imperial Shipping that Flanagan had first started with her funds. She now had a ten percent share in the parent company as a Rourke descendant.

"You're a rich girl, so make your life decisions wisely...this payment is from six years' worth of shareholder payments...you can expect at least an additional five million each year from now on."

"Oh my god!" Quinn's hands were shaking.

"So you can do whatever you like, travel the world...you don't need to stay with these two, the world is your oyster."

Maya gave Cillian a little whack of displeasure while Reese grit his teeth and glared at him.

Quinn silently folded the piece of paper up and put it back into the envelope. She stood up and both Cory and Reese looked at each other before looking up at her curiously as she faced Cillian with a stern expression.

"I thank you for this, I understand that Sean Flanagan took my inheritance to secure property and shipping rights in Boston so I assume that this all comes from that? However I am also aware that the outcome of that initial investment is billions..."

Cillian chuckled, delighted to see this girl had a backbone after all. "Quite, however that came with being able to expand and gather more investors over those six years...your share is held in a collective agreement that fifty percent be reinvested, twenty percent be invested into other family interests, resulting in a fair payout after tax."

Quinn nodded. "Good, I'm glad to hear this money is legit. However I fail to see how I can continue to hold shares when, as you say, the family don't want me any longer due to what happened in Boston."

Cillian let out a long breath. "You seem to be well informed..." He glanced at Reese who just grinned at him with pride in his little alley cat. "Do you wish to sell your shares?"

"I don't know...I'll talk to my partners about it...and let you know, until that time I expect a place at the next shareholders meeting and to be able to have the chance to speak on matters from my point of view."

Cillian laughed, slapping his thigh. "I see the attraction now...you are a smart girl." He looked at Reese and Reese flicked his head like he was giving permission for something. He knew if this girl showed up at the board meeting she would have them all eating out of her hand.

"Very well...I'll let the board know since I have taken control of Boston in the interim."

"Thank you...and I thank you, Maya for the opportunity too...I have a lot to think about, but I'm quite tired from the whole experience, and the plane trip...to be honest I'm feeling a bit faint."

Reese and Cory were on their feet immediately showing their concern.

She smiled at them and took their hands in hers. "We'll be leaving now, Mr O'Shea...thank you again, I would like to extend an invitation to dinner once we have moved and settled in."

Reese let her hand go. "Cory, take her out to the car."

Quinn looked at him with a frown but he stroked his fingers down her cheek. "I'll just be a sec."

He waited for them to leave the room before looking back at his father. Cillian gave him a strange look with an eyebrow raised in amusement. "Quite the little spitfire once she gets going..."

"She's smart, like you say...I don't have any qualms that once the others meet her they will know she belongs in the family, and with a business degree under her belt in a few years she could be an asset."

Cillian nodded, scratching his jaw. "I think you may be right, but what if you are wrong?"

"I can protect her, dad...but I think your right, publicly she should be seen as being with Cory. She should also be kept in legit business only."

"Good...you're doing the right thing..."

Epilogue
Five years later

Quinn got out of the taxi in front of the apartment building on the Upper East Side of Manhattan. She glanced up at the twenty story building with a whimsical smile on her lips. She had just arrived back in the US after spending fashion week in Paris modeling for a new fashion designer under a new brand called Eval Logic, edgy clothing that she loved to wear so much she had invested in it. After investing she inadvertently became the face of the brand so when the designer got invited to join fashion week in Paris as one of their featured young up and comers of course Quinn had to go as the model. It had been a blast and a whirlwind, but now she was nervous. Even though the planning had taken a month and she had spoken of it to her boys, she had just left in the end without them because they were busy. She had pissed them off and now she was back to face the consequences.

She glanced at her bodyguard, Trent, as he glared at her for pausing on the street as he lifted her suitcase.

It was good to be home, really good, she had missed her boys.

She stepped up to the security door and put in her pass code, then made her way to the elevator with Trent in tow.

Reese had bought this building two years ago under a guise company, completely renovated the top floor into one huge penthouse and made it their love nest, putting ownership under Cory's name. Their peaceful sanctuary away from prying eyes, a place they could all drop their public personas and finally be themselves...

She couldn't wait to let them know she was home, she hadn't told them she was coming back a day early, she wanted it to be a surprise.

She looked at her watch and saw the time was 8pm, both Reese and Cory should be home by now...but one never knew with their busy lives.

As she entered the apartment and stepped through from the foyer she saw Cory sitting on a stool at the kitchen island, holding his phone like he had been looking at it. He had glanced up to hear the front door, a frown of concern on his face that soon turned to a huge smile. He had obviously only just got home himself as he was still wearing a dark grey suit, his tie loosened and askew. He looked good.

"Quinn?" He stood up and dashed over to her, picking her up in his arms like she was a doll and twirled around in a circle with her. "Quinn, your home!"

He smelt even better.

He shouted out through the apartment. "Rice! Quinn's home! You were right!"

Quinn pouted at him as he put her down and kissed her lips. "What do you mean he was right?"

Cory rubbed the back of his neck. "Damn...I owe him a thousand dollars..."

"What? Are you still betting on me?"

Reese stepped into the room with a sexy chuckle. "I told him you were on your way home...did you forget I track your position?" She took a moment to look him over, he was wearing those notorious grey sweat pants and they hung low on his hips. He wasn't wearing a shirt, his tattoos in full view and he was dabbing his face with a cloth like he had been working out. She swallowed hard as her pussy throbbed.

"Oh..." Quinn pouted her bottom lip out. "I wanted to surprise you."

Reese came up and cupped her cheek, swishing his thumb over that pouting lip and grinned down on her. "I have a surprise for you instead."

"Really?" She gave him a cute little look of interest as her green eyes sparkled with the heat of desire. "I might just have a surprise for you guys too..."

Reese looked up at Trent. "You can go now..."

Trent bowed his head. "Yes, sir."

"Thank you, Trent...I hope you had fun in Paris." Quinn said with a smile.

He gave her a curt smile back. "I did. Have a good night, Miss O'Malley. I will be back on Monday." He gave a nod to Reese and Cory before leaving.

Reese picked Quinn up and threw her over his shoulder, making her squeal in surprise and then giggle as he started off down the hall. "We missed you...how dare you go away for so long without us."

Cory grinned and followed.

"You were both too busy to go..." Quinn complained. "Cory had that case for the Doyle brothers..." They were a small family associated to the O'Sheas, Cory hadn't become a prosecutor instead he had become one of the youngest lawyers to have his own firm, representing high profile cases usually involving people from the Mob, much to the ire of his father. "And you...you had that hotel/lodge deal up in Lake Placid..."

"But you just went." Cory grumbled. "We figured you would at least try to persuade us to take time off or something...but you never mentioned it again and then you were gone."

"Really? I knew you couldn't take the time." Quinn looked at Cory. "This was really important to me so..."

Reese smacked her ass making her gasp in a breath of shock and her body to jolt. "Stop yapping, Quinn...you already know from our multitude of phone calls that you're in trouble."

"So my surprise is actually something to do with punishing me?" She asked as he put her down on her feet in the bedroom and she looked up with large luminous eyes.

"Absolutely." Reese said with that sexy lick over his teeth. He spun her around to reveal a new piece of furniture in the room next to the Tantra chair by the window.

Quinn felt a million butterflies take off and swirl around her stomach as a deep heat expanded through her groin and made her clit pulse. There was a spanking bench in the room and on the bed was laid out a paddle, a flogger and a horse riding crop.

"You're going to spank me...with those?" Quinn asked in a husky voice as it stuck in her throat.

Reese chuckled darkly. "Oh yes..." He came behind her and placed a hand on her belly, pulling her back into him as he brought his mouth to her ear. "I can tell already that you're looking forward to it, baby."

Her skin goose bumped at the deep husky tone he used.

Cory dropped to his knees in front of her removing her heeled sandals and ran his hands up her bare thighs, dragging her dress up to reveal her panties then pressed his face to her pussy inhaling her scent and letting out a satisfied thrum in his throat.

"You smell divine, bunny...I can literally smell your arousal..."

She dropped her chin to look down at him and smiled, ruffling her fingers into his hair. At the same time she grabbed Reese behind her around the neck and leaned back into him. "I missed you guys so much..."

"We can see that..." Reese chuckled, kissing her neck. He ran a hand up the back of her skirt to palm her bottom as Cory pulled her panties down her legs. He suddenly groaned into her neck with a sigh of needy pleasure. "Oh, fuck...you didn't?"

Quinn grinned as his fingers found her surprise. Cory looked up with a curious frown. "What didn't she do?"

"It's what she did do...our little sex crazed minx is already one step ahead of us..." He pulled her over to the bench and pushed her face down over it, flicked her skirt up to reveal her naked ass and Cory saw the flanged end of a butt plug wedged inside her.

He laughed, as Quinn lifted up onto her forearms and looked back at them both with a wicked smile. "That's our good bunny...shit, was that your surprise?"

"Yes...now..." She stood up before them and started to remove her blouse. "I'm assuming that this punishment is going to be a full session?"

Reese's eyes darkened immediately as he licked his tongue over his teeth. "You need it, princess?"

Cory slung his arm over Reese's neck as they watched her undress then drop naked to her knees and hold her wrists out. "I need it...I deserve it for being a bad girl." She breathed with an alluring smile up at her two alpha males.

Reese gave her a smile back as he stepped closer and tilted her chin up with his fingers, brushing her lips with his thumb before sticking it into her mouth to suck.

"Alright, baby...we'll give you what you need, I'm glad you decided you need this punishment...but let's just reiterate...safe word?"

"Sapphire." She breathed as he took his thumb out of her mouth.

"Good girl...Cory, get the black leather cuffs with the fluffy inside...she's going to be cuffed for a while." He moved his hand to encompass her throat and lifted her to her feet then up on her tip toes as he pulled her up to his mouth and kissed her hungrily, taking everything she had as he lashed his tongue into her mouth savagely leaving her panting for breath.

Cory had gone to a set of drawers in the room dedicated to their toy collection returning with cuffs in hand. Reese gazed into Quinn's hooded eyes seeing them sparkle with anticipation. "Behind her back I think..."

Quinn bit her lip as she slow blinked at him and he smirked. "Oh, yes...you, my little minx, are in serious trouble tonight."

The End

Thank you for reading!

Italian Translations

Brara rageizza – *Good girl*
Petalo – *Petal*
Bambina – *Baby*
E cosi bello il mio piccolo cannolo – *It's so beautiful, my little cannoli*

BOOKS BY THIS AUTHOR

Tygarya Saga

(Epic Fantasy)

Book 1 – Destiny Finds You

Book 2 – Loyalty Binds You

Book 3 – Betrayal Frees You

Book 4 – Destiny's Shadow Defines You

Redeemable Series

(Stand alone mafia suspense romance stories)

Caught in the Middle – Curry & Rice

Unwanted Attention – Mad Dog

Collateral Damage – Raven

COMING SOON

Black Butterflies Series

(Stand alone paranormal/fantasy romance stories)

The Vampire in My Mirror

Dimitri's Little Fox

Little Jaguar

The Dragon's Wolf Omega

To Love A Vampire Queen

(Paranormal/Fantasy Romance Trilogy)

Book 1 – Houses of Shadow and Wolf

Book 2 – Land of Myth and Fantasy
Book 3 – Realm of Fire and Nightmare

ABOUT THE AUTHOR

ANNETTA LINCOLN

Annetta lives in New Zealand with her son in the lovely rural community of North Canterbury.

She loves walks on the local beaches and through the natural native bush that surrounds her little piece of paradise.

In 2019 Annetta was diagnosed with a rare SCC cancer and has battled with ongoing treatments, operations and scans. In 2023 she was told it had now traveled to her lungs at Stage 2, palliative care and more chemotherapy treatment would be needed.

Currently Annetta is living comfortably in a stable remission.

Annetta loves animals and owns two cats at present, barn rescue kittens they are brother and sister, Roman and Lily.

Annetta spends the rest of her spare time enjoying Anime and K-dramas, she is a great reader of fantasy and horror genres and loves listening to her son playing the guitar.

Annetta likes to spend her days writing in the hopes she brings a little joy to those who discover and read her books.

Instagram – annettalincolnauthor

Don't miss out!

Visit the website below and you can sign up to receive emails whenever Annetta Lincoln publishes a new book. There's no charge and no obligation.

https://books2read.com/r/B-A-IZPME-RJIWG

BOOKS 2 READ

Connecting independent readers to independent writers.

www.ingramcontent.com/pod-product-compliance
Lightning Source LLC
Chambersburg PA
CBHW070539030726
47505CB00001B/92

9781067109578